THE

DANIEL
OPTION

THE
DANIEL

A NOVEL

OPTION

#1 *NEW YORK TIMES* BESTSELLING AUTHOR

MIKE EVANS

TimeWorthy
BOOKS

P.O. Box 30000, Phoenix, AZ 85046

The Daniel Option
(a novel)

Copyright 2019 by Time Worthy Books
P. O. Box 30000
Phoenix, AZ 85046

Design: Peter Gloege | LOOK Design Studio

Hardcover:	978-1-62961-194-5
Paperback:	978-1-62961-193-8
Canada:	978-1-62961-195-2

This book is dedicated to
Jared and Ivanka Trump Kushner,

two very special friends who love and support
our beloved nation and the nation of Israel.
These are two of the most intelligent and kindest
people I've ever known. Over dinner at the
Jerusalem Embassy Gala, I said to both,
"You are senior advisers to the President.
Who is the senior adviser at home?"
Both laughed and pointed to the other saying,
"He is/she is." Evangelicals have never
had access to a president as we have
with Donald Trump. Two of the reasons are
Jared and Ivanka Trump Kushner.

PRIMARY CHARACTERS

IRAN

Ayatollah Ali Khamenei	Supreme Leader of Iran
Hassan Rouhani	President of Iran
Mahmoud Alavi	Iranian minister of intelligence
General Mohammad Bagheri	Commander of all Iranian armed forces

ISRAEL

Benjamin Netanyahu	Israeli prime minister
Avigdor Lieberman	Israeli minister of defense
General Gadi Eizenkot	Israel Defense Forces Commander
Yossi Cohen	Mossad director
Nadav Argaman	Shin Bet director

UNITED STATES OF AMERICA

Donald Trump	President of the United States
John Kelly	White House chief of staff
James Mattis	US secretary of defense
Dan Coats	Director of National Intelligence
Gina Haspel	Director of the CIA
John Bolton	National Security Advisor

CHAPTER 1

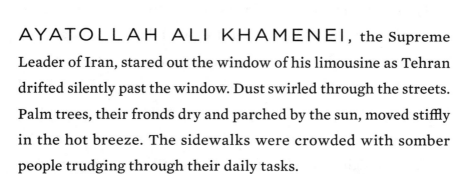

AYATOLLAH ALI KHAMENEI, the Supreme Leader of Iran, stared out the window of his limousine as Tehran drifted silently past the window. Dust swirled through the streets. Palm trees, their fronds dry and parched by the sun, moved stiffly in the hot breeze. The sidewalks were crowded with somber people trudging through their daily tasks.

Despite the insular life he led, Khamenei saw them—and not just that day. From the window of his residence at the Beit Rahbari compound, when he rode to the mosque on Friday for worship and prayer, and as he came and went about his daily business. He saw it. The dusty, dirty streets that once had been lush, verdant corridors of beauty. The sparse, listless clusters of two or three at the open markets, where once there had been teeming, thriving crowds. But now all around him there was only decay. And he felt it was all directly attributable to Donald J. Trump, the president of the United States.

Not five years earlier, things were very different. Led by Barack Obama, the youngest man ever elected to the US presidency, the Americans had spearheaded an international effort to maneuver Iran away from its program of nuclear development. Khamenei had been reluctant at first, thinking it was merely another ploy of the West to keep Iran under the imperialists' thumb. But when his own negotiators became convinced they could obtain a workable arrangement—one that offered the *appearance* of compliance with world expectations, but enough ambiguity for continued clandestine nuclear activity, and removal of economic sanctions—Khamenei had allowed them to proceed. And they were magnificently successful. An agreement was reached. Money flowed to Tehran once more. Purchases long delayed had been made. Improvements in infrastructure had been well on their way to completion. The entire country seemed to breathe a collective sigh of relief. But then Barack Obama's term in office came to an end.

Donald Trump, the next American president, was a businessman from New York who took office with a very different outlook. As a staunch supporter of the Free Iran movement, Trump had stressed the need to revoke the deal with Iran and reimpose sanctions. Time and time again during his campaign for office he groused that the deal was a gift to Iran and a bad deal for the world. New negotiations were required. Renewed sanctions would make that happen. Americans saw it as good policy.

Khamenei viewed the American stance as yet another attempt to humiliate his country and he wasn't one to suffer humiliation lightly. "They will know that soon enough," he mumbled to himself. "And they will rue the day they did this. Allah will avenge our cause."

Moments later the limousine slowed, then turned from the street and passed quickly through the gates at the Beit Rahbari compound. A crowd was gathered there and waved to him with genuine enthusiasm, a stark contrast to what he'd seen just a few blocks away. Khamenei waved back, mustering a smile as if greeting old friends, before the gates swung closed and the car wound its way along the drive toward the center of the compound.

As the car came to a stop outside the main building, Hassan Rouhani, the Iranian president, stepped forward and opened the rear door. He held it in place as Khamenei rose from the back seat and stepped out to the pavement by the curb.

"I am glad to see you, Supreme Leader," Rouhani bowed his head when he spoke and he meant it, too. Unlike many who pretended a reverential attitude, Rouhani was sincere. Of all Iran's politicians and religious leaders, Khamenei was truly his favorite.

Khamenei seemed not to notice the solicitous tone in Rouhani's voice or the posture of his body. In fact, he didn't seem to notice Rouhani at all except to speak with the assumption that Rouhani knew the comments were directed to him. "They are here?" Khamenei asked.

"Yes," Rouhani replied. "Assembled and waiting." Khamenei was already moving up the steps and Rouhani left the car, its door still standing open, to hurry after him.

"You did not tell them why they were summoned?"

Rouhani shook his head. "Not a word."

"Very good."

With Rouhani at his side, Khamenei made his way inside and up to a third-floor room reserved for working sessions with key government officials. About the size of a large conference room, it was on an interior hallway with no windows to the outside. In the center was a long table and at the far end there was a large chair that sat on a raised dais, placing it well above the others. Khamenei entered and walked toward it.

Everyone who'd gathered there—the room was packed that day—stood and waited until the Supreme Leader was seated. Rouhani took a seat next to him and once both men were settled in place, the others returned to their chairs.

After what seemed a long time, Khamenei began. "As you are well aware," his voice was heavy and his cadence deliberate, "the Americans have chosen to cancel our previous agreement and once again impose sanctions against us such that the latest restrictions are even more severe than the first. This is no easy thing for our people to bear. All across the city and, indeed, throughout the nation, we see indications that these acts of aggression against us—and make no mistake about it, that is precisely what they are—we see indications that these acts of aggression are having a decidedly ill effect on our people. The Americans are attempting to strong-arm us into accepting the rules of the infidels. But as difficult and reprehensible as all of that may be, their actions have placed us in an even far more dangerous position.

"Historically, the people of Israel have perceived us as their greatest enemy—the one nation in all of the Middle East with the will to destroy them. And they are correct. For a long time, their zeal against us has been kept in check by American presidents who have restrained the Israelis from implementing their desire to launch a preemptive attack on our most valued assets.

"Now, with this infidel Trump as the new American president, the Israelis have perceived a shift from the ways of the past to an American president who is far less inhibited in his support of them. They sense in him a new moment; a moment of opportunity opening to them. And that makes them very dangerous. Attacking us with a devastating first strike is no longer impossible for them as they expect a friendly American government will gladly support such a move." Khamenei paused to look around the room, letting his eyes fall on each one before continuing. "This is a very dangerous time for us. They might very well do this thing they have wanted to do for so long, and the American masses might very well support them."

Bijan Rasouli, the foreign affairs minister, spoke up. "Even the Israelis must know they cannot conquer us with military might! They haven't the strength for an invasion, nor the air force to obliterate our military."

"That is correct as to the Israelis," Khamenei acknowledged. "But with American assistance, they can inflict great misery on us. Destroy our domestic economy. Set back our nuclear development by decades. And there are many US politicians who would like to do just that."

Rouhani nodded in agreement. "Well said, Supreme Leader. Many in the United States think if they inflict enough misery on us, our people will rise up in revolt, as they did against the shah."

Khamenei assented, "And they might, but we cannot allow that to happen. We have done much to please Allah. We cannot fail him now." He paused a moment and sipped from a bottle of water, then continued. "I have called you here because, as I have said, this is a crucial moment for us. We must not cower or run from it, but rather turn this moment to our advantage. What the Jews perceive as their greatest advantage also might well be their greatest weakness. We must find that weakness and exploit it to the fullest." He paused again, then turned to where the nation's most powerful generals were seated. His gaze focused on General Mohammad Bagheri, commander of the general staff of the armed forces.

"General Bagheri," he began. . .

Bagheri jumped to his feet and stood at attention in almost comical fashion. "Yes, Supreme Leader."

"Your task is to produce a plan that will turn this moment against the Israelis and give us the strategic advantage we need."

Bagheri immediately responded. "Yes, Supreme Leader."

"Return to me in three days with a plan that will do that."

Without saying more, Khamenei stood and everyone in the room rose with him. They waited in silence once again, while he made his way through the room to the door and disappeared down the hall.

✦ ✦ ✦

Three days later, Bagheri and the Iranian generals returned to the room on that third floor of the main building in the Beit Rahbari compound. As before, Khamenei's key advisors and officials were assembled. They all stood as Khamenei entered the room and took his place in the chair at the far end of the table. And they watched with rapt attention as Khamenei turned to General Bagheri. "You have something you wish to say to me?"

General Bagheri pushed back his chair and stood, then turned to face Khamenei and began. "As you have indicated before, this is a moment given to us by Allah. However, it is a moment for cunning, not brawn."

Khamenei seemed intrigued. Several who were present that day later said he even smiled. "What do you have in mind?"

Bagheri cleared his throat. "As a preliminary matter, we must pre-position additional troops in Lebanon and Syria. This is a cautionary measure to ensure they are in position to prevent a ground assault by the Israelis against Hezbollah, in a potential Israeli response to what is coming. Having them in position in advance will give us additional options should events unfold in an unforeseeable manner. We will deploy these troops incrementally and in ways that do not attract great attention to their arrival."

Khamenei interrupted. "Our current strength in these countries is not enough?"

"It is sufficient for what we have been doing in the past," Bagheri explained. "But not for what we may face as a result of our complete proposal."

Khamenei thought for a moment, then gestured for Bagheri to continue.

"At the same time as we strengthen our troops in Lebanon and Syria, we will insert operatives into Israel—men who have been trained by our Revolutionary Guard but who have no traceable connections to us. Capable men who know how to do the things we ask them to do."

Mahmoud Alavi, the intelligence minister, spoke up. "And how will this happen? The Israelis are quite vigilant against people of this nature."

Bagheri looked suspiciously at Alavi. They had clashed before on questions of policy and military strategy. "We will use various means and methods." Bagheri was guarded in his remarks and careful not to commit himself to anything specific. "Perhaps with the help of our Russian contacts we will send some as Russian Orthodox priests."

Some in the room smiled at the mention of this—the very thought of a Shia Muslim, playing the part of a Christian priest to infiltrate the Jewish homeland.

"Or," Bagheri added, "as diplomats from some of the countries that are friendly with us." Several in the room took this more seriously and nodded their approval. "Or even posing as Jewish refugees exercising their right of free return." Bagheri seemed to have overreached with that remark and some raised some eyebrows at that suggestion, but Khamenei nodded and seeing that he was not upset the others quickly nodded approvingly, too. "We can work the details of that out later," Bagheri continued. "It will not be a problem."

"If we begin inserting these men immediately, we can pre-position dozens in a matter of weeks without calling attention to their arrival. These operatives will work to assist in the things that are to come—recruiting, informing, supplying, facilitating inside Israeli territory—using members of Hamas and Arab Israelis whom we know, and are waiting to assist us."

Bagheri seemed to warm to his topic and spoke with confidence. "At the same time, and in preparation for what is to come, our operatives—and those whom they recruit to assist them—will create an air of tension regarding the Palestinians. Tensions that begin low but rise higher and higher to set the Israelis on edge. Creating a sense of foreboding, as if something big is in the offing but the Israelis will not know what that something is."

Khamenei became. "And what is that *something*?"

Bagheri responded, "When all is ready, our operatives will launch five simultaneous attacks by Hamas from Gaza against Israel's western border. These attacks will be disguised as Gaza protests and will occur at the same time on the same day. A surge of thousands of people from Gaza moving toward each of the five border checkpoints. With the help of our operatives, these protestors will be instructed to cross the border at all costs to occupy land on the other side, thus ensuring they approach and surge through the checkpoints in an aggressive manner. Our operatives will make certain that women and children are at the front of those protest groups.

"By these great surges of humanity, and in the air of tension previously created, we will provoke IDF soldiers to shoot them at the border in an apparent attempt to stop them from crossing, as they did in previous protests. Only this time, the IDF will slaughter hundreds at each checkpoint. Thousands more will be injured. Thus, the casualty count will be five times higher than at any time in the past.

"Through our media contacts, we will make certain that international news agencies cover the events. Scenes of these actions will be broadcast around the world and presented in a light that portrays the Israelis as the evil oppressors we know them to be. We will make certain these reports are repeated through the news cycle for many days."

Bagheri had their attention now and he knew it, which left him feeling pleased with himself. "At the same time, our operatives will facilitate a large protest by Israeli citizens—those who favor the cause of peace and freedom for our people. This protest will take place in Jerusalem, and will ensure a large crowd is present in the streets of the city. On the day of the protest, we will infiltrate Jerusalem with children—perhaps a hundred or so, a group large enough to be effective but small enough to avoid raising suspicions. These will be Arab schoolchildren—old enough to be useful, young enough not to ask too many questions. They will spread out among the public, particularly in the Old City where streets are narrower and more confined. Many of the children will carry backpack bombs that can be remotely detonated. Others will carry only backpacks. But all of the children will appear the same—schoolchildren with backpacks. As the bombs are detonated around the city—some here—some there—more over here—then dozens more over there—the Israeli police will be provoked to take action. If we do this correctly, many of the policemen will react in fear and begin shooting at all children wearing backpacks, most of whom will be merely unarmed children with backpacks, not bombs.

"Through our various media contacts, we will make certain the international news agencies are present to broadcast all of this, in Gaza and in Jerusalem, to televisions and Internet devices around the world. As the images of slaughtered and wounded women and children are replayed again and again—in broadcasts and on social media—outrage will build among the citizens of the world. Sympathizers and politically liberal constituents in the West will make certain these news stories get repeated and that the dead children are not forgotten or overlooked.

"As global outrage builds, our friends at the United Nations will call for sanctions against Israel. You will remember when President Ahmadinejad saw the green light at a UN meeting. He said no one in the room blinked for thirty minutes." Bagheri's cadence changed and many who heard him speak later said he sounded like one of the prophets of old. "Just as the Mahdi aided him, so he will assist us. All members of the Security Council will agree to those sanctions, including Russia. But the United States will come to Israel's defense and veto those sanctions, promising support to the Jews and defending the Israeli government to news reporters.

"Then all the world will become outraged and all of the nations will demand justice on behalf of the slain Arab children. And instead of the United States bludgeoning the nations of the world to impose crippling sanctions against us, as they are now, the nations of the world will rise up against the Americans and impose sanctions against the United States.

"The European Union, China, perhaps even Russia will see this as their moment to turn the tables on the Americans. China, in particular, would welcome an opportunity to assert itself as the world's leading economic superpower. They will jump at the chance to impose the severest sanctions. Sanctions that will amount to a virtual worldwide halt in trading with the US. Those sanctions will shock the American economy. Exports to and from the US will tumble, the US stock market will collapse, American consumers will stop consuming, and the American economy will fall to the ground.

"And when the American economy collapses from lack of international trade, and its allies abandon it to turn their allegiance to others, the once-mighty US military will no longer be free to roam the world imposing its will on us. Then we will be free to destroy Israel, once and for all. There will be no one to stop us!"

The room was quiet when Bagheri finished. Everyone sat in stunned silence. With all eyes fixed upon him, Bagheri slowly turned to face Khamenei, and bowed respectfully. "That, Supreme Leader, is the strategy we propose."

"Very well," Khamenei responded. "I will take the matter under advisement." With nothing more, he rose from his seat at the table, made his way to the door, and was gone.

Bagheri gathered his things and followed the others from the room. Still, no one said a word to him or offered even the simplest greeting as they shuffled to the hall and made their way to the steps.

Though they did not speak or utter a word of praise in the presence of those who had attended the meeting, several generals—Kayhan Alizadeh from the army and Jalal Elahi from the air force, among others—accompanied Bagheri through the hall to the main corridor and down to the sidewalk outside the building. When they were safely away, General Alizadeh asked, "Do you think he will approve it?"

"No one can say for certain."

"And what if the strategy does not succeed?"

General Elahi interjected, "If the strategy fails, it won't matter."

Alizadeh looked perplexed. "And why not?"

"Because," Elahi replied, "if it fails, we will all be dead."

The others chuckled self-consciously. "Relax," Bagheri urged. "It will not come to that."

"And if it does?"

"If it all falls apart, we always have the Mahdi option."

Everyone smiled and nodded with a sense of relief. "Yes," they all agreed, "We always have the Mahdi option."

The following day, Khamenei issued a memo approving the plan proposed by General Bagheri. It was communicated to him by a courier who brought the memo in an envelope bearing the wax seal of the Supreme Leader.

Six months later, three operatives, specially selected by Bagheri and trained specifically for his purposes, arrived in Tel Aviv. Each held credentials and a passport from France, and a background on record as an executive from a medical technology company. Nothing about them gave even a hint that they had ties to anything Iranian. By the time they were settled, three more were on their way.

CHAPTER

2

FOUR MONTHS AFTER the first Iranian operative arrived in Tel Aviv, Shahram Markazi, traveling as a Qatari diplomat, entered Israel from Jordan as part of the Economic Review Committee, an international delegation authorized by the United Nations. The committee was created to assist the Palestinian National Authority with economic development in the disputed territories. The delegation crossed the border from Jordan via the Allenby Bridge near Jericho and made its way to Jerusalem. Traveling with an Israel Defense Forces escort, they traversed the disputed territories without incident.

For the next two days, Markazi and his fellow committee members met with representatives both from the Palestinian National Authority and the Israeli government, exploring points of agreement that might be used as the basis for building economic cooperation between the two parties. No one associated with the committee could account for the committee's activities on the third day of the trip, but on the fourth they traveled from Jerusalem to Gaza, crossing the border fence at the Eretz checkpoint located at the northern end of the Strip.

In Gaza, the committee met with representatives from Hamas and three key non-governmental organizations that were active in providing relief to Gaza residents. Their discussions focused on the need for economic development in the region and the necessity of reducing or eliminating cross-border acts of violence as a precondition to the expansion of further economic activity.

After a day of discussions, some of which were quite intense, members of the committee retired to accommodations prepared by Hamas near Al-Azhar University. After settling into his room there, Markazi slipped away to meet privately with the executive committee of the Izz ad-Din al-Qassam Brigades, the military wing of Hamas.

"I come to you under the direction and authority of Ayatollah Ali Khamenei, the Supreme Leader of Iran, and I bring you greetings in his name and in the name of Allah."

The group replied in unison, "As-salamu alaykum."

For the next ten minutes, Markazi outlined the planned protests—thousands of Gaza residents surging through each of the five border crossings, entering into Israel and occupying territory beyond the border fence. He did not provide all of the details, mentioning nothing about how many would be killed in the effort, but offered a broad presentation of the plan that was designed to motivate Al-Qassam leadership for enthusiastic participation.

"This is the will of the Ayatollah as prescribed by Allah," Markazi explained. "Protests at all five border crossing checkpoints, all occurring at the same time on the same day. All protesters must approach the border with the intention of crossing into Israel. And we must have women and children in front."

Abdullah Al-Hadi, one of the younger members of the executive committee, was seated to one side. He wore a linen robe of the kind preferred by Bedouins and a *keffiyeh* of the same material covered his head. "This will require more people than we've ever used before," he noted.

Markazi rejoined, "No. Which is why you should begin now to prepare for it."

"Our people are always ready," another spoke defiantly.

Markazi differed. "Not for what we have in mind. For this, you must educate your people and you must organize them to respond in very large numbers. You must get them ready. They must know the objective is to cross the border. Not merely to throw rocks at the Israeli soldiers and then run away, but to push through the checkpoints and actually move beyond the fence to the other side."

"That will not be easy," someone added.

"Many will die," another commented. "The Israelis will respond with deadly force."

"Listen to me," Markazi retorted. "It will be impossible to do this if you don't prepare."

"And how are we to do that?" Another member of the group asked.

"Work in smaller groups first. Groups that can meet in homes and apartments under the leadership and guidance of carefully selected people. Instruct those leaders and get them to understand that the objective of these protests is to actually move out of Gaza. To show the Israelis we will not be confined to Gaza by a wall that imprisons us like criminals or slaves. Then guide those leaders as they recruit participants. Help them as they choose additional participants for instruction, take them out for protests in small numbers, and make sure they work toward the goal of getting everyone ready."

Al-Hadi spoke up. "Small events leading to a big event?"

"Yes. Have these groups take their people out in small protests, not just to harass the Jews, but so they can gather information about the Israeli response—where they position themselves as you approach, how close you can get before provoking a response. Show them that they can go very close to the fence—closer than they thought possible before—and still live to tell about it."

"And then we use these small groups to build larger groups?"

"Yes. Once you train those initial groups," Markazi explained, "you send out each member to recruit, establish, and train their own group."

"Ahh." Al-Hadi had a look of realization. "Four becomes sixteen. Sixteen becomes sixty-four. And so on."

"Exactly. This will multiply your numbers quickly and dramatically."

"And how many do we want for the major protest?"

"Thousands," Markazi stated emphatically.

One of the older members shook his head. "I don't know . . ." His voice trailed away in a skeptical sigh. "This seems like a lot to do."

"That is why I'm telling you," Markazi persisted, "you must organize. You will not be able to gather the crowds we need at the last moment. Get organized and get busy now. These protests must work."

✦ ✦ ✦

The next day, Al-Hadi sent for Mohammed Khalafi, a twenty-something and an up-and-coming member of Al-Qassam, the military wing of Hamas. An aide located Khalafi in a neighborhood near the beach in Khan Yunis, a community at the southern end of the Gaza Strip. Although nervous at being summoned by a member of Al-Qassam's executive leadership, Khalafi joined the aide without protest. After a time-consuming ride north, he was brought to a building in Gaza City and taken to a safe room in the basement. A single lightbulb hung from the ceiling, and chairs were arranged along one wall. Otherwise, it was starkly bare.

A few minutes after Khalafi arrived, the door to the room opened and Al-Hadi entered. He closed the door behind him. The two were totally alone.

"If I did something wrong," Khalafi urged with a nervous voice, "please tell me and I will do my best to make it right."

"Relax," Al-Hadi replied with a disarming wave of his hand. "You are not in trouble."

"Then why did you send for me? Why am I here?"

Al-Hadi brought a chair for Khalafi to sit and took one for himself, too. "Your work has been noticed," he assured. "Because of that, you have been selected for a great honor."

The words Al-Hadi used did little to calm Khalafi's fears. Among Hamas operatives, phrases like *special honor* were not always a positive thing. He waited until Al-Hadi was seated, then took a seat opposite him. "What honor is that?" he asked.

"We are preparing for a major protest," Al-Hadi explained. "And we need your help."

Khalafi remembered participating in large protests before. He'd been there when hundreds marched to the border fence in protest of the United States relocating its embassy to Jerusalem. It was a sight to see. So many moving as a group, shouting and chanting. Then the soldiers opened fire with live rounds. Several of his friends were wounded and he saw others killed.

"I was with them when we protested the US Embassy move," Khalafi boasted proudly.

"That was a very effective action," Al-Hadi acknowledged. "But we intend to stage something much larger."

"Larger?"

Al-Hadi nodded. "This will be the largest protest ever held in

Gaza. And to do it we need to prepare ahead of time."

Khalafi was eager. "What do you have in mind?"

"We intend to protest with thousands of people at every border crossing."

"All five crossings?"

"Yes. All five. Thousands at each site. All protesting at the same time on the same day."

Khalafi was wide-eyed with excitement. He'd never heard of such a thing. "That will require a lot of people."

"So you can see," Al-Hadi continued, "we must get organized."

"How can I help?"

"We want you to organize the protest at the Sufa Crossing."

Sufa was a community in southern Israel not far from the Egyptian border and very near the Gaza border fence, directly opposite Al-Buyuk in Gaza. The crossing near it, named for the nearby kibbutz, had been used intermittently for cargo, mostly in the form of agricultural exports from Gaza. Access to Gaza through that crossing had been irregular. Khalafi wasn't sure it was open just then, but he didn't think he had the latitude to raise that issue at the moment.

"Your role," Al-Hadi continued, "is to gather a group of people who can form a cadre—a core group that can recruit the numbers you need. Instruct them on the basic plan, then lead them in several protests to get them ready. Lead them to the border, gather information about the crossing, and assess IDF responses to your presence."

"We are always ready to challenge the soldiers."

"Yes, but you will need thousands to join you this time. Not hundreds. Gathering a crowd of thousands takes time. Your efforts must be intentional and always focused on the goal: Thousands surging through the crossing checkpoint."

For the next ten minutes, Al-Hadi gave Khalafi detailed instruction about what was expected. Thousands surging toward the border, through the checkpoint, crossing into Israel, occupying as much land as possible on the other side, women and children leading the way.

"And one more thing," Al-Hadi added. "News cameras will be recording you."

"That is good," Khalafi agreed. "Protests are waged as much in the media now as on the ground."

"And that is why you won't simply go out and throw rocks at the guards or fly kites with gas bombs over the wall. If we want to be successful, we have to do this in a way that creates an image. A spectacle. An event of horrendous proportions. One that will carry itself across all media platforms and get repeated by millions of viewers worldwide, many of whom could not locate us on a map but who will be inspired by what they see."

Khalafi grinned. "This will be a good thing."

"This is your job." Al-Hadi stood. "Create a compelling image for the world's media and the protest will be broadcast to the entire world." Khalafi followed him toward the door, then Al-Hadi turned to face him. "This must not fail."

Khalafi knew precisely what he meant. Succeed or die trying—or death would await him another way.

✦ ✦ ✦

In an effort to build a cadre of protesters capable of gathering a crowd of thousands, Khalafi gathered a group of a dozen Hamas operatives. Men who were about his own age whom he knew well, and whom he perceived to be somewhat lower in rank than he. They had been involved in Hamas activities—flying kites over the border fence with gas bombs attached and on one or two occasions launching rocket-propelled grenades into the nearest Israeli villages, but they had never been in the tunnels or into Ashkelon for bombing raids.

After contacting each of the operatives, Khalafi gathered them at a house in Umm al-Kilab. Over a light meal he laid out the plan Al-Hadi had given him for the protest. Some of it, at least. He left out many of the details, such as the thousands of participants needed, and that many of them would die in the process. Instead, he concentrated on the notion that this should be a highly organized effort and that participants should be prepared in stages. "The first thing we need to do is to probe the crossing."

"Probe the crossing?" someone asked in a sarcastic tone. "What are you talking about?"

"I'm talking about getting close without getting *too* close," Khalafi explained. "Close enough to observe the guards at the checkpoint but not close enough to provoke a response. That will allow us to determine the nature of their operation. What they do. How they do it. Then slowly make our trips closer and closer, noting how our advances change their responses."

Samir Jubran spoke up. "We know what they'll do. They'll shoot us." Several in the room laughed at the comment.

Khalafi was unfazed. "They won't do that if we're at a distance."

"But we *know* the ultimate response." Jubran gestured to those in the room. "We all know. They'll shoot at us. That's what they'll do. That's what they always do."

"We need to document it," Khalafi insisted. "Look." He paused to glance around the room. "We have to do this one differently from the way we've done things in the past."

Hisham Shomali joined in Jubran's response. "Why? Why do we need to do all this . . . planning? Let's just ride out there and harass them."

"Listen to me," Khalafi demanded. His tone was more strident than before. "This operation comes from the top."

"You mean from the executive committee," Shomali said.

"No," Khalafi replied. "From the Ayatollah himself."

Jabra Shahid laughed out loud. "The Ayatollah?"

"Yes."

"The Supreme Leader of Iran gave an order that has come all the way down to you?"

"Yes."

"And from you to us?"

"Yes."

Right," Shahid scoffed. "Like that's for real."

"It is for real," Khalafi said. The look in his eyes was intense and the tone of his voice serious. "And if you play around with this, you'll be playing around with your life."

"Whoa," Shahid retorted. "Are you threatening us? Are you threatening *me*?"

"No," Khalafi replied. "I'm not threatening you. I'm warning you."

Shahid struck a defiant pose. "And who's going to back up that warning?"

"The executive committee of Al-Qassam," Khalafi replied flatly.

Shahid scoffed once more, "They don't even know we exist."

"They do now."

Shomali interrupted their exchange. "You gave them our names?"

"I gave them to Abdullah Al-Hadi."

Shomali's eyes were wide. "Why did you do that?"

"Because I was given this task by Abdullah Al-Hadi and he wanted to know who I recruited for help."

That the Ayatollah would give Khalafi an order seemed insane to everyone in the room. Men like the Ayatollah didn't deal with people like them. But Abdullah Al-Hadi was a different matter. All of the men assembled that evening with Khalafi had seen Al-Hadi at least once, though none but Khalafi had ever spoken to him.

Still, they knew who he was and they had seen him on the streets of their neighborhoods. They also knew of his ruthless reputation. That he might be involved was too plausible to ignore.

Jubran's tone seemed to soften. "You met with Al-Hadi?"

"Yes." Khalafi took a drink and swallowed slowly before continuing. "Let's focus on the task at hand. They want thousands to participate in this demonstration. It's our job to figure out how to do that."

Ibrahim Atweh glanced at Khalafi with a look of disbelief. "They want thousands to participate?"

"Yes," Khalafi said. "Thousands at each of the crossings."

"Why so many?"

"Because they don't intend for us to simply walk up to the fence and lob a few rockets over. They want us to cross into Israel and occupy the land on the other side. They want to make a statement."

Jubran spoke up again. "How much land are they talking about?"

"As much as we can take."

"But look at us." Atweh gestured to the room. "We are only a dozen people."

"That's why we're having this meeting. Do what I tell you to do, follow the directions, and we'll grow to thousands." Khalafi looked over at Atweh. "Do you have a problem with that?"

"No." Atweh shook his head, no longer willing to argue. "Not at all."

They sat in silence a moment, then Shahid returned to the topic at hand. "So, what are you telling us to do?"

"The first thing we need to do is to find out how IDF operates. Get as close as we can without provoking them. Determine the point at which they will respond. And we need to document it. Analyze it. Be deliberate about it. Make sure that what we think will happen is actually what will happen. Then we'll know how to create a strategy that will allow us to move thousands of people to the border without getting them killed before they can get past the guards." Khalafi looked around at each of them. "This is a big operation."

"Pictures might help," Shahid suggested with a cooperative tone.

"Great idea," Khalafi praised. "You can be in charge of that. Make sure we get plenty. And video, too."

✦ ✦ ✦

For the first of their approaches to the border fence, Khalafi's group met at the house in Umm al-Kilab, then climbed into a pickup truck and drove toward the Sufa Crossing. Several cargo trucks were already there waiting in line to cross the border. Khalafi brought the truck to a stop behind them and sat there a moment, studying the landscape. That quickly proved futile and after observing the checkpoint and a few pictures, he steered the truck out of line and drove past the others.

When their approach did not bring an immediate response,

the men riding in back began throwing rocks and bottles at the soldiers guarding the border crossing. When Khalafi realized what they were doing he felt a surge of anger. Then in almost the same instant he saw soldiers at the checkpoint begin to move into place and realized, however unwittingly his companions may have acted, they had induced the IDF soldiers to react at just the right moment—close enough for observation, far enough away to likely avoid a deadly confrontation.

As the pickup truck continued forward, soldiers at the checkpoint took up defensive positions behind a concrete barrier near the edge of the road. Moments later, a tear gas canister burst directly over the truck. At the same time, live gunfire aimed in the direction of the pickup, but not intended to strike them, hit the ground, kicking up puffs of dust all around them.

Finally, though, one of the shots struck the pavement just ahead of them. A second hit the mirror on the truck's passenger side. Instantly, Khalafi wheeled the vehicle around, pressed the gas pedal to the floor, and started in the opposite direction. His eyes burned from the tear gas and his heart was racing from the adrenalin rush of the moment, but he was glad to have taken a step toward completing the task Al-Hadi had assigned him.

By the time they reached the house, the thrill of the moment had begun to fade, as had the irritation from the tear gas. That's when Khalafi began to process all that he had observed that day. And that's when he and the others with him realized that organizing a protest at the Sufa Crossing would not be easy.

As with most of the other crossing points, no one lived near the border fence. Certainly not in the immediate area around the checkpoint. But unlike areas farther north in Gaza, the area in the south was predominantly agricultural, especially near the fence where there was nothing but fields and farmland. The nearest housing area dense enough to provide anyone for a protest was more than a kilometer away. And even there he wouldn't find the thousands that he needed.

"Even if we had the people," Atweh said, "getting them from where they live all the way up to the border where the checkpoint is located would be impossible."

"What do you mean?" Shahid asked.

"Busses," Atweh replied. "I'm talking about busses."

"What about them?"

"To stage the protest envisioned by Hamas leadership," Khalafi explained, "we would need to bus people to the border."

"So," Shahid said, "we bus them."

Atweh looked over at him. "Thousands?"

"Yeah."

"That could never happen."

"Why not?"

"We don't have that many buses."

"Oh," Shahid reacted as the energy drained from his voice. "I didn't think about that."

"What we need," Khalafi suggested, "is a way to motivate the people to come, rather than invite them or ask them or demand that they come. A way that makes them *want* to come no matter how far it is."

"No," Shomali replied. "That's not how it works." He looked over at Khalafi. "You know how they do these things. You've been involved in more of these than the rest of us." He glanced around at the others. "We are Hamas. We will tell them to come and they will come."

"Yeah," someone joined in. "We'll tell them it's their service to Allah. Their own Jihad. And they'll respond or else."

"Exactly," another added.

"This is how it has been done before and it's how we will do it."

Khalafi shook his head. "We could do that and get a crowd the scope of the ones we've had before. Which was perhaps a hundred. That's not what we want here. It has to be much larger."

Shomali argued. "They had thousands when we demonstrated against the American Embassy move to Jerusalem."

"Yes." Khalafi nodded in agreement. "And it took weeks to organize. And it was just one location. And they were all motivated by the desecration of Jerusalem. We don't have that advantage."

"Then we'll have to find one," Atweh stated flatly. "I don't think it will be that difficult."

Khalafi decided not to argue the point any further. The men with him that day were the best available to him. If the demonstration was to be as successful as Hamas leadership expected, these men were the ones who would pull it off. But he knew from hearing their discussion that he had a difficult task ahead. And he knew for certain that he needed a new way to motivate others to participate. Something different from the way they'd done it in the past. Something that would bring a crowd of its own volition to the border. Something that would make them want to be there no matter how far it might be or how overwhelming the obstacles. He just didn't know yet what that something was.

✦ ✦ ✦

Farther north in Gaza, near the Erez Crossing, Khalil Farah was recruited to lead a similar protest. Like Khalafi, he gathered a group of Hamas operatives with whom he was well acquainted and began a series of reconnaissance trips to the crossing, traveling as close to the border as possible by vehicle, then walking forward on foot. Checking the IDF response, noting their troop strength, their position, and plotting their response.

A friend who crossed the border at the checkpoint for medical attention in Ashkelon was recruited to take pictures and video with a cell phone, capturing images from both sides and of the actual crossing procedure. He brought those images to Farah, who downloaded them to a laptop, then spent hours with his group huddled over the images, studying every detail.

Over the following weeks, Farah and his team made repeated trips to the border crossing. At the same time, each of his men organized their own groups, telling their people, "We are staging the largest protest ever. The Ayatollah himself has ordained it.

And not just a protest, we intend to cross the border into Israel and continue our protest on the other side by actually occupying land beyond the fence, even if only a small area."

When some noted that many would die in the effort, Farah and his men responded, "Yes. It is true. Some of us will die. But others of us will make it across and whether we make it across the border or not, we will let the Israelis and the world know the true nature of our situation and the oppression that we face here. You must join us in this work. Allah is with us."

Unlike other crossing locations, the one at Erez had been the scene of numerous protests, demonstrations, and clashes with IDF troops. The checkpoint had been challenged many times and people who lived near it were always eager to participate. Also unlike the other crossings, this one was located much closer to densely populated residential areas. That meant gathering protesters in the thousands would be a much easier task.

Consequently, hundreds joined in what quickly became almost daily protests, the crowds growing larger, more vocal, and more violent every day. Some only shouted and threw rocks or bottles at the guards. Others, however, tossed homemade Molotov cocktails at the checkpoint. Though they landed some distance from the soldiers, they created a noticeable explosion followed by a plume of black smoke that seemed to please the growing crowds.

At the same time, others prepared kites that they released to fly over the border fence. Attached to the kites were gas bombs that were ignited by cell phone. They landed on the other side and set fire to fields and even a few houses, creating more than a nuisance to residents who lived on the Israeli side of the fence.

Farah's men cheered at the sight of all of it—the crowds, the flying rocks and bottles, the exploding gas bombs and resulting fires. And the sound of their voices only served to increase the crowd's enthusiasm as tensions in the region continued to rise. Everyone sensed that an explosive moment was coming, but no one seemed certain what that moment would bring.

✦ ✦ ✦

Back in southern Gaza, Khalafi continued to wrestle with how to attract a large crowd for a protest at the Sufa Crossing. As he did, the enthusiasm of the dozen men he'd managed to recruit seemed to lag. In an effort to keep them engaged, he visited a cargo container he used for storage and retrieved a dozen rocket-propelled grenades, then loaded them in the pickup truck and brought them to the house in Umm al-Kilab. Shomali, Atweh, and the others he'd gathered as his core group met him there and they became excited when they saw the rockets. "Now, this is what I'm talking about!" Shomali exclaimed. He picked up one of the rockets and held it like a trophy. "This is how you let the Jews know what you mean."

Using the house and surrounding neighborhood as a shield, Khalafi and his men fired one of the rockets in the direction of the border crossing. Moments later, they burst into laughter at the sound of the rocket exploding somewhere in the distance.

"But we don't know if it hit anything," Atweh complained.

"We need a spotter," Shahid decided. "Someone to get closer to watch and tell us how to adjust our aim."

Khalafi volunteered. "I'll go. The rest of you stay here and be ready when I call." He'd done this a hundred times as a kid. In fact, it was one of the ways he'd first participated in a demonstration, spotting rocket fire for a group of older guys.

From the house in Umm al-Kilab, Khalafi drove in the pickup truck to within sight of the border crossing, then turned onto a road that led between the many farm fields that covered the area near the fence. When he'd gone far enough to suggest he was just a farmhand, he brought the truck to a stop, then got out and lay flat on the ground.

Using a cell phone, Khalafi placed a call to Atweh. "Okay. Let the next one go."

Moments later, Khalafi heard the whistling sound of a rocket as it sailed overhead. It landed near the checkpoint and exploded with a loud thud that even from that distance he could feel. But it landed in the open and did no damage.

Khalafi spoke into the phone. "Adjust a little to the right."

The next rocket landed on the other side of the checkpoint. Like the first, it made a loud noise and kicked up a cloud of dust, but did no damage. "That's too far right," Khalafi ordered. "Come back to the left."

The next rocket came down on the road squarely in front of the checkpoint but well within the Gaza side. "Okay," Khalafi said.

"Hold that position but make the next one longer."

A few minutes later, a rocket landed atop a truck that was stopped at the crossing. The truck exploded in a ball of fire that sent the checkpoint guards scrambling for cover. Khalafi snapped a picture of it with his cell phone. "Okay. That's enough. Better get out of there before they shoot back." As he spoke, he crawled back to the truck, turned it around, and drove toward the house.

Khalafi was certain his men enjoyed the exercise. This was the kind of thing they'd been doing long before Al-Hadi asked him to lead a massive group demonstration. But he was equally certain it did little to further their cause. Rocket attacks only harassed the Israelis, and even when they hit something they only damaged a single structure or, as in this case, a single vehicle. It did much to provoke the IDF to retaliate, but little to further the Palestinian cause. They needed a new way to express themselves. And Khalafi continued searching for a new way to build enthusiasm among his people.

CHAPTER

3

IN NEW YORK CITY, Davoud Hatami, an Iranian-born American citizen, sat in his office and looked out on Madison Avenue. As he gazed down at the people and traffic below, he thought back over his life, remembering how he had flourished since coming to America and how he had come to think of himself not as an Iranian, but as a New Yorker.

Hatami had been brought to the United States by his parents, both of whom had been loyal to Shah Reza Pahlavi and fled Iran in the early 1970s before the Shah's government collapsed. After arriving in New York, Hatami's father obtained a position with a firm that had longstanding ties to the Iranian oil business. Even after the collapse of the government, his position afforded the family a comfortable lifestyle in an apartment just a few blocks from where Hatami now worked. The area of the city between

Midtown and Murray Hill was his childhood neighborhood, the place where he grew up and the place he thought of as his hometown.

After high school, Hatami enrolled at Columbia University where he majored in advertising. Following graduation, he took a job at Adams-Merken, one of the city's premier advertising agencies. Later, with financial backing from his family and with the help of the family's international connections, he established an agency of his own—Madison Park and De Heer, named after his favorite New York City streets and one of New York's original settlers.

From an inauspicious beginning, Hatami's business grew to become the go-to organization for some of the world's largest corporations, especially those attempting to avoid—or recover from—devastating public relations fiascos. But as Hatami looked out over his beloved New York, he faced his own challenge.

Hatami's parents were of Arab descent, but having been born and reared in Iran, they came to view themselves as Persian, adopted the Persian culture, and eschewed religion of any sort. While in high school, however, Hatami began attending Friday prayers at a mosque in Brooklyn. Not long after that, a friend introduced him to Muhsen Jadid, a Muslim cleric who was associated with a radical Alawite cell operating in New York. Before long, Hatami was not only a practicing Shia Muslim but also fully radicalized.

Under the direction of Jadid, Hatami finished high school,

enrolled at Columbia, and followed a traditional American career path, taking care not to involve himself in overt Islamic activity of any kind. He even stopped attending prayers at the mosque and ceased meeting directly with Jadid. Instead, the two maintained contact by means of cryptic messages passed through friends and later, when the Internet became widely available, through the chat feature of an online video game.

Jadid's goal had been to create in Hatami an American citizen who was above reproach but who secretly and inwardly was as radical as any Islamic fighter in the Middle East. To that end, Hatami had been a willing participant and the plan had succeeded completely. He became known to marketing professionals around the world as an advertising genius and to politicians and business leaders as a trusted advisor. Along the way, he had enjoyed a fairytale life. But until the day the phone call came, he did not realize how deeply American culture had seeped into his mind, will, and emotions, nor how addicted he'd become to it.

The call that came that day was from Rifaat Kanaan, CEO of a software startup and one of Hatami's clients. Unlike Hatami, however, Rifaat attended services at the Brooklyn mosque and was a frequent go-between for Jadid. Kanaan had been short and to the point. "We need to hire your services." With those six words, Hatami knew his world was about to change.

Three hours later, Hatami met with Kanaan at a cafe in Jamaica Queens. Over a traditional Iranian meal, Kanaan outlined Jadid's request. "Make certain news crews are available to cover demonstrations in Gaza set to occur near the end of the month. See that their coverage is broadcast around the world."

"I will need to provide specific dates and times."

"We don't have those yet," Kanaan replied. "I will contact you when we do. But you should get busy laying the groundwork for this now."

Hatami bristled at the abrupt comment. He didn't need Kanaan or anyone else to tell him how to do his job. But instead of retorting in anger, as he really wanted, he forced a smile. "Yes. I will get right on it."

"And," Kanaan added with a whisper, "I have been instructed to tell you this comes from the top."

"The top?"

Kanaan smiled. "The Ayatollah himself has authorized this."

The remark seemed over the top, even for Jadid, and more than a little unnecessary. Hatami had always done whatever Jadid asked and he had done it without question. There was no need for such a statement . . . unless he meant it as an honor. To tell him that the Ayatollah had approved a plan that included him. Perhaps that's what it was? Certainly, he was known well enough that someone in Iran might have heard of him.

"Very well," Hatami said in response. "Report that I will be pleased to do as the Ayatollah wishes."

With numerous major corporations for clients, and having been involved in many of the most important events of the past twenty years, Hatami had a vast array of media contacts. However, choosing the right person for the coverage Jadid requested was a bit of a challenge. If he gave it to one of the major networks, they would expect an immediate crisis. Most of their coverage was oriented toward current incidents. The craft of uncovering a story before it became known, then reporting on it as it developed was not really their forte. What he needed was a news organization with extensive relationships in the Middle East, reporters who were committed to telling actual stories and not just the pop fluff served up in a three or four minute news spot, that also had the resources to ferret out the details and then stick with a situation as it unfolded over a period of weeks, not days. Only one organization like that came to mind—ISD News Service.

Founded in 1941 as a clearinghouse for independent photographers, ISD had slowly expanded from merely photographing events to reporting them and developed into a network of independent stringers that gradually became a news service. By the 1990s, the company provided a large portion of the reporting shown on daily television broadcasts. John Gleeson was ISD's president. Hatami knew him well. A few days after talking to Kanaan, he invited Gleeson to lunch at the National, a popular upscale Midtown restaurant.

After catching up on the latest about family and friends, Hatami turned the conversation to the topic of Gaza. "Are your people covering these latest incidents in Gaza?"

"We have a few people there," Gleeson replied. "Seems to be just the typical stuff, though." Then his eyes opened wider and he looked over at Hatami. "Why? Have you heard something?"

Hatami had a knowing smile. "I hear this might not be the typical situation."

"What do you mean?"

"Sources tell me the people of Gaza plan protests at all five border crossings, and we think they intend to do them all at the same time, too."

"We?"

Hatami did his best to appear vague while also delivering a hint. "Our firm has been hired by an Israeli company."

"What kind of company?"

"A biotech firm."

"And why would a biotech firm be interested in protests along the Gaza border?"

"Well . . ." Hatami gave him another knowing look. "They have close ties to the prime minister's office."

Gleeson leaned away, as if taking a moment to think about that comment. Then a look of realization came over him, as if he realized Hatami was giving him an inside scoop at the suggestion of the Israelis. Perhaps even the prime minister himself!

For his part, Hatami was nervous about making such an insinuation, especially since it was blatantly untrue. But seeing the look on Gleeson's face, he felt a sudden sense of satisfaction at having apparently pulled it off.

"This will take a few weeks to develop but they anticipate huge crowds," Hatami continued.

"How huge?"

"Larger than anything ever seen before."

"And you're getting this from the inside?"

"Yes," Hatami replied.

Gleeson was obviously intrigued. "What are the Israelis going to do about it?"

"I don't know, but whatever they do, it is expected to be big." That part was a deviation from the directions he'd been given by Kanaan, but Hatami didn't care. As far as he knew, Kanaan could be making the whole thing up for his own purposes. Hatami was the one with the risk, placing the reputation of his firm on the line for this meeting. And since it was his firm, he felt the liberty to ad lib as seemed necessary.

"I suppose in Gaza," Gleeson noted, "Hamas can do anything it wants."

Hatami took a coy tone. "This might not be just Hamas."

Gleeson frowned. "Then who is it?"

"This appears to be the work of the residents of Gaza themselves."

"That seems impossible."

"That's what everyone else says, too," Hatami agreed. "But our sources indicate otherwise."

"That has never happened before, has it? I mean, it's always been Hamas who instigated this sort of thing, never merely private citizens, hasn't it?"

"It would seem so."

"This could represent a dramatic change in Gaza."

"You should look into it," Hatami strongly urged. "Get your people in place. Dig out the details. Get ahead of the competition in breaking the coverage."

"Yes," Gleeson agreed. "I think you're right."

✦ ✦ ✦

Meanwhile, Hossein Rajabian, one of the first Iranian operatives to enter Israel pursuant to General Bagheri's strategy, began carefully recruiting Arabs in the West Bank. Sleeper agents sent to Israel years earlier. Fully trained, always ready, living unremarkable and unassuming lives. Waiting for just such a moment as this when someone would come and awaken them for service in the cause of Arab nationalism.

This group became Rajabian's core source of support, similar in function to the ones recruited by Khalafi and Farah in Gaza. These, however, brought a different skill set to the task. They were bomb makers, primarily. People whose painstaking work required the most time, attention, and specialized resources. Others in the group would see that they had what they needed. Capable people, adept at acquiring the large quantities of the items operations like this required—precursor chemicals for the explosive devices, backpacks to carry them, and transportation to ensure that bombs, backpacks, and children arrived at the correct time and location. And also people who were able to do all of that without drawing attention to themselves.

After Rajabian established a group that could facilitate and support the technical aspects of the Jerusalem protest, he moved on from working solely with members of the Arab community to making contact with liberal Israelis. This was perhaps the most delicate part of his assignment. It was potentially riskier than building the bombs or recruiting the children to carry them. He'd recognized this from the beginning and pushed back, arguing that they should avoid this part. An Iranian, in Israel on a diplomatic pretext, having direct contact with Israeli Jews, for the purpose of organizing a civic protest, based on issues that appealed solely to Israelis—it was too much, too cute, too dangerous. One slip and they would discover who he really was and then the entire operation would collapse. Gaza, Jerusalem, it would all fail. But he was assured that Bagheri had thought of this himself and insisted they go forward with it.

For the next several weeks Rajabian spent each day and many nights talking, listening, and observing the discussions and activities of various Israeli organizations—feminists who supported women's rights, gays and lesbians who advocated for equal rights, others who wanted legalized nonreligious marriages, and on, and on—hoping to find a group with a cause he could use as the rallying point for a massive civil demonstration in Jerusalem. Something that would attract a crowd on the day of the children's demonstration and pack the streets of the city with thousands of people who would become victims of the bombs in the backpacks carried by the children he had yet to recruit. Just thinking of how the idea would play out seemed like proof enough that it was too nuanced to work, but he had done his best to make it happen. And he got nowhere.

After weeks in the coffee shops, cafés, and lecture halls of the city, Rajabian came to the conclusion that he could easily stage a demonstration on any one of several topics that would attract a few hundred protesters each, but getting a crowd significantly larger than that would be almost impossible. There simply was no single issue capable of galvanizing liberals and moving them to action in overwhelming numbers. Hundreds, yes. But not the thousands they had wanted.

No doubt, he thought, *it is the reason the conservatives have remained in power. If the liberals had an issue that empowered them and put them in the streets to demonstrate, they would have put themselves in office years ago.*

Faced with the futility of planning a political protest using Israelis—a matter that was always ancillary to the primary focus of his mission—Rajabian decided to abandon the effort. If Bagheri or anyone else in Tehran wanted to organize a protest, they could come to Israel and do it themselves. He was finished with it. Instead, he turned his attention to the most important work he'd been sent to accomplish—that of organizing a Jerusalem protest led by children.

For that, Rajabian needed to locate an Arab school, with lots of Arab children, in a location that was a part of Israel but outside the disputed territory. An Arab enclave that had never been a source of trouble to the authorities and one that prided itself on that fact. And he knew precisely the correct location—Rahat, an Arab city not far from Beersheba.

Overwhelmingly Arab, the people of Rahat enjoyed the same liberties and freedom of access afforded those who lived in every other city and town in Israel. A peaceful place where social and economic advancement were at least as important as remaining distinctly Arab. Where parents stressed the need for a child to make good grades in school, rather than encouraging them to throw rocks and bottles at Israeli troops. It was the perfect place to find the children he needed for the Jerusalem protest and, no longer bound by any need to remain in Jerusalem, he headed there at once.

CHAPTER

4

WHEN GENERAL BAGHERI presented the Ayatollah with his strategy for an attack against Israel, he did so as if the proposed deployment of Iranian troops to Lebanon and Syria were a new idea. In reality, it was nothing new at all. Iranian troops had been continually deployed to and rotated through both countries on an ongoing basis for years in support of Syrian president Bashar al-Assad's regime. Most recently, that support had been provided to shore up the regime in a conflict with Syrian rebels that devolved into a long-running civil war. A war that began as an offshoot of the Arab Spring, it had only recently reached an apparent end.

In the months that followed the adoption of Bagheri's strategy against Israel, the nature of Iran's military involvement shifted from that of supporting the Syrian government to one of positioning Iran's best troops for an assault on Israel. A strategy designed for the purpose of finally achieving the radical Iranian dream—a dream held by many but openly articulated most memorably by Iran's former president Mahmoud Ahmadinejad—the dream of wiping Israel off the map, once and for all. Having endured a long and costly war, Assad was all too happy to have an Iranian presence in his country and readily acceded to Bagheri's plans.

As Iranian troops moved out of Iran and into Syria and Lebanon in increasing numbers, Bagheri convened an operational meeting at his office in Tehran. That meeting was attended by General Alizadeh from the army, General Elahi from the air force, and Mahmoud Alavi, the Iranian intelligence minister. The others were already present when Alavi arrived. He seemed surprised when he entered the room and glanced around suspiciously before turning his attention to Bagheri. "Where is everyone else?" he asked with a puzzled expression.

"This is all," Bagheri replied. "You were expecting someone else?"

"Rasouli, Rouhani. Certainly Hassani." Alavi was referring to the other relevant ministers with a stake in the planned military action. Mehran Hassani, was the minister of defense, a person to whom Bagheri was nominally accountable. "I cannot participate in a defense ministry meeting without the defense minister present. You report to him. Not to me."

"I work with Hassani, but I do not report to him," Bagheri

said. He spoke with a dismissive and arrogant tone, as only one used to giving orders and having them obeyed could manage. "I report to the president and Supreme Leader."

"Relax," General Alizadeh soothed. "No one will report you."

The others chuckled, but Alavi looked uneasy. "I will sit," he said. "But do not expect me to participate."

"We were discussing our progress with the strategy against Israel," Bagheri informed him. "And that is what this meeting is about. We are deploying our troops in accordance with the Ayatollah's plan."

For certain, the plan originated with Bagheri and it was his future and, indeed, his life that was on the line should it fail. But once approved by the Ayatollah, the plan became the Ayatollah's, especially in the event of great success. All success was his. All failure was someone else's.

"We have designated the units we will use," Bagheri continued, "and we are training them for their mission. That and their deployment is proceeding according to schedule. The big issue— the one we were discussing when you arrived—is—"

"What will the Americans do?" Alavi cut him off and finished the sentence. "You want to know how the Americans will respond when they realize what you are doing." Again he looked over at Bagheri. "I tried to warn you about this very topic before you presented your strategy to the Ayatollah and the ministers."

"I considered what you had to say."

"And then you ignored it." Alavi looked to the others. "The

strategy is brilliant except for one thing. There is no way to check an American reaction. The Russians can tell us about it as it unfolds. The Chinese can tell us about it, too. But neither of them can stop a US response. And that is the problem with this strategy that no one in any of the meetings bothered to point out to the Supreme Leader."

General Elahi spoke up, ignoring all that Alavi had just said. "You are the head of intelligence. Will we know about the American response in advance? Before the bombs start falling on our heads."

"I assure you," Alavi answered with confidence, "we will know what the Americans are doing long before they do it."

"And you can say this, how?" Bagheri asked.

"I cannot say. I should not have said this much. I should not even be here."

"Relax," Bagheri said. "No one will tell."

"Certainly not us," General Alizadeh interjected.

Bagheri let his eyes bore in on Alavi. "How will we know?"

"You should ask Hassani."

Bagheri gave a dismissive gesture. "Hassani is opposed to the strategy. You know that already."

"Nonsense," Alavi retorted. "He can't possibly oppose it."

"But he does," General Alizadeh argued. "And not only that, he is lobbying the Ayatollah to rescind the entire plan."

Alavi frowned. "We can't rescind it." He glanced in Bagheri's direction. "Can we?"

"They can give the order," Bagheri responded. "But our operatives are too far into the plan to bring them back. Some of them can no longer be reached, even if we wanted to stop them ourselves."

"Even if the Ayatollah himself wanted to stop them," General Alizadeh added.

Alavi nodded. "As I thought."

"So, tell us," Bagheri insisted once more, "how is it that we will know the American response before they execute it?"

Alavi had a look of resignation. "Because," he sighed, "we have sources in America."

"Some of those famous television executives you brag about?" General Elahi needled.

Elahi gave a mocking look of horror. "VEVAK is relying on newspaper reporters?" VEVAK was an old term for the Iranian intelligence service.

"This has nothing to do with news reporters," Alavi answered curtly.

"Then, what?" Bagheri was growing impatient. "How will we know?"

"We have a source," Alavi said finally. "Someone high up in the US intelligence community."

"And who is that someone?" Bagheri badgered.

"That is all I will say." Alavi stood. "And this is as long as I can stay in this meeting." He started across the room toward the door. When he reached it, he paused and glanced back at them.

"You're certain we cannot recall our operatives?"

Bagheri shook his head. "Not the ones that matter."

Alavi lingered a moment longer, as if considering the topic, then jerked open the door and stepped out into the hall. When he was gone, Elahi turned to Bagheri. "I think you just got your way."

"How's that?" General Alizadeh looked bewildered. "What are you two talking about?"

"Alavi is on his way to see Hassani this very minute," Elahi explained.

"And that is good?"

"Yes," Bagheri nodded. "It's time Hassani realized that others in the government know what he is up to. And we aren't going to let him get away with it."

"You think Alavi will get him on board?"

"I think Alavi knows what to do next."

Mehran Hassani lived on an estate in eastern Tehran that included a five-hectare plot—five hundred acres by American measure. It was lavishly appointed with gardens, groves, and a variety of animals, all made possible by the family fortune in which he shared. For many generations his family had enjoyed great success in the textile business, with offices and manufacturing facilities in Egypt, India, Bangladesh, and Pakistan. That success allowed them to accumulate a fortune of which they secreted away in Switzerland, Luxembourg, and even in New York, where it remained safely out of the reach of Iranian authorities and obscured to the prying eyes of Americans wishing to impose their sanctions on it.

Hassani, of course, denied any connection to the business, but he lived as though he controlled it all.

One week after the meeting in Bagheri's office, Hassani went for a walk. As was his custom, he strolled among his gardens and made his way to a beautiful meadow where three zebras grazed. As you might expect, Hassani's walk did not end well for him. No one knows for certain how the end came to him, but he was reported missing that evening and the authorities conducted a citywide search. It was, of course, a totally pretentious effort—no one expected him to be found and certainly not found alive. It was, however, a useful escapade nonetheless.

President Rouhani used it as an occasion to round up key members of the People's Mojahedin, a dissident political group that had vigorously opposed Rouhani in the previous election and vowed to defeat him in the next. Its leadership council was brought in for questioning, then locked away in Evin Prison.

Foreign affairs minister Bijan Rasouli used the manhunt as a pretense for securing the Italian ambassador in a suite at the Espinas Hotel. It was a luxury suite, of course, and the ambassador had been in no great danger, but he had been at the hotel to spend the evening with his mistress, a relationship of which the detention put on public display. It proved quite an embarrassing incident for the ambassador and his paramour, which was the sole point of the detention.

In spite of all the show and running about the city searching and looking, the police never found Hassani alive. Six days after he disappeared, his decomposing body was found in a refuse pile at a tannery on the western side of the city. Forensics experts from Tehran University were called in to help identify the body. They used dental records and a birthmark on his back, which his wife confirmed was his. His wife remained on the family estate, living in the care of her very large staff.

After Hassani's body was discovered, President Rouhani appointed Farshid Monzavi as the new defense minister. Two weeks after the appointment, another meeting was convened in General Bagheri's office. Present that day were Monzavi, Bijan Rasouli, the foreign affairs minister, General Alizadeh from the army, General Elahi from the air force, and Mahmoud Alavi, the head of Iranian intelligence.

Monzavi began. "I understand from General Bagheri that most of the operatives are now working in Israel and are beyond our direct control."

"We can reach some of them," Alavi informed. "But it is difficult and not easily accomplished."

"I take that to mean it cannot be accomplished in a timely way, either."

"That is correct," Alavi confirmed. "Sending directions from here to the operatives in Israel would be a cumbersome matter."

"And if you *do* communicate with them, you do so through operatives working in Gaza, correct?"

Bagheri spoke up. "Yes, that is how we maintain contact for timing."

Monzavi had a questioning look. "Timing?"

"The attacks from Gaza must coincide with an attack in Jerusalem," Bagheri explained. "Which must be timed to cover our advances in Syria and Lebanon."

"You mean, it must all occur at the same time."

"More or less."

"The key to our success is the use of missiles," General Elahi explained.

"Hezbollah's missiles?"

"Yes," Elahi answered. "But our own, too."

Monzavi had a grim expression. "The Supreme Leader must authorize that. And he has not been forthcoming in that regard."

"We are aware of that," Bagheri noted. There was a stern tone to his voice and he seemed bothered by the subject.

"And how do you propose to convince him this time?" Monzavi asked.

"We have a plan," Bagheri answered.

Monzavi glanced around the room at the others. "A plan?"

General Alizadeh chimed in. "An option, actually."

"Ah." Monzavi's eyes brightened in a knowing look. "The Mahdi option."

"Yes, the Mahdi."

Monzavi smiled. "General, you do not seem a religious man to me."

"I use whatever works," Bagheri replied.

CHAPTER

5

A FEW KILOMETERS east of Masyaf, a city near the coast in the southwestern region of Syria, Shafiq Giladi went about his task as a night attendant at the Awada Petrol Depot. There, he loaded petroleum transfer trucks and cleaned up from the day crew's activities. Giladi enjoyed working at night, when the hot desert air cooled, the workload was the lightest, and fewer people were around to bother him.

Giladi, an Iraqi Jew, had arrived in Syria when the Americans invaded his native Iraq to bring down Saddam Hussein. Having lived in fear of Hussein's Baathist Muslims since an early age, he had wanted to leave the country earlier but could never find the means or contacts to settle anywhere else. Finally, though, as reports reached his Baghdad neighborhood that the American army was preparing to invade, he and a friend pooled their money, stole a car, and drove toward the Syrian border. After bribing a guard at the border checkpoint, they made their way to Aleppo, then drifted south to Damascus where they found a friend who had emigrated from Erbil with his family years earlier. Through their contacts, Giladi found work as a laborer in a restaurant, then landed a job with Awada.

Not long after taking the Awada job, Giladi was approached by a man who identified himself as Rafet Wassef. Slender and of medium build, he spoke Arabic well, but it was not his first language and Giladi detected a hint of an accent he was certain was Israeli. In the following months, the two became better acquainted—often meeting for coffee or attending soccer games together—and that's when Wassef made his play. "I have friends who would be interested in any information you could provide."

They were seated in a coffee shop not far from the depot where Giladi worked and he glanced around nervously, checking to see if any of his coworkers were present. "What kind of information?"

"You work for Awada."

"Yes."

"My friends would be interested in anything you can tell them about what you see, what you hear, what goes on there."

Giladi frowned. "You mean. . .about their business?"

"Whatever you see or hear." Wassef was intentionally vague. "That sort of thing."

"I am merely an attendant at a fuel depot," Giladi replied. "I work at night. Not much happens at night."

"You load trucks?"

"Sometimes." Giladi glanced around suspiciously once more, "But mostly I just clean up after they are finished making deliveries."

"Good, no one will notice you. No one will suspect anything."

Giladi took a sip of coffee, "Who are your friends?"

"The less you know about them, the better."

Giladi liked Wassef but he was glad not to know who these *friends* were. Still, he was curious now about whether he'd been set up from the beginning. "How did you find me?"

"I met your father."

Giladi was taken aback. "My father?"

"Moshe. The merchant in Baghdad. I met him when I was there on business. He told me about you."

The remark troubled Giladi deeply. Since coming to Syria, he had told no one about his family for fear there might be reprisals against them. In the old days, many family members of those who left Iraq met with harsh treatment from Hussein's henchmen. Giladi had wanted to spare his family that misery so he kept quiet and even changed his name. How did Wassef make the connection of him with his father? And how was he to understand Wassef's reference? Did he mean it as a threat? Did he really know his father? And why was he interested in information from the fuel depot? He was in no position to provide much.

"I can pay you a small amount," Wassef added. "Not much, but even small amounts can help over time."

They talked awhile longer, but Wassef gave no further details about the kind of assistance he expected from Giladi, just information. Whatever Giladi could provide. No matter how trivial it might seem at the time. By the time Giladi had finished his coffee, he had agreed to Wassef's proposal.

A few days later, Giladi returned to his apartment to find a cell phone on the table by his bed. There was no note with it, but when he checked the screen he saw that a message had come to the phone an hour earlier. He opened it to read, "Coffee tomorrow?"

Giladi replied, "Where?"

Almost immediately came the reply. "Same place." And with that, Giladi became an informant for Mossad.

That evening at the fuel depot, Giladi walked, as he always did, to a storage building in back and retrieved a large push broom. With the broom handle propped on his shoulder, he made his way to a row of loading stations and began sweeping up the day's sand and trash from the concrete pad beneath them. Although it wasn't late yet, Giladi was tired, which made the evening seem later than it really was.

Not long into his shift, Giladi heard the rumble of heavy trucks as they approached on Highway 35, the road from Hama that ran along the front of the depot. The sound grew steadily louder, and moments later he watched as convoy of dark green military transports rumbled past. Heavy trucks with dual axels in back and canvas coverings over the beds. Through the flaps of the canvas, he saw soldiers seated inside dressed in fatigues with combat helmets on their heads. He was certain they would each hold a rifle in their hands.

The soldiers could have been from anywhere, but the markings on the truck cabs indicated they were Iranian. Probably units of the Revolutionary Guard, Giladi thought. He had seen men like that in the area before. Masyaf was home to several military installations that the Iranians seemed to guard.

Giladi watched the trucks move past until they disappeared from sight, then he turned back to his sweeping. Thirty minutes later, he finished with the first loading station and sat down on a concrete barrier to take a break. Alone in the quiet of the evening, he took the cell phone from his pocket, found the number from the earlier text—the only number in the contacts list—and, using the code he and Wassef had worked out at their most recent meeting, sent a message that read, "8-789."

Seconds later, the message from Giladi arrived on Wassef's cell phone. Though it appeared to be nothing more than numbers, Wassef understood it immediately. He put aside the matter he was working on and, using a secure satellite phone, forwarded the message in decoded form to a Mossad analyst section in Tel Aviv for verification. "Eight-truck convoy traveling southwest on Highway 35 toward Masyaf. Believed to be Iranian Revolutionary Guard troops. Perhaps at company strength."

An hour later, the analyst section responded. "Review of existing information indicates troop movements in Syria are fresh troops replacing existing units that have been in the country for an extended deployment. We have added this to the database and will continue to monitor."

Wassef was unconvinced. Something in the back of his mind found the analyst section's report unsatisfying. So he took another cell phone from his satchel and sent a message to Avi Safra, a Mossad agent embedded with US troops who, although greatly reduced in number, remained on deployment in eastern Syria. The text read, "4812203252."

✦ ✦ ✦

Avi Safra was seated on an upturned five-gallon bucket outside a tent on a US Army base near Ain Issa. The base, situated due east of Aleppo on Highway 4, was home to a unit of Army Rangers from Fort Benning, Georgia. Safra had been embedded with the Rangers for six months and, although he respected and enjoyed their company, he found it necessary to spend a few minutes each day to himself. That evening, as he sat on the bucket, he sipped from a cup of tea he'd brewed over a Sterno™ flame. The tea, sent from the United States and included in an MRE (Meal, Ready to Eat), did not taste as good as what he remembered from Kadosh, a café in Jerusalem he frequented whenever he was home, but it was tea nonetheless. He'd learned to tolerate it and, on occasion, to enjoy it.

As Safra took a sip of tea, the satellite phone vibrated in his pocket. From the single vibration he knew he'd received a text message. He grabbed the phone, and glanced at the screen to see that the message was from a caller identified by his device as 246—the designation for Wassef. The text read, "4812203252." He understood it immediately as a request for him to report on the latest troop movements in his area. Wassef, it seemed, was particularly interested in any information he might obtain about Iranian troops.

Safra took another sip of tea and thought about what the message meant. He knew what Wassef wanted and he knew why he was interested. For the past two months Mossad agents and operatives in Syria had seen Iranian troops moving into position to join the advancing Syrian army regulars—the Syrians cleared an area of rebels, then Iranian army units stepped in to occupy the newly conquered territory while the Syrians pressed forward to new areas. All of which required the addition of more Iranian troops. By Safra's count, six new Iranian divisions had entered the country in the past two months, but that was just a guess. He didn't have the data to back it up. The Americans had the data, though—which was what Wassef really needed—and he wondered how he might obtain that information.

Just then, Colonel Atwood appeared from around the corner. Tall and broad shouldered, Atwood was the stereotypical American soldier. Handsome, angular, and self-assured. A soldier's soldier. Firm and fair, but no nonsense. And when he wanted his men to obey to the letter, he gave his orders with language they didn't forget. He commanded the Rangers at the base and, in Safra's estimation, did a very good job of it.

Safra shoved the phone into his pocket and turned to face Atwood. "Everything okay, Colonel?"

Atwood looked down at him. "We're about to head out. Are you coming with us?"

"Where to?"

Atwood gestured over his shoulder. "Come with me and I'll tell you about it."

Cup in hand, Safra followed Atwood to the base command tent—a canvas-over-frame structure with a raised wooden floor and air-conditioning. Worktables lined the walls, their surface covered with laptops, notepads, and documents of every kind. Analysts and technicians were seated, busily sorting through the constant stream of information that kept Atwood and his staff abreast of the latest activity in the region.

A map was pinned to a board on the far side of the room and Atwood made his way to it. "This area right here." He pointed to the map. "We've had reports of a significant ISIS presence there. We're sending recon units into the area to determine if the reports are accurate."

"And I suppose, as usual, the Syrians are facilitating their activity?"

"The Syrians are still playing all ends against the middle."

"What about the Iranians? Any sign of them in that area?"

Atwood shook his head. "Not here. Nearest Iranians are ten kilometers to the west of us." He stepped to a table, picked up a folder, then handed it to Safra. "Everything you want to know about the Iranians is in here."

Safra quickly glanced through the file and saw that Atwood was correct. Everything he wanted to know indeed was right there. Estimates. Photos. Reconnaissance reports. In fact, there was so much information in the folder that Safra began to wonder if Atwood had been tipped to the message he'd received from Wassef. But then, why give it to *him*? Why not just share the information directly from Langley to Tel Aviv? Unless Langley didn't have it. No, he realized, that couldn't be the reason. The CIA had agents in Syria. NSA had listening stations trained on the region. The US Army had satellite and airborne battlefield control systems that detected everything. They had more information than anyone. At times, more information than they could process.

And then Safra thought of the interagency rivalry that plagued the Americans. The CIA unwilling to share its information with Defense Intelligence. Neither of them willing to cooperate with NSA. Maybe someone at the CIA, or the DIA, or the NSA knew what Mossad wanted but didn't feel comfortable sharing it directly, agency to agency. Maybe they didn't have orders to do so, but thought it was necessary and wanted to share it anyway. Maybe Wassef knew all of that and Atwood was simply the messenger, while he was merely the courier. And the message he'd received was only intended to put him in a useful position rather than a request for him to develop his own information. And of course, how could he develop the kind of specific information Wassef wanted anyway?

Atwood interrupted Safra's thoughts. "We need to go. You can look at that file when we get back."

"Right. I'll do that."

"Sure thing." Atwood took the file from him and laid it on the table near where they'd been standing. "It'll be right there waiting for you." He glanced at the map once more, then turned to leave. "Come on. We gotta go."

✦ ✦ ✦

Early the next morning, Wassef received a response from Safra. Based on information from US sources, fresh Iranian troops had been arriving in Syria at a steady pace. Safra included numbers derived from the data in Colonel Atwood's file, his own observations, and information he'd received from sources in the region. In addition, US information indicated some Iranian units were being moved to Lebanon. Wassef forwarded the report to Tel Aviv immediately.

Mossad analysts in Tel Aviv confirmed Wassef's report through agents in Lebanon, then checked those reports against satellite images from the past two weeks. Over several days, they expanded their review and noticed additional tents being erected at several Hezbollah training sites in southern Lebanon. New buildings were being constructed there as well, indicating the troops intended to remain there indefinitely and further supporting agent contentions that Iran was expanding its involvement in Lebanon.

In the course of normal operating procedure, Mossad analysts prepared their findings in a report that was forwarded to their supervisor. Information from that report was included in the daily security briefing provided to the Israeli prime minister, Benjamin Netanyahu. When the briefing concluded, Netanyahu met privately with Avigdor Lieberman, the minister of defense.

"I'm concerned about this buildup of Iranian troops," Netanyahu admitted.

"As am I," Lieberman replied.

"I suppose they could offer some justification for being in Syria. I don't agree with it, but they could give a strategic reason. Supporting Syrian army operations. Propping up Assad. But increasing their strength in Lebanon . . ."

"None of it bodes well for us."

Netanyahu agreed. "This doesn't seem to be merely a defensive posture."

Lieberman arched an eyebrow. "You are concerned about their offensive capabilities?"

"Yes." Netanyahu looked over at him. "Aren't you?"

"I am now," Lieberman acquiesced. "And I have been for quite some time. Having Iraq on our border was bad enough. But now the Iranians . . . It can only mean trouble."

"We need to know more about what they are doing."

Lieberman nodded in agreement.

"You will find out what's going on?"

"Absolutely."

CHAPTER

6

AFTER CONCLUDING his work in Jerusalem, Hossein Rajabian arrived in Rahat. He settled first in a hotel and began searching for an apartment, but found Rahat too provincial for his tastes. He was committed to the Islamic cause, but Arabs in Rahat were predominantly Bedouin and he found their culture somewhat off-putting. "Rather like living among Saudi Arabians," he had noted in a rare text to a friend.

One week after arriving in the region, Rajabian located an apartment in Beersheba, twenty kilometers north of Rahat. As part of Israel in which travel between villages was not restricted— he was free to make the drive to Rahat as often as he wished. The commute turned out to be a pleasant, relaxing time.

In Rahat, Rajabian went looking for the Allah Hu Madrasat Muqadasa, a private school with classes from kindergarten through twelfth grade that catered to Rahat's upscale Arab community. Rashid Masalha, a fifth grade teacher at Allah Hu, had been chosen by Jalil Majidi—Rajabian's handler in VAJA, Iran's ministry of intelligence—to lead the children's planned protest in Jerusalem. Rajabian had little trouble finding the school.

In addition to having access to the requisite number of children necessary for the protest, Masalha had been chosen to lead it because he had no obvious connections to Hamas or any other radical organization, and because he had been living peacefully in Rahat for more than a dozen years. A modern-day Nizari, he lived a normal, unassuming life—going about his work as a teacher in the same manner as any other, waiting quietly for the day when he would be called upon to act.

Masalha had come to Israel as a student at Al-Quds University in Jerusalem. After graduation, he wanted to remain in Israel and applied for a teaching job through a program sponsored by the ministry of education. The program offered new non-Israeli graduates a path to permanent residency in exchange for teaching at an Arab school. Allah Hu Madrasat Muqadasa needed teachers, Masalha needed a job. They were a perfect match.

During his first year at Allah Hu, Masalha took a trip to Istanbul. While there, he was approached by Iranian intelligence agents who met him through a mutual friend. They wanted him in the service, but not as an active asset.

"We want you to remain in place as you are," they explained. "That is all. Following a career as a teaching professional. Perhaps we shall never need you. But if that day comes, we will expect your absolute loyalty."

"But won't the Israelis know I am working for you? Even if I'm not, as you say, *active*?"

"Unless you are needed, you will never hear from us again. It is a simple matter. You make yourself available to us now. We use you only if we need you."

Masalha smiled. "And what do I receive in exchange?"

"We will make discreet deposits to an account only you control."

Masalha had a puzzled frown "An account?"

"Perhaps a Swiss account."

"And no one will be able to find it and know the payments are coming from you?"

"Not if it is in Switzerland," they assured.

True to their agreement, the Iranian intelligence apparatus made regular payments to Masalha through a numbered account. He kept track of it but never accessed it. Holding it instead against that day when, should it ever come, he might need to disappear.

When Masalha returned to Rahat, he went about his work as before, doing his best to be the best teacher possible. Through his position at the school, he came to know parents, teachers, students, and imams throughout the southern region of Israel. Each one he cataloged in his mind, then in a file on his laptop, according to their potential usefulness—parents who tended toward disaffection with the status quo, students who were oriented toward obtaining his approval. Noting those who identified with the Palestinian cause and agenda—and those who did not. Just in case the day should come when he would be called upon for some as yet unknown activity on behalf of his native Iran. Though he did not know it at the time, that day was fast approaching.

A few days after locating the school, Rajabian appeared at Masalha's apartment. Using a prescribed series of questions and statements—a defined litany familiar to them both with set questions and well-defined answers used as a means of verifying each other's identity and credibility—Rajabian identified himself as an Iranian operative who'd come to give Masalha his orders. The day of service had finally arrived.

They sat at a table in the kitchen and, after listening to Rajabian's outline of the planned protest—children wearing backpacks filled with explosive devices, on a school-related trip to Jerusalem—Masalha said in a knowing tone, "This was General Bagheri's idea."

Rajabian had an amused grin. "You are familiar with him?"

"Yes."

"That strikes me as strange but not altogether unexpected."

"And why is that?" Masalha asked.

"You have been here a long time. I should have thought establishing a relationship with someone as deeply involved in our government as Bagheri would have been rather impossible for a man in your position."

"My position?"

"A teacher. In southern Israel."

Masalha did not like the implication. "Yes, well, I do not need a relationship with a man to know how he thinks."

The tone of Masalha's remark did not set well with Rajabian and he began to wonder if Masalha wasn't more connected than he'd been led to believe. Many from Iran went abroad to live, assumed other identities, and established lives with no traceable connection to Iran, all the while remaining deeply connected to events there—some even with relatives in Tehran who held important government positions.

Masalha continued the conversation. "Tell me something. These devices you wish to strap to the backs of my students—how will they be detonated?"

"We will take care of that," Rajabian assured.

"And the bombs?"

"What of them?"

"How will they be constructed? Who will construct them?"

"That is not your concern."

"And how do you propose to get these backpack bombs onto the backs of my students?"

"We have people for that," Rajabian repeated. He was quickly tiring of this line of questioning.

"You will force them?"

"No."

"Good." Masalha sighed. "Very good," he whispered.

Rajabian looked over at him. "You are fond of your students?"

The two men stared at each other a moment before Masalha finally said, "Yes. I am fond of them."

"Will that pose a problem for your involvement?"

Masalha looked down at the tabletop, and then responded with a quick shake of his head, "It will not be a problem."

"Any other questions, then?"

"Just one."

"What is that?"

"Typically when we take trips with the students, parents accompany us. Not all of the parents, but some. Will they be allowed to come on this trip?"

Rajabian had not thought of that and he took a moment to consider the matter. Masalha noticed the look of hesitancy on his face. "That troubles you?"

"No," Rajabian replied. "As long as they are not apprised of the full story."

"Most people in Rahat, even though they are Arabs," Masalha explained, "have not been radicalized. They feel as though they have a stake in the success of the region."

Rajabian frowned, the asked sarcastically, "What does that mean?"

"They are not like Palestinians in Gaza or even the West Bank. They don't spend their time throwing rocks and bottles at the Israeli soldiers. They want their children to succeed in the typical way and they are involved in their lives."

Rajabian gave a dismissive gesture. "Do not worry about that.

Organize them in any way that suits your situation. We need about a hundred participants. And we need them to travel to Jerusalem."

"When should this trip take place?"

"I will tell you that when the time comes." Rajabian was now having second thoughts about whether Masalha was the correct person for the job. He seemed unusually attached to his students, and Rajabian wondered if he would be able to follow through on the plan, knowing that they would die in the end. He looked over at Masalha. "You can do this? You can create this trip? This event for your students?"

Masalha nodded. "Yes. But I don't have a hundred students in my class. No one does. I will need to involve at least one other class. Perhaps two. Which means involving the teachers for those classes."

"You know these teachers?"

"Yes."

"If you must use them, then that is what you must do. But tell them only about the trip. Not about me or about anything we have discussed."

A few days later, Masalha introduced his class to the idea of a trip to Jerusalem, working the topic into the class curriculum. As instructed, he told them only the kinds of things he would have told them for any other proposed class trip—their planned destination, what they would see, how long the trip would take. Normally, he would know the date of the trip at the time he first started discussing it with them. In this case, however, he was forced to say, "We don't have an exact date right now. We are still working out the details."

Later that week, parents began approaching him with questions about the trip. Some raised the issue of how safe an event like that might be. "We have seen many acts of violence recently," they told him. " More than usual, it seems."

"I can't guarantee it will be tension free," Masalha revealed. "But we are going there to see the historic sights and to talk about history—the history of the region and the history of our people—as we have done with classes in previous years. The places we intend to visit are all public places. They are heavily guarded and visitors are carefully screened before anyone is let inside. Our children need to see the sights and hear the stories. That's all we are trying to do. We'll go up and back in the same day."

As expected, parents of Masalha's students saw nothing unusual about the proposed trip, and readily agreed to allow their children to participate. Several volunteered to accompany the group as chaperones. Masalha was glad to have their support but felt a twinge of guilt at the thought of betraying their confidence. These were not like the radical Muslims he'd been taught to appreciate, and certainly not like the Palestinians who saw martyrdom as the ultimate expression of their faith.

CHAPTER
7

IN GAZA, Masud Darwaza left his apartment at Khan Yunis in the southern end of the Gaza Strip. The same area where Mohammed Khalafi was assigned to organize the protest at the Sufa Crossing. A Palestinian with close ties to members of Hamas, he had nevertheless avoided direct participation in their activities. Protesting—throwing rocks and bottles at Israeli soldiers guarding the border crossing checkpoints—or the other popular activity— taking videos of those doing the throwing and selling those videos to media outlets—never interested him. Life in Gaza was miserable, and he had no interest in profiting from anyone's misery at any level.

Although he lived in the same area as Khalafi and, in fact, knew Khalafi, though not well, Darwaza was not involved in the organizing effort for the Sufa Crossing protest, but he had heard about it from a friend. Rumors about the protest seemed to be everywhere, too. In the coffee shop, among the neighbors who sat on the stoop outside Darwaza's building at night, even at the mosque. So prevalent were they that he asked around and learned that, indeed, a protest was being planned for the Sufa Crossing, but not just for Sufa. Protests were being organized at all five Gaza border fence crossings.

At the same time, Darwaza heard reports of new Iranian operatives arriving in Gaza. "They have come to assist with the protests," someone said.

"Something big is in the making," others suggested.

People were talking about it. Word was spreading. There seemed to be tension in the air, but Darwaza couldn't find a single person who had actually seen one of the alleged Iranians for themselves. Only reports and rumors about things someone else said they'd heard from another source.

The fact that Iranian operatives were in Gaza was nothing new. Iranian operatives worked and lived in Gaza all the time. Some were there on a more-or-less permanent basis, attached to one of the UN relief agencies active in the area. But this seemed different. The rumors he'd heard were more intense, the excitement more palpable, and Darwaza was determined to learn the truth about what was going on.

Secretly, Darwaza was a spy. An Arab who lived in Gaza, but who had been recruited by agents from Shin Bet, Israel's internal security agency. For three years he had passed on information he'd learned about various Hamas activities, the location of key personnel, the smuggling operations that kept the extremists supplied with weapons, including the rockets they regularly launched over the border against IDF troops and Jewish villages.

Darwaza had lived in Gaza all his life, but unlike many of his friends and family he was not bitter with the Israelis for the misery he endured, even though he'd been injured during an IDF sweep of an area inside the Gaza Strip where Al-Qassam stored large caches of weapons. During an exchange between Hamas operatives and an IDF patrol, an unexploded rocket-propelled grenade became lodged in Darwaza's thigh.

No medical facility in Gaza was qualified or equipped to extract the device, and at first none in Israel would accept him as a patient. Finally, though, the director of a hospital in Ashkelon heard about Darwaza's injury and assembled a team to treat him. A Jewish doctor and three nurses risked their lives to remove the device and repair the damage to Darwaza's leg, then a Jewish charity in Tel Aviv covered the cost of his rehabilitation.

While still recovering in a rehab unit, Darwaza began receiving visits from a hospital volunteer named Aaron Lavie. Over the next several weeks Lavie and Darwaza became friends. Before Darwaza returned to Gaza Lavie identified himself as an agent with Shin Bet and announced, "We know about you. We think you could help us."

"Help you with what?"

"We know you don't like what Hamas is doing to your

people. If you are interested in helping us change that, let me know."

Later, when Darwaza was released and sent back to Gaza, he found a cell phone in his belongings. He'd never owned a cell phone before and at first he thought it was a mistake, but then a text message arrived to the phone. The message was from Lavie. Darwaza had been an informant for Shin Bet ever since.

Now Lavie was gone, killed in a shootout near Haifa. Since his death, Darwaza had been handed off to Yaakov Auerbach, a Shin Bet agent who worked from an office in Beersheba. They had met in person only once, communicating instead by means of the Internet and by text using the cell phone Darwaza had received from Lavie. Even so, he knew Auerbach would be interested in the things he'd heard about Iranian operatives and demonstrations planned for the crossing checkpoints, but he needed something definite. He needed real information, not just rumor. What he needed was a source.

One of Darwaza's many friends was a man named Wasif Sayed. Somewhat older than most in the ranks of Al-Qassam, Sayed had trained as a violinist at a time before the partition of Palestinian lands and before the Gaza border fence limited access to the outside world. Forced to abandon a musical career, he supported himself and his family by working as an assistant for Hamas leadership. Most recently, he had been assigned to work with Abdullah Al-Hadi.

Darwaza knew Sayed worked with Al-Hadi but was unaware of Al-Hadi's involvement in the rumored protests about which he had been hearing. He only knew that Sayed could be a source of information—if Sayed would talk.

Contacting Sayed posed a measure of risk to Darwaza. Though they were friends, the two did not socialize frequently. Hence, Darwaza had some assurance his name never came up in conversations Sayed might have with others. Likewise, Darwaza had never asked Sayed or any other member of Al-Qassam for a favor. Probing him now for information was akin to asking for a favor. But perhaps, if he posed his inquiries carefully, he could raise the issue with Sayed in a context that was more like an earnest subject seeking to know how to please those in power. "I've heard these things," he could say. "And I want to know if they are true so I can be ready to act when the time comes." But even that sounded like too much.

Still, I can't learn what is really happening without talking to someone, Darwaza told himself. *And Sayed is the least-risky person to contact.* He would simply have to contact Sayed, meet with him, and let things progress.

Later that week, Darwaza contacted Sayed and they met for coffee. After catching up on the latest news of family and friends, Darwaza turned the conversation to the real point of their meeting. "I have heard many things over the past few weeks," he began. "I wanted to ask you about them because I think you know the truth."

"Ahh," Sayed grinned. "I wondered why you asked to see me."

"I really wanted to touch base with you," Darwaza countered. "We haven't spoken in quite some time."

"But you also wanted to ask me some questions."

"Yes. That is true," Darwaza admitted.

"Okay, what is troubling you?"

"I have heard rumors that new protests are planned for the border crossings."

"People protest at the border all the time. Why is that suddenly important?"

"These rumors seem to indicate something different."

Sayed looked serious. "Masud," he said in a parental tone, "you have never participated in any demonstration before." He arched an eyebrow. "You wish to join one now?"

"If there is trouble coming," Darwaza answered, "I would like to know before it happens. Last time one of these major events occurred, I wound up with a rocket lodged in my thigh."

"So, if there is trouble, you wish to be somewhere else?"

"The thought occurred to me."

"Tell me, what sort of rumors are you hearing?"

"That something is being planned. Some say a protest. Others say it is more than merely a protest. That this time the attacks against the Israelis will be much larger, more violent, and that they are planned to occur simultaneously at all five crossing points."

Sayed appeared unmoved, which told Darwaza that what

he'd heard was more true than not. "Where have you heard such things?" Sayed asked.

"Almost everywhere. People in my building talk about it. People I see on the street. I overhear it in a conversation at the table next to mine in a café."

"What else have you heard?"

Darwaza leaned closer and lowered his voice. "I also have heard that new Iranian operatives have arrived to assist with these proposed demonstrations."

"And that troubles you even more."

"Yes. This is the kind of thing that incites the Israelis to even more drastic action than normal. And I don't trust the Iranians."

"Why not?"

"We are Arab. They are Persian. They live in relative freedom. We do not. They have access to money. We do not."

"And you do not like them for it?"

"I am suspicious of them for it. They come here and incite our people to do acts of violence. Acts of violence that fit into Iranian plans, not Palestinian."

"So, you think they take advantage of us."

"Yes."

"Tell me something. If one knows he is being taken advantage of, does it not mean the one supposedly asserting his will against another has become the tool of the other?"

"You are saying that Hamas knows the Iranians are playing them?"

"I would not use that term, but yes. They know the Iranians are taking advantage of them, but they also know they get things from the Iranians they cannot get anywhere else. So," Sayed added with a shrug, "that is the price they pay."

The conversation with Sayed confirmed for Darwaza most of the things he already had heard. That protests were planned for all five border crossings. That protests would be massive in size, far larger than any ever staged before. That Iranian operatives were assisting in organizing those protests. Based on the things he'd learned, he signaled Auerbach that he had information to share.

A few days after Darwaza contacted Auerbach a Jordanian businessman traveling under the name of Fayez Ensour arrived in Gaza on his way from Egypt to Amman. He paid Darwaza a visit at the warehouse where Darwaza sometimes found work unloading delivery trucks, though that kind of work had become less frequent than in previous times. After identifying himself through prearranged authenticating dialogue—much like the method the Iranians used when contacting their sleeper agents—Ensour said to Darwaza, "I understand you have something for me." This wasn't Darwaza's first time communicating through an intermediary, and he understood precisely what Ensour meant. He'd come to collect the information Darwaza had implied when he signaled Auerbach.

Speaking quickly, Darwaza told Ensour what he had seen and heard about protests Hamas was planning, and about the presence of new Iranian operatives in Gaza. Ensour listened patiently, then said, "Pictures would be very helpful for my associates."

"Pictures?"

"Images speak much more clearly than words."

"Okay," Darwaza agreed. "But that's the reason I wanted to meet in person."

"What do you mean?"

"I think someone is monitoring my cell phone. Not just the Israelis or the Americans, but someone with the phone service provider."

Ensour nodded thoughtfully. "Perhaps that is true. But we need confirmation of the things you have just mentioned. Particularly about the Iranians. No one can act on merely your words. They need some sort of confirmation."

"I understand that. But I will be placing my life at risk."

"By capturing a few images on your phone?"

"No. By being too obvious."

A few days later, Darwaza finally caught sight of a man he was certain was one of the Iranians. He was talking to a man Darwaza knew to be a Hamas operative. Darwaza captured images of them with his cell phone and later confirmed the man's identity through another friend. Later that evening, he forwarded those images to the messaging account that he and Auerbach used to contact each other.

✦ ✦ ✦

When Darwaza captured the images of the Iranian operative, he took precautions to make certain he was not discovered by his subjects. However, others were present that day and one of them noticed what he was doing. The person who noticed relayed that information to Samir Jubran, one of the men working with Mohammed Khalafi to organize the Sufa Crossing protest.

When news of Darwaza's conduct reached Khalafi, he was disturbed by what he'd been told and by the fact that he did not know Darwaza, nor had he ever even heard of him. That some-one—Darwaza—lived in his area, with the requisite skill and understanding to determine the identity of an Iranian operative, and who knew the identity of Khalafi's fellow Hamas members as well, had escaped Khalafi's notice. It seemed impossible, but he was determined to learn more about this person.

For the next five days, Khalafi tailed Darwaza at a distance, paying close attention to the people with whom Darwaza associated but making certain Darwaza did not see him. Even then, based solely on the things he observed, he could not determine whether Darwaza was doing anything wrong, or even what Darwaza was doing at all. Nor could he determine whether Darwaza had friends in Hamas. He heard only the story told to Jubran about Darwaza photographing someone with his cell phone, and scattered reports of him asking questions about rumors he'd heard regarding a protest being planned as the largest Hamas had ever staged.

If Darwaza was indeed photographing one of the more recent

Iranian operatives, it could mean only one thing—he was a spy gathering information for relay to his handler. Most likely, that handler was an Israeli contact. The Palestinian Authority did not like the way Hamas took over Gaza, but they would never spy on them. Not like this. They had no need to spy. They already knew what Hamas was doing, often before the rank-and-file Hamas operatives were informed. The Egyptians, who shared the border with Gaza to the south, had no need to spy, either. They were not the object of Hamas's operations. Only the Israelis would do such a thing.

At any rate, everyone knew that some residents of Gaza regularly engaged in espionage. Some did it for money—life in Gaza was very difficult and everything was in short supply. People engaged in all sorts of activities they might not otherwise be involved with simply in order to survive. Others did it for political reasons, genuinely hoping the Israelis would provide a solution to the Gaza situation that would rid the region of Hamas. Regardless of the reasons, so prevalent was the activity that members of Hamas took special precautions to screen those with whom they associated. Khalafi had thoroughly vetted the men he'd recruited to work with him, leaving nothing to chance even though he'd known most of them since childhood.

If Darwaza was spying, he deserved only one thing—death. No trial. No hearing. Just a bullet to the head—if his executioners were feeling generous. If not, he would die by the blade. But that was not Khalafi's decision to make. Someone else would make that call, especially given the fact that he had not observed Darwaza in the act of doing anything really suspicious. Khalafi wasn't worried about killing him, per se. He just didn't want to kill someone who had connections with Hamas leadership. That would be bad for Khalafi. It would also be bad if he received a report of suspicious activity and did nothing. So he decided to do what every good soldier did—he would report what he'd heard to Abdullah Al-Hadi and let Al-Hadi handle it.

The following day, Khalafi met with Al-Hadi. "One of my men told me that Darwaza was taking pictures of one of the Iranian operatives. Another said he was asking questions about the protests—the details, and trying to find out who else might be involved."

"Word is getting out," Al-Hadi replied. "No one expected you to fully contain news of the event you're organizing. In fact, this may help you with recruiting in your area. You've had difficulty with that, have you not?"

Khalafi was worried about that last remark. He did not realize Al-Hadi knew of the trouble he'd encountered. "It has not been easy. But nothing worthwhile ever is."

"This is correct."

"I just didn't know what to do about this guy, Darwaza," Khalafi continued. "They said he was taking pictures. I followed him a day or two to see what he was doing."

Al-Hadi's eyes seemed to bore in on Khalafi. "You followed him instead of coming straight to me?"

"Yes."

"And what did you intend to do if you saw him doing it again? Taking pictures or asking questions?"

"Confront him."

"And?"

Khalafi shrugged. "And do what had to be done."

"Good," Al-Hadi said with a smile.

"So, what shall I do now?"

"Leave it with me."

Al-Hadi, who had been reclining against a pillow on the floor, moved to stand, but Khalafi raised his hand, and then continued. "Are we certain the men who claim to be Iranian operatives really are Iranian operatives?"

"Why would they not be?" Al-Hadi asked. "Could they get to us here in Gaza if they were not?"

"I suppose not. But did someone check them out?"

Al-Hadi chuckled. "I assure you, the men who are assisting us are legitimate. We have nothing to worry about in that regard." He then rose from his pillow and walked with Khalafi toward the door. "Do not worry about this Darwaza matter. You did the right thing in coming to me. Now, leave this matter to me."

✦ ✦ ✦

Despite the casual way he'd handled Khalafi, Al-Hadi was disturbed by what he'd heard. He, like everyone else, was well aware that a few Palestinians spied for Israel. Some of them were, from time to time, discovered and executed. Others were known only by rumor, but Hamas was always on the lookout for them. Once discovered, Hamas usually followed a methodical procedure to trace their contacts thoroughly, learning as much as possible about their activities before executing them. With this operation, however, Al-Hadi felt there wasn't time for all of that and he wanted to proceed without consulting anyone.

Still, killing the wrong person—even in Gaza—could result in trouble for Al-Hadi. Perhaps even his own death. And so, against his better judgement, he decided to report the matter and seek permission in dealing with Darwaza.

Two days later, the response came back. "The committee has made no allowances for delay. Proceed to eliminate all obstacles and threats."

That afternoon, Al-Hadi assigned his best operative—Sliman Nafar—to deal with Darwaza, once and for all. "Locate him," Al-Hadi ordered, "and end him—as soon as possible."

"Any particular manner in which you would like him to die?" Nafar asked.

"You may choose any method you like. But perhaps it should be a death that sends a message. Something that says, 'This is how you will die if you are a spy or a traitor.'"

"Very well."

"And make it quick. We don't have time to waste on him."

"As you wish," Nafar affirmed.

That same day, Nafar located Darwaza's apartment and hid

outside to observe the target's coming and going. Very quickly, he learned that Darwaza lived alone, which made the task of killing him much easier. No need to worry about a spouse or, worst of all, children. He hated it when they called on him to execute men with children. A clean job meant killing everyone present. Yet when it involved children, he still had a soft spot for them. . .even after all that he'd been through.

That evening, Darwaza returned to his apartment, as was his normal routine. Nafar waited until the entire building was dark, then entered Darwaza's apartment and shot him in the head while he was asleep in bed. *I have to kill him,* Nafar thought as he squeezed the trigger on his silenced 9mm handgun, *but I don't have to make him suffer.*

After shooting Darwaza, Nafar sat down on a straight-backed chair and smoked a cigarette. Giving the spirit time to leave, he called it. When that was done, he rubbed out the butt in the floor with the heel of his boot and rummaged around the apartment. In short order he found two cell phones and an assortment of Hamas documents in an envelope behind a dresser near the bed. He set those aside, then returned to the bed where Darwaza's body lay.

Using a length of rope he brought for the task, he hung Darwaza from an exposed pipe that ran overhead, then found a knife by the kitchen sink and began to carve on Darwaza's back. *He's dead,* Nafar thought to himself. *He can't feel a thing. Just like carving up a carcass in the butcher shop.* Dark red blood dripped from Darwaza slowly soaking the mattress below his body.

When Nafar finished, he rinsed his hands at the sink and wiped them on a towel, then retrieved the cell phones and envelope from the table where he'd laid them. He stuffed the phones in his pocket, tucked the envelope under his arm, and opened the door to the corridor outside. He left without closing the door. Al-Hadi wanted to send a message. He was sure the body hanging in the apartment would do just that.

✦ ✦ ✦

The following day, Yaakov Auerbach, the agent from Shin Bet who served as Darwaza's handler, checked the message account to see if Darwaza had sent any new information. Auerbach had been briefed by Fayez Ensour, the supposed Jordanian businessman who talked to Darwaza, and was hoping to find out more regarding the things Darwaza had said.

Auerbach had volunteered for IDF service the summer after graduating from Hebrew University in Jerusalem. Actually, service in the military was compulsory. At the end of his first enlistment he was recruited for IDF Special Forces where he served an additional two terms. As that time came to an end, he was offered a position with Shin Bet, which he readily accepted. Auerbach received extensive training through Shin Bet and later with the CIA at its training facility in Langley, Virginia. Fluent in at least four languages besides Modern Hebrew and English, he had been posted to several places in Israel and abroad before landing at the office in Beersheba.

Two days after Darwaza's last upload, Auerbach checked the message board and found the images he'd taken—pictures of the person Darwaza thought was an Iranian talking with a man Auerbach already knew was a ranking member of Al-Qassam. He uploaded the images to a file in the Shin Bet database, then left a cryptic reply for Darwaza asking how many others he had seen.

Using facial recognition software, he began a scan of the unknown man in the image—the one Darwaza thought to be Iranian. Late that afternoon the software completed its scan and Auerbach learned that the person Darwaza photographed was Akbar Ansari, a person whom Shin Bet's database knew all too well.

Ansari had been a student in Milan for a while. Most recently, he was arrested and released in Paris in connection with an investigation of a protest held outside the headquarters of Charlie Hebdo, the satirical weekly. Auerbach studied the report and wondered if he should send Darwaza another message, asking for additional information. "Or perhaps it is time for us to meet in person," he said to himself.

After thinking about it, though, Auerbach decided against an in-person visit. Traveling into Gaza was extremely risky, especially for a Jew, and bringing Darwaza out would be a one-and-done proposition. He wouldn't be able to return, and even then he'd live the remainder of his life always looking over his shoulder. Darwaza probably already did that. Before leaving for the evening,

Auerbach circulated the information he'd developed about Ansari among agents who were present in the office, then sent an email to others he thought might be helpful, asking if they had anything more recent about Darwaza, including recent reports placing him in Gaza.

CHAPTER

8

AS PLANS FOR PROTESTS along the Gaza border moved forward, Khalafi continued to wrestle with the logistical problem of how to get a sufficient number of Palestinians to the Sufa checkpoint. In the past, Al-Qassam members simply circulated information about a protest, then moved through a neighborhood on the appointed day announcing the protest and urging everyone to join. If that wasn't successful, they turned from cajoling to threatening and herded residents out to the fence. That strategy produced crowds in the hundreds. This time, however, that wouldn't be enough; the situation required more. Hamas leadership, after all, expected Khalafi to create a crowd of thousands.

Previous trips to the Sufa Crossing had made obvious to Khalafi that the distance from where people lived to the area near the border fence was much greater than at most of the other locations. That, and the need for a greater number of participants, along with the expectations of his superiors—expectations that also were a threat—made the task of organizing his part of the protest seem overwhelming.

As Khalafi thought about the situation and discussed it with members of his group at the house in Umm al-Kilab, Ibrahim Atweh mentioned an online article he'd read about the American civil rights protests from the 1960s. "Those were highly organized events," he pointed out. "As were protests in America against the Vietnam War. They were organized events that only seemed to be spontaneous."

"That's what I was telling you about earlier," Khalafi agreed. "I think successful protests have always been orchestrated in advance. Even here. At least the biggest ones. I know we sometimes went out and threw rocks or bottles or flew kites over the wall without being urged to do so at the time. But I think the really important protests were planned long before they happened. Maybe what we remember from the old days wasn't really as spur of the moment as they made it seem."

Hisham Shomali spoke up. "Then what we need is a cause to rally the people."

This was the kind of thing Khalafi had tried to tell them before, when no one wanted to listen. Now they seemed to think of it themselves and he was tempted to remind them that it was his idea first, but rather than argue about who thought of it, he let them continue as if it were their own idea.

Jabra Shahid spoke up, "How about the people the Israelis killed at the border before. That is something that angers many."

Hisham Shomali shook his head. "We've already mentioned that as the reason."

"That ought to be enough," Shahid urged. "They have killed hundreds of us and—"

"Thousands," Shomali corrected.

"Okay," Shahid conceded. "Thousands. That makes my point even better."

Ibrahim Atweh joined in, "But even *that* hasn't been enough to rally mass protests of the kind we're talking about."

"It is true," Shomali conceded. "Our people should be storming the fence every day. Forcing their way across. Refusing to be contained. Forcing the Israeli soldiers to shoot us or be overrun. Yet our people do nothing of the sort. Only the occasional protest and only then with a few rocks and bottles."

They sat in silence a moment, then Khalafi spoke up. "Back to the issue. What can we use to rally a crowd?"

Samir Jubran had been listening to them without comment, but now he spoke, "Maybe we're going about this the wrong way."

"What do you mean?" Khalafi asked.

"Maybe we shouldn't be looking for an actual issue. We just need an issue. It doesn't have to be real." The others frowned. Jubran continued. "What if we created a reason?"

"You mean, a rumor."

"Yes," Jubran replied. "A rumor."

"What kind of rumor?"

Atweh spoke up. "That the Israelis mean to kill us all."

Everyone laughed. "That's not a rumor, that's a fact."

"It needs to be more specific," Jubran insisted, ignoring them.

"And something big," Khalafi added. "Something that will get an immediate reaction."

"Like the Israelis plan to blow up the Dome of the Rock?"

"Yes. But not that. It's too much."

They thought for a moment, then Shomali offered, "Al-Aqsa."

"What about it?"

"A rumor," Shomali explained slowly, "that the Israelis plan to demolish Al-Aqsa and replace it with a synagogue."

Atweh shook his head. "They would never do that."

"But they might build a synagogue somewhere else on Haram esh-Sharif."

"Yes," Atwah agreed. "They might."

Khalafi pointed to his laptop. "Look at this."

They gathered around the screen and read an article from a news site about the desire of some Israelis to build the Third Temple. A spokesman for a messianic Jewish group was quoted, suggesting that the Temple could not be built until the Messiah returned but that a synagogue could be built on the Mount. "And one ought to be constructed," the spokesman had intoned. "Above the Western wall, even if it means destroying Al-Aqsa Mosque."

A rabbi was quoted as saying, "Muslims already have the Dome of the Rock. Why should they have two or three places of worship on the Mount and we Jews have none?"

"Print that article," Shomali instructed. "We can make fliers with it about how the Jews want to destroy Al-Aqsa and replace it with a synagogue."

Atweh turned aside. "This is crazy. No one will believe it."

"Yes, they will," Khalafi insisted. "We have just enough from that article to form the kernel of a rumor. We can build whatever we want around it. This is what we want. The Jews plan to destroy Al-Aqsa and replace it with a synagogue. We must not let that happen. When our people hear this they will believe it, and no one will be able to stop them from storming across the fence. Tell them we must protest this atrocity. That Hamas has ordered it. That Allah requires them to do it. That we are going to march as a group to the border and all the way to Jerusalem to protect Al-Aqsa. Haram esh-Sharif. The Noble Sanctuary must *not* be defiled by the Jews. Tell our people this is their Jihad. This is their duty. They must join us."

✦ ✦ ✦

Meanwhile, Al-Hadi met with Sliman Nafar to discuss the Darwaza matter. "Did someone finally dispose of the body?"

Nafar reassured. "That has been taken care of."

Al-Hadi gestured to Darwaza's cell phones, lying on a nearby table. "One of those phones contained images." Al-Hadi retrieved the phone from the table and turned the screen to show Nafar. "You reviewed these?"

"Yes."

"And the calls he made on it—did you recognize any of the numbers?"

"There was only one number," Nafar replied. "And it was not familiar to me."

Al-Hadi tossed him the phone. "Find out the details about that number and anything else in there."

A few days later, Nafar returned to Al-Hadi. "The account mentioned in Darwaza's cell phone was for a Catch-Up messaging service."

Al-Hadi seemed puzzled. "Catch-Up?"

"It's a private messaging board. We use them all the time. Access to the board is limited to members authenticated by a moderator, but even then people who have an account can arrange to communicate through sub-accounts that only the parties to a particular conversation control."

"Where is this message board located?"

"The IP address indicates it is operated on a site maintained by a company known as IAT Communications."

Al-Hadi seemed surprised. "IAT? In Gaza?"

"Yes," Nafar said. "I checked with them. They acknowledged that the message board operates on their servers."

"Can we find out who Darwaza sent those pictures to?"

Nafar shrugged. "I doubt it. Anonymity is the reason message services like that exist. But," he added with a smile, "We have the phone."

Again Al-Hadi seemed puzzled. "What do you mean?"

"We could send a message back to that account."

"And say what?"

"Ask for a meeting."

Al-Hadi's countenance brightened. "That's a good idea."

"I think we have nothing to lose by trying."

"Nor do I," Al-Hadi replied. "Pose as Darwaza. Send a message to the account. Ask for a meeting. Do it the way he did it in those other messages and let's see what happens."

Later that week, Auerbach checked the message account and saw what appeared to be a new message from Darwaza that read simply, "We need to talk."

To anyone else reading it, the message sounded like a request for a face-to-face meeting. By prior understanding with Darwaza, however, the message meant that he needed to pass information to a courier. No agent from Shin Bet ever met personally with him.

As was their standard procedure, Auerbach replied to the message agreeing to the request. His reply, however, made no mention of how or where they would meet but simply said, "I will see you in a few days."

When Nafar received the reply from Auerbach, he realized from the nature of the text that Darwaza and his handler, if that is who the person on the other end really was, probably had a prearranged way of communicating. And apparently a way of doing so that did not involve the phone. A closer check of the cell phone's contents confirmed this, as none of the messages requesting a meeting ever included a response indicating details by which that requested meeting would take place.

In order to figure out where and when Darwaza met his handler, Nafar went back to the neighborhood where Darwaza lived and began asking around among those who lived in his apartment building. Nafar was an ominous character and everyone in Darwaza's neighborhood knew he was the one who left Darwaza's body hanging in the apartment. As a result, they told him whatever it took to get him satisfied and out of the way. After a day of talking, Nafar learned nothing that tipped him to how Darwaza communicated with his handler.

✦ ✦ ✦

A few days later, a relief worker traveling on a Norwegian passport in the name of Olav Borgen, and with credentials from the UN Relief and Works Agency, came to Darwaza's neighborhood. Under the guise of relief assessment and evaluation, Borgen interviewed people from the block where Darwaza's apartment building was located. He questioned residents in each of the buildings about living conditions, the treatment accorded them in general, and whether they had any special medical issues.

Taking his time, moving from floor to floor, building to building, Borgen finally arrived at the apartment building where he'd already been told Darwaza lived. Even after almost ten days in the neighborhood he found no sign of Darwaza.

In the apartment building, Borgen began on the ground floor and worked his way methodically through each apartment, conducting a housing assessment as any other aid worker might. Taking one floor at a time, one apartment at a time, one person at a time, in a meticulously thorough effort to hide the real reason he'd come—to make contact with Darwaza and to do so in the privacy of his apartment. It was a risky attempt, but one that Auerbach and, Noga Milgrom, his Shin Bet supervisor, thought necessary. They wanted to know what additional information Darwaza had obtained about the Iranian agent and the supposed demonstration that was apparently in the offing.

After days of painstaking thoroughness so as to give no hint of his true purpose, Borgen located the apartment where Darwaza was supposed to live. He knocked on the door but no one answered and when he tried again, the door moved open a little way. Borgen grasped the knob and found the door was unlocked, so he went inside.

The apartment was empty, bare walls without a single piece of furniture. It had recently been cleaned, too. Quite thoroughly, from the scrub marks and bleached tile on the floor. But an odd odor hung in the air and as Borgen paused to sniff it he realized the smell that tweaked his nose was the smell of death. Human death. The odor of a dead body. One that had been left to decay in the heat and had already begun to decompose by the time it was removed. He knelt to examine the grout lines between the floor tiles but found no blood residue. Nor did he find any fragments of bone or skin. But even so, he was certain Darwaza was dead and that he had died in his own apartment.

Just then, a woman appeared at the door and Borgen glanced in that direction. She was older than most people he'd seen so far and he looked at her with an unassuming pose. "How long has this apartment been empty?"

"I do not know," the woman replied. She seemed nervous, and there was tension in her voice.

"You live here?"

She shook her head and gestured defensively with both hands. "Too many questions. You ask too many questions."

"But something happened here."

"No . . . no," she stammered. "I cannot say." Then she disappeared down the hall.

Borgen left the apartment and made his way down the hall, stopping at each apartment to interview the residents, as he had before, only now he included questions about the empty apartment and the odor he'd encountered there. The neighbors cooperated until he asked about Darwaza, then they backed away from him. They refused to say more, and abruptly slammed their doors.

Finally, one person—a man Borgen thought was at least seventy years old—who lived near the end of the hall took him into his apartment. "You are risking your life by asking too many questions," he whispered. "The one you ask about—Darwaza— he is dead. There is nothing you can do for him now. Nothing anyone can do for him. And you will be dead too if you keep asking about him."

"You are certain he is dead?"

"Yes," the man whispered. "I saw his body with my own eyes. Everyone did."

"You knew him?"

"Yes."

"And you saw his body?"

"His body hung in the apartment for five days. The door was open for us to see."

"For you to see?"

"That is how they sometimes send us the message, 'Mind your own business or you will get the same.' And that is the message I am giving you. Mind your own business or you will end up like him." Then the man hustled Borgen to the doorway, urged him into the hall, and closed the door behind him.

✦ ✦ ✦

Not long after Borgen visited the building where Darwaza lived, Nafar learned that a UN relief worker had been present at the apartment building, asking questions about what happened. Concerned that someone outside Gaza might know of Darwaza's demise, Nafar returned to the neighborhood and questioned the residents of the apartment building. Everyone denied talking to the relief worker. Nafar didn't really believe them but decided to take no action and let the matter go. He'd learned from prior experience that torture produced little in the way of reliable results. People would say anything just to end the agony, but they didn't always tell the truth or give an accurate version even of the truth they told. Instead, he let the matter slide with the residents but he could not let it pass with Al-Hadi, and reported the matter to him at once.

When he learned of the relief worker's presence and the questions he'd been asking, Al-Hadi seemed unconcerned and told Nafar not to worry. He would get to the bottom of the matter and find out what happened. In reality, he was deeply troubled by the potential risk wider dissemination of information about the murder might have on the planned attacks.

After checking with other sources Al-Hadi learned that, just as Darwaza's neighbors had reported, a UN relief worker named Borgen—genuine and appropriately credentialed, as far as anyone could determine—had visited Darwaza's building but was no longer present in Gaza.

"Some say he has been here before," one contact reported. "Others say this is his first time."

An inquiry with officials from the Palestinian National Authority indicated a worker by that name had been cleared for travel to Gaza by the UN and already had arrived and departed the Strip. "He came with a group from Finland and left with them three days ago," the responder said. "That much is certain and beyond doubt. As to whether he has been here before, we do not know."

None of their reassurances satisfied Al-Hadi. *He could just as easily have been an Israeli,* he thought to himself. *An asset sent to meet with Darwaza after Nafar sent that text message.*

For two days, Al-Hadi did nothing more about the matter. He had plenty of other details to occupy his time. At night, however, as he lay upon his mat and stared into the darkness, he thought about Darwaza, Borgen, and Nafar. Alternately suspicious and dismissive, he considered the equities of the matter.

Darwaza had made choices, and he bore the consequences of those decisions. There were rules to the life they lived and Darwaza had violated those rules. What he got was only what he knew he would receive when he chose the course of action he had taken. Al-Hadi had no regrets about ordering his death.

Borgen was someone he could not reach. Not now, anyway. And maybe not ever. He would keep his name tucked away in the recesses of his mind and, should Borgen ever return to Gaza, Al-Hadi would make sure that trip was his last.

Nafar, however, was another matter. Nafar had been with Al-Hadi for three years—quite a long time in the life of an Al-Qassam operative. Still, the same rules that applied to Darwaza also applied to Nafar. Directives regarding the planned attacks on the IDF border checkpoints came from the highest authority—the Ayatollah himself had approved the plans and mandated their implementation. The attacks must succeed. There could be no impediment to that success. Which meant no loose ends along the way.

Aside from the fact that Al-Hadi had ordered Nafar to kill Darwaza and to do so in a manner that sent a message to his neighbors, someone other than Darwaza's neighbors now knew Nafar's identity. What Borgen might do with that information, no one could say, but the group of people who knew what Nafar had done was now wider than merely Palestinians living in Gaza. The neighbors knew Nafar. A UN relief worker knew about him, too. Which meant Nafar was now a loose end.

The following day, Al-Hadi summoned Nafar to a building in Al Zahra that Hamas used for storage. As Nafar came through the doorway, he caught sight of Al-Hadi and greeted him with a smile. "How may I be of service to you?" he asked as he stepped closer.

When Nafar was only a few feet away, Al-Hadi drew a pistol from beneath his robe, pointed it squarely at Nafar's forehead, and squeezed off a single shot. The bullet struck Nafar between the eyes while the smile was still on his face.

For a moment, Nafar seemed to stand there, as if the gunshot had been of no effect, then his knees buckled and he fell face forward onto the ground. Al-Hadi stood over him and fired two more shots into his body. One struck Nafar in the back of the head. The other entered his back directly behind his heart. Blood streamed from the wounds and slowly pooled on the concrete floor around him.

As Al-Hadi returned the pistol to its place inside his robe, two men entered the building. They made their way to Nafar's body, took hold of him by the legs and arms, and carried him away.

CHAPTER 9

THE CONTINUED MOVEMENT of Iranian troops into Syria and Lebanon did not go unnoticed. In Washington, it caught the eye of Mike Pitman, an analyst at the CIA.

"I'm not sure what this means," Pitman muttered as he scrolled over an image on the monitor at his desk.

Bradley Carter, who sat at the next workstation, turned to see. "Did you find something?"

"We've been looking at images from the Middle East. And here." Pitman pointed to the monitor screen, "This makes no sense."

"Isn't that larger than what we saw last month?"

Pitman said. "That's what I'm talking about. The civil war in Syria is winding down, yet Iran continues to add troops there." He pointed to the screen again. "This is today and . . ." He paused to switch images. "This is from last month." A second image appeared on a split screen, showing both views side by side.

"You're right," Carter agreed. "They've definitely increased the size of those units."

Pitman changed to a regional image. "And they're doing the same thing in Lebanon, only they're repositioning them farther south." He changed the view again and tapped the screen for emphasis. "Look right here."

Carter studied the screen a moment and nodded. "You're right. They have moved them."

"This is the kind of thing we've dreaded."

Colin Harper came from across the room. "What situation is that?"

"Iran," Pitman replied. "Moving additional troops into Syria and Lebanon."

"Iran has always had a good relationship with them," Harper pointed out.

"The problem isn't with them," Carter explained.

"Then what's the problem?"

"Israel."

Harper studied the screen. "I see what you mean, but you think this means they're preparing to move against Israel?"

"I think the Israelis will see the same thing we see," Pitman said. "And *they* will think of it as a threat."

Harper looked concerned. "Do we need to alert someone?"

"We should tell Jenkins," Carter decided.

Pitman scooted back from his desk and stood. "I'll go find him."

Bryce Jenkins was the analyst supervisor for their division. Pitman found him in the conference room across the hall, where he was busy studying memos from the day before. He followed Pitman back to the workstation and reviewed the images. After a moment to look at them, he ordered, "Write it up and we'll let senior staff have a look at it."

Later that day, Jenkins received a memo from Pitman detailing his analysis of the satellite images. Jenkins made a copy of the memo and slipped it into a pocket inside his briefcase. He placed the other copy in a filing cabinet behind his desk and locked it.

That night, Jenkins drove to a bar in Odricks Corner, Virginia. He parked on the far side of the parking lot and waited. Twenty minutes later, the passenger door opened and Vasily Gorchakov took a seat beside him.

Gorchakov was a cultural attaché to the Russian Embassy. He and Jenkins had become acquainted when Jenkins was stationed at the CIA office in Berlin. Gorchakov, older and more experienced, was all too eager to show Jenkins the German nightlife. By the time Jenkins' tour ended, he was a pawn in the Russian intelligence game.

Jenkins handed him the Pitman memo. "Tell Bagheri his troop movements have been noticed."

Gorchakov glanced over the memo. "This man, Pitman." He pointed to the paper. "He is a problem?"

"He is not a problem. Just an analyst doing his job."

"Yes," Gorchakov nodded. "And doing it well, I see. Did you report this?"

"Not yet," Jenkins replied. "But I will have to soon."

"Give me a day."

Jenkins acquiesced. "Okay, but that's all. One day."

"That's all I will need."

Gorchakov reached for the handle to open the door but Jenkins put out his hand to stop him. "I can finesse this on our end for a while, but there's not really anything I can do about the Israelis."

"If Bagheri gets his act together, he can take care of the Jews." Gorchakov opened the car door. "I'll be in touch." He stepped out, closed the door behind him, and was gone.

✦ ✦ ✦

Early the next morning, Mahmoud Alavi, the Iranian intelligence minister, called General Bagheri to a meeting at Alavi's office. "The Americans have noticed our troop movements in Syria and Lebanon."

Bagheri seemed unfazed. "What do they plan to do in response?"

"Nothing, for now," Alavi replied. "We have the situation contained. But you must be more careful."

Bagheri had a dour expression. "There is no careful way to move an army."

"Then you must get this accomplished quickly."

"It is impossible to move an army that far very quickly. Quickly and carefully are impossibilities. This is a dangerous business, but don't worry. We always knew we would be discovered."

"But not this soon."

"It is nothing," Bagheri waved dismissively. "I understand there was some trouble in Gaza."

Alavi had a questioning frown. "Trouble? As I said, we have the situation contained for now."

"Not with the Americans. An informant in Gaza."

"Oh." Alavi looked away. "That has been dealt with."

"I understand his name was Darwaza."

Alavi frowned. "How would you know his name?"

Bagheri smiled. "I have my sources, too."

"Is that a problem?"

"You do not recognize the name?"

"What was it?"

"Darwaza," Bagheri replied. "Masud Darwaza."

Alavi's eyes opened wide. "He is—"

Bagheri grinned. "He is the son of Azita Darwaza. The Supreme Leader's niece. You should have thought of that when they contacted you. Our communication with Gaza is not so bad that you could not have prevented his death."

A look of terror came over Alavi and his skin turned pale. "Does the Supreme Leader know about this?"

"I do not know," Bagheri answered slowly. "But you should hope that he does not find out."

"Surely," Alavi consoled himself, "he is not concerned about his niece's son."

"The man you killed was the Supreme Leader's great-nephew."

Alavi gave a dismissive gesture. "These things do not count for much."

Bagheri chuckled. "I understand he was present when the man you killed learned to walk."

"I did not kill him."

"But they contacted you first. And without your approval, he would not have died." Bagheri seemed to enjoy needling his friend.

Alavi leaned back in his seat and closed his eyes. "Oh, the trouble your plan has caused us."

Bagheri laughed. "I did not tell you to murder anyone."

"And neither did I."

Now it was Bagheri who looked stricken. "They killed this man and you did not give the order?"

"He was not living there as one of our operatives," Alavi explained.

"Did they know who he was?"

"Not completely."

"Then you must find out who gave the order. Place the blame on them."

Alavi shrugged. "I suppose I must."

"And do it quietly. We don't want anyone to find out about this."

"Especially not the Supreme Leader."

"And not Rouhani, either."

"President Rouhani," Alavi corrected.

"I am old enough to be his father," Bagheri snarled. "And I've been in the army longer than he has been alive. I will call him whatever I please." He paused a moment. "And I will not have him disrupt our plans, so make certain he does not find out about this issue."

CHAPTER
10

A FEW EVENINGS LATER, Yaakov Auerbach and his wife, Yarden went out for dinner at a café in Beersheba. They were joined by friends they had known for many years—David and Ada Schapiro along with Elias and Shafi Racah—who had moved to Beersheba at about the same time. During the course of the evening, the conversation turned to the way life in Beersheba had changed. "Everything changes," Auerbach mused. "That is the nature of life."

Elias agreed and gestured to those at the table. "People move. Look at us. We lived in Jerusalem, now we live here."

"But *life* seems different now," Ada said. "Not merely people moving from one place to another. No one lives in the same place all their life anymore. But this seems different."

"Lots of new people here for sure," David added.

"From everywhere, too," Yarden obsessed. "Not just relocating from another part of Israel but coming here from other countries."

"We've lived and grown on the ability to attract new people," Auerbach explained. "That was one of Ben-Gurion's major points from the beginning. 'Come home to Israel.'"

"But the people coming here now aren't just Jews returning to Israel," Ada replied, "which is what Ben-Gurion was talking about. They're coming from everywhere now and they don't have much in common with us. Just the other day I saw someone in the store who was from Iran, of all places. I mean, aren't they the same people who want to wipe us off the earth?"

"Not the Iranian people," David corrected.

"Just the Iranian *leadership*," Elias added.

The mention of Iran caught Auerbach's attention. "How do you know he was from Iran?"

"For one thing," Ada replied, "he looked different."

"Nah," Elias chimed in. "You can't tell by that."

"Yes, you can," Yarden argued. "Not all of us look the same."

"I don't mean it like that," Elias said defensively. "I'm not a racist."

"I didn't say you were a racist," Yarden replied. "But we don't all look the same."

"There was more to it than that," Ada continued. "I mean, the guy gave me the creeps, but then I heard him talking to the clerk and he had an accent."

"You can't tell he was from Iran by his accent, either," Elias chided. "Everyone has an accent."

Ada refused to concede the point. "This was distinct. I'm not making it up. I have a friend—Yael—who is married to an Iranian. This man sounded like her husband."

"They're from an area in northwestern Iran," David explained. "They speak Azeri much of the time, especially at home."

"Which is what this man was using," Ada noted.

Elias still was skeptical. "Azeri?" he asked.

"An older language," David replied.

"I know." Elias shook his head. "But that language is extinct."

"That's what linguists say," Ada responded. "But it's not extinct. They still speak it."

Elias looked over at her. "You seem to know a lot about it."

"Not really. I'm mostly just repeating things I've heard. I only became interested in it because Yael is my friend and she's married to a man who speaks that language."

After all he'd learned from Darwaza, his contact in Gaza, Auerbach was keenly interested now. "So, you heard a man in the store using this language?"

Ada nodded.

"And something about him struck you as different."

"Yes."

"How so?"

Ada shrugged. "I don't know. I just didn't feel right about him."

"Where did you see this mystery man? What store?"

"Tiv Ta'am."

Auerbach recognized the name. "The grocery store?"

"Yes." Ada shifted positions uncomfortably in her chair. "Look, it was probably nothing. It's just—"

Auerbach cut her off. "No, no! Don't feel bad about bringing it up. We're supposed to talk about this."

"People from everywhere live here now," Elias interrupted. "It's not like the old days. High-tech industries. Medical industries. That's what makes us great."

"It also makes us vulnerable," Shafi joined in the conversation.

Auerbach, still thinking about the man in the store, looked over at Ada. "Did anything about him stand out?"

"No," Ada replied. "I guess it wasn't so much the way he looked as the way he looked at *me*. The way he made me feel." Everyone except Auerbach chuckled. Ada shrugged them off. "I know it sounds strange, but after all that's happened this past year . . ." The look on her face was serious. "They tell us to be alert. Aware of our surroundings. I'm just saying he seemed out of place."

Elias spoke up again. "Maybe he just arrived here. Maybe *he* felt out of place."

Yarden grimaced. "You mean maybe we should change our policy from 'come to Israel' to 'stay away'?"

Elias glared at her but did not respond and the conversation continued. Auerbach's mind, however, was far away. To him, Ada's comments weren't mere comments, nor were they the comments of a woman with a heightened sense of feminine acuity, as Elias seemed to think. Her comments were the kind of thing he'd been trained to listen for, the kind of anomaly others readily dismissed but that later proved to be a hint of things to come. With Darwaza and all he knew about that, and the constant stream of threats that came through the office . . .

Already Auerbach's thoughts were on a list of targets that might be at risk, and as he glanced around the room he thought of the people who might be at risk, too. Then he thought of his own children, and suddenly he wanted the evening with friends to end so he could get home to his family.

✦ ✦ ✦

Later that night, when Auerbach and Yarden were at home and getting ready for bed, Yarden said, "You got rather quiet tonight toward the end."

"I couldn't say too much."

"Why not?"

"You know why not. I work for the government."

"What's that got to do with—" Yarden stopped short as a look of realization came over her. "You know something, don't you?"

Auerbach glanced away. "What do you mean?"

"About what Ada said. You know something, don't you?"

He avoided her gaze. "I can't say."

"But you'd tell me if we were in danger, wouldn't you?"

"Everything I do is to protect you."

"So I'm right. What she said, it wasn't just conversation to you."

"Do they know?" Auerbach looked at her now. "Do they know who I work for?"

"You said we were never to tell anyone."

"That's right. And don't."

"Okay, but you can't have it both ways."

Auerbach had a puzzled look. "Both ways?"

"Them knowing and not knowing at the same time. It doesn't work like that."

"I know," Auerbach snapped. "I know."

"What's the matter?"

"I don't know," he sighed. "It's just . . . the whole thing. Life's changed. *We've* changed. I'm always listening. It's what I do. But now we're looking at people. Do they seem out of place? Do they seem okay?"

"And this," she said sarcastically, "coming from a man who makes his living out of being suspicious."

"I know," he sighed once more. "But sometimes when I hear it from someone else, it doesn't sound so good. Like we're changing who we are."

Yarden gave him a disarming smile. "You don't think Israelis in the past were suspicious of new people?"

"I suppose they were."

"And isn't it your job to be suspicious? That's what you're always telling me."

"Yes. It *is* my job, but it didn't sound so nice coming from Ada tonight at dinner."

"It doesn't always sound so nice coming from you, either."

"Coming from me?" When Yarden did not respond Auerbach became insistent. "Go on. Say it."

"It's not about that," she replied. There was a note of hesitancy in her voice.

Auerbach was unwilling to let the matter drop. "Then, what?"

Yarden looked at him. "I saw someone like that, too."

"Where?" he asked, suddenly alert.

"Any number of places. I see people all the time who are from any number of places. But I've had the same experience as Ada had and wondered who that person was and why he was here."

"Beersheba is an active place." Yarden caught his eye and frowned. "What now?"

"That is not your usual response," she noted.

"Well, I can't go off on a rant every time something scratches a place in my mind, can I?"

They stared at each other a moment, then burst into laughter. He took her in his arms and kissed her, then she pushed against his shoulders with both hands and they tumbled onto the bed.

"We're going to wake the children," she whispered.

"They aren't children anymore," he replied. "They're teenagers. They never sleep."

"I know, but they might come in here."

"They know better," he said, then he kissed her once more.

✦ ✦ ✦

The next day, Auerbach still was curious about the conversation from dinner the night before, especially after talking to his wife later that evening. And he was concerned about the Iranian operative Darwaza had photographed in Gaza. And that meant there might be others. In Gaza or elsewhere. Could be. Might be—that was a bad way for a government to make policy, but Auerbach wasn't the government and it was precisely the area in which he and Shin Bet operated. *Might be.* It was their job to peer into the world of "might be" and "could be" and stay ahead of trouble.

In the midst of that, Auerbach's supervisor, Noga Milgrom, who also managed the Shin Bet office in Beersheba, received a report from Borgen, the UN relief worker who had arrived in Gaza and was asking about Darwaza. Borgen, it turns out, really was a UN relief worker and he really was from Norway, but he wasn't a Shin Bet asset. Not really.

During World War II, Borgen's grandfather had been a member of Sivorg, a Norwegian civilian resistance group. Through him, Borgen learned of the civilian efforts to smuggle Jews out of Norway before and during the Nazi occupation. Borgen's grandfather was a Christian, and as Borgen grew up he learned from his grandfather the importance of praying for the peace of

Jerusalem. Later, when the opportunity for access to Gaza arose, he made himself available to Shin Bet to gather information and relay reports. He'd been to Gaza half dozen times and each time he either delivered information or retrieved it. His involvement, however, was purely on a voluntary basis and he reported through a Shin Bet office in Tel Aviv.

Milgrom appeared at Auerbach's office and handed him the report. "It's grim."

"How grim?"

"Read it for yourself," Milgrom urged. "It's not very long." Indeed, it comprised only two pages. Auerbach read it quickly.

From interviews with Darwaza's neighbors, Borgen learned that Darwaza was dead. Although no one told him in explicit details, he came to suspect that Darwaza's death also involved mutilation of his body. From the condition of the apartment, the body probably had remained on display for several days afterward.

By the time of Borgen's arrival, the apartment had been cleaned and all items related to Darwaza had been removed. Any information Darwaza may have obtained was presumed to be lost with him.

Borgen had also learned that subsequent to his visit to Gaza his name had become known to at least one Hamas official— Abdullah Al-Hadi—who had been inquiring about his identity.

When Auerbach finished reading the report, he glanced over at Milgrom. "This isn't good."

Milgrom shook his head. "It's not."

"We lost Darwaza *and* Borgen."

"So it would seem," Milgrom replied. "Darwaza for certain. And if Borgen returns to Gaza, no one could keep him safe."

"They knew Darwaza was working with us."

"It would appear so."

"But was his death merely the routine reprisal, or to protect something?"

"Those are good questions, and we are working all sources to see if anyone has even a hint of something in the works there."

"I think they're planning something," Auerbach sighed.

"I think so, too," Milgrom agreed.

"Something really big is coming. I can feel it."

Milgrom nodded thoughtfully. "The question, though, is what is it?"

✦ ✦ ✦

In the days that followed, Auerbach asked around the office about reports of suspicious people in the area. "Anyone talking about foreigners in the area? Someone who looks out of place? Any mention of Iranians arriving here that has made someone uncomfortable? Anything like that?"

No one seemed to know anything about reports of suspicious people, other than the usual complaints and rumors. There was always someone up to something, and always someone who saw something they felt compelled to report. They investigated each of those, but most of it turned out to be of no use.

After canvassing the office, Auerbach found nothing that lent credence to the things he'd heard at dinner a few nights earlier. Nothing and no one that is, except for Elon Harel, the youngest and newest agent in the office.

When Harel heard of Auerbach's inquires, he came to Auerbach's office. "You are interested in reports about suspicious people?"

"Yes," Auerbach replied dismissively. "But you work with Michael Geller and I talked to him already. He said there was nothing."

"Geller doesn't know everything I know," Harel replied. "And much of what I tell him he dismisses because he thinks I'm young and inexperienced."

Auerbach grinned. "You *are* young."

"Yes," Harel conceded. "But I am not as inexperienced as he thinks. Just the newest person in the office."

Auerbach was mildly impressed by Harel's brash attitude. "What did you want to tell me?"

Harel stepped inside the office and closed the door behind him, then took a seat across from Auerbach. "I heard two other reports of new faces showing up at odd places," Harel began quietly. "Both people reported the same description—sharp features and an accent they had never heard before. I ran a check through the foreign office. They have foreign nationals arriving in the region every week, but I looked through all of their relevant files and no one stood out as obviously suspicious." Harel shrugged.

"Not even someone who seemed interesting."

"That's it?"

"I could never find enough to focus on anyone in particular."

Auerbach sat there a moment, lost in thought, then all at once his eyes opened wider. "Does the Tiv Ta'am grocery store have security cameras?"

Harel shrugged. "I don't know. Why?"

"The person I heard talking about this said she saw someone in the store." Auerbach stood and reached for his jacket. "I'm going over there to find out. Want to come with me?"

"Sure, but don't I need to tell Geller?"

"Nah," Auerbach replied with a dismissive gesture. "He'll never miss either of us."

Twenty minutes later, Auerbach and Harel arrived at the grocery store. Auerbach found the manager, identified himself, and asked about the store's security cameras. The manager pointed to the ceiling. "On the inside, we have cameras in the corners. One over each register. Two pointed toward the door. Several along the front and back walls that are aimed down the aisles. And there are a couple more outside."

"Good, I need to see your footage from the past month."

"That's a lot to review," the manager grumbled.

"Yes," Auerbach acknowledged. "I'll take a copy of it and we can review it at the office."

"Okay," the manager replied. "It's in the back. We monitor the system from an office back there." The manager turned in that direction, then hesitated. "Shouldn't I call someone to ask about this?"

"Call anyone you like," Auerbach shrugged. "I just need the images from your cameras for the month."

The manager led the way to an office off the stockroom where a single employee sat facing a bank of monitors, each one wired to a camera in the store. "The cameras record digitally," he explained. "You wanted this month's images?"

"Yes," Auerbach answered.

After a phone call to the store's owner and a few minutes with the system, the month's security images were downloaded onto two flash drives, which the manager handed to Auerbach. Auerbach placed them in his pocket, shook the manager's hand, and left with Harel following behind.

CHAPTER
11

BACK AT THE OFFICE, Auerbach and Harel loaded the grocery store security video onto the office computer system and used facial-recognition software to scan it for a match with photos in the agency's database. While that program was running, Auerbach contacted Ada Schapiro and asked her to come to the office. She was surprised to learn where he worked.

"I had no idea," she said with amazement.

"I did my best to keep it quiet," Auerbach replied.

"I suppose I can understand why."

"Things like knowing where someone works tend to change the way people perceive you," Auerbach explained. "This job in particular. I wanted to have some part of my life that was *normal*."

"Well," Ada conceded, "in light of that, I guess you want to continue the conversation we were having at dinner the other night."

Auerbach nodded. "I was wondering if you could tell me where in the store you saw the man you mentioned."

"I saw him in several places, but the place I noticed him the most was in the line at the cash register. He was standing across from me and he kept looking at me. I didn't like it."

"Do you remember what day that was?"

"It was a Thursday."

"Of this month?"

"Yes. Last Thursday . . . I think."

Auerbach turned to the monitor on his desk, pressed a key on the keyboard, and the security camera footage appeared on the screen. Using the mouse, he advanced the images forward to the correct date. "What time of the day was it?"

"About ten, as best I can remember. It was in the morning, before lunch."

Auerbach advanced the images on the screen until the date and time stamp indicated ten o'clock on Thursday morning. The tape played and they watched together, then Auerbach sped up the images a little. At the 10:35 mark Ada leaned forward, and pointed to the monitor. "Back it up a little." Auerbach ran the images backward until she tapped the screen once more. "There." He froze the image on the screen. "That one right there." She tapped the image of a man waiting at the cashier's register.

The store had two checkout lanes, and the man she pointed to was in the lane across from the camera. The image captured Ada from the side but provided an unobstructed view of the opposite lane. Auerbach advanced the footage frame by frame until a clear image of the man's face came into view. "You're sure that's him?" Auerbach asked.

"Yes," Ada replied. "I don't know if any of this means anything, but that's him."

Auerbach isolated the image of the man on the screen and was about to move it into the facial-recognition program when there was a tap on the office door. He opened it to find Harel standing in the hallway, gesturing for Auerbach to step outside. Auerbach joined him in the hall.

Harel whispered, "We got a hit on a face from the software analyzing the security tape."

Auerbach pulled the office door closed behind him. "Who is it?" he asked.

"Come in here and I'll show you."

Auerbach followed Harel to his office. Harel pointed to the monitor on his desk that showed an image of a man standing in line at the grocery store checkout. "That man right there is in the system."

"Ada just identified him as the man she told me about. Who is he?"

Harel switched to a screen showing a file from the Shin Bet system. "Hossein Rajabian. He's in the system."

Auerbach glanced at the screen, then turned back to the door. "All right. Let me send her home. You get started finding everything there is to know about him."

Auerbach returned to his office. "Okay, sorry for the interruption."

"This is an exciting place to work," Ada noted.

Auerbach smiled. "At times. . .most of the time it's just long periods of boredom."

She pointed to the screen again. "Is he someone of interest?"

"I'm not sure. But now that we have his image, we can find out more about him." Auerbach stood, indicating it was time for her to go. "Thank you for telling me about this and for coming in today."

She stood also. "I hope I'm not making something out of nothing."

"On the contrary," Auerbach replied. "I hope you are."

She frowned. "I don't understand."

By then they were in the hallway and he walked with her toward the exit. "You did exactly what we want people to do. You saw something that bothered you and you spoke up about it. We investigate all of these issues completely, until we either find trouble or find nothing. We always look for trouble, but we always hope there is none."

"That sounds like a life of tension."

"Yes, very much so at times."

When Ada was gone, Auerbach returned to Harel's office. Harel had the agency's file on Rajabian on the monitor. "Anything interesting?" Auerbach scooted his chair next to Harel's and sat down to read the information on the screen.

"I'm not too far into it," Harel replied.

The agency's file indicated Rajabian was born in Tehran, Iran, but said nothing about his education. As an adult, he had worked for several firms in Iran, none interesting enough to be suspicious and none more recently than two years ago.

Auerbach leaned away from the monitor. "Anyone else have anything on him?"

"Not that I can locate."

"And he's not in the foreign office system?"

"No."

"So that means he didn't come in through immigration," Auerbach mused.

"Or," Harel added, "he entered properly and someone has masked that information from us."

"When you checked with the foreign office, did their system say we were blocked from seeing his file?"

Harel shook his head. "No."

"Shin Bet has access to everything we want or need," Auerbach noted, "but if they *had* blocked us from seeing a file, wouldn't their system tell us we're blocked?"

"Yes."

"So we can assume this guy isn't supposed to be here. We need to find him, then," Auerbach declared. "It might be nothing. There might be a logical explanation for why he's here and not in the system. But we need to find him."

✦ ✦ ✦

While Harel searched for details about Rajabian, Auerbach called Yousef Farsoun, a Palestinian who lived in the nearby town of Umm Batin but worked in Beersheba. After a brief conversation, they arranged to meet later that afternoon.

Farsoun, a Bedouin from the Abu Kaf tribe, was the first member of his family to graduate from high school and then the first to obtain a university degree. He returned to live at Umm Batin but found employment with a technology firm located on the southern edge of Beersheba.

As confidential informants went, Farsoun was not particularly well placed to provide the kind of information usually associated with clandestine work. Nevertheless, Auerbach found him helpful at times. Farsoun was married and apparently lived a typical Israeli life. His children were of school age and he was active in a mosque. All of which meant he had friends in places and among people Auerbach could never reach and he provided a view of Palestinian life and culture from a non-radicalized Arab perspective.

From the office, Auerbach drove to an area near where Farsoun worked and parked the car on a side street. A short while later, Farsoun appeared at the passenger door. He opened it and took a seat across from Auerbach. "You said this was important?" Farsoun was all business but did not seem nervous.

Auerbach took a photograph of Rajabian from his pocket and handed it to him. "Have you ever seen this man before?"

Farsoun glanced at the photo, "No, I have not."

"Can you ask around? Find out if anyone knows anything about him?"

Farsoun looked over at him. "What do you want to know?"

"I need to know where he is."

"Do you have a name to go with the photograph?"

"Yeah," Auerbach nodded. "Hossein Rajabian."

"I will ask around and see what I can find." Farsoun gestured with the picture. "I can keep this?"

"Of course."

Farsoun placed the photo in his pocket, then opened the car door and climbed inside. "I'll be in touch."

A few days later, Auerbach received a text message from Farsoun that read simply, "We need to talk."

Auerbach replied with the cryptic, "Same place."

Late that afternoon, Auerbach once again drove to a side street near where Farsoun worked. He hadn't been there long when Farsoun arrived and took a seat beside him. "The person you are looking for is staying somewhere in Beersheba," Farsoun retorted. "I am not sure of the location, but he has been meeting with a man named Rashid Masalha, a teacher at a school in Rahat. You should have no trouble locating Masalha."

Auerbach was pleased. "Any idea what Rashid Masalha looks like?"

Farsoun took a cell phone from his pocket and swiped his thumb across the screen to open it. He held the phone toward Auerbach, "That's him."

Auerbach glanced at it. "Send me that picture." Seconds later, his phone vibrated to indicate he had received a message. He checked for incoming messages and found the image of Masalha. He pressed the image to save it to his phone. "What's the name of the school?"

"Allah Hu Madrasat Muqadasa."

Auerbach looked over at him. "In Rahat?"

"It's a private school," Farsoun explained. "I think the classes are from kindergarten through twelfth grade. My sister's children attend there."

Auerbach glanced again at the photo of Masalha. He pointed at the image on the screen. "This was taken really close. You know him?"

Farsoun sighed. "Masalha, I know him."

"How?"

"It's a long story."

"I've got time. What do you know about him?"

"Masalha is an Arab, but he is also an Israeli citizen. Fully integrated into Israeli culture. I'm not sure of his past, just that he is a teacher at Rahat."

"How did you meet him?"

"Like I said, my sister's children attend that school. I met him through them." Farsoun looked over at Auerbach. "There is one more thing, though."

"What's that?"

"People say the man you asked about before—Rajabian—they

say he might be a member of the Revolutionary Guard."

Auerbach frowned. "Impossible."

"Maybe so. But that is what they say."

"Who says that? What people?"

Farsoun shrugged. "You have your sources. I have mine. And that is what they are telling me."

On his way back to the office Auerbach thought about what Farsoun had told him. It seemed impossible that anyone with even the remotest connection to the Revolutionary Guard would be allowed to enter the country. "Stranger things have happened," he mumbled to himself. "But I don't see how this could have gotten past someone at the foreign office or the point of entry or . . . us. We share information with every other department of the government."

A few minutes later, Auerbach arrived at the office and went straight to his desk, then accessed the agency's data system to see what information they had on Rashid Masalha and the school where he worked. Very quickly, however, he learned that the agency had only Masalha's name and basic information—a record of his birth, education, and current job—and equally cursory information about the school.

Auerbach muttered to himself as he switched to another screen on the monitor, "This is exactly the kind of person who poses the greatest threat to us—someone who is unknown, who has no history of anything, yet possesses citizenship papers and goes about an unassuming life in an unassuming manner raising no flags whatsoever."

As those words came from his lips, Auerbach realized that the description he'd just muttered to himself described just about everyone, making the entire population of Israel—even the population of the world—a potential suspect. *Might not be a way to govern,* he thought. *But it's the job I'm assigned to do.* So he clicked the cursor on an icon for the Internet search engine and began looking for more information about Masalha.

The next day, with still no new information on Rajabian or Masalha, Auerbach decided to try the old-fashioned approach—personal observation and footwork. That afternoon, he took a digital camera from the cabinet in his office, stuffed it and his laptop into a leather satchel, and drove to Rahat. The GPS app on his phone guided him to Allah Hu where Masalha taught and he found a parking spot with a clear view of the building's entrance.

Not long after he arrived, classes were dismissed for the day. Students and teachers came from the building to the vans and cars that awaited. Using the picture he'd received from Farsoun, Auerbach identified Masalha as he stood outside the school building, directing traffic and assisting students.

Auerbach lowered the car's sun visor to obscure himself from view, then focused the camera on Masalha and pressed the shutter button. In a matter of seconds he captured dozens of images of Masalha, the parents he greeted, and others that he talked to. The camera was Internet capable and he used that feature to upload the photos to his office email account.

In a little while, Masalha appeared again outside the school. This time, he walked to a well-worn BMW and got inside, then drove away. Masalha followed him at a distance, taking care not to be observed, as they wound their way through the streets of Rahat to an apartment building a few miles from the school. The building had an open stairway that led to three upper floors. Auerbach parked a little way from the building and watched as Masalha paused on the second floor, opened an apartment door, and stepped inside. He took a photograph of the building and made a note in his phone of the location, then put the car in gear and drove away.

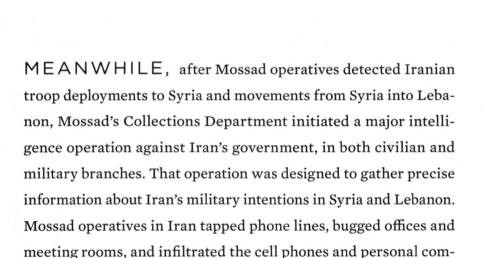

CHAPTER
12

MEANWHILE, after Mossad operatives detected Iranian troop deployments to Syria and movements from Syria into Lebanon, Mossad's Collections Department initiated a major intelligence operation against Iran's government, in both civilian and military branches. That operation was designed to gather precise information about Iran's military intentions in Syria and Lebanon. Mossad operatives in Iran tapped phone lines, bugged offices and meeting rooms, and infiltrated the cell phones and personal computers of key Iranian officials.

At the same time, Mossad technicians on the ground in Tehran and at facilities near Tel Aviv, launched cyber-attacks on the Iranian government's computer systems at multiple levels, inserting spyware and creating user accounts that gave them access to the deepest levels. By these and other means, including airborne, land-based, and space-based listening capabilities, Mossad operatives and technicians intercepted phone calls, read emails, and tracked the movements of all Iranian military units, top Iranian military officers, and key government officials both in the region and throughout the world.

Within hours of infiltration, Mossad's efforts produced a torrent of information and data on Iranian activities, all of it streamed back to the Mossad operations center in Tel Aviv, where a team of analysts under the direction of Yona Landau, went to work determining what it all meant. Almost immediately, their review of data confirmed that Iran was involved in a major operation, not only involving troops in Syria and Lebanon but also operatives in Israel, including the disputed territory and Gaza.

After a day for the analysts to get up to speed on the data stream, Landau came to the analysts' control room where the primary work was being done. "Okay," he said. "Tell me what we know so far."

Moshe Haick spoke up. "Iranian troop movements in Syria and Lebanon are only part of the problem."

"What do you mean? Explain it to me."

Moshe gestured to someone near the front of the room, and a map appeared on a screen. "We've noted troop movements here in Syria," Moshe pointed out, "And in Lebanon."

"Right," Landau said.

"And we have communications regarding Iranian operatives in Gaza. Here." Moshe again pointed to the map. "And here."

"Confirmed?"

Benjamin Dudai spoke up from across the room. "Yes, we have reports of actual sightings."

"And how do you know this? We don't have anyone there."

"Correct. Internal security is beyond our purview of operations, but not beyond our knowing."

Landau looked amused. "You got this from Shin Bet."

Benjamin nodded. "Certainly."

"And what do they know?"

"Not the entire picture, that's for certain."

"No one has the entire picture," Shafi Gottstein added. "But here's what they have." She came from her workstation and pointed to the map. "An Iranian operative here, in southern Gaza. A dead Shin Bet informant here, in Umm Batin. Also in southern Gaza. And . . ." She paused to move her finger to Beersheba. "Another Iranian here."

Landau arched an eyebrow. "An Iranian operative?"

"And," Moshe observed, "he's made contact with an Iranian asset here." He pointed to Rahat on the map.

"You know this for certain?" Landau asked.

"Shin Bet is developing the information as we speak."

"Who do they have on it?"

"Yaakov Auerbach," Shafi answered. "And a young man named Harel."

Landau frowned. "I'm not familiar with Harel. But Auerbach will follow this to the ground, one way or the other."

"That's our plan."

Landau continued. "So, the Iranians have placed operatives in Gaza and within our borders. Anyone in the West Bank?"

"No one seems to know yet."

Just then, the door opened and Amos Shalvi, team leader for the analysts, entered with a file tucked under his arm. "Collections confirms most of what we have."

Landau turned in his direction. "You have signals intelligence?"

"Yes," Amos replied. "And reports from operatives on the ground."

"They have operational specifics?"

Amos shook his head. "We can determine operational specifics for the troops in Syria and Lebanon, but not for the operatives here."

"And what about those troops?"

"Based on communications intercepts, satellite images, troop movements, strength, armaments—and the work of everyone here in the room—it appears Iran is positioning those troops for a major offensive."

Landau nodded. "Against our northern border."

"Yes."

"An invasion," Moshe added.

"So it would seem. And the operatives?"

"There is no way to know for certain what they plan to do, but it would appear that they are engaged in a coordinated effort."

Landau seemed satisfied but continued, as if wrapping up the discussion. "Any communication directly from Tehran to the operatives working inside our borders?"

"No, sir."

"Then I think we can assume they were sent here with objectives, but the specifics of how to accomplish their goals were left to their discretion."

"I believe that is correct," Amos agreed.

Landau turned toward the door to leave. "Write this up in a report that I can send to the director. I need it in two hours."

Later that day, as requested, a report from the analysts on the latest developments in Syria and Lebanon reached Landau's desk. He reviewed it and forwarded the document up the chain of command where it was delivered to Gavriel Merin, supervisor of Mossad's analyst section. Merin, in turn, delivered the report to Yossi Cohen, the director of Mossad. Merin and Landau briefed him on the contents.

When the briefing concluded, Landau departed but Merin lingered a moment. "Other agencies should know about this. Shall we disseminate it through the usual channels or wait until after tomorrow's briefing with the prime minister?"

"Send it now," Cohen directed. "Make sure it goes at once to all relevant agencies. I will see that the prime minister is informed, though I'm not sure we should wait until morning."

"It is rather urgent," Merin noted.

"Foreign operatives working within our own borders? I should think so."

When Merin was gone, Cohen placed a phone call to Nadav Argaman, the director of Shin Bet, and requested a meeting, then called for a car to take him to IDF headquarters.

From his office at Mossad headquarters, Cohen drove across town to the ministry of defense where he met with Avigdor Lieberman, the Israeli defense minister, and General Gadi Eizenkot, the IDF commander. The meeting was primarily to make certain everyone understood the information being provided in the Mossad report but also to ensure that Lieberman and Eizenkot—key players in any action that might prove necessary—understood Mossad had the lead on the matter at the moment. "The situation is sensitive," Cohen repeated more than once. "We cannot afford to have anyone acting on their own, in an uncoordinated manner."

When he finished with Lieberman and Eizenkot, Cohen drove to Jerusalem where he met the prime minister at his official residence. Nachum Reuben, one of Netanyahu's closest advisors, also was present.

Cohen briefed them on what Mossad had learned from the data retrieved from Iran. Information that confirmed earlier reports from covert operatives—that additional Iranian military units were being positioned in Syria and Lebanon and that new Iranian agents were operating with Hamas in Gaza and within Israel's borders.

As Cohen's presentation concluded, Netanyahu was attentive and serious. Concerned but not shocked. Before he could respond, however, Reuben spoke up. "We should strike them now," he said in a matter-of-fact tone.

The prime minister frowned. "Strike whom?"

"Iran."

Netanyahu seemed perturbed, both by what Reuben had said and by the way he blurted it out. He was about to say something when Reuben waved him off. "I know. I know. We can't do that right now. It's just very frustrating to deal with this every day."

"With what?" Cohen asked. He also was put off by the interruption.

"With Iran. Every day they threaten us. Question our legitimacy. Vow to wipe us off the map." Reuben growled. "It gets to be a little much sometimes. And now this."

"That is the life we lead," Netanyahu smiled indulgently. He now seemed the calmest person in the room as he turned to Cohen. "Do we know where the agents are? The ones who have infiltrated our borders."

"No, Mr. Prime Minister," Cohen replied. "We haven't even identified them yet. We just know they are here and that more are coming."

"And we've confirmed that they are moving more troops into Syria and Lebanon."

"Yes, Mr. Prime Minister. Additional units have arrived and more are on their way."

"Do they have enough to invade?"

"No. Not right now. But their force is building."

"But right now they have enough for . . . what?"

"You're asking about the threat level."

"Yes."

"Right now," Cohen explained, "they have only enough to mount a credible defense of their current location."

"You've discussed this with General Eizenkot?"

"Yes."

"And he concurs?"

"Yes."

"I'll need to meet with him."

"Certainly."

Netanyahu had a questioning look. "Why are the Iranians doing this?"

"We're not sure," Cohen replied. "We're not certain about a lot of things, Mr. Prime Minister. It's a fluid situation and we're very early in this."

"What do you recommend?"

"I recommend we sit tight. Do nothing in the way of overt response yet. As I mentioned before, I've discussed this with General Eizenkot and with Lieberman. We have issued the report to all of the relevant departments and agencies. And I have a meeting with Nadav Argaman over at Shin Bet when I leave here."

"Shin Bet is aware of this situation?"

"Yes. They became aware of the Iranian operatives about the

time we noticed increased activity in Syria and Lebanon."

Netanyahu smiled. "That's good. Everything is working as it should."

Cohen nodded. "Everyone is doing their job."

"You think we should let this develop further."

"Yes, Mr. Prime Minister. If we take action now, we'll only tip the Iranians that we know about them and we still won't be able to take down their entire operation."

"Very well," Netanyahu concurred. "You'll monitor the Iranians for further information?"

"Yes, sir. Always."

"And you'll discuss this with Argaman?"

"I'll see him within the hour."

"Good."

✦ ✦ ✦

Cohen left the prime minister's residence and returned to Tel Aviv. On the northern side of the city, he made his way to Shin Bet headquarters. Nadav Argaman, Shin Bet's director, was waiting in his office when Cohen arrived.

"You are aware of our report regarding the latest Iranian troop movements in Syria and Lebanon?" Cohen asked.

"I read it an hour or so ago. Troubling, to say the least. But even more so, the indication that there are Iranian operatives among us."

"I suppose we always knew they were present in Gaza."

Argaman thought the remark might have been a slight against Shin Bet. A backhanded way of saying, 'If you had done your job . . .'" Argaman was well aware of the work Yaakov Auerbach and the office in Beersheba had done to uncover and track down Iranian agents. He'd received updates several times each day since Darwaza, an agency informant in Gaza, was confirmed dead. He knew all of that and more, but he wasn't ready to reveal everything to Mossad. Not yet. Mossad had no authority to work domestically. That was solely within the mandate given to Shin Bet, at least as far as the national government was concerned.

Argaman pushed aside his immediate reaction. "Yes, we did."

"This evening I spoke with the prime minister at his residence—"

"You saw him alone?"

"Yes. Well," he corrected, "Nachum Reuben was there." Argaman seemed to wince at the mention of that name. "You have a problem with that?" Cohen asked.

"Not with you, personally. It's just contrary to accepted protocol. Except in matters of gravest concern, agency directors—even those like you and me with walk-in privileges—usually brief the prime minister in the company of another person." As director of Shin Bet, Argaman reported directly to the prime minister.

"As I said, Nachum Reuben was present. At any rate," Cohen was clearly growing tired of this exchange, "I didn't think this should wait."

"When you were with the prime minister. Did he decide on any action?"

"No," Cohen replied. "None, other than that we should continue gathering information."

"We?"

"Mossad and Shin Bet."

"Good." Argaman seemed to relax. "We should make certain our agencies share their findings at every level. This is a troubling situation and we will need each other's assistance to do our jobs well."

"I agree," Cohen nodded. "Which is why I wanted to see you tonight."

Argaman looked over at him. "Has there been a problem in that regard?"

"None."

"Good." Argaman leaned back in his chair. "I shall strive to keep it that way on my end."

Cohen stood to leave. "As will I."

Argaman looked up at him and their eyes met. "This is an act of war, you know."

A frown wrinkled Cohen's brow. "What is?"

"Positioning their troops along our border. Sending agents into our country. They aren't here to harass us, as in the past. Hamas can do that on their own now. Those agents are here to coordinate and facilitate an attack against us. This is war."

"I don't think anyone else is ready to say that."

"They should be," Argaman argued, "And if no one else does, you and I should. That's our job."

✦ ✦ ✦

When Cohen was gone, Argaman convened a meeting of his department heads and reviewed the content of the Mossad report with them. After a thorough discussion, he ordered each of them to devise a coordinated plan to step up their search for the Iranian operatives.

Not long after that meeting ended, Auerbach received a text message. It was early evening. He was at home with his family preparing for dinner. Auerbach read the text message, then looked over at his wife, Yarden. "I have to go to the office."

"But you just got here," she complained. "We haven't eaten dinner."

"I know." He leaned close, gave her a kiss, and whispered, "This can't be avoided."

The phrase was their code for a matter that required his immediate attention. Something serious enough that he might not be returning home soon. Yarden's shoulders sagged with a sense of resolution. There was no use fighting about it. He had to go.

Auerbach lifted the cover from a platter that sat on the kitchen counter and took a chicken leg. "I can eat on the way," he grinned as he returned the cover to its place. Yarden swatted him as he headed toward the door.

The message on Auerbach's phone was from Noga Milgrom, his supervisor. It read, "Tonchenco kuchenko." A nonsensical phrase to anyone else, but to members of Shin Bet at the Beersheba office it meant, "Come now, immediate threat." Also known around the office as, "If you don't come within the hour, look for a new job." But no one had ever lost their job over it because no one had ever failed to respond.

When Auerbach arrived at the office he found everyone gathered in the operations center—the one room in the facility large enough to hold them all. Milgrom was already there and as Auerbach entered he announced, "Okay, as most of you are aware, several of our agents have been working to identify suspected Iranian operatives who are alleged to be working in the area. As of now, they are no longer supposed or alleged. They are here."

Milgrom told them of the information being developed by Mossad. It was a condensed version, but alarming just the same. By the time he'd run through the report, a somber mood had settled over the room. "The Iranians are here, there is no longer any doubt about that, and it is our job to identify them and figure out what they are doing."

"Yaakov has already been working on this," someone spoke up in a lighthearted manner. "He probably has it all figured out by now." Everyone chuckled in response.

"And Harel, too," another chortled.

"Now we need the first team," another called out and the room burst into laughter. Harel might be the youngest and least-experienced man in the office, but Auerbach was the class of the place. No one had more experience or expertise in fieldwork than he.

Milgrom brought the meeting back to order. "We need a coordinated effort now."

For the next twenty minutes they discussed what they knew about rumors and reports of suspicious people in the area. Not the usual criminal mischief—a strange car on a neighborhood street or kids out at night on a weekday—but genuinely unsettling incidents. Contacts who had met with Iranians who appeared to be organizing for something, though no one knew just what. New people who appeared at the house next door, going and coming at all hours, living well but apparently without jobs. And the now-familiar chatter about *something big* being planned in Gaza.

"Let's develop a suspect list," Milgrom directed. "And work up dossiers on each of them. Run the background. Friends and family. Surveillance operations. All of it as usual. You all know your roles. Coordinate everything through the operations center. We all need to stay informed of what each other is doing so that nothing and no one gets overlooked. So make sure you update the data in the system. I want to know what everyone is doing and I want you to know it, too."

The meeting was somewhat chaotic, but as the evening grew late things settled into the hum of a major operation as Milgrom set about methodically organizing his agents. By midnight he knew what each of them was doing, who their persons of interest were, and how they planned to proceed. And each of the agents had a general understanding of what the others were doing, too, which was precisely what they needed in order to work the problem in a systematic fashion.

As the group in the operations center began to dwindle, Milgrom took Auerbach aside. "Look, Sussman and Elazar have an informant who has suggested that what Hamas is planning next is more like a civil demonstration. Merely a protest. Nothing violent."

Auerbach had an incredulous expression. "Civil?"

Milgrom shrugged. "That's what the guy is saying."

"This is Hamas," Auerbach argued. "Iran might be involved. They might have operatives here helping them. But whatever they're planning, it's Hamas all the way. The groundwork is coming from Hamas, the people will be coming from Hamas. And they have *never* conducted a single protest that wasn't a violent attack against us and our people from beginning to end."

"That's what I said," Milgrom replied. "But Sussman and Elazar seem to think their guy might be on to something."

"So, what are you saying?"

"I'm just telling you what's going on. And think about this—just consider it because this is where we are—everyone is working this situation hard and we aren't passing up anything that looks suspicious, but other than your guy Rajabian and that other fellow. . ."

"Masalha," Auerbach finished the sentence.

"Other than those two, we don't have a lot to go on down here."

"So, what are you saying?"

"I'm saying, if there's something to this Rajabian angle, find it fast."

Auerbach added, "Speaking of that, we don't have much information on either of them in the system. We need to check with some other agencies. FBI. Interpol. CIA. Find out if they can help us."

"You can send those requests yourself. You don't need me for any of that except the CIA."

"You'll ask?"

"Yeah. Write it up and get it to me."

"We also need to send a tech team into Masalha's apartment," Auerbach noted. "They need to install the full package—cameras and listening devices, whatever else they have. So we can keep tabs on what happens there."

Milgrom agreed. "Get me the particulars and I'll get them started on it."

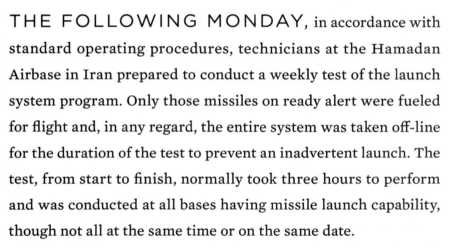

CHAPTER
13

THE FOLLOWING MONDAY, in accordance with standard operating procedures, technicians at the Hamadan Airbase in Iran prepared to conduct a weekly test of the launch system program. Only those missiles on ready alert were fueled for flight and, in any regard, the entire system was taken off-line for the duration of the test to prevent an inadvertent launch. The test, from start to finish, normally took three hours to perform and was conducted at all bases having missile launch capability, though not all at the same time or on the same date.

Testing the system at Hamadan required sending a launch order, complete with authorization codes, to each of the base's launch stations. Generating that code required the authorization of General Asghar Modiri, the base commander. He was present for the test, as was his usual practice.

Well past sixty, Modiri was a holdover from the time before the Islamic Revolution. He'd managed to survive by walking a fine line between military career, political struggle, and radical Islamic faith. Like many in the Iranian army, however, Modiri believed only in himself and had gone to great lengths to preserve his life and his future. It proved a successful course. He'd risen to the rank of general, which was much further than many of his peers had attained, most of whom were executed in the purge that followed by the shah's ouster and the Ayatollah Khomeini's return in 1979.

Colonel Emkanian, the launch control officer, was much younger and far more attuned to the way modern armies had developed. He had graduated from Tehran University with a degree in engineering and quickly distinguished himself as an expert in areas related to the use and development of digital technology. He directed the staff at Hamadan's launch control center, which had responsibility for oversight of each of the base's firing stations.

When the test was prepared and ready, Emkanian gave the order to launch from all the bases' twelve missile stations. The system responded as expected, generating orders to each of the firing stations that required fail-safe responses. When those responses were entered they should have caused a simulated launch, but nothing happened. Emkanian ordered the system reset and tried again, but when they reached the same point in the process they received the same response—nothing. After a third attempt, the system generated an error message that read, "Unable to complete requested action."

Modiri appeared dumbfounded. "What is the meaning of this?"

Emkanian was bewildered. "I do not know. It has never happened before."

"You can figure out the problem?"

"Yes," Emkanian replied. "But it will take a while."

"How long?"

"Hours, if we are lucky."

"Hours?" Modiri frowned. "You think this is serious?"

"I think we must run diagnostic programs to discover the source of the issue. The program that operates the system contains millions of lines of code. Examining each of them for corruption will take time."

"We don't have time." General Modiri turned to an aide who stood nearby. "Notify headquarters immediately and make certain General Bagheri is aware of this issue. And see if any of the other bases have reported a similar problem."

✦ ✦ ✦

When General Bagheri learned of the problem at Hamadan, he was concerned but not overly so. However, when he discovered that all of the nation's missile bases had encountered similar difficulties he ordered a review of the entire system. Homayoun Rousta, a technology advisor who had trained in Paris and

Moscow, was placed in charge of that inquiry.

While the investigation proceeded, Bagheri met with Alavi at the ministry of intelligence. "The Americans have hacked our computers," Bagheri announced.

"I heard there was an issue," Alavi replied. "You are certain it was the Americans?"

Bagheri took a seat across from Alavi and sat slouched to one side. "Rousta is getting to the bottom of it." He sounded tired and there were dark circles under his eyes.

"But you have no proof it was the Americans," Alavi countered.

"No, we do not have the proof yet."

"Then keep your opinions to yourself." Alavi spoke with a stern tone. "We don't want to tip the world that we are defenseless."

Bagheri was taken aback by the abrupt tone in Alavi's voice. "You're telling me what to do now?"

"I'm telling you we must make certain of the facts that support the things we say publicly. And we must make certain *before* we speak. So keep quiet until Rousta completes his work."

"It *has* to be the Americans," Bagheri argued. "Who else but the Americans would have the capability to do such a thing?"

"Many are capable. Some of them even more so than the Americans."

"The Russians, certainly," Bagheri acknowledged. "But they would never do such a thing."

"And the North Koreans. And the Chinese," Alavi added. He spoke with a sarcastic tone that belied his opinion of Bagheri's rant.

"The Koreans and the Chinese are our friends," Bagheri noted. "They buy oil from us even when the world imposes these stupid embargos. They would not attempt such a thing. It would serve them no purpose." He gave a heavy sigh. "It was the Americans. It *has* to be."

"Or the Israelis," Alavi suggested.

Bagheri's eyes opened wide. "The Israelis," he whispered, as if only just then considering the possibility. They sat in silence a moment, staring at each other, then Bagheri asked, "Do you suppose the Americans informed the Israelis of their suspicions about our activities in Syria and Lebanon?"

Alavi shook his head. "My sources say they have not."

"You checked with your *sources*?"

"Yes. They say the situation regarding your troop movements remains contained on the American side."

"What does that mean?"

"None of the information prepared by the analysts has been included in the president's daily briefing."

"Has anyone else in their government been briefed on the matter?"

"No, this problem with our missiles did not arise from American suspicions. It came from somewhere, or someone, else. And if the Israelis are behind it, they did it on their own."

"Could the Israelis have infiltrated our system on their own?"

"Yes," Alavi nodded.

"You give them much credit."

"They have proven adept at this sort of thing in the past."

"But they would need a reason. Could they have discovered our deployments on their own?"

"They have their own satellites," Alavi noted. "And Jews are sneaky people."

"Yes," Bagheri agreed. "They use money to corrupt our people into helping them."

"So," Alavi shrugged, "anything is possible."

"Anything is possible."

✦ ✦ ✦

Late that evening, General Bagheri received a preliminary report from Homayoun Rousta regarding the issues that affected Iran's missile launch system earlier that day. "We have discovered a problem."

Bagheri raised an eyebrow in a questioning look. "A problem."

"Yes."

"Not *the* problem?"

"We are not sure if this is the sole issue. Based on what we have found, there may be others."

Bagheri leaned back in his chair. "What did you find?"

"Five days ago, someone inserted a flash drive in a computer at the Physical Science Center at the University of Tehran. At one time, the center's system was connected to our system in order to allow scientists at the university to use extra space on our servers for research into subatomic particles."

"Subatomic particles?"

"It was a program the Ministry of Intelligence was interested in at the time. I do not know much about it and only learned about it when attempting to locate the source of our current issue."

"And how does this previous computer connection affect us now?"

"The link between the two systems was never removed. The university stopped using it when they acquired greater computer capacity of their own, but the link was still there. The hacker used that link to access our system."

"What does that mean?"

"The university had an account that allowed one official to serve as administrator of their program. This permitted that administrator to create accounts for individual users. The hacker gained access to that administrative function and created a user account. With that account, the hacker then gained access past the partition that separated the university's use from our use. Once past the partition, the hacker inserted a program to monitor our usage of the entire system."

"They gained access to everything?"

"Yes."

"Launch codes?"

"More than that."

Bagheri's eyes opened wide. "What more is there?"

"Everything," Rousta spoke in a matter-of-fact tone. "Launch codes. The launch system program. Internal email. Files. Databases. All of it."

"And they have used this program to neutralize our launch ability?"

"No." Rousta shook his head. "They *corrupted* the launch program."

"What is the difference?"

"Our technicians do not think the hacker knows the full extent of his actions."

"Oh?"

"The program the hacker inserted into our system is one designed to monitor activity. It does not have a function designed to directly interdict our use, but when the program wrote itself onto our server it changed some of the code in our programs. We found multiple lines of code where this occurred."

"A by-product of their snooping, not a direct attack on our ability."

Rousta nodded. "So it seems at the moment."

"Then, what do we do?"

"Our technicians have moved our users to an alternative server, one not connected to the system we were using. It was prepared for just such a circumstance as this."

"The missiles are functional now?"

"Yes. They have been for hours. We have also corrected the

programing errors on the server we were using before, which has enabled it to return to normal function, too. The hacker is operating on that site, while we are operating on the alternate server."

"He thinks he's in the real system?"

"Yes. It looks like our system but is only there to make the hacker think it's the real thing."

"And this site where the hacker is located, it is separated from our current system?"

"Completely different location."

"Won't they know we've discovered them, now that no one is using the system they are on?"

"We have a demonstration program running on that site."

"A demonstration program?"

"It's been modified to generate random activity that appears to be normal usage but is really only computers talking to each other. Anyone good enough to obtain access to our system will eventually figure out what has happened, but for now they seem not to know."

"And who is this hacker?"

"We do not yet know."

"But someone is investigating?"

"Yes, our technicians are continuing to mine the metadata left by the hacker. And when we realized what had happened we notified NAJA. They are reviewing the matter as well."

"They have technicians who are cleared to do this sort of thing?"

"Yes, but they are focusing on the physical aspect."

Bagheri frowned. "Physical?"

"The hacker gained access by inserting a flash drive into one of the university's academic computers. The university has security cameras, and witnesses have come forward with information about the person's identity."

"Do you think the hacker realized the issue they created when we took the system off-line?"

"Nothing we have seen indicates that," Rousta explained. "It was Monday. We test the system on Monday. Everyone in the world knows that and we made sure of it in order to prevent them seeing our activity and misunderstanding its nature. Given the kinds of tests we run on that day, anomalous activity would not appear abnormal."

"But we were off-line for an unusually long period of time."

"Yes, but we are back now. And so far as the hacker knows, we came back online within the usual time. It does not appear to have caused any alarm on his end."

"Very well."

CHAPTER
14

OVER THE NEXT several days, Shin Bet agents in Israel learned more about Hamas's proposed action in Gaza. Through diligent footwork and by scouring social media, online chat rooms, and hacking email accounts, they learned the identity of each of the Hamas operatives organizing the protests, including Mohammed Khalafi. A vetting of those operatives showed that, though they were part of the rank-and-file membership, they all were up-and-coming Hamas notables being groomed for greater roles in the organization.

As part of the ongoing investigation, Milgrom held periodic briefings to keep all agents in the Beersheba office apprised of the latest information. They were making progress, and all indications pointed to the planned Hamas events as violent in nature—potentially the most violent ever. Even so, the suggestion of some that these events would be merely civil demonstrations persisted.

Auerbach was adamant that whatever Hamas was planning would be the opposite. "I don't doubt that there are Arab residents of Israel who would be interested in participating in a protest that was merely a march," he argued. "But the rumors we are hearing are about protests coming from Gaza. This is Hamas we are dealing with, and Hamas has never staged a mere protest."

Sussman spoke up. "But so far, all we have are your informants who say that."

Auerbach shrugged. "That simply means there's more to this than we know."

Sussman shook his head. "You never give up."

"No," Auerbach snapped. "I never give up."

"And you always think you are right."

"Look, I'm not saying I can't be wrong. I just have a feeling about this."

Sussman rolled his eyes. "A feeling?"

"That there's more to this than we know right now. That we haven't figured it all out yet. That it's too early to jump to conclusions and think we know it all." He was shouting by then.

"Okay, gentlemen," Milgrom intervened. "It *is* too early to draw conclusions and rule anything out. So keep digging. All of you. Find out the rest of the story. And get to the bottom of it."

✦ ✦ ✦

When Milgrom's briefing ended, Auerbach walked down the hall to his office, dropped into the chair at his desk, and leaned back as far as the chair would allow. Dealing with this case had been frustrating, partly because time was of the essence and partly because, although he had pursued every lead, he still had only identified two Iranian operatives. He was certain there were more. But even with those two, he knew very little about them and almost nothing of the details about what they were planning.

The first of those operatives was Akbar Ansari, the Iranian identified by Darwaza, his informant in Gaza who was murdered. Information about Ansari remained sparse but based on the little information they had, he still was in Gaza. Finding him there, however, would be quite difficult, if not impossible.

The other operative was Hossein Rajabian, the Iranian working with Masalha, the teacher in Rahat. With them, things had developed somewhat better.

With the help of Yousef Farsoun, Auerbach's Palestinian informant from Umm Batin, and by dogged observation, Auerbach had identified the location of the school where Masalha taught and ascertained the location of the apartment where he lived. A covert team had installed listening devices in the apartment, spyware on his personal computer, and hacked his cell phone. That allowed Shin Bet analysts access to an audio feed from inside the apartment as well as access to Masalha's phone conversations and computer activity. In addition, cameras placed strategically inside and outside the apartment provided video coverage. And, while they were in Masalha's apartment, the covert team also cloned the hard drive from his personal computer. Yet, thus far, none of those efforts had yielded a single clue as to what Masalha and Rajabian were up to.

At the same time, the suggestion that Hamas might somehow have turned the corner from its violent past and was planning an American-style civil demonstration—a protest march with signs and slogans and nothing more—seemed ludicrous to Auerbach. There had been no indication of that. Quite to the contrary, there was every indication of the opposite.

For one thing—and this seemed the most obvious point to Auerbach—was the presence of Iranian operatives. Hamas could stage an orderly march without need of outside assistance. If they wanted Gazans to carry protest signs while marching around shouting slogans, they could organize that on their own any time they chose. The suggestion that the Iranians had come to assist with organizing such an event, or even a series of those events, struck him as absurd. That Sussman continued to promote the idea was even more ridiculous, and the more he thought about it the angrier he became.

Finally, with no new developments, and growing more frustrated by the moment, Auerbach's thoughts turned once again to the techniques he'd learned years ago, before electronic devices had become such a large part of their work. *Human intelligence,* he thought. *That's what this situation needs. Human intelligence.* By which he did not mean the application of a superior intellect to the problem, but the craft of gathering street-level, personal information. Human information. The kind that came from personal interaction with the subject, whether informants working under-cover or simply by observation. *Legwork. We shall apply ourselves to legwork and get us some useful human information.*

As he had several weeks earlier, Auerbach went to the closet in his office. From it he gathered a digital camera, long-range microphone, and his laptop, then started up the hall toward the building exit.

Just then, Milgrom came from the operations center and caught sight of him. "Where are you going?"

"To follow Rashid Masalha," Auerbach replied.

Milgrom looked puzzled. "The teacher in Rahat?"

"Yes."

"We have his apartment covered, you know. Video and audio devices throughout. All the other things you requested."

"I know," Auerbach admitted. "But he is the only viable lead I have right now and I'm running him to the ground. One way or the other, he will lead me to Rajabian. And Rajabian will take us to the bottom of this matter."

Milgrom smiled. "Okay. But you can't do it by yourself. I'll get you some help."

"Good. Give me Harel."

The smile vanished from Milgrom's face, replaced by a genuine look of concern. "Are you sure? Harel is young and not experienced at this sort of thing. More suited to those drones he's always talking about and a dozen other gadgets. This could get rather close and . . ."

"Personal?"

"Yes."

"I've worked with him a little," Auerbach noted. "He has potential—and he's not married."

A frown winkled Milgrom's forehead. "Not married?"

"Sitting in a car all night watching someone's apartment won't be a problem for him," Auerbach explained. "He has the time for it, and no one at home to complain."

"Okay," Milgrom conceded. "If you want him that much, he's yours."

Auerbach went to Harel's office and delivered the news. "You're working with me now."

"I thought I already was."

"This time it's official."

"Good. What are we doing? I was thinking we should—"

"We're staking out Masalha's apartment," Auerbach interrupted.

Harel grinned. "I was just about to suggest that."

"Well, then, you'll be glad I came along." Auerbach took a slip of paper from Harel's desk and scribbled a note, then handed it to him. "This is the address. Be there to relieve me around five this afternoon. I'll call you if things change."

"Okay, but this isn't exactly what I had in mind."

"Oh," Auerbach suddenly understood. "You meant those drones."

"Yes."

"Well, put some in place if you like. They might come in handy. But be there at five to take my place."

"Okay."

Auerbach noticed a hint of skepticism in Harel's voice. "It works," he relayed in a business-like tone. "You'll see. There really is no substitute for this sort of thing."

"We could hover a drone over his house."

"I'll hover the drone high enough that he won't hear it. Or notice it. It won't be a problem."

"Like I said." Auerbach wasn't budging. "Place your drones. And be there at five to relieve me."

"You really don't like drones, do you?"

"No. I don't like them. Used one once. Someone saw it and it ruined the whole operation."

"They won't see it at night."

"Don't like 'em."

Harel had a twinkle in his eye. "You realize Masalha lives in Rahat."

"What of it?"

"Rahat is an Arab city. You're Jewish. You'll be way more obvious than a drone to anyone who cares to notice."

Auerbach turned toward the door. "Just be there at five," he snarled. "And make sure those drones stay out of my way."

"You do realize, don't you, that I don't actually fly the drones."

"What are you talking about?"

"We have people who do that sort of thing. They're really very good at it."

Auerbach looked perturbed. "Just be there at five," he growled, and then he was gone.

✦ ✦ ✦

For the next week, Auerbach tailed Masalha by day and Harel covered him at night. They were joined part of that time by drones that, thanks to an excellent flying staff that controlled them from the operations center, did indeed hover high enough to go unnoticed. Yet despite their efforts, they still hadn't learned anything new about Masalha, except that he had few friends and seemed to keep mostly to himself after work.

Finally, just as Auerbach was beginning to wonder if they'd been wrong about him all along, Masalha left school in the afternoon and, instead of returning home, drove to a park on the north side of Rahat. He left the car near the park entrance and walked toward a fountain near the center.

Auerbach tailed him to the park, then found a space in the lot as far from Masalha's car as possible but one that still afforded a clear view of him. He watched as Masalha lingered a moment near the fountain, then drifted off to a side trail. As he started down the trail, Auerbach grabbed the long-distance microphone, exited the car, and followed after him.

The trail Masalha had taken led to a children's playground, and as it came into view Auerbach saw it was empty. For a moment he thought Masalha had spotted him, used the park as a distraction, and slipped away. But as he scanned the playground he saw a pavilion located some distance away. Masalha was seated beneath it at a table, as if waiting.

A line of trees and a low brick wall extended from the trail toward a clump of shrubs a hundred yards away. He ducked below the height of the wall, using it to shield himself from view as he made his way toward the shrubbery. When he reached it, he spread out flat on the ground, used the bushes for cover, and pointed the long-distance microphone toward Masalha. With it in place, he reached for the camera, then remembered he'd left it in the car. Angry with himself for not bringing it, he nevertheless captured an image of Masalha with his phone, then waited.

Not long after that, Rajabian appeared on the trail. He stopped near where Auerbach himself had paused and, after checking the grounds, proceeded to the pavilion and took a seat across from Masalha.

Auerbach connected the cord from a pair of earbuds to the base of the microphone, and trained the microphone on Masalha and Rajabian. He slipped the earbuds into his ears and pressed a button to begin recording in the microphone's memory.

"The parents of my students are growing impatient," Masalha said. "This work has reached a peak. We need a date for the event in order to keep them all together."

"You told them this was a school trip?" Rajabian asked.

"Yes," Masalha replied. "I told them just as you directed. That we are going up to Jerusalem to visit historic sites. That we will go up and back in a single day. They are all excited."

"That's all you told them?"

"Yes. That is all."

"No hint of anything else?" There was a hint of skepticism in Rajabian's voice.

"No," Masalha insisted. "Nothing else."

"I can't give you a date yet. We're having a little difficulty with a few other things. Things you do not need to know about, but it all has to occur at the same time. So, wait and I will get back to you."

"What do I tell the children and the parents?"

"Tell them we checked with officials in Jerusalem and there are a couple of events planned there already." Rajabian stood. "Tell them officials in Jerusalem said they will get back to you with a good date for the trip. But that it will be soon."

Rajabian walked away without saying more and Auerbach prepared to leave, too, thinking they would walk out together. Masalha, however, remained at the table awhile longer and Auerbach was forced to remain where he was in order to remain unseen. Five minutes passed, then ten, and finally Masalha rose from the table and made his way back to the trail toward the fountain in the center of the park. Auerbach waited a little while longer, giving him time to get a safe distance ahead, but he was frustrated that by then Rajabian was far away.

When Auerbach was sure the way was clear, he hustled from

his hiding place and hurried back to the parking lot near the park entrance. He opened the car door, put the equipment on the passenger's seat, then got in behind the wheel, but he still was frustrated by the way things had turned out. "I had him." He bumped his fist against the steering wheel. "He was right there in front of me. All I had to do was follow him and find out where he lives. And he got away."

In the distance he caught sight of Masalha's car and slowed to keep from getting too close. He continued to review what had happened in the park. It was good to have a recording of their conversation. And he now had an idea of what they were planning to do—an event in Jerusalem involving children from Masalha's school—but he had wanted Masalha to lead him to Rajabian so he could find out more about Rajabian.

"We may never get another chance like this. And I blew it." As he made his way through traffic near the center of town, Auerbach used his cell phone to call Harel. He wanted to make certain Harel was present at Masalha's apartment to take over surveillance.

Harel answered on the first ring. "We got him!" he blurted out in an excited voice.

The repose took Auerbach by surprise. "Got who?"

"Rajabian."

Auerbach felt his heart skip a beat. "We picked him up?"

"No," Harel replied. "But we know where he lives."

"Where?"

"An apartment in Beersheba. The drone crew has the address."

"Drone crew? How did they find him?"

"One of their drones followed you when you followed Masalha to the park," Harel explained. "They were watching the live feed from the camera and when they saw him meeting with the guy in that pavilion they used the facial-recognition program to scan an image of his face. The program matched the image of the guy in the park to the one we have on file for Rajabian. So when Rajabian left the park, they followed him with a drone. Tracked him all the way back to his apartment."

"We're sure it's his apartment?" Auerbach asked.

"Yes," Harel replied. "It's his."

"We need to get some people over there," Auerbach decided.

"Milgrom has a team over there now."

"Good."

"I guess drones aren't so bad after all, huh?" Harel sounded proud and vindicated.

"Yeah," Auerbach admitted. "They worked out pretty well this time."

Actually, they worked better than well, but Auerbach wasn't ready to admit that much. And he wanted to make sure he kept Harel under control. Not that he'd ever shown any indication of being out of control, but still . . . He'd worked with a young agent before—*one* young agent—and had given him a free rein. Things went well for a while, but the kid got sloppy and now, well, there was a grave marker at a cemetery in Haifa to remind him of that mistake. He didn't want to repeat it.

190

✦ ✦ ✦

An hour later, Auerbach arrived at the Shin Bet office in Beersheba. Milgrom was excited about the progress they'd made in locating Rajabian and about the way everyone had worked together. "This is good. And once we have a grasp of his daily routine, we'll send in a team to plant surveillance devices inside."

"They should give him lots of room, though," Auerbach cautioned. "I don't think this guy is like many we've seen before."

"You saw him at the park."

"Yes," Auerbach replied. "And I recorded him."

Milgrom's eyes opened wider. "Great! Let's hear what he had to say."

"I'll get the audio ready and be back in a minute."

Auerbach walked to his office and stowed his gear, then uploaded the file from the microphone to his laptop. After listening to it to make certain it was useful, he copied the file into the office system and returned to the operations center where he played it for Milgrom.

"These guys really are planning something big," Milgrom noted.

"Multiple somethings," Auerbach added. "He was telling Masalha that whatever he's doing has to be coordinated with the others."

"Right."

"The whole thing is going to come off at the same time."

"But what is it?" Milgrom asked.

"I don't know what's coming in Gaza, but the thing they have planned for Jerusalem involves students from Masalha's school."

"Young children."

"And some of the parents, too."

They listened to the recording again. "A class trip to Jerusalem," Milgrom commented. "Hamas and Iranians," he sighed. "They insist on indulging human depravity to its fullest."

"And when it happens this time, it won't be good."

"I agree," Milgrom nodded. "Have you had any response from Interpol or the FBI?"

"No. What about the CIA? Have they responded?"

"No." Milgrom shook his head. "Not a word."

"I'll check with my contact."

Auerbach and Milgrom replayed the audio recording from the park, then Milgrom forwarded it to the analyst section. "They're pretty good at mining this stuff for things we miss."

"Let's hope they can find a lot more."

When they were finished in the operations center, Auerbach returned to his office and placed a call to Vincent Binoche, his friend who worked at Interpol's office in Lyon, France. "I haven't heard from you on that request we sent," he began.

"These things take time," Binoche replied.

"I really need whatever you have on him," Auerbach lamented.

"I understand."

Something in his voice, though, made Auerbach suspicious. "What are you not telling me, Vincent?"

Binoche lowered his voice. "We cannot respond on the Iranian."

"Why not?"

"There is a hold on his information."

"Who placed it?"

"The Russians."

"Why?"

"No one ever says why with these things. They place the hold and that is that. You know how these things work."

"Can we get it released?" Auerbach asked.

"You can ask."

"Who do I ask? The Russians?"

"Yes," Vincent said.

"No chance of that happening."

"I am sorry, my friend."

"What about the other one?"

"Him I can give you," Vincent responded, his voice now at normal levels. "With no problem."

"Good. Send me everything you have on him. We have a situation developing here."

"I will deliver it to you as soon as possible."

CHAPTER
15

AS AUERBACH and others in the Beersheba office continued to develop leads regarding Iranian operatives in southern Israel and the kind of attacks they were planning, Milgrom briefed his supervisor who, in turn, forwarded the briefing to Nadav Argaman, Shin Bet's director. Other Shin Bet offices did the same and after reviewing the agency's most recent information on the matter, Argaman contacted Yossi Cohen, the director of Mossad. They met at the Mossad office in Tel Aviv to review the matter.

After listening to the audio recording of Masalha and Rajabian from the pavilion at the park in Rahat, Cohen said, "This is bigger than we thought."

"It is much bigger."

"Have your analysts reviewed the information?"

"They are doing that now. I think yours should work on it,

too. They need to know what we know, and they might be able to extract something from it that we missed."

Cohen agreed. "That is an excellent suggestion. Send me what you have and I'll get them started on it at once."

"I suppose it's a little early yet to brief the prime minister."

"We don't know enough details to bring him into it yet. And apparently from the conversation we just heard, whatever they're planning isn't going to happen immediately. So we have a measure of time to work with."

Argaman agreed. "That's right. So we should allow our staffs time to work this up. You get your team's results. I'll get mine to look at it and we'll compare notes. Then we'll brief the prime minister." Argaman looked over at Cohen. "We need whatever you have that might relate to this situation."

"Okay." Cohen seemed suspicious.

"We discussed this sort of thing before."

"I know."

"So we'll need to see the latest threat assessment regarding the situation with Iran. Any new information you're developing about Iranian movements in Syria and Lebanon."

"Yes," Cohen replied. "Of course."

Argaman left the meeting concerned that Cohen might not be as forthcoming with Mossad information as he suggested, or as Shin Bet needed. In fact, he might cut Shin Bet out of the presentation to the prime minister altogether. He'd already briefed him once on his own regarding this and related matters. *But that was a briefing about Mossad's own work,* he thought. *Not about Shin Bet. He doesn't know about our work. Not all of it.*

On the ride back to the office, Argaman pushed those thoughts from his mind and focused on the work that lay ahead. This situation with Hamas and the Iranian operatives posed a serious threat to Israeli security and it was Shin Bet's job—his job—to stop it before it ever came to pass. To do that, he needed to be working to coordinate the agency's efforts, not ruminating over internal politics.

✦ ✦ ✦

Two days later, Auerbach was parked outside Rajabian's apartment in Beersheba when his cell phone vibrated. He checked the screen and saw the call was from Milgrom, his supervisor.

"We just got word of an explosion at a house near Jerusalem," Milgrom reported. "Ripped the place up pretty bad."

"What do you think it was?"

"Police think it was a bomb. We have a team from the office up there on the scene, but they thought someone from our office ought to take a look at it since we're working that Hamas-Iran situation down here."

"You want me to go?"

"Yeah, maybe you should take Harel with you. Where is he?"

"At home sleeping, I imagine," Auerbach replied. "He was over at the teacher's house in Rahat all night."

"I'm gonna get you two some help on that. Both of you need to be working the bigger picture. Someone else can stake out those locations."

Forty-five minutes later, Arik Shavit arrived to take Auerbach's place and Auerbach left for Jerusalem. Milgrom sent him the address for the house in a text message while he was on the way.

As had been reported, Auerbach found the house was badly damaged from an explosion. With only a cursory scan of the structure as he stepped out of his car he could see it had been damaged on three sides. Windows were blown out at both ends, most of the rear wall was gone, and the roof hung at a precarious angle. Everything inside appeared to be charred black and covered in soot.

As Auerbach closed the car door, he was approached by Yoram Imry, one of the Shin Bet agents from the Jerusalem office. After a brief introduction, Imry pointed toward the house. "I'm not sure how safe it is to go inside. We took a look from the door and from the back but we thought we ought to call you guys before we disturbed everything."

"Good, has *anyone* been inside?"

"No," Imry replied. "We didn't go in and we didn't let anyone else, either. Secured the back so we can search for debris later, since it appears the blast went in that direction. Police were a little upset they couldn't get in there, but we told them they had to stay out."

Auerbach took a pair of rubber gloves from his pocket and

slipped them on. "I need to get in there and have a look around. Care to join me?"

"Sure."

With Imry following close behind, Auerbach stepped through the front doorway and picked his way among the charred remains of the front room. It had the least damage of any of the house but even so, the furniture was broken up and shoved in a heap against the front wall. All of it was littered with debris and ash. Auerbach glanced through it, taking care not to disturb anything other than the place where he stood.

Several books lay among the rubble—two volumes on European history, a biography of David Ben-Gurion, and a copy of the Quran. Beneath a chair he noticed an overturned box of magazines—written in English, he assumed, by the appearance of the cover.

"You have a team to process all of this?" Auerbach asked.

"They're waiting outside. Those are their vans parked by the street."

Auerbach glanced out a window in that direction. He hadn't noticed the vans before. "They'll need to get in here as soon as we're done."

"Right. We held them up like everyone else when we heard you were coming. Secured the area and waited."

"I appreciate that."

After a moment, Auerbach continued past the front room to the room at the back of the house that apparently had been the kitchen. The entire back wall was gone, giving a clear view of the yard behind the house and those on the next street.

"Anyone injured?" Auerbach asked.

"No. Houses on either side suffered minor damage."

"Minor?"

"Broke a couple of windows. Scattered glass inside. But no one was injured."

"Did you secure those as well?"

"Yes." Imry nodded. "No one was home in the house on the right. Occupants of the house on the left have been taken to the station. We secured both houses."

Auerbach glanced around the room. On one wall was a sink and next to it a counter. Three pieces of galvanized pipe, each about five centimeters in diameter and thirty centimeters long, lay next to the sink. Auerbach pointed to them. "Why weren't these blown out with the rear wall?"

Imry moved to a spot near the center of the room and stood facing the place where the rear wall had been. "If the blast originated here and went in that direction"—he pointed toward the back of the house—"then everything on either side would have been in the wake of the blast. Not in its direct line."

Auerbach thought for a moment, then looked over at Imry. "This was a bomb-making lab."

Imry nodded. "I believe it was."

"It might resemble a kitchen," Auerbach frowned. "But whoever lived here was a bomb maker." He pointed to the pipes on the counter. "And he intended to make more. Any idea how many detonated?"

"Neighbors said they heard what sounded like three explosions."

"In succession?"

"I think so. That's the only way they could have heard three. And if that's the case, he was working on a total of six."

"We need to process this scene now," Auerbach directed. "And we need to figure out what the explosive charge was made of. And find out who lived here."

"Do you want to take the lead?"

"No. I need you to do this. Run it to the ground. Find out everything you can about the people who lived here. What they were doing here. Everything."

"Sure," Imry replied. "I'll take care of it."

"Work fast," Auerbach added. "If this is related to the things we're working on, we don't have a lot of time." He started toward the front of the building. "And keep me informed of what you find. If he was doing what I think he was doing, he was just one of several like this."

For the remainder of the day and part of the next, Shin Bet agents sifted through the wreckage of the house. In the rubble they found documents addressing a variety of issues, including the size limitations of pipe bombs and plans for ways to accentuate their effectiveness. Receipts for pipe and other parts. Receipts for cell phones and pieces of the boxes they came in. In all, agents collected two dozen boxes of documents and items from the house, all of which they transported to a Shin Bet lab in Jerusalem where forensics specialists examined things in minute detail. From them they learned that the occupant of the house was a man named Khalil Kanafani, a Palestinian who had been born and reared in Jerusalem. Dental records from human remains found behind the house confirmed his identity.

A laptop recovered from the house was damaged, but technicians recovered the hard drive and examined the contents. On it they discovered files that included copies of emails between Khalil and someone named Alireza Farsad. Most of the messages were written in innocuous language, but analysts familiar with communications used by terrorist groups determined that the parties were discussing the creation of bombs that could be detonated remotely. Other messages discussed locations in Jerusalem's Old City and included data about which days were most crowded in the surrounding neighborhoods.

Later that week, Imry came to see Auerbach at the office in Beersheba. "I thought we should talk about that house in Jerusalem."

"I saw the report from the forensic team about the laptop," Auerbach noted. "Any information about Farsad?"

"Iranian. Born in Tehran. Grew up in Tabriz. Doesn't appear he ever lived anywhere else. No one seems to know how he arrived here or where he is now. Mossad offered to track down information about him in Iran."

"That might be helpful. What about the person who lived there in the house?"

"Now, that's where things get a little interesting." Imry was intrigued. "As best we can determine, the explosion that destroyed the house came from three pipe bombs and originated about where I suggested when we were in the back room. At a spot near the center of the back wall of the house."

"What kind of explosive did they use?"

"Fulminated mercury."

Auerbach arched an eyebrow. "Mercury?"

"Very effective."

"Most of the people we encounter use something more mundane. Something they can obtain easily," Auerbach responded. "Isn't mercury hard to come by?"

"Not if you have access to a laboratory."

Auerbach's eyes opened wider. "He was a scientist?"

"No. But his brother is."

"Were they working together?"

"I don't know. We haven't located the brother yet."

"Who are we talking about? I think you found the name of the man in the house."

"Khalil Kanafani was the man in the house. His brother is Jamal. The house was owned by Khalil. Jamal was the scientist. He works at a private research lab in Haifa."

"Kanafani . . . They're Arabs?"

"Yes."

"And the brother is gone?"

"Didn't show up for work three days ago."

Auerbach looked puzzled. "Why did they use mercury? As I recall, isn't it unstable?"

"I think it was simply the kind of explosive they could obtain easily. And, yes. It is unstable. But stability can be improved by using a crystal form, which is what we think this was."

Auerbach nodded. "This was a sophisticated approach."

"The bombs were just pipe bombs. Same as the others we've seen before. But using mercury for the explosive is definitely a step up in effectiveness. And there's more."

Auerbach frowned. "More?"

"We recovered pieces of the bombs from behind the house. They were wired for remote detonation. We found parts of three different cell phones and pieces of the boxes they came in."

"So, why did these bombs go off at the house?"

"I think Khalil just made a mistake."

"Was he experimenting?"

"Perhaps. But there's one more thing. When we processed the scene we found half a dozen backpacks."

"Okay," Auerbach said slowly, unsure what Imry meant but gesturing for him to say more.

"These were backpacks of a kind that a child might take to school."

Auerbach had a sinking feeling in his chest and he leaned back in his chair. "Masalha," he whispered.

"The teacher from Rahat?"

"You know about him?"

"We've been getting the memos on your work. Agency emphasis and all."

Auerbach nodded. "And you actually read them."

"That's how we knew to call down here when the bombs went off, to ask if your office wanted to participate."

"Oh," Auerbach reacted, remembering the sequence of events. "Sorry. My mind was lost on the backpacks."

"I think you're right about Masalha and Rajabian."

"I do, too," Auerbach agreed. "And I think it was a wise decision not to simply take them down. If the bomb maker was dealing with yet another Iranian, there's no telling how many there are in the country."

When Imry left, Auerbach went to see Milgrom in the operations center. Milgrom was seated at his desk sorting through the latest reports from field agents tailing Rajabian. "What did Imry have to say?" Milgrom asked.

"A lot."

"I saw that they had uncovered some items up there, but I haven't read the reports yet. Two brothers involved with the bombs?"

"Yes."

"Anything that connects that incident to the men we're following?"

"The explosive they were using was mercury."

Milgrom looked attentive. "Fulminated mercury."

"Right."

"Different from what we usually see."

"Yes. One of the brothers made the bombs. The brother worked at a lab. That's how they had access to the mercury."

"Anything else?"

"They found maps and messages on the hard drive of a laptop. The one making the bombs Khalil Kanafani was working with was an Iranian named Alireza Farsad."

Milgrom put aside the file that lay on his desk. "An Iranian? Why haven't we heard about this already?"

"It's in the report. I think they're releasing it now. Probably on the system."

Milgrom turned to a computer, entered his password, and scanned down the screen. "Here it is. I'll read it in a minute." He folded his hands in his lap and looked over at Auerbach. "This is getting bigger by the minute."

"I think it was always bigger than we realized. We're just seeing more and more of it. From the messages on Khalil's laptop, it looks like they were planning to use the bombs in Jerusalem. Somewhere near the Old City."

"Security in Jerusalem would never let them in there."

"I know, but they were scouting areas around there. Looking for the most crowded places and the most crowded times."

Milgrom shook his head in disgust. "One more thing," Auerbach added. "They found a number of backpacks at the house.

They say they're the kind of backpack a child would carry to school."

"What does that mean?"

"Smaller. Probably bright colors. Not a backpack like a hiker would use. Or one of us, for that matter."

"Students," Milgrom grumbled.

"Yes."

"And that's where Masalha comes in."

"Looks like it."

"There could be other teachers with other classes full of other children." Milgrom pointed to Auerbach's midriff. "What is that infamous gut of yours telling you?"

"I think the guy in that house in Jerusalem was making bombs to use in whatever Masalha and Rajabian are planning. It could be bigger than just Masalha and bigger than just his students. And I'm beginning to think the protests we've heard being planned for Gaza are a diversion."

Milgrom looked puzzled. "A diversion? From what?"

"From whatever they have planned for Jerusalem."

"Why do you think that?"

Auerbach pulled a chair up to the desk where Milgrom was working and took a seat. "For a long time I've been thinking about how the Palestinians in Gaza fire their rockets at our soldiers and at the villages near the border. They come up to the border fence and throw rocks and bottles at the men guarding the crossings. Those are acts of frustration. They can't effect change that way.

They can't force us to do anything merely by throwing rocks at us. It's just a statement of frustration, a way to vent, and I think they know it."

Milgrom looked skeptical. "And an incident in Jerusalem would be more than merely a statement?"

"When Al-Qaeda attacked New York City, the attack destroyed the tallest buildings in the United States. It was a big, bold move."

Milgrom shrugged. "But it didn't deter the United States from responding. Saddam Hussein is dead because of it. His country has been totally transformed because of it. Afghanistan, too. And Osama bin-Laden, the mastermind behind it, is dead, too."

"But the attack very nearly brought the US economy to its knees," Auerbach pointed out. "The stock market closed for a week. When it opened, more than a trillion dollars in value was wiped out. And more critically, US consumers stopped buying. Businesses stopped their long-range projects. All of that was caused by the uncertainty created by those attacks."

"You think Hamas is trying to do that with us?"

"This isn't Hamas," Auerbach cautioned. "This is Iran. Hamas uses small-minded tactics because they have no way of doing more. Iran has a much larger vision and the resources to pull it off. As a result, they think bigger. Whatever they're planning in Jerusalem, it's way bigger than protests along the border fence."

"Okay," Milgrom huffed. "Write it up and I'll take a look at it."

Auerbach winced. "Write it up?"

"You know how the system works. If you're right about this, we can't address the problem on our own. Shin Bet doesn't have the resources to hold off Hamas in Gaza, deter the Iranians in Syria and Lebanon, and thwart a major attack in Jerusalem. So write up your idea and I'll see that it gets circulated." Auerbach stood and started toward the door. Milgrom called after him, "And do a good job with it. Serious people are going to read whatever you write."

✦ ✦ ✦

Auerbach spent the remainder of the day preparing a memo about the evidence they'd uncovered thus far on pending Hamas attacks and the involvement of Iranian operatives in that effort. The memo included the suspicion he'd shared with Milgrom that attacks in Gaza were meant as a diversion from the real focus, which he thought was a catastrophic attack in Jerusalem. The memo was tightly written, well argued, and factually accurate.

After the memo was reviewed by Milgrom, the document was forwarded through proper channels until it reached the Shin Bet director's office where it was brought to Argaman's attention. He found it fascinating and eerily convincing. When the analysis department concurred with Auerbach's opinion, Argaman made sure it was circulated among all other related government agencies and departments.

Late Thursday afternoon, Argaman, Cohen, and General Gadi Eizenkot, the IDF commander, met to discuss the situation.

Afterward, they went together to brief the prime minister.

Cohen provided an update with Mossad's latest information on Iranian troop movements in Syria and Lebanon, along with a review of additional information intercepted from their eavesdropping operation in Iran. Argaman gave Shin Bet's assessment of the explosion at the bomb maker's house near Jerusalem, details about the bomb maker and his weapons, and an update on Masalha and the meeting with Rajabian that Auerbach had observed and recorded; then he outlined the argument presented in Auerbach's memo.

"And you think the attack planned for Jerusalem is in conjunction with an outing for Masalha's students?" Netanyahu asked.

"Yes."

"And what about the protests planned at the Gaza border crossings?"

"As I indicated, we now believe those were planned as a diversion for the attack in Jerusalem."

Netanyahu seemed puzzled. "Can't we stop them?"

"We can arrest the two suspects we've been tailing—Masalha and Rajabian," Argaman explained. "But we don't know the extent of their operation, and based on information gleaned from the wreckage of the bomb maker's house, we think other Iranians were involved. He was working with an Iranian whom we know very little about."

"Our operatives in Iran are working on that," Cohen added.

"But the children attend a school at Rahat, don't they?" Netanyahu asked.

"Yes, but they aren't involved in this, other than to be the first victims."

"You don't think this will work the other way around? The children in Jerusalem as a distraction from an attack somewhere else?"

"They were making pipe bombs, Mr. Prime Minister. And we recovered remains of several backpacks from the scene. The kind of backpacks a child might take to school."

Netanyahu had a pained expression. "Bombs in the backpacks of students?"

"Yes."

"How old are they?"

"Masalha teaches the fifth grade."

Netanyahu looked deeply troubled. "And fifth graders will agree to blow themselves up?"

Argaman sighed. "It appears the bombs were being made to detonate remotely."

Netanyahu's expression changed to one of anger. "And you don't want to simply arrest these two?"

"We would prefer to follow them right now. As best we can determine, there still is time before the planned attack. We would like to use that time to learn precisely what they are doing and whether they have other things planned."

"I don't know," Netanyahu mused. "I'm not sure that's the

right thing to do. I mean, we're talking about fifth graders." They all were silent a moment, then Netanyahu looked to General Eizenkot. "We should close the border gates immediately."

Eizenkot nodded in agreement. "Yes, sir."

"And redouble our troop strength at all of the crossings."

"Yes, sir."

Netanyahu turned to Argaman. "Do we know for certain they plan a protest action in Jerusalem?"

"Yes, Mr. Prime Minister."

"Do we know the date?"

"Not yet. And based on the most recent information, they don't know the date, either."

Netanyahu nodded. "But we know for certain the teacher is behind it. He is at least *one* of the people behind it."

Argaman concurred. "In the conversation we recorded, the Iranian working with him indicated this was to be an event coordinated with *all of the others*. We don't yet know the extent of what that means but if we take them down, anyone else out there will disappear and we'll never find them."

Netanyahu understood. "So, what would you like to do?"

"As I mentioned, we would like to follow Masalha and Rajabian awhile longer. They aren't ready to make their trip to Jerusalem yet. We have time."

"Very well," Netanyahu said, then he shot a look at Eizenkot. "But close the border crossings immediately."

"Yes, Mr. Prime Minister. I'll give the order now."

✦ ✦ ✦

In the days that followed, Shin Bet transferred additional agents to the Beersheba office. Milgrom employed some of them to help monitor Masalha and Rajabian, freeing his own agents to delve into the background of Alireza Farsad and to broaden the investigation in an effort to figure out precisely what Hamas and the Iranian operatives were planning to do.

One of those new agents was Eli Faiman. He and Auerbach were friends from a time years earlier when they worked together at the Shin Bet field office in Tiberias. Auerbach invited Faiman to his office and brought him up to speed on what they had learned so far. They discussed the information Auerbach had collected on Masalha and the meeting he had recorded between Masalha and Rajabian, and on the information gleaned from the wreckage of the house in Jerusalem. In the course of their conversation, Auerbach showed him pictures of both Rajabian and Masalha.

Faiman glanced at the picture of Rajabian and quickly shook his head. "I've never seen him before." With the image of Masalha, however, he took more time. "He looks familiar."

"Really?"

"I think . . . I think I investigated him several years ago. There was an incident in Jerusalem. A car bomb that someone found. It didn't go off and a guy with a tow truck found it." He pointed to Masalha's photo. "This guy's name came up and we took a look at him but never found anything incriminating."

Auerbach was interested. "You have a file on him?"

"Yeah. It's in the system."

Auerbach was doubtful. "I looked, but I didn't find anything on him."

Faiman took a laptop from the satchel he carried and opened it. With a few moves of the cursor, a picture appeared on the screen. He turned the screen for Auerbach to see. "That's your guy, isn't it?"

"Yeah." Auerbach nodded. "That's him, but I didn't find this in the system. Why isn't it in there?"

"That's because I entered him under the name we had for him at the time." Faiman pointed to the screen again. "He's in there under the name of Kashua."

"Kashua?"

"When I investigated him, that's the name he was using. Rashid Kashua. And sometimes he used Ibrahim. Ibrahim Kashua. We didn't know him as Rashid Masalha."

Just then, Milgrom appeared in the doorway. He looked over at Faiman with an irritated expression. "We need you in the operations center." There was an edge to his voice. "We have several leads that need to be investigated. And they're talking about setting up surveillance in another place."

"Okay," Faiman stood and made his way past Milgrom, then disappeared up the hallway. When he was gone, Milgrom turned to Auerbach. "You should probably get in on this, too."

"On what?"

"We're working on the bomb maker in Jerusalem and his

connection to the Iranian, Alireza Farsad. Someone spotted him here in Beersheba two days ago. If we push it, we might get a lead to whatever Masalha and Rajabian are planning."

"I want to stay in here and work on this," Auerbach replied, pointing to the monitor on his desk. "Faiman investigated Masalha a few years ago but had him under a different name. There's quite a bit of information on him in the system after all, just under a different name. I want to review it."

Milgrom seemed perturbed. "I thought you said we had nothing on him."

"That's because they had him by a different name."

Milgrom frowned. "A different name?"

"Yeah. They had him as Rashid Kashua. So when I searched for him under his current name, nothing came up." Auerbach glanced in Milgrom's direction. "You have plenty of people working on the bomb maker. I have work to do on this and I need to finish it."

Milgrom seemed dissatisfied. "You do remember that I'm the one in charge around here?"

The remark struck Auerbach as out of place. "Is something wrong?"

"I got people everywhere and none of them know how to work together."

"You asked for them."

"I know I asked for them. And we need them. It's just frustrating getting them to fit in to the way we operate."

Auerbach grinned. "You got us to work together. I think you can handle them without me." Milgrom glared at him a moment, then turned away.

Auerback called him back. "Look, the people we're after—Iranian operatives, Hamas operatives—they aren't stupid. Whatever they're working on is complex. They didn't come up with plans like this on the spur of the moment. When they do this kind of thing, it's always with a view toward the long term. They've been working on this for a while and they've involved a lot of people. We can crack this thing wide open, but not by rounding up the usual suspects. We have to work smart and we have to stay on task." He grinned. "And I'm not just making that up. I learned it from you."

Milgrom's shoulders sagged. "Okay, keep at it. But make sure you keep the rest of us informed."

When Milgrom was gone, Auerbach rechecked the Shin Bet computer system and reviewed the information that Faiman had entered in the file for Masalha. All of it was under the name of Ibrahim Kashua, but the system hadn't been updated to connect that name with Rashid Masalha—the name by which Auerbach knew him. Auerbach made sure to correct that error and cross-reference the names. The remainder of what he read was far more enlightening, though, than merely his name.

From the new information, Auerbach learned that Masalha had attended school in London where he was friends with someone named Emile Shammas. Shin Bet didn't have much information on Shammas but his last known address was in Paris. However, when Auerbach checked the address he learned that Shammas no longer lived there. In fact, the apartment had been re-leased several times since Shammas had lived there and was currently occupied by two art students from the United States. Still, Auerbach was encouraged by what he found and focused his attention on Masalha and his relationship to Shammas.

An hour or two later, just as he had exhausted every possible avenue of exploration into Shammas, Auerbach received an email from Vincent Binoche, his friend who worked at Interpol's office in Lyon, France. The email read simply, "See attached file." A single file was attached and Auerbach clicked on it to open it.

From the contents of the file he learned that Rashid Masalha's real name was Ibrahim Kashua—which he already knew. That Masalha attended school in London where he was friends with Emile Shammas—which Auerbach also knew. But then he noticed an entry that indicated Shammas was the cousin of Mohammed Khalafi, a person Shin Bet had long known was a member of Hamas's Al-Qassam Brigades. Auerbach was excited. "Now we have a connection!" he exclaimed.

Updated addresses in the Interpol file indicated that Shammas had lived in Paris for a while but now resided in Nicosia, Cyprus. A photograph of him was also included.

In a rush, Auerbach gathered his laptop from the desk and stuffed it into a leather satchel. He took the camera from the cabinet, checked to make certain the battery was fully charged, and put it in the satchel, too, then hurried out to the operations center to find Milgrom.

Milgrom wasn't in the center but Harel was there, reviewing surveillance footage from inside Rajabian's apartment. "Anything interesting?" Auerbach asked.

"Not really. Where were you this afternoon?"

"Working on a new lead."

"What kind of lead?"

"I don't have time to tell you all of it. But look at the file on Masalha and you'll see. I updated it to cross-reference some new information." He turned toward the door. "Tell Milgrom I'll be back in a few days."

Harel had a startled expression. "A few days? Where are you going?"

"Cyprus," Auerbach called over his shoulder as he stepped into the hall. "Tell Milgrom I'll call him later."

CHAPTER

16

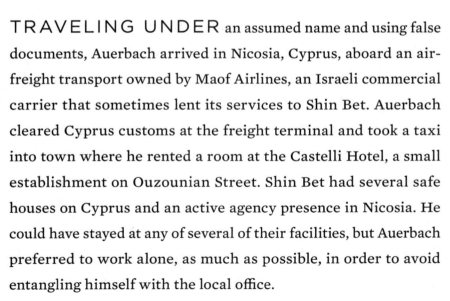

TRAVELING UNDER an assumed name and using false documents, Auerbach arrived in Nicosia, Cyprus, aboard an airfreight transport owned by Maof Airlines, an Israeli commercial carrier that sometimes lent its services to Shin Bet. Auerbach cleared Cyprus customs at the freight terminal and took a taxi into town where he rented a room at the Castelli Hotel, a small establishment on Ouzounian Street. Shin Bet had several safe houses on Cyprus and an active agency presence in Nicosia. He could have stayed at any of several of their facilities, but Auerbach preferred to work alone, as much as possible, in order to avoid entangling himself with the local office.

The next day, Auerbach located Emile Shammas's residence in an apartment above a neighborhood grocery store a few blocks from the hotel. A stairway near the store's entrance led up to the second floor. Auerbach took a seat at a table outside a café near the center of the block and sat facing the grocery store. From his position, he had a clear view of the stairway.

For most of the first day, Auerbach sat quietly at the café, noting Shammas's comings and goings. On the second day, he moved to a four-story building up the block. Once inside, he took the stairwell to the top floor, then used a service door to access the roof of the building. Perched next to a cooling unit, he had a view of Shammas's building that allowed him to avoid detection by anyone on the street below. He brought the camera with him that day, too, and used it to record images of Shammas's goings and comings.

On the first day, Shammas left in the morning around eight and returned in the afternoon around five. Both times he was alone. On the second day, however, he arrived in the afternoon in the company of a man about his own age but slightly taller and very much thinner. They were in the apartment for about an hour, then the visitor emerged and walked up the street. Auerbach captured an image of him with the phone, then watched as he made his way for two blocks, then rounded a corner and disappeared from sight.

That evening, after dark, Auerbach descended from the roof and returned to his hotel. He showered and relaxed for a few minutes, then reviewed the images from the camera. Several of the shots showed a view of Shammas's visitor that Auerbach thought might be identifiable by the facial-recognition program at the office in Beersheba. He transferred the images to his laptop, then emailed them to Harel along with a note asking him to identify the person in the photos.

Once the email was sent, Auerbach placed the laptop in his leather satchel, then hid the satchel on the closet shelf behind a stack of extra blankets. Once it was secured, he went downstairs, crossed the lobby to the street, and walked to a café on the next corner for dinner.

After his meal, Auerbach returned to his hotel room. As he entered the room he caught a whiff of something—a sweet scent with a hint of an herbal aroma. *Someone has been in here,* he thought.

A check of the room showed nothing missing, but several things were out of position. The shaving kit that he'd left on the dresser top was a few centimeters to the right of where he'd left it. The bathroom door was ajar but sitting at a different angle now. Worried that someone might have taken the laptop, he opened the closet door and glanced up at the blankets on the shelf. They seemed undisturbed and he felt behind them to check. The laptop was still there, just as he left it.

Auerbach brought the laptop out of the closet, set it on a table near the bed, and opened the lid to turn it on. As it powered up, he pressed a button to take it off-line to prevent it from connecting to the hotel's Wi-Fi system. When the machine was ready, he checked the user log and saw that no one had attempted to access it.

The realization that someone had entered the room left Auerbach unsettled. It could have been simply the housekeeping staff making a nightly check to make certain all was in order. In most places, however, that would have included turning down the bed, which had not been done. Just to be safe, Auerbach slipped the laptop beneath his pillow that night and slept with it under his head. It was an uncomfortable way to rest, but at least he knew no one could take it without awakening him first.

On the third day, Auerbach returned to the rooftop of the building across the street from the grocery store. This time he brought the laptop with him, carrying it in the leather satchel. It was not the ideal situation. The laptop might be damaged by exposure to the afternoon heat, or it might get jostled about too much, but leaving it in the hotel room while he was out no longer seemed a viable option. So he brought it with him and set it in the shade beside the cooling unit, then took his position nearby to surveil the building once more.

As on the other days, Shammas followed his regular schedule. He left in the morning and returned around five, but this time with a different young man. They made their way up to the apartment and about an hour later the visitor reappeared, walked up the street, and disappeared around the corner. Auerbach was curious about what they had been doing in the apartment and about where the men went when they left. They all departed in the same direction and disappeared at the same corner. "Strange," he said to himself.

Collateral matters, however, were not his focus or the reason he'd come to Nicosia. His mind was fixed solely on gaining access to Shammas's apartment and finding out whether he'd been in contact with his cousin, Mohammed Khalafi. Auerbach was searching for any connection between Shammas and the threats that Shin Bet now perceived as coming from Hamas and Iran—which he was certain were imminent.

By the fourth day, Auerbach was confident Shammas would stick to his familiar schedule. When he left that morning about eight, Auerbach gathered up his things, made his way downstairs to the street, and walked around the corner to an alleyway that went behind the grocery store. A dumpster was located a little way down the alley and he paused there, hiding behind it while he waited to see if he had been followed. When he was certain he had not been noticed, he continued down the alley to the fire escape that led to a second-floor window above the grocery store.

Shammas's apartment was a two-room efficiency with a room in back for a bedroom and one up front that served as a kitchen. A bathroom was located in back and attached to the bedroom. Auerbach entered through a window in the bedroom and immediately went to work searching for anything suspicious or interesting.

There was a bed with a nightstand on one side. Across from the foot of the bed was a dresser. Auerbach checked the nightstand drawers but found nothing, then looked beneath the bed and saw only dust. The drawers in the dresser held only clothes and he found nothing of note in the closet.

In the front room, however, Auerbach found a table with a laptop resting atop it. Papers lay loosely alongside it with a half-empty coffee cup. Auerbach lifted the lid of the laptop and waited for it to load the operating system. When the screen brightened, he pressed the return button and a login page appeared. Auerbach pressed the return key again and the home page appeared. "Great," he sighed. "No password to break." He took a seat at the table and scrolled through the laptop's directory.

The laptop contained documents, photos, and video. Auerbach did a cursory check of them, then took a flash drive from his pocket and inserted it in the computer's USB port. In a matter of minutes, he cloned the hard drive, removed the flash drive, and returned it to his pocket.

Papers on the table were mostly about a class Shammas appeared to be taking—an engineering course at a college across town. Auerbach used the camera on his cell phone and took pictures of each document, then returned them to a cluttered stack beside the laptop.

A sink was located on the front wall with a window over it that looked out on the street below. Three cabinets were positioned above the window.

Next to the sink was a small refrigerator. A one-burner stove stood nearby. Auerbach checked the cabinets and looked inside the refrigerator but found nothing. As a second thought, he opened the oven door and looked inside. An automatic pistol lay on the top rack. He thought about checking it more closely, then decided to leave it alone. Better not to tamper any more than necessary. It was enough to know that it was there.

Across from the kitchen area, two chairs were positioned near the back wall of the room. They sat next to each other with a small bookcase to one side. Auerbach moved to the bookcase and glanced over the spines of the books that were stored there.

Tucked between the books he found a brochure for the 2017 Pan Arab Games. The flier had been created by a Lebanese tourism committee. The cover image showed Camille Chamoun Sports City Stadium, the largest stadium in Lebanon. He opened the brochure and inside found a ticket stub from a match between Qatar and Algeria. Auerbach studied it a moment, then closed the brochure with the stub inside and returned it to its place on the shelf.

A glance at his wristwatch told Auerbach he'd been in the apartment long enough. There still was time to do more but with the hard drive from the laptop cloned onto the flash drive, he was sure he had obtained all that he needed. Now the only choice was how to leave—stairway or fire escape. Auerbach chose the stairway.

The apartment was separated from the stairs by a wooden door. Auerbach gripped the leather satchel, then draped the strap over his head and let it rest on his shoulder. With the bag out of the way, he reached for the door to unlock it. As he grabbed the knob, he heard the door open downstairs at the street. "He's early," Auerbach whispered.

Without another thought, he turned from the door and hurried to the bedroom, raised the window and ducked through the opening to the fire escape. He heard the sound of the door lock as he closed the window and stepped onto the ladder.

Auerbach was four rungs down from the second floor when he heard the window open above him. "Who's out there?" a voice called in Arabic. Auerbach kept moving until his feet hit the final rung, then he dropped onto the pavement below and walked down the alley in the opposite direction from which he'd come earlier.

There was no way to know if he'd been seen, and Auerbach wasn't about to look back and give himself away. Instead, he kept his head down and focused on reaching the street without delay.

When he reached the street, Auerbach turned and ran to the next corner. A taxi was parked there and he opened the rear door. "Take me to the Cyprus Museum," he ordered as he climbed into the back. He'd seen a brochure about it in the hotel lobby and that was the first thing that came to mind. The driver waited until Auerbach closed the door, then put the car in gear and started forward.

At the next corner, Auerbach saw Shammas standing near the crosswalk, glancing from side to side as if searching. Auerbach slid low in the seat and turned away, hoping he was not recognized.

When the taxi reached the museum, Auerbach glanced out the window a moment, then said, "Okay. Now take me to the Castelli Hotel." The driver glanced at him in the rearview mirror but pressed the gas pedal and the car started forward once again.

✦ ✦ ✦

Back at the hotel, Auerbach inserted the flash drive into his laptop and pulled up the directory for Shammas's computer. He opened the main directory and checked several of the files at the top in an effort to see whether he had collected anything of interest. Nothing in those files seemed noteworthy, but as he scrolled through the remainder of the file list he came to another directory. In it he found files that contained copies of emails Shammas had received from an account identified only by a series of numbers. The messages were instructions about someone he was to contact in Jerusalem to discuss his work. The messages did not identify the person in Jerusalem by name. Nor did they disclose the nature of the topic he was to discuss, but seemed to reflect a mutual understanding that both parties were well aware of who that person in Jerusalem really was.

After perusing the files further, Auerbach connected his laptop to the hotel's Wi-Fi service and forwarded a sample of one of the messages taken from Shammas's computer to Harel with a note asking him to have someone identify the account and the server from which those messages came. Once the message was sent, he again took his laptop off-line and continued trolling through the files.

Several dozen files later Auerbach came to a collection of documents that described methods for manufacturing Sarin, a highly lethal nerve gas capable of being mixed on a small scale with relative ease. Seeing that information discussed in such practical and frank terms sent a pang of worry through Auerbach's chest. He'd witnessed the effects of Sarin on civilians in Syria where it was used against those who supported various political factions rebelling against the al-Assad regime. *No one should be treated that way,* he thought.

Indeed, the world had been outraged by the Syrian army's use of the gas and the United States seemed ready to act. But when other Western powers faltered, the US stepped back. That's when Mossad launched an extensive operation to locate and destroy Syria's nerve gas stockpiles. They succeeded in finding much of it, but a significant portion had been whisked away to safety in Lebanon.

Further into the directory were articles addressing the instability of the final Sarin gas product and the limitations of its shelf life. One of the articles noted that both of those problems could be largely addressed by storing Sarin in its component form, rather than as the final product, delaying mixing the components together until shortly before the time of use. This, it was suggested, presented an optimal solution to both issues because the components were quite stable in their singular form and tended not to degrade rapidly. Several diagrams were included showing easy-to-assemble methods for combining the components to produce the gas in a relatively short time.

Auerbach spent several hours reading Shammas's files. By then his eyes were tired and watery from staring at the screen. He was about to quit for the night when he noticed a directory with photographs. Instinctively, he tapped the cursor on the directory icon and scrolled through the images. That's when he saw a picture of Shammas standing with Khalafi outside the soccer stadium in Beirut, their arms around each other's shoulders, both men grinning broadly.

"This was taken at that game advertised on the brochure I saw in Shammas's apartment," Auerbach mumbled. "The one with the ticket stub. They attended that game together." A frown creased his brow. "But how did Khalafi get out of Gaza and travel to Beirut?"

As he stared at the image, thinking about that problem, the magnitude of what he'd discovered became apparent. Khalafi had been present in Lebanon—with Shammas. Khalafi was a member of Hamas. Shammas was someone with knowledge of Sarin gas. And both of them were recently in Lebanon where they could have easily obtained access to quantities of Sarin gas or its components.

Suddenly, Auerbach wished he had access to the technical experts in Beersheba—immediate access. They could dissect every file on the flash drive. Analysts could review it. If they had the information now they could have answers by sunup.

Auerbach glanced down at the key on the laptop that activated its Wi-Fi connection. With one press of that key he could go back online and upload everything on the flash drive to the Shin Bet system . . . but that could take a long time. Some of the files appeared to be rather large and the hotel's Internet connection wasn't that fast. It also wasn't secure. He'd already taken a risk sending the two emails to Harel.

After considering the matter further, Auerbach decided that sending the files over the Internet was not wise. That meant the only option open to him was to get out of Nicosia as quickly as possible and return to Beersheba to deliver the flash drive in person. By then, however, there was one more problem. It was late. Any office in Nicosia that might arrange air travel for him would be unreachable until morning.

Rather than wait until then, Auerbach used his cell phone and sent a message to the office in Beersheba. The message said only, "I need a ride home."

Twenty minutes later his phone buzzed with a response. "08:50 at the freight terminal."

Auerbach checked his watch. It was a little past ten in the evening. Zero eight fifty was a little before nine the next morning He had to remain alive eleven hours—and get to the airport before nine. "Easy," he said to himself. It was more a statement to buck himself up than one of confidence, and his memory replayed images of Shammas standing on the corner, searching as he rode by in the taxi.

As he had the night before, Auerbach placed the flash drive in his pocket and put the laptop beneath his pillow. He then lay on his back—head on the pillow, hands folded across his chest—and tried his best to remain awake. Doing so until morning would be a challenge, but he'd once stayed awake for seventy-two hours straight. Eleven ought not to be that difficult.

Auerbach was beginning to doze when he felt his cell phone vibrate in his pocket. He took it out and glanced at the screen to see that a text message had arrived from Harel.

"Email account was created with a laptop using an IP address located in Jerusalem. No further information available."

Auerbach stared up at the ceiling. Now the connection of things *really* bothered him. Not any actual connection but just the mention of those things together—Shammas, Khalafi, Lebanon, Sarin, Jerusalem.

Maybe his wife was right; maybe sometimes he worried too much. It would be a distraction to worry about the wrong things. Then he thought of his family, the neighbors, and the friends of his children. And then he knew, it didn't matter if people thought he worried too much. There was too much at stake not to worry, and if there was even the remotest chance something might happen to those he loved, he would investigate it to the very end.

CHAPTER

17

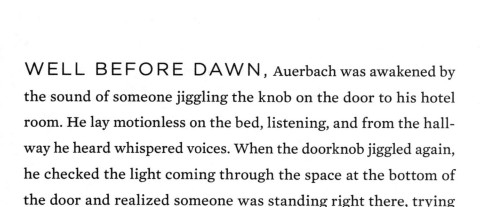

WELL BEFORE DAWN, Auerbach was awakened by
the sound of someone jiggling the knob on the door to his hotel
room. He lay motionless on the bed, listening, and from the hallway he heard whispered voices. When the doorknob jiggled again,
he checked the light coming through the space at the bottom of
the door and realized someone was standing right there, trying
to enter his room. At least one person, maybe more.

Carefully and quietly, Auerbach rolled on his side, slipped
from the bed, and started around the end. As he passed the table
where he'd been working the night before, he picked up a ball-
point pen and flipped off the cap. Holding it like a dagger, he crept
across the room to a spot at the corner by the closet, near the door
but out of sight. Anyone entering the room would pass right by
him without seeing him immediately.

Just as Auerbach slid into position against the wall, the door to the room opened and two men entered. The first was Shammas—he recognized him immediately. The other was the man Auerbach had seen coming and going from Shammas's apartment on the second day. In an instant, Auerbach stepped out from hiding and stabbed Shammas in the right eye with the pen, driving the pen inward until it lodged against the bone of Shammas's skull.

Shammas screamed in agony and clutched at his face. Blood and fluid from his eye oozed down his cheek in a thick dark stream, but Auerbach paid him and it no attention. His sudden appearance and ruthless attack on Shammas, coupled with the screams and gore, startled the second man, causing him to hesitate for the slightest moment. In that moment of hesitation, Auerbach head-butted the second man in the nose with all the force his body could generate. Instantly, blood splattered across the man's face and he grabbed at his nose with both hands, shouting and swearing angrily in Madani Arabic, an urban Arabic dialect spoken by Palestinians who lived in Gaza.

By then, Shammas had recovered somewhat and, with the pen still buried in his eye, grabbed Auerbach and placed one arm around his neck. Holding on with all his might, Shammas snatched the pen from his eye and stabbed Auerbach with it in the neck. Electric pain shot down Auerbach's right arm but he ignored it and reached back with his left hand trying again and again to grab hold of Shammas, even as Shammas pulled him backward and squeezed his arm tighter and tighter against Auerbach's neck. They stumbled across the room until they collided with the rear wall of the room.

The second man, blood dripping from his chin, charged toward them. His face was contorted in anger, his eyes fixed on Auerbach, a low growl rising from somewhere deep in his throat.

While the second man still was a meter or two away, Auerbach lunged toward him and leaned his body forward. Shammas, who still gripped him from behind, was lifted from his feet. Summoning all his strength, Auerbach rolled his right shoulder down and lifted with his right arm. At the same time, he stopped his forward motion, bent forward even lower, and used the leverage of his body to hurl Shammas over his shoulder toward the onrushing second assailant.

It all happened in mere seconds and the suddenness caught both men by surprise. Shammas sailed through the air, collided with the second man, and sent them both crashing to the floor. Before they could recover, Auerbach snatched a lamp from a nearby table and, wielding it like a club, struck Shammas in the back of the head with all the force Auerbach could manage. It made an awful crunching sound as it hit, and Shammas's body went limp.

The second man scrambled to his feet and reached for the lamp to take it from Auerbach's grasp. Auerbach stepped backward, causing him to miss, then swung it at him but the swing was short and the second man took hold of it. Auerbach held tight to the lamp with one hand and gave it a strong tug. The other man, refusing to release his grip on it, was drawn toward Auerbach. As they collided, Auerbach reached with his free hand and took hold of the second man by the hair.

Using the man's hair as a source of leverage, Auerbach spun him around and slammed his head against the wall, then quickly wound the lamp cord around his neck and pulled it tight. The man struggled and flailed in a desperate effort to free himself, but Auerbach held the cord tight as the energy slowly drained from the man's body.

Thirty seconds later, the man collapsed to the floor beside Shammas. Auerbach knelt over him, his knee in the center of the man's back, and pulled the electrical cord even tighter. He held it in place and waited until the man stopped breathing, then waited a moment longer just to be sure.

With both men on the floor, Auerbach tossed the lamp onto the bed and staggered to the bathroom. He groped with his hand along the wall until he switched on the light, then stood before the mirror to check the wound to his neck. Despite Shammas's repeated efforts to injure him, only one jab with the pen penetrated his skin deeply enough to cause a problem. He used a towel to dab the blood that flowed from it, then washed it with soap. Thankfully, it seemed the pen had missed the arteries and a few minutes later the bleeding stopped.

As Auerbach turned away from the mirror toward the bathroom door, he heard a shuffling sound coming from the bedroom and darted out to find Shammas standing at the end of the bed.

He held an automatic pistol in one hand and swayed from side to side, barely able to stand, the pistol loosely at his side. They both stared at each other a moment, then Shammas attempted to lift the pistol high enough to aim at Auerbach.

Without thinking, Auerbach rushed forward, snatched the pistol from Shammas, and struck him in the head it with it. Shammas's knees buckled. He dropped to the floor with a heavy thud, then flopped forward landing facedown on the carpet. That's when Auerbach noticed the deep hole in the back of Shamma's skull and knew he didn't have long to live.

Auerbach dropped to the floor beside Shammas and leaned near his ear. "What were you planning?" he asked. Shammas tried to respond but his voice was weak. "What were you planning?" Auerbach repeated. "With your cousin Khalafi. With the Sarin. What were you planning to do with it?"

Shammas lifted his head ever so slightly. "I will never tell you," he croaked.

"You are going to die," Auerbach argued. "Your friend is already dead. Why are you doing this?"

Shammas managed a weak smile. "You can choke all of my friends," he gasped. "But before the week is out, thousands of Jews will join us in death and there is nothing you can do to stop it." He held the smile a moment, then his chin hit the floor and his body went limp. Auerbach checked his neck for a pulse but found none.

A glance at his watch told Auerbach it was not quite three in the morning. Too early to leave for the airport, but he didn't want to sit in the room with two dead bodies. As he stood from beside Shammas he stripped off his shirt, took a clean one from the leather satchel, then folded the soiled shirt inside out and laid it on the bed beside the lamp.

In the bathroom, he washed his hands again, then his face and chest to rid them of blood and sweat from the fight. After he'd dried himself, he returned to the bedroom and stashed his shaving kit in the satchel, then took the laptop from beneath the pillow and put it in there, too. Finally, he put on the clean shirt and stuffed the dirty one in the satchel with the other things.

Standing at the foot of the bed, with the bodies at his feet, he paused a moment, mentally inventorying the room to make certain he'd packed all of his belongings. He felt his pocket for the flash drive and confirmed it was there, then thought of the trace evidence he'd left in the room. There wasn't much he could do to erase his presence but he took a towel from the bathroom anyway and used it to wipe down all of the hard surfaces—tabletop, nightstand, headboard, dresser, bathroom counter—then he noticed the lamp lying on the bed and wiped it off, too.

Confident he'd done all he could do, and certain he should spend no more time at the hotel, Auerbach switched off the bathroom light, then stepped out to the hall and pulled the door closed. He walked briskly but calmly to the stairway and made his way down to the lobby.

As he came from the stairwell, he saw the other man from Shammas's apartment, the one who'd been there on the third day.

He was leaning against a post on the far side of the lobby. Auerbach avoided looking at him and crossed the lobby to the street. When he was away from the hotel, he glanced over his shoulder to see if he was followed, but saw no one.

Relieved to at last be away from the room, Auerbach used his cell phone to call Harel. The call was answered on the first ring. "I'm in trouble," Auerbach reported.

"What happened?"

From the sound of the call Auerbach imagined that Harel was seated in his car, probably outside Masalha's apartment, and for a moment he wondered why Milgrom hadn't gotten them the extra people he'd promised, but there was no time for all of that just then. "They made me."

"Where are you?"

"Listen," Auerbach snapped, cutting him off. "The protest at the Gaza crossings is a ruse. It's just a diversion."

"A diversion? For what?"

"An attack in Jerusalem."

"They told you that? It's not just a hunch? What did you find?"

"I don't have time to explain it, but there's no doubt they mean to do it and I think they intend to use Sarin."

"Who?" Harel sounded anxious. "Who means to use it?"

"Mohammed Khalafi. The Iranian helping that guy in Jerusalem. The teacher in Rahat. And Rajabian. They're all part of the same thing. Working on the same attack."

"You have—"

Auerbach cut him off again, "Listen! Shammas, Khalafi, Rajabian, they're all connected. Hack into that email account I sent you and see what you can find. I gotta go."

"Are you okay?"

"No."

"Do you need a ride?"

"I have one. On my way to catch the bus now."

Auerbach ended the call and shoved the phone into his pocket. A little way up the block he came to a taxi parked at the curb. The engine was off but the driver was sitting in the front seat, though he was sound asleep. Auerbach opened the rear door and the driver awakened with a start. "Take me to the airport."

The driver roused himself and started the engine. "I do not think the airport is open yet."

"Take me to the freight terminal for Maof Airlines. You know where that is?"

"Yes, sir," the driver replied. "I know it well." He put the car in gear and steered it away from the curb.

As the taxi continued up the street, Auerbach heard the wail of a police siren behind them. He glanced over his shoulder in time to see a police car come to a stop outside the hotel. Moments later, another car arrived, and before the scene disappeared from view the street was filled with cars, officers, and onlookers. Auerbach turned to face forward and slid lower in the seat. The driver glanced at him in the mirror, then looked quickly away.

✦ ✦ ✦

Thirty minutes later, the taxi came to a stop at the Maof freight terminal. Auerbach paid the driver, grabbed his satchel from the seat, and went inside. He was met at the door by a young man who appeared to be about twenty-five. "Come with me," he said. Auerbach hesitated. "Hurry," the young man insisted. "There's no time to waste."

Auerbach followed him down a hall and into an employee locker room. The room was deserted. In fact, the entire building seemed deserted, too.

Around the corner from the entrance they came to a space lined with lockers on either side. A wooden bench ran down the middle between them. The young man opened a locker and pointed to a stack of clothes resting inside on the bottom. "Put these on."

Auerbach glanced inside and saw a Maof flight crew uniform. "A uniform?" he asked with a curious tone.

"Yes, put it on. And give me your documents."

"My documents?"

"Yes." He held out his hand. "Give them to me and get your clothes changed."

Auerbach was puzzled. "Why do you want my documents?"

"So that if the police question you, you can avoid arrest. Give me the documents. Haven't you done this kind of thing before?"

Reluctantly, Auerbach took his passport and ID card from his pocket and handed them over. The young man took them and stuffed them in his pocket, then pointed to the shelf in the locker above the clothes. "Your new documents are up there. Read them and memorize them before you leave the building. You have about ten minutes."

"Ten minutes?" Auerbach glanced at his watch. "It's a long time before the flight takes off."

"You can't wait until then. Get moving," the young man urged.

"Where am I going?"

"Out to the plane." The young man moved close and lowered his voice. "You will be traveling as a crew member, but you can't wait until the others arrive. You must be on the plane before the authorities get here."

Auerbach frowned. "The authorities are on their way here?"

"Yes. They are setting up checkpoints all over the city. We think they will close the passenger terminal within the hour. Eventually, they will come here."

"But why?" Auerbach was certain no one could have discovered the bodies in the hotel room.

"They know what happened," the young man answered.

And then Auerbach remembered the man in the lobby. He must have gone to check on his friends and found them, then reported it as a crime. No telling what he told the police.

The young man noticed the look on Auerbach's face. He smiled and patted him on the shoulder. "But don't worry. You will be long gone by the time they think to check the airplane."

Then just as quickly, the young man's expression turned serious and stern. "But only if you get moving," he snarled. "Put on the uniform. Leave your old clothes in the locker. And come out to the main hall when you are ready."

Ten minutes later, Auerbach came from the locker room and found the young man seated in the hall. He stood as Auerbach approached and gestured for him to follow. "You read the documents?"

"Yes."

"And what is your name?"

"Isaac Doron."

"Where are you from, Captain Doron?"

"Haifa."

"And how long have you been with us?"

"Seven years."

"Very good. You read the note included with your documents?"

"Yes."

"Then tell me, what is the reason you are included on this flight?"

"Reviewing the crew's performance."

"And why are you doing that?"

"I'm one of the company's training staff."

"Very good."

Auerbach followed him through the building and out to the tarmac. An Airbus A300 was parked fifty meters beyond the door and they made their way toward it. Stairs extended from the fuselage to the pavement and when they reached them the young man moved in front to lead the way up to the fuselage door.

At the top of the stairs, he opened the door and pushed it out of the way, then gestured for Auerbach to enter. Auerbach stepped inside and the young man followed.

He pointed to a seat on the right side of the cockpit. "You will sit up here."

When Auerbach was seated, the young man backed away. "You should sleep now. The remainder of the crew will be along later. You will be safe in here and if anyone should open the door, they will certainly awaken you." He stepped through the cabin doorway, then turned back one last time. "And don't turn on the lights. No one must know you are in here." With that, the young man stepped through the fuselage door, closed it tightly, and dropped down to the ground.

Sometime later Auerbach was awakened by the sound of the fuselage door opening. He sat up straight and glanced out the window to see the sun shining brightly in the east. Seconds later, the pilot and crew appeared and entered the cockpit. They shook Auerbach's hand and greeted him as they passed by but took their seats in the cockpit without saying more and before long started through the departure checklist. Thirty minutes later, the plane was airborne without any incident from the Cyprus authorities.

An hour after takeoff, the airplane landed in Tel Aviv. Auerbach came from the fuselage, made his way down the steps to the tarmac, and crossed to the freight terminal at a deliberate pace. As he neared the terminal door, he touched the front pocket of his trousers to make certain the flash drive still was there.

Auerbach made his way through the terminal to a locker room where he changed back to his street clothes. He placed the uniform in a locker and found a small envelope on the top shelf. In it was a car key. He put the key in his pocket, checked to make certain he had everything, then grabbed the leather satchel and headed outside.

A car was waiting outside for Auerbach. He got in on the driver side, started the engine, and steered the car toward the street. Two hours later, he arrived at the Shin Bet office in Beersheba.

Milgrom was waiting in the hall as he came inside. "Are you out of your mind?" he railed.

Auerbach had a sheepish smile. "It was a good lead. I had to go."

"This isn't how we do things."

"I know. But I didn't think it could wait. And I was right."

"About Jerusalem."

"Sarin."

"Yes."

Auerbach handed him the flash drive. "I cloned his hard drive. We need to get someone to analyze the files on this."

"Right," Milgrom replied.

"And we need to work fast. Did Harel tell you about the Sarin gas and the Hamas connection?"

"We're working on it now." Milgrom turned away. "Go home. Kiss your wife and take a shower," he called. "But get back here as fast as you can."

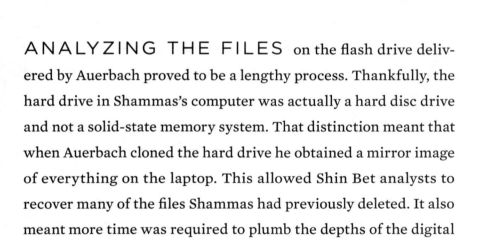

CHAPTER
18

ANALYZING THE FILES on the flash drive delivered by Auerbach proved to be a lengthy process. Thankfully, the hard drive in Shammas's computer was actually a hard disc drive and not a solid-state memory system. That distinction meant that when Auerbach cloned the hard drive he obtained a mirror image of everything on the laptop. This allowed Shin Bet analysts to recover many of the files Shammas had previously deleted. It also meant more time was required to plumb the depths of the digital trove.

As an initial conclusion, however, analysts determined that Auerbach was correct when he suggested that Shammas, Khalafi, and Rajabian were working together in an attempt to develop bombs for use in Jerusalem. They also confirmed that, based on files from Shammas's computer, those bombs were designed to be of a size and kind capable of being carried and detonated by an individual, and that Shammas and his cohorts were intent on using those bombs to disperse Sarin gas. The files also supported Auerbach's assertion that the attack being planned by Khalafi and Rajabian appeared to be imminent, though nothing in the files specifically corroborated the time frame alluded to by Shammas moments before he died. All of this information, along with the conclusions drawn by Shin Bet analysts, was prepared in a report that was funneled up to the Shin Bet director, Nadav Argaman.

After reviewing the report and conducting a thorough discussion of its contents with senior leadership, Argaman distributed copies of the document to Yossi Cohen, the head of Mossad; Avigdor Lieberman, the Israeli minister of defense; and General Gadi Eizenkot, the IDF commander. Along with the report, Argaman requested an updated status report from each of them in accord with their previous agreements to cooperate and share information.

The following day, Argaman received status memos from Mossad, the defense ministry, and IDF. Late that afternoon, the heads of those organizations and their senior staff members met in a conference room down the hall from Lieberman's office to discuss the situation regarding Hamas, Iran, and the troops massing in Syria and Lebanon.

Everyone in attendance that day was convinced that Iran was continuing to strengthen its military presence in Syria and

Lebanon, that those troops were being positioned for an advance toward Israel's northern border, and that the anticipated attacks along the Gaza border and in Jerusalem were no more than a week to ten days away. Their opinions about what they should do in response to the situation were slightly less cohesive.

"We should launch an immediate operation to prevent the attacks in Jerusalem from ever happening," Argaman opined. "We can't wait for bombs to go off in the street."

"And what would that entail?"

"Arresting the people we know about."

"Taking down the two . . . Rajabian and . . . the other fellow."

"Masalha," Cohen said. "Masalha and Rajabian."

"You think arresting them will end the threat?"

"I think it will end the threat from *them*."

"Is it not likely they have others involved with them?" Lieberman asked. "I understand this plot involves a group of schoolchildren. Transporting them would require assistance. I'm just thinking, there must be others involved."

"That is probably true," Argaman acknowledged. "There probably are others involved that we don't know about. But the risk is now at a level that we cannot let this go on any longer. Earlier, I was of the opinion that we had time and we should use that time to investigate further before making arrests. Now, with the new information we've obtained, we have reached a point that it is no longer prudent to delay. We should prevent the ones we know about from doing any harm."

"This gets to another matter," General Eizenkot added.

"What is that?"

"We can't make ultimate decisions about this ourselves. The stakes are too high. We must brief the prime minister."

"But we need to present a coordinated plan." Cohen looked over at Argaman. "You would tell the prime minister that Shin Bet wants to arrest these men?"

"Yes."

"I don't have any problem with that," Lieberman commented. "I don't think that impinges on the situation along our northern border. And I agree, we cannot sit by and watch while they detonate bombs in the streets of Jerusalem. Especially now that we know they intend to use Sarin."

After airing their views further, the four department heads—Lieberman, Cohen, Argaman, and Eizenkot—arranged to brief Netanyahu early that evening. They gathered in the prime minister's office in Jerusalem. It was a solemn occasion with the four men standing before Netanyahu's desk while he remained seated. Cohen and Lieberman outlined the situation regarding Iranian troops in Lebanon and Syria and the threat those troops posed. After they'd finished, Netanyahu turned to Eizenkot.

"General, what does this mean?"

"Iran can't simply invade us and accomplish a military objective," General Eizenkot explained. "The troops they have in place now are not of sufficient number to overrun us by that means alone."

"They could cross the border and that would be it."

"Basically. And even if Hamas attempted to move out of Gaza against us in mass numbers it would have a very limited effect, either alone or on the combined attack with the Iranian troops now on hand. Al-Qassam isn't armed well enough to pose more than a momentary threat."

"So neither of these two elements even working together can cause us more than a limited problem."

"Yes," Eizenkot acknowledged. "None of these—Hamas, the Iranians, even suicide bombers in Jerusalem—none of them taken separately has any hope of ultimate success. What the Iranians must do, if they truly want to succeed against us, is to coordinate *all* of these various elements in a combined attack and, at the same time, launch an all-out missile attack against us."

Netanyahu raised an eyebrow. "A missile attack? From Iran?"

"From every location," Eizenkot replied. "Missiles launched from their bases inside Iran. And missiles launched by Hezbollah forces in Lebanon. With an invasion by the troops they have placed in Lebanon and Syria. With a massive surge of humanity led by Hamas from Gaza. Plus suicide bombers in Jerusalem in large numbers and in a way designed to yield mass casualties in the most compelling manner."

"Gas."

"Yes. And all of that timed to occur on the same day and at roughly the same time. If they did that, they would pose a serious threat to our stability. We would be sorely challenged to handle all of that simultaneously."

"And you think a missile attack would be part of it?"

"Most certainly, Mr. Prime Minister. Iran wouldn't commit this kind of troop presence without it. Hezbollah has more than a hundred thousand rockets of its own—precision-guided missiles. Syria has tens of thousands still at its disposal, even after their lengthy civil war. If Iran wanted to attack us from their current posture, and do so with the intention of destroying us, they would need to use all of those missiles—the ones in Syria and the ones in Lebanon—plus the missiles Iran has at its bases within its borders."

"Which seems rather impossible for them to pull off," Cohen interjected, raising a sense of skepticism he had not mentioned earlier.

"Difficult," Eizenkot countered. His conciliatory tone masked the anger he felt that Cohen was undermining his position. "Challenging, perhaps, but not impossible." He delivered the final line with his eyes focused directly on Cohen in an unmistakable glare.

Netanyahu remained focused on Eizenkot's point. "And we don't have the capability with our Iron Dome Defense to halt a missile attack like the one you've just outlined, right?"

"That is correct, Mr. Prime Minister, if they are able to launch," Eizenkot advised. "We could not shoot down that many missiles if they became airborne in substantial numbers and at a sustainable rate. To prevent widespread damage, we would need to launch a preemptive attack and destroy most of their missiles before they ever leave the launch racks. That is why long ago we adopted the strategy of a preemptive attack as our primary defense posture."

Netanyahu looked to Cohen. "Hezbollah still has possession of Syria's nerve gas stockpiles?"

"Yes," Cohen replied. "Assad moved their nerve gas to Lebanon for safekeeping after the United States attacked them in response to Syria's use of gas against Syrian civilians."

"And you're confident of that?"

"Yes, Mr. Prime Minister. We have an inside source. Syria relinquished its nerve gas to Hezbollah. Perhaps not for Hezbollah's indiscriminate use, but they have the gas in their possession."

Netanyahu turned back to Eizenkot. "How much time do you need to launch a preemptive strike against the missile threat?"

"We would need two hours to get our planes in the air for a strike against Hezbollah missile batteries in Lebanon. A day to launch a widespread attack on Syria's capability. And—"

Netanyahu interrupted. "Why the difference? Why hours against Lebanon and a day against Syria?"

"Syria has a better air-defense system," Eizenkot explained. "And they have Russian advisors on the ground. We would need to work around both of those variables."

"And what about with the missiles inside Iran?"

"That is more complicated," Eizenkot cautioned. "The flight

time from here to there is about six-and-a-half hours and we would need to fly through Saudi Arabian air space."

"And what is the possibility we will destroy all of their missiles?"

"Zero," Eizenkot replied.

Netanyahu asked thoughtfully. "Zero?"

"Yes, Mr. Prime Minister," Eizenkot replied. "It would be impossible to destroy all of the missiles at all of these various sites."

"We have estimates for total numbers, but no definitive location for all of them."

"Correct. Many of them are on mobile launchers. And the volume of devices involved is simply beyond our capacity. We would need help."

Netanyahu nodded. "I agree." He looked over at Cohen. "What about this attack in Jerusalem? Where are we on that?"

"Mr. Prime Minister," Cohen began, "we have uncovered information that indicates an attack in Jerusalem could be widespread. We don't know the full extent yet. But we know bombs are being made and the—"

Netanyahu cut him off. "You found the bomb maker, though, didn't you?"

"We found *one* of them. At the house where several bombs detonated while he was in the process of making them."

"And you found backpacks that indicated these bombs were to be carried by schoolchildren."

"Yes. As you are aware, we have been following two of the people behind that plot in the hope of uncovering others that might be working with them. That effort has led us to a third person. That third person had connections to an additional Iranian operative and connections to interests in Lebanon."

"Interests. What does that mean?"

"We're not certain," Cohen replied. "But this person was discussing the use of Sarin gas in conjunction with the bombings in Jerusalem with each of the others."

"Sarin?"

"Yes, Mr. Prime Minister. We've collected quite a bit of information from this person about this part of the plot but we haven't finished processing all of it."

"You have this third person in custody?"

"No," Cohen answered. "We are following the original two people we identified previously. The third person is dead."

"But you think he was involved?"

"Yes. He died as a result of a struggle with our agent who was investigating him."

Netanyahu looked concerned. "Your agent is okay?"

"Yes. He was not seriously harmed."

"Okay." Netanyahu leaned back in his chair. "So," he sighed. "What should we do, gentlemen?"

General Eizenkot spoke up. "I think we should put our forces on alert, Mr. Prime Minister."

"Won't that tip our hand?"

"Yes. I suppose it would. But we can't defend if we aren't ready."

"I'm a little reluctant to do that just yet. Not before we've brought our allies up to speed." Everyone in the room knew he was referring to the United States. "Iran hasn't started moving its troops toward the border, have they?"

Eizenkot shook his head. "No, sir, not as far as we can determine."

"If we put our troops on alert, we'll not only tip our hand that we know what they're doing, we'll also raise the level of engagement. I don't think we want to do that. Not officially. Not right now."

Eizenkot nodded. "Then I would at least like to reposition some of our units. Move some from the south and west up to the north."

"So ordered," Netanyahu replied.

"And we need to prepare our missile defenses. Make certain our anti-missile systems are in the correct locations. Ensure that shelters are stocked and ready."

"Yes," Netanyahu agreed again. "Do you need an order for that?"

"No, Mr. Prime Minister."

"So ordered anyway." Netanyahu glanced over at Argaman. "Nadav, what would Shin Bet like to do about these pending attacks in Jerusalem and along the border with Gaza?"

"You've already ordered the border crossings closed and I think that has been done."

"Yes," Eizenkot spoke up. "They're closed now."

Argaman continued. "I think we should arrest Masalha—the

teacher we think is working on the Jerusalem plot—along with the Iranian operative who is helping him."

"You've completed your investigation?"

"No, sir, but we've reached a point where we need to act on the information we've gathered. The threat is too real to delay a response now. We need to take them into custody."

"And that will end the threat in Jerusalem?"

"No, Mr. Prime Minister. If they have others assisting them that we don't yet know about, the attacks could go forward. But we can't wait any longer."

"Right." Netanyahu sighed. "So, this is where we are."

They all agreed.

"Okay." Netanyahu stood. "Move the troops. Prepare the missiles and shelters. Take those two into custody." He paused a moment before saying, "We can only do so much by ourselves. For a complete response, we will need help."

"The Americans," Cohen added quietly.

"Yes," Netanyahu said. "Which is why I want each of you to brief your American counterpart on where we stand. Share these reports with them." He gestured to the collection of reports lying on his desk. "Make sure they have our most recent information. It's time for us to act and in order for us to do that effectively, we need the Americans on our side. So brief your American counterparts and impress upon them the gravity of the threats we face and our need for their support."

As the meeting broke up, Netanyahu asked Lieberman to

remain behind. When the others were gone, Netanyahu closed the office door. "I want you to go to America tonight."

Lieberman seemed taken aback. "Tonight?"

"Yes. I want you fly to Washington and brief the US secretary of defense in person."

"Very well. But I'm not sure he can see me that quickly."

"He will make the time for you," Netanyahu assured. "Especially if you arrive on his doorstep. And you can call ahead while you're in the air."

"Yes, Mr. Prime Minister."

Netanyahu put his arm around Lieberman. "Avigdor, I need you to sell our situation to them. The nation needs you to convince them. Get Jim Mattis to understand what we are facing and get him in a posture of cooperation with us."

"Certainly."

"You have to convince him that they must join us."

"I'll do my best."

"No," Netanyahu urged. "This is it. I've read the reports and I've seen your internal analysis. We face a threat to our very existence. The Iranians and Hamas aren't attempting to merely harass us. Not this time. This time they really mean to destroy us. Do you believe that?"

"Yes, Mr. Prime Minister. I do."

"We'll need help from the United States to survive what's coming. And we need them adequately informed from the beginning so we're working together when we begin our response."

"Right."

"Don't wait until tomorrow to leave," Netanyahu stressed. "Leave now and arrange your meeting while you're in the air."

"Yes, sir."

✦ ✦ ✦

Despite the lateness of the hour, as Argaman drove away from the meeting with Netanyahu he thought about the things they had discussed and about what must happen next. So far, he and Cohen had driven the nation's policy options. Their agencies uncovered the plot. Their employees tracked down and identified the people involved. However, if Iranian troops advanced on the northern border, that relationship would change.

If Iran attacked with its troops, defending the nation would take precedence over all else. Eizenkot and Lieberman would become Netanyahu's primary advisors. IDF's priorities would gain veto power over every other aspect of the government until the crisis was addressed. In that event, Shin Bet shouldn't be in the way. And regardless of whether the attack actually occurred, the nature of the threat couldn't be met without the involvement of the IDF and the defense ministry. That had the effect of changing the status quo between the agencies. Henceforth, the path forward for Shin Bet would be one of cooperation. For that to take place, people down the line should know the details.

Perhaps not everyone, Argaman thought. *And not every detail.*

But those involved in the effort, particularly those at the office in Beersheba, needed to know. He'd dealt with Auerbach before and found him to be headstrong. The prospect of an agent running roughshod over the case, especially with the prime minister wanting to involve the Americans heavily, left him uneasy.

Before he reached home, Argaman phoned his office. An overnight clerk took the call and provided Argaman with the home telephone number for Milgrom. As Argaman's car came to a stop in the drive outside his house, he placed a call to Milgrom.

"We should meet," Argaman said.

Milgrom was flattered to have personal contact with a Shin Bet director, but the phone call struck him as odd and not a little out of place. Argaman was head of the agency. He reported directly to the prime minister. Milgrom was an operations supervisor temporarily doubling as manager of the Beersheba office because the person who had been in charge retired for medical reasons without much notice.

Even as manager of the office, Milgrom received official policy priorities through the agency's established chain of authority. In the normal course of business, his instruction and oversight came from the supervisor for Shin Bet's southern district, not from the director himself. Still, Argaman was the director and if he wanted to meet, Milgrom had no choice but to attend.

"What time?" Milgrom asked.

"Now. But not at the office. Meet me at Beit Guvrin. It's halfway between us."

Milgrom agreed and Argaman ended the call. As he slipped his cell phone into his pocket, Milgrom mumbled to himself.

His wife, just coming in to the room, looked in his direction. "What was that about?"

"Nothing. Just talking to myself."

"You do a lot of that lately."

"I know. And I'll probably do a lot more." Milgrom started from the room and made his way toward the front of the house. His wife followed him to a coatrack near the door where Milgrom took a jacket and slipped it on. "I have to go out. It might be late when I return. Don't wait up for me."

She reached up to straighten the jacket. "Why do you rush off into the night like this?"

Milgrom kissed her gently. "Part of the job."

"They should pay you more," she replied.

"Yes." Milgrom turned away and opened the door. "They should pay me a lot more."

Beit Guvrin was a farming collective located fifty kilometers north of Beersheba. Driving there took Milgrom an hour. As he neared the village, he received a text from Argaman that read, "BG Technologies."

Milgrom located the facility and turned in at the gate. A guard saw him and for a moment Milgrom wondered what would happen next, then the gate opened and he saw a gray Mercedes sedan parked on the other side. He drove past the gate, parked in front of the sedan, and got out. The dome light inside the Mercedes came on as he stepped toward it and he saw Argaman seated behind the steering wheel. Milgrom got in on the passenger side.

Argaman began without introduction. "This man you have working on the case . . ."

"Auerbach," Milgrom offered.

"They tell me he's a bit of a rogue."

"He's a good agent," Milgrom said.

"But he had some issues in Tiberias. A shooting. Something about a man he locked in a closet. And a woman, I believe."

"The shooting was justified," Milgrom explained. "He was defending himself and his partner."

"And the man in the closet?"

"I don't know about that," Milgrom replied. "No one does. That part might be true."

"And the woman?"

"That was a complete fabrication given by a witness who later proved to be false on every point of information offered. The witness was later implicated in a bombing arranged by members of Hamas."

"You believe him?"

"Yes."

"And you trust what he has told you about this trouble with Hamas and the Iranian operatives?"

"Absolutely."

"Then you need to know the latest."

For the next twenty minutes, Argaman outlined for Milgrom

the most recent developments—Iranian troop strength in Syria and Lebanon, the chatter from intercepts obtained by the team that infiltrated the Iranian communications system, the determination that the anticipated attacks from Hamas in Gaza and the bombings in Jerusalem would portend an invasion by Iran from the north, and the prime minister's desire to involve the Americans in a coordinated defense.

When he finished, Argaman looked over at Milgrom. "I want you to know these things so that you can direct your agents as necessary. This situation is shifting toward a military response, and we must find our place in a strategy that increasingly will be dominated by IDF and the defense ministry."

"Should I tell Auerbach?"

"That is at your discretion. I would suggest you tell him as necessary. On a need-to-know basis. But make certain your office works with the greater situation in mind. And we have authorized you to arrest the two primary people you've noted. The teacher and the Iranian."

"Masalha and Rajabian."

"Yes. Have your men detain them immediately."

Milgrom nodded. "I will do as you wish." He opened the door to leave, then paused. "This is a real danger to us, isn't it?"

"It is more serious than ever before."

CHAPTER
19

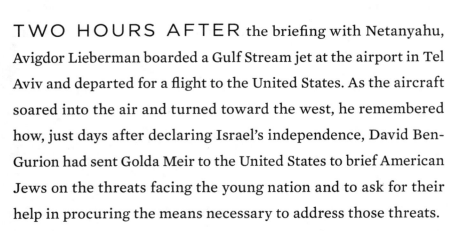

TWO HOURS AFTER the briefing with Netanyahu, Avigdor Lieberman boarded a Gulf Stream jet at the airport in Tel Aviv and departed for a flight to the United States. As the aircraft soared into the air and turned toward the west, he remembered how, just days after declaring Israel's independence, David Ben-Gurion had sent Golda Meir to the United States to brief American Jews on the threats facing the young nation and to ask for their help in procuring the means necessary to address those threats.

Now, though the nation of Israel was established and in much better shape militarily than it had been in the past. The country nevertheless faced an existential threat of a kind not seen in a long time. As he glanced out the window at the lights below, Lieberman had the deep and abiding sense that the hopes and dreams of many lying in bed that night in Tel Aviv, Haifa, Jerusalem, and thousands of other communities throughout Israel were traveling with him. In his heart he was certain the future of Israel depended very much on the outcome of the meetings that lay ahead.

A little before eleven the following morning, Lieberman arrived in Washington and reached the Pentagon twenty minutes later. He was met at the building entrance by Jim Mattis, the US secretary of defense, and the two men rode the elevator up to the secretary's office. For three hours, Lieberman laid out the scenario that faced the nation of Israel.

"We've had reports from our own sources about Iran troop buildup in Syria," Mattis related when Lieberman had finished.

"You knew about the infiltration of our territory by Iranian operatives?" Lieberman asked.

"Nothing you haven't already told us."

Lieberman felt Mattis was being guarded in his response, certainly less than candid, but he chose not to press the matter just then. Israel needed American support for any military response the prime minister might order. He'd been sent to get that support, not to confront US officials about the continuing need for transparency in their relationship.

After a late lunch, Lieberman and Mattis turned to the details of Israel's response. This time, Lieberman was the one being coy, sketching an Israeli military response in the broadest terms, but providing none of the specifics the Americans would need if they were to join Israel later. Israel needed US support. Israel wanted

US support. Lieberman, however, was concerned that if he gave Mattis too much information at the beginning, their conversations would be diverted into a critique of the details rather than a consensus about the objective. Still, he provided enough to put Mattis on notice—Israel intended to defend herself to the fullest extent of her ability.

Late that afternoon, Lieberman returned to Israel. The information he delivered, however, already was being reviewed by US intelligence analysts. Overnight, the reports were vetted and verified. A summary of that analysis was forwarded to senior staff at the National Intelligence office for inclusion in the president's daily intelligence brief being prepared for the following morning.

✦ ✦ ✦

At five o'clock the next morning, the White House telephone that sat beside the bed of President Donald Trump began to ring. He reached for it in a drowsy slumber and brought the receiver to his ear. "Yeah," he answered.

"Good morning, Mr. President," a pleasant voice spoke. "This is your wake-up call."

"Does this mean they haven't let me go home yet?" he quipped.

"No, sir, Mr. President," the voice responded in a similar manner. "You're still president of the United States."

"Thank you," he replied, then hung up the phone, threw back the covers, and rolled out of bed.

Trump—less than six months into his first term—had been

elected to office on the wave of a conservative backlash against economic policies that resulted in two decades of job exodus as the globalization of trade gave American manufacturers access to cheap labor markets abroad. The policy proved enormously profitable for corporations but left thousands of US workers unemployed, a consequence that politicians had failed to address. Trump was elected largely on the promise to fix the problem and put American workers back to work.

Although Trump won the election, he had not come to office with a popular-vote majority. The sense of division that electoral divide engendered made for a challenging start for the new administration. After a series of personnel changes, however, the White House staff was beginning to right itself and Trump was beginning to settle into the rhythm of a presidential day.

An hour after his wake-up call, the president was dressed and ready for the day. He made his way downstairs from the residence and over to the Oval Office, where he was greeted by Linda Miller, his personal secretary. She reviewed the day's schedule, making certain he understood the demands on his time and giving him a heads-up about several items that might take longer than scheduled.

As Mrs. Miller finished, a door to the left opened and John Kelly, the White House chief of staff, appeared. After graduating from Annapolis, Kelly began his career in the Marine Corps where he rose to the rank of four-star general and commanded one of the United States military's ten unified combatant commands. He'd come to the White House to help instill discipline to the decision-making process.

Kelly stood near the president's desk. "Are you ready for your security briefing?"

"I suppose," Trump replied.

Kelly had an amused expression. "Why the hesitancy?"

Trump came from the coffee tray where he'd been talking with Mrs. Miller and took a seat behind his desk. "These intelligence guys are okay, but I never know if they're telling me the unvarnished truth or something they *want* to be true."

"That's a healthy skepticism, sir. But remember, the content of these briefings comes through the director of National Intelligence. He's been a longtime acquaintance of yours."

"Dan Coats is a good man," Trump replied, referring to the director. "I just wonder sometimes . . . Let's hear what he has to say today. Send him in." There was a hint of resignation in his voice but a confident smile on his face.

Kelly ushered Coats into the room, then took a seat on a sofa across from the president's desk. Sitting there placed him close enough to hear anything that might be said to the president but out of the visitor's line of sight.

That morning, Coats arrived carrying a memo of about a hundred pages in length. Two sheets on top summarized the most critical issues. He took a seat to the right of the president's desk in a chair positioned to place his back to the room and left him facing only the president. With little in the way of personal greeting, Coats launched into a review of the memo.

The briefing covered a broad range of global issues and events. Much of it, however, was devoted to the information provided by Lieberman regarding threats against Israel. When they'd worked their way through the details, Trump commented, "We've confirmed that the Israeli information is accurate?"

"Yes, Mr. President," Coats replied. "Their assessment is in line with ours."

"We have our own Iranian communications intercepts that bear that out?"

"Yes, sir." There was a hint of defensiveness in Coats's voice, as if he was suddenly on guard. "We have intercepts picked up from bases inside Iran, from installations in Syria, and from Iranian units operating in Lebanon. Was there something you thought might be incorrect?"

The president shook his head. "No, I think you've done a good job with this, Dan."

Coats raised an eyebrow. "But?"

"I just want to make sure that the information we're working with is accurate, that's all. I don't want to say something this morning, only to have a hundred reporters talk all afternoon about how incorrect my statements are."

"Yes, sir, Mr. President," Coats acknowledged. "The information that the secretary of state received from the Israeli minister of defense was thoroughly examined and confirmed by our own sources. CIA, NSA, DIA, my own staff. All of them agree with the assessment reflected in today's memo."

"Okay." Trump stood, indicating the meeting was over. "Keep me informed as the day goes along. I'll expect regular updates on the situation."

"With the Israelis?" Coats asked as he rose from his chair. The briefing covered multiple issues and he wanted to be sure he understood correctly.

"Yes."

"Very well," Coats acknowledged.

When he was gone, Trump took a seat at the ornate Resolute Desk once again. Kelly stood nearby. "Anything you might want to do about the situation with Israel?"

Trump thought for a moment. "You should instruct the various intelligence agencies to coordinate with their Israeli counterparts. Make sure we give them whatever they need. Ask them to let us know what they are doing ahead of time so we can maintain a supportive position."

"Certainly," Kelly replied. "But perhaps you should telephone the Israeli prime minister and offer our assistance directly, rather than merely telling our agencies to coordinate at a staff level."

A frown wrinkled Trump's forehead. "You think I should get personally involved in this?"

Kelly nodded. "I think you're going to be involved with it sooner or later. We might as well get ahead of the situation while we have the opportunity. And there are things that can be done now that can't be handled very well later. We should consider those as well."

"Such as?"

"Such as providing Israel with additional defense technology before the bullets and missiles start flying. Repositioning our carrier groups. Forward deployment of troops. That sort of thing."

Trump frowned again. "Forward deployment? You mean move them close so they can get involved quickly if needed."

"Yes."

"The United States has never deployed troops to Israel."

"Not combat troops," Kelly replied. "No, sir."

Trump looked puzzled. "We sent other troops?"

"A small peacekeeping force on at least one occasion."

Trump shook his head. "I'm not interested in a peacekeeping mission."

"I understand."

Trump leaned back in his chair and glanced toward the window as if in thought. "So, I should call the prime minister?"

"Yes, sir. Talk to him. Offer access to our intelligence capabilities, any special weapons or equipment they might need. Things like that."

"Okay, sounds like a good idea. What time is it in Jerusalem?"

Kelly glanced at his wristwatch. "About two in the afternoon."

"Good. Set up the call and let me know when it's ready."

Thirty minutes later, Trump was on the phone with Netanyahu. The Israeli prime minister was blunt and straightforward about the difficulty his country faced and about the nature of the attacks they now viewed as a certainty. "This is nothing less than an attack against us by Iran. An act of war."

"We've analyzed the intelligence and we agree," Trump replied.

"They have strengthened their position in Syria and moved troops into Lebanon."

"Which places them along your northern border."

"Yes. And in addition to that, they have infiltrated our country with agents."

"Our people say those are Iranian operatives."

"Correct, Donald. These are not mere religious radicals of a variety we see on a regular basis from Gaza. These are actual Iranian intelligence operatives, highly skilled and very well trained, who are planning an extensive action against us."

"I know you've had protests before but our people say this is—"

"This isn't just another protest" Netanyahu interrupted. "This is a military action perpetrated against us by the government of Iran."

"What do you plan to do?"

"We are developing a strategy for our response right now. Which is why I sent Lieberman to see Secretary Mattis. To make sure you understand the challenges we face and to keep you informed as we respond."

"Lieberman suggested Hamas plans major demonstrations at

the Gaza border checkpoints."

"We think that will be a diversion."

"From the bomb attacks against Jerusalem."

Netanyahu added, "Information we have suggests they are planning to use schoolchildren in those attacks."

"I saw that in the reports."

"And we are certain now that the attacks in Jerusalem will involve the use of Sarin gas."

"That is outrageous," Trump replied heatedly. "We've responded with force against Syria over this sort of thing. I understand there's some evidence they moved their Sarin stockpiles to Lebanon. Do you think that's where this group of bombers plans to get their gas from?"

"Yes, that appears to be the case."

"What do you want to do about it, Bibi? Can't we stop this before it occurs?"

"There are many things I might *want* to do," Netanyahu replied. "But as I mentioned earlier, we are still formulating a plan."

"We should have our defense people talk with yours," Trump suggested. "At a ministerial level and at the operational level."

"That would be very helpful," Netanyahu acknowledged. "We should—"

Trump interrupted. "We'll get you whatever you need. If we have any capabilities you need, we'll be glad to supply them for your effort."

"That would be welcome, Donald. I'll make certain our officials cooperate fully."

When the call with the prime minister ended, Trump summoned Jim Mattis to the White House. Mattis took a helicopter from the Pentagon and arrived within minutes. They met in the Oval Office.

Mattis talked about the situation in Israel as Lieberman had presented it and the intelligence developed from US sources that confirmed the Israeli view. Much of what he said was a review of the information in the president's morning briefing book. Trump relayed the gist of his conversation with the prime minister.

"We're certain this is an Iranian operation?"

Mattis nodded in response. "All of the information we presently have supports the prime minister's view. This appears to be the work of the Iranian government and not merely the spontaneous act of a radical Islamic sect."

"Even though the operatives aren't part of the Iranian army?"

"That is correct. This is a planned military strategy effected by asymmetrical means."

Trump grimaced. "Say it in plain English, Jim."

"This is a strategy that originated at the top. It was developed as a military operation but designed to be carried out by this sort of non-regimental approach. Iranian military leaders are orchestrating these actions against Israel, their military is behind it and supplying all of the logistical support, but they aren't using rank-and-file soldiers to do it. Instead, they're using members of Hamas's Al-Qassam Brigades as their people on the ground."

Trump nodded thoughtfully. "A tactic they developed in Iraq and Syria with ISIS."

"Yes. And before that, they did this sort of thing with Hezbollah."

"We've seen it in Yemen with the Houthi, too," Trump noted. "You and I have discussed that."

"Right."

Trump had a dour expression. "I've tried to convince the world that Iran is a serious threat to everyone. Not just to Israel. People in the Middle East have understood. Jordan, Egypt, and Saudi Arabia agree with my assessment, but I haven't had much success in convincing the Europeans."

"It isn't so much that they don't believe Iran is a threat," Mattis explained. "It's just that they don't live under the immediate threat of annihilation the way Israel and other countries in the Middle East do."

Trump nodded in acknowledgment. "Our European allies seem afraid of Iran."

"They're afraid of a Muslim backlash if they say or do too much against Iran," Mattis noted. "In private, they understand quite well the threat Iran poses, particularly if they are armed with nuclear weapons. It's just not a military threat to them the way it is to the countries of the Middle East. For European countries, the threat is what will happen to their civilian population on the streets of their major cities."

"Terrorist attacks."

"Yes, Mr. President. European leaders fear terrorist attacks. Nations of the Middle East worry about military attacks."

Trump looked over at Mattis. "What do you think we should do about this situation with Israel? It seems unwise to simply wait until something happens and then try to catch up."

Mattis agreed. "We should begin to craft our response now. Put ourselves in position to respond militarily, if necessary. And give ourselves multiple options. We don't want just one tool in the toolbox."

"What did you have in mind?"

"I think we should reposition the *John F. Kennedy* carrier group to the Mediterranean. They've just come off refueling at our base in Virginia and already are crossing the Atlantic. They could be on-station in the Mediterranean in three days."

"Okay."

"And," Mattis continued, "we should add additional planes to our base at Aviano, Italy. We already have a fighter wing there but I would like to move perhaps an entire air group to that location, if the logistics can be worked out. Each of our groups has airborne refueling capability. If one of them is positioned in Italy, the refueling capability and the additional aircraft will give us the ability to strike targets anywhere in the Middle East with turnaround times short enough to maintain constant sorties if necessary."

Trump understood this was a massive realignment of forces. "Anything else?"

"We should move the *Forrestal* carrier group, currently in the Indian Ocean, up to the Persian Gulf and we should probably do that right now. They can be in position in a day. And, if the Israelis can fully integrate their battlefield system with ours, we should offer them access to our management system. Perhaps man it for them."

Trump had a puzzled look. "I thought they already had a system like that."

"They have *some* of the command-and-control planes. But if this threat is as serious as it seems, this sort of strategic command will be crucial to success on the ground. We should make sure they have this capability and then integrate them with our satellite system, if they think that would be helpful."

"Good. So ordered. Anything else?"

"Yes, Mr. President. There is one more aspect of this situation that we need to discuss."

"What is that?"

"Iran is ruled politically by religiously minded leaders. Its military, however, is run by men who understand the strategic use of force as a means of accomplishing an objective. If Iran intends to invade Israel from the north—as seems to be the case—they don't have enough men on the ground to accomplish that goal."

"What does that mean?"

"Either they intend to bring in place an even larger ground

force than the one they already have in place, or they intend to use a smaller ground force—like the one they have positioned in Syria and Lebanon—but combine that with an all-out missile attack."

"You mean launch missiles from Iran?"

Mattis nodded. "And from Lebanon."

Trump frowned. "They have missiles in Lebanon?"

"Iranian troops stationed there have a few, but Hezbollah has thousands."

Trump nodded thoughtfully. "I remember that from a briefing. More than a hundred thousand, as I recall."

"That is correct, Mr. President. If what we see right now is preparation for an attack against Israel with the intention of invading and occupying, using the kind of force they have right now in the region, Iran will need all of Hezbollah's missiles plus the ones they have at their bases in Iran."

"That seems like a lot of missiles," Trump commented.

"It would be an attack of a size and scope never seen before."

"Can Israel defend against that?"

Mattis shook his head. "No, Mr. President. Not if Iran gets to the point of launching them. Not even with our help."

Trump had a perplexed expression. "So, what can we do?"

Mattis looked him in the eye. "Take out Iran's missiles ahead of time."

"A preemptive attack."

"Yes." Mattis nodded. "An extensive, widespread attack

designed to hit Hezbollah's missiles *and* the ones at bases in Iran before they can be launched."

"Can we get them all?"

"That would be doubtful, even if we used nuclear weapons. Too many sites, over too broad of an area. And many of the sites are well fortified."

"But we could get most of them."

"Yes, Mr. President." Mattis nodded. "We could get most of them."

"And what about their nuclear research facilities? Any way we could include that?"

"Our reconnaissance indicates they've been steadily moving their development operation to hardened underground sites, which makes eliminating them problematic. We could hit some of them with conventional weapons—"

"Bunker busters?"

"Yes. That would work on some of the sites, but some of them would require a nuclear warhead, and even then I'm not sure we could completely eliminate the sites."

"When you say nuclear, what are you talking about? Widespread destruction? Hiroshima?"

"We've come a long way since Hiroshima. Probably the best option in a case like this would be our B61-11 nuclear bomb. It has a selectable yield that allows us to dial in the kind of explosion we want to create, has smart technology that will put the ordnance on target with the kind of accuracy we expect today, and it is designed to penetrate underground facilities of the type we believe Iran has."

Trump was intrigued. "So, less damage to the surrounding area?"

"Certainly less than we would have seen in the past. These bombs have a maximum yield in kilotons, rather than megatons. Thousands rather than millions. The older version of our nuclear bombs had yields of about nine megatons. Millions of tons. These are kilotons. Which is thousands of tons. Considerably smaller in size, but the penetration capability and precise targeting feature more than make up for it. And when these bombs detonate after penetrating an underground facility, most of the effect is confined to the ground."

"And we're talking about a bomb," Trump noted. "As opposed to a missile."

"Yes."

"So, we would need to deliver this weapon with an airplane."

"Yes, Mr. President."

"Isn't that risky?"

"We can alleviate some of that risk. Strike their air defenses first with cruise missiles. Initiate a cyber-attack on their system so they can't see us when we're coming. Then use our stealth bombers. All of that will reduce the risk but, yes, Mr. President. Using bombs comes with a much higher risk to our personnel than striking them with missiles."

"Missiles to take out missiles," Trump mused.

"Rather ironic, I suppose."

"Do we know where Iran has its missiles? The ones they have in Iran?"

"We know the location of most of them. And we know the key sites for their command-and-control system. We wouldn't be able to guarantee one hundred percent destruction but we could eliminate most of them and prevent them from launching most of what remained."

"What about in Lebanon and Syria?"

"We have a better grasp of the missiles in Syria. Those are under the control of the Syrian army and we were in there for an extended period of time while fighting ISIS. The missiles in Lebanon are controlled by Hezbollah. Our intelligence there is good. We know more about the missiles in Iran and in Syria than we do in Lebanon."

Trump thought for a moment, then stood to indicate they were through. "I appreciate you taking the time to talk with me." He shook Mattis's hand. "Put our people to work on the things we've discussed. We need to be ready when the time to act comes. And keep me informed as your plans develop."

"Yes, Mr. President."

CHAPTER

20

NOT LONG AFTER President Trump's meeting with Jim Mattis ended, Jim Linderman received notice of it. Linderman was a terrorism consultant with the office of the director of National Intelligence. Although his office was located up the street from the White House, his security clearance provided him with access to all of the director's files and databases. One of those databases included recordings from the Oval Office.

As part of his routine duties, Linderman reviewed recordings of meetings held in the Oval Office that were thought to bear on matters of national security. As a matter of due course, a verbatim transcript of Mattis's meeting with the president regarding the situation in Israel was prepared and entered into the database, making it available for review by appropriate officials before the end of the day.

As a supervising analyst at the CIA, Bryce Jenkins routinely accessed reports prepared by Linderman and others at the National Intelligence office. One of those reports included a reference to President Trump's meeting with Mattis and a blurb summarizing their discussion as, "Review of Iranian action in Syria with a possible response." Jenkins wasted no time in locating the file of the meeting transcript and opened it immediately.

After reading the transcript, Jenkins printed a hard copy and placed it inside a manila envelope, then sealed the envelope closed. Late that afternoon, he sent a text message to Vasily Gorchakov and arranged to meet with him, this time in the parking lot of a convenience store in Dawsonville, Maryland.

"Choose a place that's closer," Gorchakov groused as he got inside the car.

"Too risky," Jenkins replied.

"You said you had something."

Jenkins handed him the envelope. "A record of Mattis's meeting with the president today."

"This is paper."

"It's a transcript."

"I like the recording better."

"Too lazy to read?"

"No. They can alter the transcript to suit their own purposes."

"They can alter the recording, too."

"But we can tell if they do that." Gorchakov gestured with the envelope. "This, you cannot tell."

Jenkins held out his hand. "Then give it back."

"No. No." Gorchakov shook his head. "I did not mean to seem ungrateful. We are glad to have it." He opened the door to leave. "But next time, choose a spot a little closer."

The following day, Alavi met General Bagheri in a secure room at Russia's Ministry of Intelligence. When they were in the room and the masking technology was activated, they were as secure as anyone could be anywhere in Iran.

"Why all the fuss?" Bagheri asked.

"I have something for you to see." Alavi slid a file across the table to Bagheri. "Read this."

"It is too thick to read. I will give it to someone else to read and they will tell me what it says."

"You cannot take this with you. It must not leave this building."

"Why?"

"Look at it and you will see."

Reluctantly, Bagheri opened the file and began to read. As he scanned through the first few pages his interest intensified. After a moment he looked up, his eyes wide with wonder. "This is true? They really discussed this?"

"As you know, Lieberman visited with Mattis two days ago."

"Yes. You told me."

"And after that meeting, Mattis met with the president. In that meeting, he reviewed the things he and Lieberman discussed and he outlined for the president what a US response would be like."

Bagheri laid the file on the table and leaned back. "So, we have their plans."

"An outline of it."

"That is all we need. We know they are deploying two carrier groups. We can determine the capabilities they bring. And we know they are moving an air group to their base in Italy. We can determine what that means, too."

"You must prepare the way for missile usage."

"Yes, the Americans are correct in that regard. We cannot prevail without the missiles. And the ones from Hezbollah will not be enough to give us the victory we desire."

✦ ✦ ✦

When Bryce Jenkins printed a hard copy of the White House transcript, the machine on which he printed it entered information about the activity in an electronic log that was regularly reviewed by employees from the CIA inspector general's office. The log entry included the date and time of the activity, the length of the document in number of pages, the person who initiated the print job, whether the document contained a classification rating, and a link to a scan of the document that was preserved when the copy was made.

Because of its length, the document caught the eye of Katherine Jones, a security specialist who happened to have the unenviable task of reviewing the log that week. To satisfy her curiosity, Jones followed the link and reviewed the actual text. That's when she noticed the document in question was a transcript of a conversation that occurred at the White House and that the file metadata indicated it bore code-word classification. Reading further, she discovered the conversation from which the transcript arose occurred in the Oval Office. And one of the participants was the president of the United States. Jones notified her supervisor immediately.

Within hours, FBI agents located Bryce Jenkins at a diner in Bethesda, Maryland, and took him into custody. He attempted to evade questioning with long and elusive responses but eventually admitted that he had created a hard copy of the document. By then, agents had used the toll tag on Jenkins' car to track his movements to Dawsonville, Maryland. A review of traffic camera video from the time showed Jenkins' car parked outside the convenience store where he met Vasily Gorchakov.

✦ ✦ ✦

News of Bryce Jenkins' arrest was kept from journalists, but Gorchakov had connections to local police departments throughout the Virginia and Maryland area. Officers at the police department in Bethesda became aware of the arrest not long after it occurred. A detective got word of Jenkins' trouble to Gorchakov while Jenkins still was still being booked at the city jail. When Gorchakov learned of it, he didn't wait around to hear the details.

Within the hour, Gorchakov boarded a Russian Learjet and flew from Dulles Airport to Berlin, Germany. He cleared German immigration on a diplomatic passport and took a car to the Russian Embassy compound where he waited to see what would happen next.

Four days later, nothing seemed to come of the incident and Gorchakov began to wonder if he had overreacted. When two more days passed without so much as an inquiry from his supervisors, he was sure he was home free.

On Saturday evening, no longer concerned the Americans might come for him, Gorchakov went to a discotheque where he drank and danced, as was his practice when in Germany. At about two in the morning, he appeared outside the club entrance and sent a valet to bring his car. The driver started the car's engine, switched on the headlights, and drove around to where Gorchakov was waiting. Gorchakov tipped the driver, got in behind the steering wheel, and closed the door. For an added measure of security, he pressed a button on the door panel to activate the car's door locks.

Suddenly, a violent explosion ripped through the car, sending the hood and trunk lid flying in opposite directions across the parking lot. A fireball engulfed what remained of the car, and dark clouds of smoke billowed into the air.

✦ ✦ ✦

News of Gorchakov's demise reached Alavi at his home late

that evening. He contacted General Bagheri and they arranged to meet outside the ministry of defense. Alavi arrived in a limousine with driver. He and General Bagheri sat in back and talked while they rode along Laleh Boulevard. A glass partition separated them from the front compartment where the driver sat.

"What was so urgent it could not wait for morning?" Bagheri asked.

"As I told you before, I had a contact in the United States."

Bagheri looked over at him. "Had?"

"Yeah." Alavi sighed wearily. "And now he is no more."

"This isn't good news, is it?" Bagheri's voice was downcast.

"No."

"What happened? Explain this *source* to me."

"A contact at the Russian Embassy named Vasily Gorchakov developed a relationship with a young analyst at the CIA." Alavi stared out the window as he talked. "From time to time, Gorchakov prevailed upon the young analyst to provide helpful information. When we began our strategy of action against Israel, I asked Gorchakov for assistance."

"So, this was your source?"

"Yes, Gorchakov obtained information from the American and relayed it to Dmitry Belkovsky at the Russian Embassy here, who then brought it to me."

"Which one of them died?"

Alavi glanced in Bagheri's direction. "Both of them." There was a hint of sorrow in his voice.

"The Americans know," Bagheri spoke flatly. "I knew it before with the missile problem."

"I think they know," Alavi admitted. "But I also think the Israelis know."

Bagheri looked concerned. "Why do you say that?"

"Somehow—and we haven't yet determined how—but somehow, the CIA caught on to what the analyst was doing for us. The FBI arrested him and are holding him in custody. He hasn't been very helpful, but the FBI continues to investigate him by other means. Gorchakov learned of the analyst's arrest and fled to Berlin."

"Where the Germans arrested him?"

"No. One might think of that. Especially given the historically close relationship between the US and Germany. But, no. Gorchakov reached the Russian Embassy in Berlin without difficulty and remained inside the compound for a week. When nothing more seemed to come of the matter, he ventured out to enjoy the nightlife."

"Russians cannot avoid the nightlife." Bagheri spoke with a condescending tone and a roll of his eyes. "It is like a magnet to them. If we owned a brothel in Paris we could learn the world's secrets." When Alavi did not respond immediately, Bagheri glanced at him and noticed the expression on his face. "We own a brothel?"

Alavi smiled. "We have a house."

"I see."

"A very useful house," Alavi added.

"You must take me there sometime."

"Perhaps."

"So, finish about the Russians." Bagheri gestured for him to continue. "This man . . ."

"Gorchakov."

"Yes. Gorchakov. He went out for a night on the town. Then what?"

"He went to a discotheque and after a night of drinking and carousing, he asked for his car. They brought it to him and when he got in his car, it exploded."

"A car bomb?"

"Yes."

"That was no accident."

"No," Alavi agreed. "It was not."

"And the Russian who lives here? Belkovsky. What became of him?"

"He was shot in the head."

"When?"

"An hour ago. I received the call about him as I was on the way here to meet with you."

Bagheri raised an eyebrow. "And you do not think this was the work of the Americans?"

"Gorchakov, yes." Alavi nodded his head. "That most certainly was the Americans. Even the German authorities think that, though they will not say so publicly. But not Belkovsky. Not here."

"If not the Americans, then who do you think did it?"

Alavi looked him in the eye. "It was Mossad."

"Why do you say that?"

"Belkovsky was shot with a .22 caliber."

"A .22 long?"

"Yes."

"A Beretta."

"Apparently," Alavi nodded.

"How did the Jews get here?"

"They have always been here."

"Yes." Bagheri sighed once more. "They have always been among us."

CHAPTER
21

WHEN LIEBERMAN returned from Washington, he went directly to the prime minister's office. Netanyahu met with him privately. "The Americans are with us?"

"Yes, Mr. Prime Minister. They are with us."

"They will follow through?"

"Yes. Did you think they wouldn't?"

"I like Trump and he seems to like me," Netanyahu advised, "but he is sometimes unpredictable. And I have enjoyed a good relationship with previous US presidents, only to be surprised by their lack of diligence when things actually start happening."

"This one won't do that," Lieberman said. "Jim Mattis won't either."

"What about Kelly?"

"I didn't meet with him but I understand he is reliable, trustworthy. A soldier's general."

"Good. I know we talked while you were on the way back but how did you leave it with them?"

"We agreed to coordinate at an operational level and move this down to the people who actually execute our respective plans."

"Moving it from the strategic to the tactical," Netanyahu noted.

"Yes. They want to know if we can integrate our battle management systems with theirs. How to share satellite feeds. I thought General Eizenkot and the staff at IDF could handle those issues best. Along with target selections as we move forward."

Netanyahu frowned. "Target selection?"

"If Iran plans to attack us with missiles," Lieberman explained, "we'll need help from the Americans. This won't be like the Scud missiles from Iraq that we've endured in the past. This won't be random explosions from unsophisticated, poorly supported rockets. Iran's Zelzal-3 missile gives them a system capable of precise targeting. If they want to hit this building, they can do it."

"Will they?"

"If they mean to invade us, they'll try to hit every key target in the country."

"And they can do it?"

"Yes. They can do it. Which is why we need the help of the Americans. We need for them to wipe out Iran's missiles before they can launch *any* of them. And that means exact coordinates for a wide array of targets. That kind of complexity has to be done at a staff level. Not ministerial."

"They know this?"

Lieberman nodded. "Jim Mattis knows how these things operate."

"So, he understands the position we're in and the help we need?"

"Yes."

"And they understand our defensive strategy is to hit first, before the other side can attack?"

"Yes."

Netanyahu pressed the point. Israel's life was at risk from an attack on the scale Iran seemed to be preparing. He was unwilling to leave any detail to chance. "The president understands this?"

Lieberman looked puzzled. "Haven't you discussed this with him?"

"On several occasions, but I just wanted your sense of the situation."

"I discussed it with Mattis. He fully understands our position, and he was scheduled to meet with the president as I was leaving."

"And he will make our situation clear?"

"Yes. General Eizenkot and his staff already are coordinating target information now."

Netanyahu was relieved. "What do we need to do next?"

"General Eizenkot asked you about repositioning troops up to the Galilee. I'm not sure how he expressed it but moving them from Central Command to Northern Command."

"I approved that already. Though as I indicated before, he doesn't need my permission."

"We need to draw some from Southern Command as well."

Netanyahu was cautious. "Is that a good idea?"

"Egypt and Jordan pose no threat," Lieberman noted. "And if they wanted to attack, they can't mount much of a threat from their current state of readiness. We can repel any attack they might launch right now."

"Okay," Netanyahu sighed. "I suppose I have no objection to moving some of the troops. But make sure we have enough to secure our border. Lots of groups in the Sinai who don't like us."

"Certainly."

"Anything else?"

"We need to reinforce our missile defenses."

Netanyahu had a questioning expression. "Don't we have them permanently positioned?"

"But we need more. Jim offered to send us additional Patriot units and missiles. I accepted."

Netanyahu smiled. "So you're not really asking my permission," he needled. "Just asking me to ratify your decision."

Lieberman backpedaled. "I can stop delivery of them before they arrive, if you like."

"No," Netanyahu replied with a dismissive gesture. "We need them. Place them as seems best."

The meeting was drawing to a close. Lieberman stood to leave.

"If Iran attacks us, we will sustain some damage. You understand that, don't you?"

"Yes. I understand that."

"And some of the damage could be quite heavy."

Netanyahu nodded sadly. "Then we need to make sure the Americans help us in a big way."

✦ ✦ ✦

After briefing Netanyahu, Lieberman went home for a shower and a nap. Two hours later, his wife awakened him. "Can't you stay home today?" She sat on the edge of the bed beside him. "You could use the rest."

Lieberman pulled himself up to sit beside her, then slipped an arm around her waist. "I could use a long rest," he said as he squeezed her closer. "But there isn't time for that right now." He leaned over and kissed her gently on the neck.

"If you expect to get to the office this afternoon," she said playfully, "you'd better stop right there."

Lieberman kissed her lightly on the lips, then stood.

"Are things getting serious?" she asked. Lieberman made a point of not sharing office details with her, even though he knew many ministers shared quite a lot with their wives. Even so, she was aware of his travel schedule and knew he'd made a special trip to Washington. She also knew from news reports the kinds of issues he likely was addressing.

"They are."

"Will we survive?"

"Israel will always survive," Lieberman replied in a valiant tone.

"I don't mean Israel; I mean us." She followed him across the room. "You and me. Physically. Is it that much of a threat?"

"We might have to go to the shelter," Lieberman sighed. By then he was to the bathroom door.

"You mean *I* might have to go to the bunker," she quipped. "You will be at the office."

"Yes." He glanced over his shoulder and flashed a smile. "I'll be in a bunker deep beneath the most likely target."

She looked cross. "Do not say things like that."

Lieberman reached for her and took her in his arms. "It's true." He kissed her. "And we both know it."

"But we don't have to say it."

He kissed her again, then let go of her and turned away. "I need to get a shower and head to the office."

"Well," she sighed, "at least we have an actual shelter with a bed and provisions. Many only have a reinforced basement or a shelter fashioned from a concrete pipe."

"At least they have some protection from debris." Lieberman turned back to face her. "I'm hungry. Anything in the refrigerator I can warm up."

"Take your shower. 'll fix something for you."

An hour later, Lieberman left home for the office. A car and driver picked him up. As he rode, he stared out the side window and thought about his conversation with his wife.

By law and regulation, all homes, apartments, and public buildings in Israel were required to have bomb shelters. Individual residences are allowed to share a shelter as long as the shelter provides adequate space for all entitled to use it. But, as his wife had pointed out, not all shelters were created equal. Some civilian shelters were designed to withstand all but a nuclear explosion. Others, however, were merely sections of concrete culvert that sat atop the ground on playgrounds and other public spaces.

When he arrived at the office, Lieberman spent time catching up on things that had reached his desk while he was away, but late in the afternoon he sent for Arnon Gadot, a special assistant who worked in the defense ministry.

A recent university graduate, Gadot had been appointed special assistant without assigned duties so that he could be free to work on projects of interest to Lieberman on an as-assigned basis. It was a coveted position because the tasks were almost always esoteric in nature and offered the assistant who held that position access to some of the most important people in the country. Most recently, Gadot had been asked to research the effect of pay rates on reenlistment in armed forces generally, and IDF specifically. That assignment allowed him entrée not only to key individuals in Israeli academia but to researchers in the United States and Europe as well.

Gadot was in the cafeteria when the call from Lieberman's office reached his phone. He responded at once.

"This is a rather last-minute assignment," Lieberman began. "But it's important."

"Yes, sir," Gadot responded. "What would you like me to do?"

"As you know, we're facing a rather grave threat from Iran."

"Yes, sir."

"If that threat materializes, we may come under a sustained missile attack."

"Right."

"I want to know the effectiveness of our sheltering system against that kind of event. And a sense of the readiness level."

"Government or civilian?" Gadot asked.

"Civilian."

"Conventional weapons?"

"Yes." Lieberman sighed. "We have very few bunkers that could withstand a nuclear blast. I doubt any of the civilian facilities would survive."

"That *is* grave."

"All the more reason for diligence at every turn."

"When do you need an answer?"

"Tomorrow would be good." Lieberman didn't flinch.

Gadot was taken aback. "Tomorrow?"

Lieberman leaned back in his chair and closed his eyes. "By the end of the week will do."

When Gadot was gone, Lieberman rested his hands in his lap and thought about what most certainly lay ahead. Missiles striking Israeli cities. Not just in the Galilee but Tel Aviv, Jerusalem even, and all the way to Beersheba. Even if they succeeded in gaining American support, as it seemed they had, and even if the Americans struck Iran's launch sites with all the accuracy of which America was capable, missiles still would reach Israel from Iran. Even more from Lebanon and Syria. No one else would intervene. No one else would move to stop them. Only the Americans and the IDF. With America's help, they could stave off the Iranians, but thousands of Israelis would die in the process. Thousands. Perhaps more. And the thought of that weighed heavily on his mind, his heart, his spirit.

After a moment to contemplate what the future might hold, Lieberman reached behind him to the credenza and picked up his copy of *Siddur Tehillat Hashem*, the Jewish prayer book. He opened it to a well-worn page that held the Prayer of Confession. Rather than read from the page, though, he took a printed card that had been stuck between the pages. On it was written an ancient prayer of confession from the *Book of Daniel*. Lieberman held the card in his hand, turned his chair away from the door, and began to whisper that prayer aloud:

"O Lord, the great and awesome One, who keeps his covenant of love with all who love him and obey his commands, we have sinned and done wrong. We have been wicked and have rebelled; we have turned away from your commands and laws. We have not listened to your servants the prophets . . ."

CHAPTER
22

MEANWHILE, in accordance with Argaman's order, Milgrom dispatched Shin Bet teams to locate and arrest Masalha and Rajabian. In an attempt to lessen the risk that one might warn the other if the plan became known, the teams coordinated their movements through the operations center in Beersheba and timed them to arrive at both apartments simultaneously.

Eli Faiman, Auerbach's friend from their time together in Tiberias, led the team that went to Masalha's apartment in Rahat. They arrived in the neighborhood a little after midnight. Working with local police, they established a perimeter that restricted access to the block, then quietly went from door to door escorting the occupants of neighboring apartments from the building.

When the residents from surrounding apartments were safely out of harm's way, Faiman and the Shin Bet team kicked in the door to Masalha's apartment and rushed inside. Operatives surged from room to room, clearing each one in a sequence that took them from front to back as they quickly occupied the premises. In less than a minute, however, the truth became obvious. Masalha was not there.

Milgrom received news of the raid at the operations center. "He's not here," Faiman reported from the apartment. "Looks like he might have cleared out already."

"It's empty?"

"No, but *he's* not here. Looks like he had a laptop. It's gone. I see the power supply on the floor and there's a printer on a table near the window, but whatever it was connected to is gone. And there's not much in the drawers in the bedroom."

"Think he's on to us and abandoned the plan?"

"I think he changed the plan."

"Or had a different one all along."

"That's possible, too," Faiman agreed. "But I think Auerbach would have figured that out by now if that were the case."

"See that you make a thorough search and inventory whatever you remove."

"Right."

The raid on Rajabian's apartment in Beersheba produced a similar result. There, however, Shin Bet operatives located two flash drives and a number of credit cards that had been left behind, leading some to conclude that while Rajabian was gone, he did not intend to leave for good. Because of that, Milgrom instructed them to photograph the room, note the numbers on the credit cards, and copy the contents of the flash drives, but otherwise leave the apartment intact. Surveillance teams were redoubled as well.

✦ ✦ ✦

Sometime the next day, Auerbach awakened with a start and sat straight up in bed. His eyes darted around the room as he struggled to determine where he was. The windows—the dresser—the bedspread . . . all seemed familiar . . . and then he realized he was at home in his own bedroom. He collapsed back on the pillow and stared up at the ceiling, remembering the fight in the hotel room, the escape at the airport. And now, here he was, back in Beersheba.

After a moment, he threw back the covers and crossed the room to a window, then pushed aside the curtains and looked outside to find it was the middle of the day. He wore house shorts and a T-shirt and as he stood there, looking out on the neighborhood, he felt in his pockets for his cell phone, but it wasn't there. He glanced back at the bed and saw it resting on the nightstand.

With a tired gait, he made his way back to the bed, picked up the cell phone, and checked the screen for the date and time. "Almost noon," he whispered. That was late in the day for him and judging from the date on the display he'd been asleep for almost sixteen hours. "No wonder my head hurts."

After showering and dressing, Auerbach walked into the kitchen. Yarden, his wife, was standing at the counter, preparing a salad. She looked up as he entered the room and smiled at him. "Have a good rest?"

"I guess. How long have I been sleeping?"

She kissed him. "You came home yesterday afternoon."

Auerbach slipped his arms around her, pulled her close, and kissed her again. Then his mind kicked in and he remembered all that had happened. He smiled, "This is very tempting. But I need to get to the office."

"Don't you want lunch first?"

"Can't." But then he saw the food on a platter by the stove and paused. "Well, maybe lunch."

Two hours later, Auerbach arrived at the Shin Bet office in Beersheba. Milgrom took him aside and briefed him on all that had happened since he returned. "They haven't told me everything," Milgrom explained, "but from what I've heard, your discoveries in Cyprus elevated the situation to a critical level."

"What does that mean?"

"The prime minister, IDF, the defense ministry are all into it. Looks like the Americans are going to help. This is a big deal now. The Iranians have troops in Syria and Lebanon."

"What about Jerusalem?"

"They took your scenario seriously. Sarin gas and suicide bombs carried by schoolchildren got their attention."

"What are they doing about it?"

"I don't know what they're doing about the military aspect. They don't tell me much about that side of things, unless it directly involves us. But we have people out now trying to locate and detain Masalha and Rajabian. Not having much success finding either of them, but our people are looking."

Auerbach had a worried look. "They're gone?"

"No one seems to know for sure."

"Didn't we have surveillance devices in both apartments?"

"Yes."

"And that didn't tell us what they were doing?"

"They never met together. Never met anyone, for that matter. At least, not in the apartments. They talked on the phone but never about anything important. Our guys have been trying to decipher that since we hacked into their devices, but haven't gotten far with it. The information on that flash drive you brought back is more than we had from the devices in the apartments."

"That's not good."

"No, it isn't. But the information you brought back is helping them figure out how they communicated. It's like a code, only it's very contextual."

"Contextual?"

"Linguistically and culturally. Quite interesting, really."

Auerbach was not intrigued by that kind of conversation. He much preferred the concrete and practical aspect of the job. "Where's Harel?" he asked, as much to change the topic of conversation as to get on with his work.

"He's in the operations center," Milgrom replied. "He's working with the tech guys, going through the files you cloned from Shammas's laptop."

"I wish I had gone back for the laptop itself."

Milgrom shook his head. "No, you did the right thing. If you'd gone back, you might not have gotten out at all. We have enough with what you did."

"Okay," Auerbach sighed. "What do I do now?"

Milgrom laughed. "You're actually asking *me* a question like that now?"

"Yeah." Auerbach grinned. "It's a little strange for me, too."

"You can help Harel and the others," Milgrom suggested. "That will get your mind going again. Then find a spot and dig in. We need to locate those two before they detonate those bombs. And we need a more accurate time for when they plan to do it. The clock has been running on what you told us Shammas said to you right before he died."

"Yeah. If he was right, the time is getting close."

After talking to Milgrom, Auerbach walked over to the operations center. Harel was there with the technicians, seated at a workstation, staring at a monitor as he scrolled down a page of text. By then he and the others were deep into an analysis of Shammas's laptop files and online accounts.

"From what we've found so far," Harel was saying, "Shammas and his contacts used an email program as a drop box. Users logged in from wherever they happened to be, wrote messages as drafts, but instead of sending them they saved them in the draft file. Other users logged in, read through the saved drafts, and added their replies to the existing messages. Or created new messages in the draft folder. This allowed them to communicate without actually sending anything to anyone. No Internet. No phone lines. Nothing to intercept except their access to the server that ran the email program."

"Rather ingenious," Auerbach noted.

"Yes," Harel conceded. "We've seen it before, but very effective. A bit cumbersome, though. There are a lot of messages to read through but I suppose if you note the date attached to the files, you could keep up with the ones that have been changed since you last logged in to the account."

"Not much of a price to pay to keep the discussion totally private."

"That's a good point. A little inconvenience for a lot of anonymity."

"So, what do you want me to do?" Auerbach asked.

"Well," Harel began, "we're reading through the messages to see what we can learn. We started at the most recent and read toward the oldest. We're down to this point." He gestured to the monitor at his workstation. "We're reading from the newest to the oldest."

"Okay, I need to know everything they've been saying. I don't see any other way to learn that except to read their messages for myself. I don't think I can skip anything."

"Right," Harel acknowledged. "You start at the most recent and read from there. We'll keep going from where we are and you can read to catch up with us, or not."

Auerbach took a seat at a nearby workstation. "Let me see how this goes and we can reassess our progress later."

For the remainder of the afternoon, Auerbach and Harel read through the messages that Auerbach had purloined from Shammas's laptop. Though the process seemed painfully slow, they gradually uncovered pieces of information that allowed them to stitch together the plan Rajabian and Masalha were following and to do so using their own words, gleaned from the messages buried in the laptop files.

Much of what they learned from the files, however, they already knew from other sources. The one thing they needed desperately to know was the date when the attacks were planned to occur and *that* they found frustratingly absent.

Not long before midnight, Auerbach and Harel took a break. They left the operations center and walked down the hall to a break room not far from Auerbach's office. The room was deserted. They sat at a table in the corner and ate prepackaged sandwiches from a vending machine. While they ate, they talked.

"Okay," Auerbach said between bites. "We know they're using backpack bombs that will be rigged for remote detonation."

Harel nodded. "And they plan to use schoolchildren to carry them."

"Disgusting," Auerbach groused.

"They should be shot for that whether they actually do it or not."

Auerbach kept going. "Apparently they wanted to use Sarin gas in each backpack but couldn't work out the logistics for obtaining the precursor materials in Israel. Which meant they didn't have enough for their original plan."

"Right. They were only able to obtain three canisters." Harel paused and a puzzled expression came over him. "Wonder how they did that? How did they get those canisters into the country?"

"I don't know," Auerbach replied. "But that's not our problem right now. We can clean that part of it up after we solve all the rest, and after this thing is behind us. Stay focused. We need to know when they mean to set them off. Did you see anything in any of the files that indicated a time for the attacks?"

"Nothing explicit."

"What does that mean?"

"They seemed to talk about it, but every time they got close to saying when they were going to do it, they dodged the issue." Harel paused to take a bite, then continued, "Did you notice how much they quoted Yasser Arafat in those first messages? The ones that are the most recent."

"Yes."

"He's been dead a long time," Harel mused. "Why do you suppose they did that? Most Palestinians their age seem to have forgotten just how close he came to solving their problems for them."

Auerbach shrugged. "I don't know, but as far as I can tell, they still seem rather devoted to him."

Harel continued the thought. "One of those messages had a long quote from the Palestinian Declaration of Independence. Did you see that? No one ever mentions that document anymore."

"I saw that." Auerbach was finished with the sandwich he'd been eating and wadded up the wrapper. "Whoever wrote that message must have been copying it from somewhere. No one can remember that much. Not word for word. Not from memory."

"But it wasn't the complete quote."

"I wouldn't know."

"This one began in the middle of a sentence," Harel noted. "Something about the justice of the Palestinian effort or something."

"Yeah."

"Why was he quoting that?"

"I don't know." Auerbach was growing tired of the banter and wanted to get back to the reading. "We should—"

"You know," Harel interrupted. "Tomorrow is Palestinian Independence Day."

"Yeah. There will probably be more—" Auerbach stopped in mid-sentence and his eyes opened wide in a look of realization. "Come on." There was a sense of urgency in his voice and he stood, scooting aside the chair with his foot. "Show me the message you're talking about."

"In a minute," Harel protested. "I'm right in the middle of eating this sandwich." He gestured with his free hand to emphasize his point.

Auerbach snatched the sandwich from Harel's hand and tossed it into a trash can that stood in the corner. "I'll get you another sandwich. Come on." He took Harel by the shoulder and guided him toward the door. "Show me that message you were talking about. The one with the quote."

When they reached the operations center, Harel took a seat at his workstation and scrolled through the messages until he came to one of the earliest. He clicked on it with the mouse and opened the text, then skimmed down to the bottom. "This is the one. It's a reply to an earlier message." He moved farther down the screen to something written by someone else. "Here," he pointed. "'The justice of the Palestinian cause and of the demands for which the Palestinian people are struggling will continue to draw increasing support from honorable and free people around the world; and also affirms its complete confidence in victory on the road to Jerusalem, the capital of our independent Palestinian State.' That's a quotation from their declaration of independence, but it's not complete. It's stated here like a complete sentence but it actually picks up in the middle of one."

"What was the message before it? The one he was replying to. Show me that one."

Harel scrolled down the screen and pointed. "There. The thing he was responding to begins right here."

Auerbach read quickly, then pointed. He tapped the screen. "This right there."

Harel read, "'Coordination coming together. Groups getting nervous about when and where. A date would be good.'"

Auerbach looked away in thought. "That's a request for a date. And then someone responded with the quote." He turned away in thought, mumbling to himself.

"A long quote," Harel noted. "Which is what I was—"

Auerbach's eyes opened wide. "That's it!" he exclaimed. "Palestinian Independence Day." He checked his phone. It was already past midnight and the date had changed to November Fifteen.

"Like I was saying," Harel noted. "Palestinian Independence Day is tomorrow."

"Today," Auerbach corrected.

Harel glanced at him with a puzzled frown. "Today?"

"It's already the fifteenth."

"Oh." Harel's shoulders sagged. "I didn't realize—"

"We need to tell someone," Auerbach decided. "We need to tell someone," he repeated, louder the second time.

"About what?"

"About the attack," Auerbach blurted. "The attack."

"We already told them. That's what we're working on."

"No," Auerbach snapped. "Not about that. About today! The attack is today! That's what I'm trying to tell you. That's what that message means. The attack is today!" He tapped an icon on his phone for the contacts list and placed a call to Milgrom.

"The attack is today!" Auerbach shouted when Milgrom answered. "We have to get to Jerusalem. The attack is today!"

"What are you. . .?" It wasn't quite one in the morning and Milgrom seemed to take a moment to collect himself. "Are you certain of this?"

"Yes. I'm positive. The border protests. The attack in Jerusalem. It all happens today. Any success in finding Masalha or Rajabian?"

"No."

"We need to send a team to intercept the kids on that trip before they leave Rahat."

"But where will they be? Any information about that in those files?"

"I don't know," Auerbach answered. "It's a school trip. Maybe they'll meet at the school. That would be a good place to start." The frustration in his voice was palpable. "We can't just sit here."

Milgrom was now fully awake. "If today's the day, they'll be leaving soon."

"Yes," Auerbach responded. "So we need to get a team over to the school, now."

"Call them in," Milgrom ordered. "You can take them over there."

"No one's here. You have to make that call. I'm leaving."

"Leaving?" Milgrom sounded startled. "Where are you going?"

"I'm going to Jerusalem. Harel's going with me."

"But what—"

Auerbach lost patience with the discussion and ended the call before Milgrom could finish the sentence. He slipped the phone into his pocket and looked over at Harel. "Come on. You're going with me."

"What for?"

"You heard the call. We're going to Jerusalem."

"Why?"

"Masalha and Rajabian are on the move."

Harel pulled free of Auerbach's grasp. "Wait! We can't just leave. We have to bring the others up to speed on what we've found."

Reluctantly, Auerbach agreed and told the technicians who still were working in the operations center what he had concluded. They understood immediately. "Dig out the particulars from the files," Auerbach told them. "And prepare a memo for Milgrom. He'll be in here shortly and he'll need to forward that memo to the director. I suspect they'll be briefing someone on this soon."

When Auerbach finished explaining, the technicians went back to work and Harel followed him out of the room and up the hall. "What are we going to do when we get to Jerusalem?"

"I don't know, exactly," Auerbach replied. "We'll make it up as we go."

"We have teams to handle this kind of thing. They can—"

Auerbach wheeled around to face him. "Look, I've been working on this case from the beginning and I'm not sitting around here waiting to find out how it ends. I'm seeing this to the end and the end is in Jerusalem."

"I don't—"

"Elon," Auerbach barked, cutting him off. "Maybe we'll see something, or someone. Maybe we'll see nothing. I don't know. But I know this for certain—we need to be in Jerusalem." By then they'd reached the end of the hall and were standing at the door to the outside. Auerbach pulled open the door and pointed. "Get in the car."

CHAPTER

23

MILGROM HAD BEEN sitting on the edge of the bed when the phone call with Auerbach ended. He stood and reached for his bathrobe that lay on a chair nearby. As he slipped it on, his wife roused from sleep. "Are you okay?"

"Yes," he replied softly. "Just business."

She looked at the clock on the nightstand. "At one-thirty in the morning?"

"You know," he quipped. "Always someone needing our help."

Milgrom tied the sash of his robe and made his way from the bedroom. He pulled the door closed behind him as he stepped into the hall, then walked a few steps to his office and switched on the light at his desk.

A secure phone sat to one side of the desktop. Milgrom lifted the receiver, entered his password on the keypad, then placed a call to Nadav Argaman at his home. Milgrom began with a summary of what he'd learned from Auerbach. Like Milgrom, Argaman had been asleep when the phone rang and took a moment to become fully awake. As a result, Milgrom had to repeat most of what he'd just said.

"And he thinks it will all happen today?" Argaman asked.

"Yes. The border protests. The attack in Jerusalem. All of it."

"What about the threat on our northern border?"

"He doesn't know about that, other than the general information provided to all of our agents."

"You didn't tell him the details?"

"He has no need to know," Milgrom answered. "You said I should only tell him if he needed to know. And besides, he hasn't even been in the office since you and I talked."

"Okay," Argaman sighed. "Well . . . we need to alert everyone now."

Milgrom agreed. "There won't be time to work this up in advance. We'll have to feed everyone raw intelligence and process it as we go."

"Right."

"I'm sending a team over to the school to see if we can interdict the students before they depart. We might catch everyone there. Might not need to take such extreme measures."

"That would be good. But we can't wait for that before we fully respond. We have to get moving. I'll start making the calls." Having been awakened from sleep by the phone call, Argaman, too, was sitting on the edge of the bed when the conversation with Milgrom ended. Argaman found a pair of house shorts hanging on a bedpost, then made his way to his study in the next room.

It was two-thirty in the morning when Argaman reached General Eizenkot, the IDF commander, and a little after that when he contacted Yossi Cohen, the Mossad director. Both men understood the urgency and agreed to join Argaman in briefing the prime minister. They arrived at Netanyahu's residence within the hour.

By then, Argaman had received a memo, created by technicians at the Beersheba operations center and forwarded to him by Milgrom, which provided the details of the conclusions Auerbach had reached. After reviewing the document, he had forwarded a copy to General Eizenkot and Yossi Cohen. Two hours later, they awakened Netanyahu.

After reviewing the memo from Argaman and hearing their comments, Netanyahu asked, "How do we stop this from happening?"

"We've tightened security at the Wall. Redoubled patrols. I ordered the gates to the Old City closed. No one is going in or out for the time being."

"Okay. We can live with the delay and confusion. Anything else?"

"We have teams from our Beersheba office looking for the students who are supposed to be a part of this. We're in the process of positioning additional air samplers around the city and in outlying suburbs. And we began overflights with drones equipped with airborne detection devices. They can detect Sarin gas."

"After it's released."

"Yes."

Netanyahu looked over at Eizenkot. "General, what are we doing at the border fence?"

"We already deployed additional troops there from your earlier order. Within the hour I have assigned additional units to join them. We're ready for whatever happens at the checkpoints."

Netanyahu nodded and looked back at Argaman. "Find these people and put an end to this. Use Jerusalem police. Circulate photos. Do what you have to do, but find them and stop this."

"Yes, Mr. Prime Minister," Argaman replied. "We're already working with the police. They have called in all of their people and have put them on the street looking for school-aged children and particularly those in groups carrying backpacks."

"Very well," Netanyahu responded. "I'll be in my office within the hour. Keep me apprised of the latest."

✦ ✦ ✦

Ninety minutes after leaving Beersheba, Auerbach and Harel arrived in Jerusalem. Auerbach steered their car down a series of side streets, both of them looking from side to side, checking the cross streets for groups of children with backpacks, until they reached a roadblock near the Old City. He parked the car to the right of the barrier and got out. Just then, a policeman approached. "You can't leave that car there. Move it."

Auerbach produced his identification and flashed it for the policeman to see. "Okay," the officer replied. "But I can't guarantee the car won't get towed."

"Someone will find it."

The officer nodded in acknowledgment and turned away.

By then, the sun was just coming up over the rooftops along the Temple Mount. Auerbach glanced in that direction. On any other day he would have been awed by the beauty and wonder of the sun and the buildings and the historic significance of the surroundings, but not this day. He and Harel had come to the city for a purpose—to stop a bombing attack before any devices detonated—and for that there was little time to wait or stare or wonder.

Auerbach pointed to his left, and instructed Harel, "Walk to that corner, and take the next street over. It runs parallel to this one." He gestured toward the next block. "Walk south and keep your eyes open. Check with me when you reach the next cross street."

"How do I do that?"

"Just stop at the corner. Look in my direction and wait until you see me before going any farther. We'll take it one block at a time."

"Won't that be slow?"

"Yes," Auerbach replied. "But it's better than trying to jump around everywhere in a rush."

"Children," Harel muttered.

"Yes." Auerbach knew Harel's opinion—that they were wasting their time trying to find Masalha and the students on foot, that they should be using drones or the security-camera system or some other idea. Auerbach knew it was a long shot, too, but he didn't see any other option and was growing frustrated with Harel's questions. The tone of Auerbach's voice made that frustration oblivious. "They'll be in a group. All of them with backpacks. They'll look like a school class on a field trip. Because that's—"

Harel cut him off and added sarcastically, "Because that's what they are."

Auerbach groaned. "Because that's what they are. Get moving."

"And what if—"

"Go!" Auerbach shouted, his patience finally at an end. "Get moving."

Harel abruptly turned away and started up a side street to the next corner. When he reached it he glanced over his shoulder in Auerbach's direction. Auerbach motioned for him to continue and they both started forward. Auerbach on one street, Harel on the next, walking parallel to each other.

Working methodically, Auerbach and Harel made their way from block to block, searching through a neighborhood that lay south of Al-Aqsa Mosque. As they did, the sun rose higher in the sky and the city slowly came to life. More and more people appeared on the streets—first the residents, then the tourists.

Tightened security made the streets even more congested than normal, with people jammed shoulder to shoulder in some places. As the morning wore on, movement from block to block became increasingly difficult.

Auerbach and Harel weren't the only ones searching the streets. Shin Bet agents from every region had been brought in to help and, as Argaman had indicated to Netanyahu, every policeman in Jerusalem who was capable of working was on the street, too. Not just in the older neighborhoods but throughout the entire city.

It seemed a hopeless task, but shortly after ten that morning Auerbach caught sight of a group of children near the Dung Gate. All of them carried backpacks and were accompanied by two adults. He rushed forward and began searching frantically through the backpacks, moving quickly from one child to another.

"What are you doing?" a parent asked in protest.

"This is a national emergency," Auerbach replied.

"Emergency?" someone asked, stepping in the way to stop him. "These are children. They are students from school."

Just then, Harel joined him. Auerbach glanced in his direction. "Get busy," he barked. "Check them all. We don't have much time."

Harel began searching the backpacks, too. When they reached the last child, Harel looked over at Auerbach. "This isn't them."

Auerbach searched one more backpack, then stopped. His shoulders sagged and he glanced down at the children, whom he realized now were staring up at him in fear. "It's okay," he told them. "I thought you were someone else." He looked over at the adults. "We're searching for someone."

"In a backpack?"

"Someone *with* a backpack," Harel offered.

Auerbach caught Harel's eye. "Come on," he said. "Let's keep moving."

"Which way? We've looked through this whole area. And anyway, there isn't much here for a group to see."

Just then, Auerbach caught sight of another group of children. This one was beyond the Dung Gate, inside the Old City. "I thought the gates were supposed to be closed."

"They are."

Auerbach pointed. "Then what about that?"

The Dung Gate was open, and through the opening a group of schoolchildren was clearly visible. Auerbach ran toward the gate with Harel close behind. When they reached it, two guards stopped them. "Who are you?" one of them asked.

Auerbach flashed his Shin Bet identification. "Why are the gates open?" he asked in a demanding tone.

The officer was taken aback. "We were told to let in some of the student groups."

"Who told you?"

The guard gestured to a radio clipped to his belt. "They called and said to let them in. We let them in."

"All of them? You let in all of the groups?"

"No, just one, actually."

"Where are they?"

The guard pointed toward the Old City. "In there."

Auerbach and Harel pushed past the guards and ran toward Rabinovich Square. As they approached the square they came upon a group of children similar to the one they'd just searched. Auerbach and Harel checked each backpack but found nothing, then another group appeared, followed by yet one more.

"They let in more than just one," Harel noted.

"I'm gonna find out who gave that order," Auerbach retorted. "But not right now."

"Maybe they're all from one group, but Masalha divided them up," Harel suggested.

"Maybe so." Auerbach pointed across the way. "There's another group right there."

After searching the fourth and fifth groups, the futility of the effort finally sank in on Auerbach with an overwhelming force of reality. Jerusalem was a big city. Not the biggest in the world, but big. Moreover, it was full of people, especially on this day. Even with the help of a police force ten times larger than the one deployed, they couldn't search every backpack on every child who was there this day. They had no way, no hope, no possibility, no— and then Auerbach caught sight of Masalha. He was accompanied by a large group of children and four adults who appeared to be parents acting as chaperones.

Auerbach stopped abruptly and pointed. "There he is."

"There who is?"

"Masalha."

As Harel turned to see for himself, Auerbach tapped him on the shoulder. "Come on." Once again, Auerbach ran toward a group of schoolchildren with Harel close behind—only, this time he was charging toward the group they'd come to find.

When they still were half a block away, though, Masalha glanced in their direction. His eyes met Auerbach's and a knowing look came over him. In an instant, Masalha turned away and ran in the opposite direction.

As they reached the group of students Harel pointed at the children, "Deal with them. I'll go after Masalha!"

Auerbach came to a stop while Harel sped past. Three policemen who'd been standing nearby heard the commotion and rushed forward. "What's going on here?" one of them demanded.

Again, Auerbach produced his identification and held it for them to see. "Shin Bet." He gestsured toward Harel. "That man over there is my partner. He's chasing a known terrorist. Two of you, go help him." The first two policemen hurried after Harel.

"What about me?" the other one asked. "What do you need?"

"Help me search these backpacks."

Still holding his identification for everyone to see, Auerbach turned to the group of children, "I need you to take off your backpacks. All of you. And I need you to do it now." For a moment, the children stared up at him but did not move. "Take off your backpacks!" he shouted. "Do it now!"

One or two of the children shrugged their backpacks from their shoulders and others were about to follow when a parent stepped forward. "What is the meaning of this?" he demanded. "You're frightening the children."

Auerbach leaned around him and shouted to the children, "Do it now! Get those backpacks off! Drop them on the street and move away!"

The parent, now angry, moved closer. "I asked you a question."

In quick order, Auerbach swept the man's legs from beneath him and dropped him to the pavement. Before the man could recover, Auerbach put his foot on the man's chest to keep him there. With the parent pinned to the ground, he pointed to the policeman. "Get those backpacks off those children, now!"

The officer did as he was told and began removing the backpacks. As he did, the children joined in, and before long most of the backpacks lay on the ground. Auerbach glowered down at the parent. "I'm going to let you up." He pointed a finger at the man for emphasis. "But stay out of my face."

Auerbach stepped over the parent, who still was lying on the pavement, and grabbed a backpack, then jerked open the flap. Inside the pack was a pipe bomb but no gas cylinder. Auerbach turned the backpack to show the parent. "This is what we're looking for."

The parent jumped to his feet, a look of horror on his face. Two children still had their packs and he yelled at them, "Do as he says! Get your backpacks off. Drop them in the street."

One of the other parents, a woman, looked over at Auerbach and pointed, "These aren't our backpacks. None of these are ours. None of the children had this kind of pack when we left for the trip this morning."

By then a crowd of curious onlookers had gathered, but when they saw the pipe bomb from the first backpack they began pushing and shoving to get out of the way. Panic quickly set in and a crowd of frightened people stampeded away from the square, shouting as they did. That's when one of the parents noticed a child was missing.

"Where is Cherien?" she asked.

Auerbach had a questioning look. "Who is Cherien?"

"My daughter," the woman explained. "She was here just a minute ago."

Auerbach was bewildered a moment, then turned to the man who confronted him earlier. "How many came with you?"

The man frowned. "How many?"

"Yes," Auerbach demanded. "How many? How many were in your group?"

"Twenty-three. Four adults and twenty-three children."

Auerbach looked over at the policeman who had been helping him. "Count the backpacks." Auerbach began rounding up the packs. "Count them all."

Seconds later the policeman reported, "I have twelve over here."

"And I have eleven," Auerbach added, and then a look of

realization came over him. He turned to the woman whose child was missing. "Did your daughter have her backpack?"

The woman was in tears and she stared at him with her hand to her mouth, then slowly nodded. "Yes," she sobbed. "I think she did."

Auerbach pointed to the pile and shouted to a police officer, "Secure the area." He turned to run after the child. "Call the bomb squad. And get these people out of the way!"

For the next ten minutes Auerbach searched the street that led away from the square, frantically checking first this street, then the next. A block or two from the square he caught sight of a group of children he felt sure were from Masalha's group, but lost them in a crowd.

Finally he came to a stop, exhausted, drenched with sweat, gasping for breath. He bent over, hands on his knees, and gulped in a lung full of air, trying to find the will and the energy to keep going. After a moment or two, he stood up and looked around, surveying the area to determine where to look next. Then he heard a whimper and the scuffle of feet against the pavement coming from his right. He trotted in that direction.

A short way from the corner, Auerbach glanced up a narrow alley and saw a young girl huddled against the brick wall of a building that abutted the alley. On her back was the same pack as those they had taken from the students in the square. Auerbach stepped forward, moving slowly and carefully. As he did, the girl looked up at him, obviously scared and worried.

"Are you Cherien?"

"Am I in trouble?" she asked in reply.

"No, you're not in trouble. We just need to get that backpack off your shoulders."

"But it has my book inside."

"No," Auerbach said. "Not that one."

"What do you mean?"

"Someone switched your backpack. The one you're carrying isn't the one you brought with you this morning."

"It isn't?"

"No."

The girl stood and slipped off the backpack, then Auerbach took it from her. "Let me see if my book is in there," she demanded.

"Not yet. Let me check first."

Auerbach opened the flap and glanced inside to find a pipe bomb with a metal canister taped to it in a configuration similar to the images he'd seen in the files from Shammas's laptop. Anger rose inside him at the sight of it. Who would do such a thing? Who would create a bomb and put it in the backpack of a child? And use that child to deliver an attack of poisonous gas?

Constructed of galvanized pipe with a cap screwed on either end, the bomb was made from the same kind of material he'd seen in the house where the explosion occurred a few weeks earlier. A house located only a few kilometers from where he stood. Holes had been drilled through the center of both endcaps and wires ran from them to a cell phone that was taped to the side opposite the canister. He stared at it a moment, wondering what to do.

Masalha was on the run. No doubt, by then he had managed to phone Rajabian. Perhaps their plans had been disrupted now and they encountered a logistical problem getting to the information they needed to send a signal to the phones. Perhaps the signals had been unable to activate the phones—some sections of the city experienced poor reception because of the narrow streets and the lack of sufficient cell phone towers. But even so, the bombs could begin exploding at any moment. The one he was holding could detonate right then and he would be blasted into thousands of pieces.

There's not time for the bomb squad, Auerbach thought. *I have to—*

Suddenly the cell phone rang. Instantly, and without another thought, Auerbach ripped the canister from the pipe bomb, flung the bomb toward the street, and shoved the young girl to the ground, covering her with his body.

The pipe made a clanking sound as it struck the pavement, then a deafening roar followed as fire, smoke, and shrapnel flew in every direction. Auerbach felt pieces of hot metal cut into his back and the acrid smell of the explosive stung his nostrils. But within seconds he realized he was still alive and the Sarin canister lay beside him, intact and undamaged.

As the dust and smoke settled, Auerbach stood and glanced down at the girl. "Are you okay?" She said something in reply but he couldn't quite hear her for the roaring in his ears. "Are you okay?" he shouted.

"Yes," she shouted back. "But my ears hurt!"

Auerbach grinned. "Mine too."

"And you're bleeding." She pointed at his face.

Auerbach ran his hand over his cheek and saw that he was indeed bleeding, though not profusely. His back, however, was another matter. Already he felt the stickiness of blood against his shirt and knew that he had shrapnel lodged near his shoulders.

Suddenly, an explosion up the street reverberated through the neighborhood. "The bombs," Auerbach muttered. "They're setting off the bombs."

Taking her by the hand, Auerbach and the girl walked slowly from the alley to the street and started toward the square. Just then, they saw the girl's mother. She was frantic and she burst into tears at the sight of her daughter. "Cherien!" she shouted.

"She's okay," Auerbach reassured her. The roaring in his ears was less than before, but he still spoke louder than normal. The mother took the girl in her arms and wept for joy.

At another time, Auerbach would have remained with them and insisted the girl seek medical attention to make certain she really was unharmed. But these were not those times. Instead, he left mother and daughter to console each other and raced away, hoping to prevent the remainder of the bombs from exploding.

CHAPTER
24

DESPITE THE DIFFICULTIES he'd encountered in getting organized and identifying a cause to rally a crowd of thousands for Hamas's demonstration, individual members of Khalafi's core group finally succeeded in developing their own following. Under Khalafi's direction they used those additional groups as a means of drawing others into the plot to stage a massive protest at the Sufa border crossing.

As the groups grew in size, enthusiasm for the protest grew also. Awareness of the effort slowly spread across Khalafi's assigned region of southern Gaza. To keep the momentum going, Khalafi asked each of the groups to assign its members a project.

Hisham Shomali and his group prepared leaflets detailing the supposed Jewish plot to destroy Al-Aqsa Mosque and replace it with a synagogue, then handed them out to residents in Umm al-Kilab, posted notices in coffeehouses, and tacked notices on every available public space. When their immediate neighborhood had been covered, they moved on to others in the sounding area.

Ibrahim Atweh and his group created a blog for the event, then sent emails and text messages to as many addresses and phone numbers as they could find, pointing the recipients to the blog. Samir Jubran and three of the men in his group joined in the online effort, working day and night to post comments on news sites, and blogs encouraging regional support for the protest, which also directed viewers to the blog created by Atweh. Their posts cited recent news articles about the desire of some groups to establish a new Jewish temple, the third such temple to occupy Temple Mount. Unnoticed at first, their comments gradually attracted attention from both sides, Jewish and Muslim, and soon an online argument raged. Hits on Atweh's blog increased, and their articles about the protest went viral across the Internet.

Jabra Shahid concentrated on developing a Muslim understanding of why this protest was critical, not just for Palestinians but for the greater Muslim world. "Al-Aqsa Mosque sits atop the mount. Haram esh-Sharif. The Noble Sanctuary," he explained. "This is a site where Abraham worshiped. It is the site visited by Muhammad when he came to Jerusalem, and it is the location from which he rose to heaven. His feet left the earth on his night journey to heaven from the rock that is atop the mountain, and now that rock is protected beneath the Dome of the Rock built over the site. If the Jews can destroy Al-Aqsa, what is there to stop them from demolishing the Dome? Only *we* can stop that from happening because only *we* are willing to risk our lives to protect it. No one else has. No one else will. The Jordanians have not. They have withdrawn as cowards to the safety of their borders. The Egyptians have not. They have made peace with the Jewish swine and have made themselves infidels seven times over for it. The Syrians are weak and reliant on the Russians, who are infidels themselves teaching their Russian Orthodoxy with their many gods and idols. The Lebanese are divided. And, in spite of what they say, Iran is too interested in spreading regional revolution and finding outlets for its oil."

Khalafi cautioned Shahid about speaking against Iran and reminded him that the suggestion the Jews were planning to destroy Al-Aqsa was a fabrication of the group's own doing. "It is not rooted in reality, other than the desire of some Jewish groups to build a third temple."

Shahid, however, was involved too deeply to retreat from the fabrication and could not be persuaded to tone down his rhetoric. After several attempts, Khalafi noticed the level of excitement Shahid's men had for their work in organizing the protest—Shahid's group was the largest of them all and still growing. Consequently, he decided the better wisdom would suggest they be left alone, which he did. "We can always address this later," he mumbled.

Later, when General Bagheri, commander of the general staff of the Iranian armed forces, learned of Shahid's remarks about

Iran he took exception to them, though by then there was nothing that he or anyone else could do regarding the situation. Nevertheless, he took solace when he learned even later of Shahid's ultimate end. *Perhaps Allah was watching us after all,* he thought.

Right then, however, no one even thought of Bagheri, only of the Iranian operatives working in Gaza. They did not mind what Shahid said about much of anything, as long as he rallied a crowd of sufficient size and herded them toward the Sufa gate, which he did very well. "His words are of no consequence to us," some said, upon being informed of Shahid's tactics. "We only want results and Shahid is producing results. Let him tell his lies."

On the same morning Auerbach and Harel arrived in Jerusalem to track down Masalha and his group of students, Khalafi and his now-expanded group of Hamas operatives gathered, along with each of their individual groups, at the house in Umm al-Kilab. With all of them in the same place the crowd was quite large and covered the space around the house, even spilling into the street. Khalafi reviewed the plan with them once more, then Shahid led them in chants that rallied them to a frenzy. When they were sufficiently excited, Khalafi sent them into the neighborhood where they went from house to house, building to building, street to street, cajoling, instructing, and demanding that others participate. "We must protect Al-Aqsa from the infidels!" they shouted. As the crowd grew and began marching toward the Sufa Crossing, they chanted in unison, "Protect Al-Aqsa! Protect Al-Aqsa!" They numbered in the thousands.

When the marchers arrived at the Sufa border crossing, they were met by television camera crews and reporters that were already in place, filming as they approached. The crossing, however, was closed, the huge steel doors locked in place, blocking the way. The crowd gathered there anyway, shouting and chanting, "Save Al-Aqsa! Save Al-Aqsa!"

Khalafi's men—the central group of ten or fifteen that he began with—found him and took him aside. "What now?" Shahid asked, gesturing to the closed gates. "The Israelis know what we are doing."

Khalafi shook his head. "They know nothing," he assured. "They close the gates all the time."

Jubran spoke up. "Did no one think to plan ahead for a time when they would be open?"

"We have no time to argue," Khalafi snapped. "Shahid and Jubran, stay with the crowd. Keep them here. Lead them in chants. Do whatever you have to do, just don't let them leave." Then he turned to the others, "Come with me."

Khalafi led the half-dozen men to the pickup truck and drove away. A short while later they arrived at Khalafi's storage container near the beach. With the men helping, they cleaned out all of the rocket-propelled grenades and shoulder-fired missiles that remained there, then loaded them into the pickup truck and went to the house in Umm al-Kilab.

When they arrived at the house, Khalafi stepped down from the cab of the truck. "Each of you, take a rocket," he instructed.

Hisham Shomali frowned. "We're going to use these now?"

"Yes," Khalafi replied as he inserted an RPG into a Russian-made launcher and prepared it for firing.

"What are we to do with them?" Shomali asked, still with a worried look.

"Fire them toward the Sufa Crossing," Khalafi explained.

Ibrahim Atweh spoke up. "But won't we hit our own crowd?"

"Not if we aim high enough."

"How will we know what is high enough? We can't see the wall or the gates. And we don't know what's over there."

"Israelis are over there," Khalafi pointed. "Get busy."

Khalafi eased to the corner of the house, raised the launcher to his shoulder, and positioned it at a low angle, then he squeezed the firing trigger. Instantly, the rocket shot from the launcher tube and as it did he shouted, "Allah Akbar!"

They all watched as the contrail from the rocket streamed upward into the clear blue sky, then arced downward toward the ground. As the rocket disappeared into the distance, Khalafi moved past the others and took another rocket from the bed of the truck. He loaded it into the launcher, then glanced over at the men who were with him. "Get busy. We don't have much time."

Just then, the sound of an explosion reached them. They all moved back to the side of the house to look toward the east and saw a dark plume of smoke rising from the direction of the border crossing. Khalafi grinned. "Like I said, get busy."

Excited now, the others took rockets and launchers from

the bed of the truck and joined in firing them toward the border. Before long, explosions reverberated from near the crossing in sequence, first one, then another, and another, and still the men with Khalafi kept firing more and more rockets, yelling and shouting as they did.

✦ ✦ ✦

At other locations along the Gaza border, protests occurred similar to those at the Sufa Crossing. At the Kerem Shalom Crossing in the extreme southeastern corner of Gaza—near the junction of the borders between Gaza, Egypt, and Israel—the heavy steel barrier gates also were closed. Thousands of Palestinians gathered there on the Gaza side just the same but were unable to cross. News crews recorded their gathering, but the participants did little more than chant loudly and throw rocks over the border barrier.

IDF soldiers manning the crossing and units patrolling the fence on the Israeli side held their fire and made no response at all. As a result, the protest fizzled and those who had gathered on the Gaza side eventually walked away dejectedly.

At the Erez Crossing in the north and the Rafah Crossing to the south, there were no heavy steel gates. In order to secure the crossing and prevent anyone from passing through, IDF trucks and tanks were parked across the road, blocking the way for vehicles. Space between the equipment, though narrow, still was sufficient for those approaching on foot to squeeze past. As occurred at the other crossings, thousands of Palestinians gathered at Erez and Rafah. Shouting and chanting, they moved toward the wall. And, as at the other locations, television cameras recorded their effort.

Unlike the other crossings, however, the crossings at Erez and Rafah were manned by IDF troops who were visible, unprotected by steel gates, only cloistered behind the trucks and tanks they'd parked to block the road. Protesters could see the soldiers. The soldiers could see the protesters. Standing eye to eye with the opposition seemed to energize the protestors in a way not found at the other sites. Likewise, seeing the protestors before them added a measure of tension among IDF troops.

As the protesters advanced closer to the border fence, IDF troops fired tear gas canisters and rubber bullets at the crowd in an attempt to stop them without doing great bodily harm. Still the groups swarmed forward, undeterred. Then from somewhere behind the crowd on the Gaza side, a rocket was launched. It landed on the Israeli side of the border fence and exploded behind the IDF troops. This was followed by another rocket, then another.

IDF soldiers manning the crossing responded with more canisters of tear gas. When that seemed to have no effect, they fired canisters of CR gas—an incapacitating agent. Within minutes, protesters nearest the front of the crowd cried out in agony as the CR gas made their skin burn like fire. Moments later, they staggered away in pain and the crowd began to retreat. After additional canisters of CR gas were fired into their midst, the crowd disbanded altogether.

✦ ✦ ✦

As Iranian leaders had hoped, and as they had previously arranged, news of the protests in Gaza appeared on broadcast channels and Internet websites around the world, alongside reports of the attempted but thwarted bombing and gas attack in Jerusalem. Israeli officials and spokespeople were on the air immediately, telling the Israeli side of the story to every news reporter and outlet available.

A representative from the prime minister's office spoke, "This was a coordinated attack by Iran against the nation of Israel. All of the attacks—in Jerusalem and along the border with Gaza—were organized, sponsored, and coordinated by Iranian operatives working on direct orders from government handlers in Tehran. In Jerusalem, they used children to carry the bombs. Children. School students. Our agents disarmed the bombs and recovered three canisters of Sarin gas. Only two bombs detonated, but they caused no loss of life or property damage due to the diligent efforts of our agents who risked their lives to defend our people. But make no mistake about it: this was a horrendous and despicable act of state-sponsored terrorism, if not an outright act of war. All of it sponsored by the government of Iran against the people of Israel and the sovereignty of the Israeli state."

Instead of calling for sanctions against Israel, as General Bagheri and Iranian leadership suggested earlier, news agencies, governments, and social commentators praised Israel for its diligence in uncovering the plot behind the attacks and its discipline in responding in a measured but effective manner.

CHAPTER

25

IN SPITE OF the positive reaction from around the world, Avigdor Lieberman, the Israeli minister of defense, was unsettled by the attacks and the reports they'd received earlier about Iranian troops massing on Israel's northern border. "I am glad we were able to thwart these attacks from Gaza and in Jerusalem, but that does not change the nature of the threat against us."

Lieberman's aide, who listened attentively, asked, "What would you like to do?"

"Ask General Eizenkot to come see me."

"Certainly," the aide replied. "Shall I tell him to come at once?"

Lieberman nodded. "Ask him to see me within the hour."

Thirty minutes later, Eizenkot arrived at Lieberman's office. Very quickly, Lieberman realized Eizenkot had been thinking much the same as he had, that Israel still faced a credible threat to its very existence.

"We don't know what's coming next," Eizenkot cautioned. "The world thinks this is over but we don't know that."

"We should have our analysts review the latest images from our satellites," Lieberman suggested.

"Perhaps we should also ask them to compare those images with data from the NSA."

"The Americans?"

"Yes. They've indicated a willingness to help. We should take them up on the offer. That would allow our people to compare what we've seen with a second source. Make sure we haven't overlooked anything, and make sure we're seeing the situation correctly."

Lieberman nodded. "That's a good idea. Do you need me to call and arrange it?"

"No, we can handle it ourselves, at an operational level."

By midafternoon on the day of the attack in Jerusalem, IDF analysts were busy reviewing images from Israeli satellites and comparing those images to ones provided by the US intelligence community. Their work indicated that Iranian troop strength in both Syria and Lebanon had continued to rise since the last review. To make that increase obvious and irrefutable, they prepared a chronology covering troop levels for the past year.

Then one of the analysts noticed what appeared to be heavy armament—tanks and mobile missile launchers moving toward the border. "Last time they were here," he pointed out. "Now they are here." Further analysis indicated Iranian troops were indeed slowly advancing toward the Israeli border.

Leo Amitsur, a supervisor, looked over the analyst's shoulder. "Can we confirm this?"

"The images confirm it."

"We need more before reporting this," Amitsur decided. "Have our operatives on the ground confirm that Hezbollah is moving cargo to the area."

"That will take time."

"And if they're moving cargo, we need to know what kind they're moving."

"Tell our operatives to confirm as much as they can," Amitsur insisted. "I'll request a drone overflight."

Within two hours more images arrived, taken by cameras aboard the drones. Meir Yonath, an analyst viewing the images, pointed to the monitor on his desk. "I think the cargo on these trucks might be rockets."

Amitsur seemed perturbed by the remark. "*Might* be?"

"We can't be absolutely certain. Not without getting inside the trucks. But Hezbollah alone has thousands."

Gideon Kahn, seated across the room, spoke up. "Make that hundreds of thousands."

"Okay," Yonath conceded. "Hundreds of thousands. And that doesn't include the ones Iranian troops would have brought with them. The trucks in these images are the kind of trucks both Hamas and Iran have used to transport munitions in the past."

Amitsur frowned. "And you think that's what they're doing now? They're bringing rockets to the border?"

Yonath nodded. "It looks like it to me."

Amitsur pressed the point. "What you're saying will likely trigger a reaction. A serious reaction. You understand what I'm saying?"

"I understand what it means."

"And you want me to pass this along." Amitsur had a critical tone. "In a report that will tell the prime minister the Iranians *might be* moving this or that toward the border?"

"I think we *must* say it," Yonath reiterated. "The conclusive proof would only come when they start firing at us. We can't wait for that. We can't take any chances with this."

Amitsur shook his head. "We need more."

"What more do we need?"

"Find out what our operatives on the ground have to say. Then check the wider region. See if anyone else is preparing for action against us."

Yonath and the other analysts checked the latest intelligence data for Jordan and Egypt, Israel's other and nearest neighbors. Finding nothing untoward from either, they reported this to Amitsur, then waited for operatives in the field to respond to their earlier request for information.

✦ ✦ ✦

Fadi Hamdan, a Druze farmer who lived in Rachaiya, Lebanon, on the eastern slope of Mount Hermon, was at work in the afternoon tending his olive groves when a message arrived for him. Delivered by a young boy, the communication came in the form of a note neatly folded and sealed in back with a thick daub of red wax. Hamdan broke the seal, unfolded it, and read, "Are they still moving? What are they hauling?"

For three months, Hamdan had observed traffic moving south through the mountains along the Rachaiya-Marjayoun Road. Heavy military trucks with canvas covering the cargo. He had observed them from a ledge above the road, carefully counting each one, noting the date, time, and location where they passed. That information had been delivered to his handler through a drop box in town.

Now Hamdan's handler wanted to know what was inside the trucks. That was a task of considerably greater danger than mere observation but one for which Hamdan had no reservations. The trucks were Iranian military trucks. The men traveling in them were a mixture of Iranian and Hezbollah soldiers. After the death of his son, Hamdan hated them both.

Late in the afternoon, Hamdan loaded a donkey with a basket of olives, then started down the dirt trail that led from his house to a farm road. If anyone asked, he intended to tell them he was on his way to deliver olives to a buyer. He expected no one to ask, but he always preferred having an answer ready that others might believe.

The road eventually wound through the mountains to the paved highway used by the trucks. When he reached it, Hamdan walked with the donkey following behind toward an intersection a mile away. A store was located there and military trucks often stopped. Traffic passed him by without incident.

By then, the afternoon had faded to dusk but, as Hamdan expected, three military trucks were parked outside the store. Walking at a deliberate but unhurried pace, he moved past the first truck, noting that a driver sat at the steering wheel, but he was asleep. The second truck was parked in front of the first, but there was no driver inside. A check of the last truck revealed the same—no driver in the cab. Certain that no one could see him, Hamdan returned to the back of the truck, put his foot on the rear bumper, and lifted himself up to look inside.

Beneath the canvas cover, Hamdan saw stacks of wooden crates. Long and narrow, they were painted green and labeled with the words *Ruchnoy Protivotankoviy Granatomyot* written in black Cyrillic letters.

"Hand-held anti-tank grenade launcher," Hamdan whispered. He knew enough Russian to translate the words. Especially *those* words.

Not far away, in Joub Jannine, a city located in Lebanon's Beqaa Valley, Abdo Kassar stood atop his house as the sun was setting. Gazing through binoculars toward a different highway he saw three military trailer trucks, their loads covered with tarps. Kassar was not deceived, though. He'd seen these trucks before and he'd watched when soldiers removed the tarps. They were Iranian Shahab missiles loaded aboard mobile missile launchers.

The trucks slowed at an intersection a short distance from Kassar's house, then turned from the highway and made their way to a military compound. Kassar had a clear view of the entrance.

Fenced and heavily guarded, the compound had been created a month earlier on a site once occupied by a vineyard owned by Kassar's cousin. Having inherited it from his father, Kassar's uncle, his cousin had worked the vineyard in peace for many years until the day Hezbollah officials visited him with a decree signed by a judge granting Hezbollah title to the farm. They paid him for it with a stack of worthless Lebanese pound notes. That was the day Kassar began searching for a better way.

Not long after that, Kassar was approached by a man who identified himself as an Israeli intelligence handler. Perhaps he was Mossad, perhaps he was IDF. Kassar did not know and helping the Israelis was no way to bring change to Lebanon, but he thought it might offer him a chance to move his family from Lebanon to Galilee. He had visited there once and thought he could grow grapes in the hills west of Tiberias. At least he and his family would be safe from Hezbollah there.

Kassar investigated the man who contacted him, as much as one could do such things in Lebanon, and followed him two or three times. Satisfied he was legitimate—as legitimate as anyone else operating in the region—Kassar agreed to help.

That evening, after his family members were asleep in their

beds, Kassar went out to the storage building behind his house. From a cabinet in the corner he took out a shortwave radio transmitter with a Morse code key. A workbench ran along the wall and he set them there, then flipped a switch to turn on the transmitter. After the radio was warmed and ready, he tapped a few letters with the key to identify himself, then broadcast his message. "Three, six, seven, nine, nine, nine." He repeated the message three times, then switched off the radio, returned it to the cabinet, and closed the doors.

Rather than return inside immediately, he settled onto a stool that stood nearby. A pouch dangled from the waist of his trousers. In it was a quantity of tobacco. He removed the pouch and took a small packet of cigarette papers from his pocket. Carefully, he poured tobacco along the center of one of the papers, then gently rolled it up, sealing it closed with a lick of his tongue and twisting the ends tightly, forming a cigarette.

After returning the pouch to his hip and the papers to his pocket, Kassar placed the hand-rolled cigarette in his mouth. He took a match from his pocket and struck it against the cabinet door. A flame formed at the head of the match and he touched it to the end of the cigarette while gently puffing on it. Smoke filled his lungs and he took a deep breath, letting it fill him completely.

The message Kassar had sent was simply a notice to his handler that he had new information. A messenger would arrive soon and Kassar would give him the news. After that, he would go to bed. Or perhaps he would roll another cigarette first.

✦ ✦ ✦

Before sunup of the next day, information from Hamdan, Kassar, and other operatives working under similar conditions reached IDF intelligence officials. That information confirmed the suspicions of Yonath and other Mossad analysts—Iranian troops in Syria and Lebanon were slowly moving south, toward the Israeli border. The information also confirmed that the cargo in the trucks that appeared in satellite images was Hezbollah missiles. And, based on reports from operatives in the field, the Iranians were moving missiles on mobile launchers into the region.

With confirmation in hand, Amitsur forwarded the analysts' report to General Eizenkot, the IDF commander. Eizenkot and Lieberman met in Lieberman's office to review the matter. "I think we can say that the Iranian troops in Syria and Lebanon now pose a direct threat to Israel."

"Beyond any doubt," Eizenkot agreed. "And that threat must be eliminated."

"You're ready to brief the prime minister?"

Eizenkot replied. "Yes. And we should do it at once."

"I'll call to notify his office."

Within the hour, Lieberman and Eizenkot arrived at the prime minister's office. They met with the prime minister and Gil Sachs, his chief of staff.

"We have a problem with those Iranian troops in Syria and Lebanon," the general began.

"What is it?" Sachs asked.

"They've continued to increase in strength and they have advanced toward our border."

"What do you think?"

"I think the protests in Gaza, the attempt in Jerusalem, the Sarin gas wasn't all they had in mind."

"Which is?" The prime minister prompted.

"An invasion."

"From Lebanon?"

"Yes. And Syria." Eizenkot showed the prime minister some of the satellite images. "Data from the NSA confirms these movements."

Netanyahu looked over at Eizenkot. "What would you like to do?"

"I would like to move some of our infantry units into Galilee. Move several squadrons up from the south. Prepare our missile defenses."

"You think we might have to strike against the Iranians in Syria and Lebanon?"

"Yes."

"A preemptive strike. Before they reach the border?"

The general nodded, "Yes. At the very least, we need to be ready to repel an invasion."

Netanyahu seemed convinced. "Is there any threat of wider attack?"

"No. Egypt and Jordan are not a threat to us."

"Have we made sure of that?"

"Yes, Mr. Prime Minister. Our analysts have reviewed the entire region. We have no information that indicates any preparation in that direction by anyone else."

"Then this is solely Iran, with its usual allies of Syria and Hezbollah."

"Yes."

"Well," Netanyahu sighed, "at last we meet our true enemy."

"They have a huge stockpile of missiles," Eizenkot noted. "As does Hezbollah, though theirs are considerably smaller in size. Still, an all-in missile attack from Hezbollah in conjunction with a similar attack from Iran could inflict heavy damage on our major cities."

"What are you saying?"

"I'm saying, if we wait to respond until they attack us, we could end up defeating their attempt but still be devastated in the process."

Netanyahu ordered, "Move the troops and planes into position. Prepare our missile defenses. And make sure the bomb shelters are open, manned, and ready. We'll plan to strike them first but not until I give the order. I'll notify the Americans."

Lieberman, who had remained silent through most of the meeting, now spoke up. "The US has repositioned a carrier group to the Mediterranean."

"Good. We may need their help."

"They've also moved one up to the Persian Gulf. And they've added planes to their base in Italy."

"I talked to the president about helping us," Netanyahu noted. "I'll call him right now. Make sure we're all working together." He looked at them earnestly. "This is beginning, gentlemen. We can't afford to lose."

"No, sir," Lieberman assured. "We won't."

When the briefing ended, Netanyahu placed a phone call to Trump. They began their conversation by discussing the attacks on Israel from Gaza and in Jerusalem. "I must say," Trump praised, "your people handled those incidents very well, Bibi."

"Thank you, Donald," Netanyahu replied. "We have trained long and hard for difficult situations like that."

"Well, it paid off splendidly. I wonder how those television crews knew to be there at just the right time."

"I think we know the answer to that," Netanyahu replied grimly. "They were told to be there. The liberal press loves that kind of stuff and Hamas has a very good relationship with them."

"They certainly had advance notice."

"Yes."

"You called me, Bibi," Trump said. "Did you have something you wanted to discuss?"

"We've confirmed our suspicions about Iranian troop movements in Syria and Lebanon."

"They're advancing toward your border."

"You've seen that already."

"I've been briefed," Trump informed. "They also tell me that there is no way Iran would do something like this unless they meant to invade. And they also tell me that they can't invade with any hope of success unless they launch a withering missile attack, too."

Netanyahu agreed. "That is correct. And that has been borne out by our analysis. Along with Iranian troop movements, we have confirmed they are relocating vast quantities of missiles and rockets to the border region. Including Shahab missiles on mobile missile launchers."

"What do you plan to do about it?"

"As you are aware, our defense policy calls for a preemptive strike. We are small in area," Netanyahu continued. "Our enemies share our border. It is not possible for us to wait until a threat becomes an attack."

"This is the scenario everyone fears," Trump commented. "A threat from one of your neighbors that you can't ignore, even if it might be only a threat."

"This is no mere threat, Donald."

"I understand."

"This is the fight. One Iran chose and one we don't intend to lose. We've war-gamed this situation from many different perspectives. Your country and mine, during previous administrations. Those mutual efforts have produced several strategies. I think we should focus on Operation Daniel."

"Taking the fight to Persia?"

"Yes. With each of our two countries addressing the aspects of the threat that they are best equipped to handle."

"Our carriers are in position to assist in whatever way seems best."

"Perhaps we should let our commanders handle it from here," Netanyahu suggested. "At an operational level."

Trump agreed. "Are your people prepared to integrate US and Israeli AWACS and JSTARS capabilities?"

"I think so, but our commanders would know more about that."

"Is there anything we need to do at our level? You and I, as heads of state. Anything we need to agree on?"

"No, I think we've already done that."

"Yes," Trump answered. "I think we just did."

CHAPTER
26

IN TEHRAN, Ayatollah Khamenei was seated at his desk when Mana Mosaffa, his chief assistant, entered the room. Khamenei looked up. "You appear worried."

"Yes, Supreme Leader, I am."

"Well." Khamenei pushed aside the papers he'd been reading and rested his hands in his lap. "Tell me. What is the matter?"

"We have received news that the protests in Gaza have failed."

Khamenei frowned. "Failed?"

"Yes, Supreme Leader. The protesters arrived at the crossing points as planned but the gates were closed."

"No one anticipated this?"

"Apparently not."

"And what of the attack in Jerusalem? Surely, at least that was successful."

Mosaffa shook his head. "No, Supreme leader. The attack in Jerusalem failed also."

Khamenei had a bewildered expression. "Both of them failed?"

"Yes," Mosaffa replied.

Khamenei appeared to struggle in his effort to comprehend the result. "Both strategies failed?" His voice was barely audible.

"Yes."

Khamenei looked toward the window. "That is not possible," he muttered in disbelief. "I reviewed the strategies myself. I sensed the presence of Allah."

"I am sure you were correct," Mosaffa reassured. "Perhaps it was not Allah who failed."

"Allah can never fail," Khamenei retorted sharply.

"But man can."

A troubled frown wrinkled Khamenei's forehead. "Something must be wrong," he mused. Still seated at his desk, he looked over at Mosaffa with a stony expression. "Tell General Bagheri to report to me at once."

"Yes, Ayatollah." Mosaffa bowed respectfully, turned immediately toward the door, and disappeared from the room. Within the hour, he returned with General Bagheri in tow.

"Supreme Leader," Bagheri began with a note of supplication. "I am—

"You failed," Khamenei snapped.

"We made—"

"You failed!" Khamenei shouted, cutting him off. His voice was so loud it startled Mosaffa. "You told me the Israelis would be thrown into a state of confusion. You told me they would be so disrupted, our troops could descend upon them from Lebanon and Syria and plunder their cities with impunity."

"I did not say—"

"You most certainly did say," Khamenei roared, interrupting him again. "And now our soldiers—valiant and dedicated warriors—are positioned for an attack they cannot win!"

"We can withdraw them," Bagheri offered.

"No!" Khamenei shouted. He struck the desktop with his fist and glared at Bagheri. "You must salvage this operation!" His voice was even louder than before and Bagheri backed instinctively toward the door. "And you must do it before the Americans intervene." He paused to take a deep breath, then looked over at Bagheri and asked calmly, "So, what will you do?"

"That part is very simple, Supreme Leader. We turn to the Mahdi option."

"And what is that?"

"A conflagration in Israel so devastating that all the nations of the world will come against us in an attempt to destroy us. And just before we are obliterated, the Mahdi will appear to protect us and restore order."

"And what would this entail?"

"Hezbollah has a hundred thousand rockets. They will launch them into Israel. While the Israelis are forced into a defensive posture from that barrage, our troops will move out from their positions in Lebanon and Syria and invade Israel from the north, as we planned. Before the Israelis can counter on the ground, we will launch an even greater barrage of missiles from our bases here, in an attack larger than any ever launched by any nation against anyone."

The Ayatollah did not immediately dismiss the idea. "And where would we launch these missiles?"

"From Lebanon using Hezbollah's rockets and missiles. And from here, using our own."

"From here?"

"Yes. Our missiles are strong and powerful. We will strike Jerusalem, Tel Aviv, Haifa, Ashdod," Bagheri enumerated confidently. "All of those cities will be devastated, first by the explosions from the missiles and then by the fires those explosions create. We know the targets already. They are programed into the launch system."

The Ayatollah folded his arms across his chest. "And an attack of this nature will be enough for our troops to invade and prevail?"

"Almost."

"You have more in mind?"

"Coinciding with the missile attack, we will prevail upon ISIS and Al-Qaeda cells already training in the Sinai to move up against Israel from the south. They will divide into two groups, the first overrunning smaller towns in southern Israel and advancing quickly on Beersheba with the kind of fast-paced attack ISIS used to overrun western Iraq. As they do so, the second group from ISIS will enter Gaza and incite the Palestinians to overrun the border crossings wherever they can."

The Ayatollah smirked. "Didn't we try this already?"

"Yes, but it was too peaceful. This would not be a protest, but a rush against the border. Many will die, but many will prevail and overwhelm the soldiers guarding the border. Those who are unwilling to offer themselves in that way will launch all of Hamas's rockets into Israel."

"Hamas has rockets?"

Bagheri nodded. "Not anything like Hezbollah but, yes, they have rockets."

"And *this* will be enough?"

Bagheri replied confidently, "It will be the most devastating attack Israel has ever endured. And the timing is perfect. The Israelis put down our earlier attempts. They think they have the upper hand. When we strike this time, our people will move with unrelenting devotion."

When he finished, Bagheri bowed respectfully, his hands folded, and stood before Khamenei in silence. Khamenei sat quietly for a moment, then finally spoke, "I will consider your suggestion."

From the Ayatollah's residence, Bagheri returned to his office where he found General Alizadeh, commander of the Iranian army, waiting for him. "Did you convince him to call off the attacks?"

"No," Bagheri replied. "I did not."

Alizadeh looked worried. "What happened?"

"He was quite upset," Bagheri related with a noticeably non-chalant attitude. "So," he shrugged, "I gave him the Mahdi option."

Alizadeh's mouth dropped open. "You actually gave him that as an option?"

"I gave it to him as a proposal," Bagheri corrected. "We discussed this earlier. Don't you remember?"

"Yes, but I did not think you would actually do it."

"You don't even believe in the Mahdi."

Bagheri had a twinkle in his eye. "Do *you* believe in the Mahdi?"

Alizadeh answered curtly. He was in no mood to play. "Of course I believe in the Mahdi, but the timing is all wrong now. We cannot bring a great war—a great *conflagration*, as you call it. We don't have enough troops in place. The missiles are not ready. Hezbollah has not been informed. Hamas is not well armed. We cannot—"

Just then, the door opened and General Elahi from the air force appeared. He was grinning at Bagheri as he entered the room. "You gave him the Mahdi option," he said with obvious excitement and approval.

Taken aback, General Alizadeh shouted, "You knew about this beforehand?"

"No," Elahi replied. "But I have a contact on the Ayatollah's staff. He told me what happened."

Alizadeh looked deflated. "News of it will be everywhere before morning." He turned to Bagheri. "There will be no way to stop this now."

"Cheer up," Bagheri needled. "The Supreme Leader hasn't approved it yet."

"Oh, he will approve it," Elahi assured.

Bagheri was caught off-guard. "How do you know that?"

"My contact said they were discussing it before you arrived," Elahi explained. "The Supreme Leader was hoping you would suggest it. He just feigned anger to make the moment legitimate."

The door opened once again and Alavi appeared. "He approved it!" he announced with glee.

Bagheri smiled. "He authorized the missiles?"

"He authorized all of it. The orders for final preparations are being drafted now. They are set to go out once official authorization has been granted."

Bagheri laughed. "I thought he really was angry with me."

Alizadeh sagged limply onto a nearby chair. "We are all dead men," he groaned, obviously distressed.

"We were dead men either way," Bagheri replied. "The original plan cannot possibly succeed now."

"But we cannot create a crisis large enough to require the Mahdi's attendance," Alizadeh lamented. "It's simply not possible now."

"Like Bagheri said," Elahi chortled, "we are dead men either way."

"And," Alavi added, "don't forget the Americans."

"What of them?" Alizadeh asked.

"They will rain down such terror upon us, the Mahdi will have no choice but to appear and stop it."

Bagheri threw back his head and roared with laughter. Alavi and Elahi joined him, but Alizadeh seemed on the verge of tears. "This will be the end of us all."

Two days later, the Supreme Leader formally approved implementation of the Mahdi option. When news of the decision reached Bagheri, he issued orders straightaway to set the plan in motion. General Elahi from the air force wasted little time directing his technicians to begin preparing missiles for launch from sites inside Iran.

Likewise, General Alizadeh from the army, though still certain the plan would fail and they all would die, did as he was told and designated additional troops for emergency deployment to Lebanon and Syria. Troops already located in those countries were directed to advance toward the Israeli border but not cross over, pending final preparations and coordination with the missile attack.

Orders also were issued to Hezbollah through intermediaries in Qatar, directing their operatives to make every rocket and missile in Lebanon available for launch against targets in northern Israel. Overnight, traffic along the roads that ran through the Lebanese mountains increased significantly as trucks began transporting munitions toward the front.

In Lebanon, that increased activity caught the attention of Israeli intelligence contacts. Fadi Hamdan, the Druze farmer who lived on the eastern slope of Mount Hermon, noticed the nearly constant flow of truck traffic along the road that ran beneath the rocky perch near his home. From his rooftop lookout in Lebanon's Beqaa Valley, Abdo Kassar noted an increase in the number of mobile missile launchers that arrived at the compound built on the site of his cousin's vineyard. Zelzal-3s, he supposed, with a range of two hundred kilometers. More than enough to reach Tel Aviv.

All across Lebanon, and in Syria, too, others working under similar conditions detected the same sort of increased activity. Those sightings and traffic counts were duly reported to Israeli handlers who, in turn, relayed the information to Mossad and IDF headquarters in Tel Aviv.

✦ ✦ ✦

Fueling of long-range rockets and missiles is an elaborate task, one not easily hidden from view. In the same way, the repositioning of troops on the scale needed for Bagheri's proposed attack was not something Iran could accomplish and hide from view at the same time, especially given the now greatly-shortened time frame within which his units worked.

As preparations got underway, satellites operated by the CIA, NSA, other US intelligence agencies captured images of the increased activity in Iran as well as in Syria and Lebanon. Listening stations operated by the NSA at sites in Iraq and Afghanistan intercepted communications that confirmed the nature of the activity. Satellite images were downloaded directly to the respective agencies' headquarters. Reports detailing communications intercepts from regional NSA operations were screened and collated at an NSA facility in Bahrain, then forwarded to NSA headquarters in Maryland.

Under rules instituted following the terrorist attacks of September 11, information collected by NSA that was deemed to be operational in nature was forwarded to CIA headquarters at Langley, Virginia, for review in light of the larger intelligence context. With Bryce Jenkins no longer available at the CIA to inhibit the flow of information, the task of evaluating the data fell to Justin Andrews.

After reviewing the reports, Andrews took the information to his supervisor, Olivia Bradley. They met in Bradley's office.

Bradley glanced up as Andrews entered the room. "You said this was important."

"I've reviewed the satellite images and the intercepts we received from NSA."

"What did you find?"

"From what I've seen, I'd say Iran is preparing large numbers of missiles for launch. Some from sites inside Iran. Others from sites in Lebanon."

"Hezbollah?"

Andrews crossed the room to her desk. "Yes, we have photos, communications intercepts, and emails." He spread an array of documents and pictures on her desk.

"Do we know where the missiles are located?" Bradley asked as she viewed the images.

"We've pinpointed twenty-five locations." Andrews handed her a list. "All of them located within Iran's borders."

Bradley looked up at him. "And these sites are all launch sites? Sites from which Iran is preparing to launch missiles? Right now?"

"Yes, ma'am, these are confirmed locations where preparation activities are taking place right now. Fueling. Arming. They're getting ready for a large-scale attack."

"You're sure it's not an exercise?"

"It's not an exercise. They've moved Zelzal-3s into Lebanon."

"And how do we know this?"

"Satellite images show the missiles being placed on permanent launch pads. Mobile launchers are being moved to strategic sites, and are positioned for launch. Missiles are being fueled. Telemetry indicates warheads are being readied."

"And we have confirmed this information?"

"Yes. NSA's satellites. Our satellites. DIA. NSA listening stations. They all indicate Iran is preparing to launch at the sites on the list." He pointed to the list he'd handed her earlier. "We know of a dozen more locations that are potential launch sites—places in Iran that we know hold inventories of missiles and from which they have launched in the past. We just haven't detected activity there in this round of preparation."

"That puts Tel Aviv within their range."

"Yes, ma'am."

"What about Hezbollah?"

"There are reports of increased truck traffic in southern Lebanon. Communications intercepts indicate they are moving munitions toward the Israeli border. But we don't know exact locations for their missiles."

"Anything else?"

"Yes," Andrews answered. "Increased troop movement."

"Iranian troops?"

"Yes. They're moving troops already in Lebanon and Syria toward the Israeli border. And they're sending additional units to the region."

"You've prepared your results in writing?"

Andrews handed her a copy of a memo. "Written and reviewed."

"Okay," Bradley decided. "I'll send it upstairs." She looked over at him. "You're prepared to stand behind it?"

"Yes, ma'am," Andrews replied. "It's accurate."

"You'll probably get called into a meeting on this. A meeting with people way above your pay grade. You're prepared for that?"

"Yes, ma'am. I've been there before."

Ten minutes after Andrews left her office, Bradley took his memo upstairs to Dylan Gray, director of the analysis section. She handed him the memo. "This is our latest information on the Iran situation. We have the backup data to go with it. Would you like to see it for yourself?"

"Yes," Gray replied. "Forward it to me."

An hour later, Gray had reviewed the information from Bradley, along with the accompanying intercepts and images, and forwarded the package to the office of Gina Haspel, the CIA director. Haspel took one look at it and arranged a meeting with Dan Coats, the director of national intelligence. They met at Coats's office in the White House.

"This can't wait," Coats asserted after reading the memo. "We have to brief the president now."

Haspel glanced at her wristwatch. "It's almost one in the morning."

"I know," Coats noted. "But this can't wait until daylight. Not if Iran is preparing to launch. We don't have much time."

Twenty minutes later, Haspel and Coats arrived at the Oval Office, where they were met by tired but alert President Trump. The president was accompanied by his chief of staff, John Kelly. The briefing took fifteen minutes. Trump asked only a few questions. He understood the gravity of the situation and needed little explanation.

Trump looked over at Coats. "You'll share this with the National Security Council?"

Coats nodded his head. "At your direction, Mr. President."

"Do it," Trump ordered quickly. "And you two stick around."

"Yes, Mr. President," both replied.

"We'll get some coffee in here and talk about this some more." Trump looked over at Kelly. "Notify the rest of the National

Security Council. Tell them to meet me in the Situation Room in half an hour."

"Yes, Mr. President." Kelly started toward his office.

Trump called after him, "And tell the kitchen to send coffee, and bring me a diet Coke."

"Yes, sir."

Trump looked over at Coats and Haspel. "We're gonna need all the help we can get."

✦ ✦ ✦

Shortly before two in the morning, President Trump entered the White House Situation Room. Coats and Haspel were there, along with the secretary of defense, Jim Mattis; John Kelly; and a dozen other officials who comprised the National Security Council. They were seated at a long conference table that occupied the center of the room.

Admiral Dewey Porter, chairman of the Joint Chiefs of Staff, stood at the far end of the room near a video screen that covered the wall. A map was up on the screen, showing an area that extended from the eastern end of the Mediterranean across the Arabian Sea to Pakistan.

Everyone stood as Trump entered the room. "Sit back down. I know it's early for some of you." He paused to glance around the room. "And late for others." They all smiled in response. "You're all aware by now, there have been some new developments with Iran and Israel. So let's get to work." He looked to Coats. "Dan, why don't you and Gina tell them what you told me and we can all get on the same page."

"Yes, Mr. President," Coats replied.

For the next several minutes, Coats and Haspel presented their briefing on the situation in the Middle East. Unlike the president, who had a variety of issues to address each day, members of the Council dealt with foreign and domestic military threats on a daily basis. They spoke and thought in intelligence jargon and were comfortable with brisk, curt analysis summaries. It didn't take long for them to understand the context they faced.

John Bolton, the national security advisor, spoke up. "Are we certain this threat against Israel is limited to Iran, Hamas, and Hezbollah?"

Haspel replied, "We have no intelligence indicating anyone else is preparing to attack."

"Nothing from Jordan or Egypt?"

"No."

Rex Tillerson, the secretary of state, spoke up. "Both of those countries have treaties and agreements with Israel. Our sources tell us they have no interest in violating those commitments."

Bolton seemed unconvinced. "What about Syria?"

"The Iranians have troops in Syria," Coats acknowledged, "but the Syrian military is still stretched thin from fighting the civil war. We've seen no indication their troops are preparing to join the Iranians."

Trump looked down the table to Admiral Porter. "Our ships are in place?"

"Almost, Mr. President." Porter turned to the screen on the wall and pointed to a location on the map. "The *John F. Kennedy* and its group are here. They're transiting down the Mediterranean and will be on station tomorrow. The *Forrestal* is here," he pointed to the screen again, "Almost to the Arabian Sea. They could join operations now, but will be in a better position in two days."

"What about the planes?"

Porter frowned. "The planes, sir?"

"The air group."

"Oh. Right." Porter smiled. "Fighters and bombers from the Fifty-First Air Group have arrived at Aviano. The remainder of their troops and equipment are being relocated there now. They could carry out the mission now, but their efficiency won't be at optimal levels until later this week."

Steven Mnuchin, the secretary of the treasury, spoke up. "In terms of the threat from Iran, we're looking at missile strikes in conjunction with a military invasion, is that correct?"

"Yes," Coats replied.

"And part of the missile threat comes from launches that would occur from inside Iran and part from Lebanon. Is that correct?"

"Yes. That is correct."

"Do we know the targets those two contingencies might strike?"

Jim Mattis spoke up. "We don't have target-specific data right now, but we know the rockets from Hezbollah can only reach targets in the northern one-third of Israel. Modified Shahab missiles launched from Iran can reach any city in Israel."

"So," Mnuchin continued, "if they coordinate their plans and attack in the most efficient manner, they would divide the targets respectively."

"Yes," Haspel replied. "But that's a big *if*."

Coats explained. "Earlier intelligence suggested the attacks from Hezbollah and Iran should have happened on the same day as the protests from Gaza and the attempted bombings in Jerusalem. That being true, coordination is apparently a problem for them."

The president spoke up. "Who's in charge of things from Iran's side?"

"General Bagheri," Mattis replied.

Admiral Porter chimed in. "We've dealt with him before, Mr. President. Not a bad general, as these things go, but he's seriously delusional about the Mahdi, and that clouds his judgment."

Trump had a questioning expression. "The Mahdi?"

Slate explained. "The Islamic belief that events will eventually transpire to bring the threat of a devastating end to Islam at which time the Mahdi, a savior figure, will appear to prevent the destruction of Islam and bring all to a belief in the true faith." Trump acknowledged him with a nod. "Mr. President," Tillerson continued, "you understand, we know the missiles are being fueled and armed. And we all agree that Israel is the apparent target. But there is no way to know for certain that this is in fact what the

Iranians plan to do."

"If we wait for absolute certainty," Trump replied, "it will be too late. Those missiles pose an overwhelming threat to Israel, but they also threaten the world. We can't let this pass without a response."

"And," Mattis added, "Israel won't wait for an attack, either. They can't. They have no option but to strike first."

"That's their standing defensive strategy," Porter spoke up.

Trump looked to Porter. "Admiral, you're clear about the threat?"

"Yes, Mr. President."

"Very well. Prepare an operation that will eliminate Iran's missile threat."

"Mr. President," Mattis said, "we already have an operation for that. We call it Operation Daniel."

Trump's eyes, however, were focused on Porter. "I'm aware of that. Admiral, whatever you need to do, get me an operation with details that will address the situation and show it to me by noon."

"Yes, Mr. President."

When the meeting ended, Trump returned to the Oval Office. He met there alone with John Kelly. "I suppose we should phone Netanyahu." His voice had a weary tone.

"Yes, Mr. President," Kelly acquiesced.

"Set it up." Trump leaned back in his chair and closed his eyes. "I don't mind an early-morning call, but this one was a little too early."

"We can squeeze in an hour for you after lunch."

"I'll be all right. Just set up the call."

"Yes, Mr. President."

Twenty minutes later, the president's phone call was ready and Netanyahu was on the line. They wasted little time on greetings. "Our intelligence indicates the Iranians are fueling and arming their missiles," Trump reported to his counterpart.

Netanyahu quickly replied. "General Eizenkot has indicated the same to me."

"We can calculate when they would be ready to launch, we just don't know when they will actually do it."

"I understand. General Eizenkot is on his way now to brief me in person. I should know more after that."

"We're planning a response," Trump continued. "Admiral Porter and the team will present the details for that operation to me today by noon, our time. We should talk again after we've both had our briefings."

"Do you intend to launch that operation immediately?" Netanyahu asked.

"We'll wait to respond until we hear from you."

"Good."

"Bibi, I think it's essential we are both prepared to act at the same time. We're in good shape for that with the work we've already done."

"Yes, Donald," Netanyahu said. "I agree."

CHAPTER

27

AT ELEVEN THAT MORNING, President Trump convened a meeting of the National Security Council to hear Admiral Porter's briefing and consider a plan to address the threat posed by Iran's activity. They met in the Situation Room. As before, Admiral Porter stood before the video screen at the end of the room opposite Trump's chair.

When everyone was present and seated, Porter nodded to an aide, and a map appeared on the screen behind him. "Mr. President, this is Operation Daniel." He pointed to red dots on the map. "These are the sites where Iran is currently preparing missiles for launch. There are twenty-five in total. Using cruise missiles from the *Forrestal* carrier group and stealth bombers from our base at Aviano, we can hit all twenty-five sites. And we can hit another ten sites that are potential locations for future launches." He pointed to the places on the map. "The ones highlighted in green."

"Aren't some of these launch sites actually hardened silos?"

"Yes, Mr. President."

"The cruise missiles . . ." Trump began. "They can penetrate hardened sites?"

Jim Mattis spoke up. "Some of them are equipped with low-grade, tactical nuclear warheads."

Trump looked perplexed. "Nuclear?"

Porter intervened. "Battlefield nukes, Mr. President."

"Right." Trump nodded. "Have we used them before?"

"Once," Mattis replied. "In Iraq."

"At the airport," Coats added.

"And that went okay?"

"They proved to be very effective," Haspel said.

Trump was concerned. "Okay, but they're nuclear weapons."

"Yes, Mr. President."

"And you can't use them without my specific authorization."

Porter answered. "That's correct, Mr. President. We also have bunker-busting conventional ordnance. I believe Secretary Mattis briefed you on that earlier."

"Yes. He did," Trump concurred. "But back to the point you were making about the launch sites. We can hit all of these sites, inside Iraq, with only twenty-five or thirty missile and bomb strikes?"

"No, Mr. President," Porter answered. "Our weapons are efficient, but they're not *that* efficient. We have about five hundred aim points. Places on which we would put ordnance. One device can't eliminate an entire facility."

"Five hundred aim points."

"Yes, Mr. President."

"So, five hundred missiles," Trump clarified.

"Something like that, Mr. President," Porter responded. "Do you need an exact count?"

"No." Trump shook his head. "Just trying to understand the magnitude of what we're doing."

"It will be a large-scale undertaking," Porter said.

"And what about their nuclear sites?" Trump asked. "The places where they've been developing nuclear weapons. Can we hit those?"

Porter shot a glance in Mattis's direction before saying, "That will expand our targeting package considerably, Mr. President."

"Because?"

"Iran has spread out their nuclear development program to dozens of locations. They have a heavy water reactor at Arak." Porter indicated the location on the map. "A reactor at Bushehr, located along the Persian Gulf. Processing and enrichment plants at Isfahan, Natanz, and Saghand. Hitting all of those locations will add several hundred more strikes to our plan."

"But it could be done."

"Yes, Mr. President. It could be done."

"How long will this take?"

"From beginning to end?"

"From the time the first hit occurs until the last—how long will that take?"

"For the plan we've proposed, the stealth bombers will go in on the first sortie," Porter explained. "They will take out Iran's radar and defense systems. A second sortie will take out their command-and-control sites. Those two attacks will happen almost simultaneously. Then we'll send in the B-2s and the cruise missiles to take out the actual launch sites."

Trump frowned. "We can get that done before they launch?"

"It will happen rather quickly."

"So, a few hours to complete the whole thing?"

"A matter of hours to take out the launch sites. But a day if we add the sites you were asking about earlier. The nuclear development sites. Perhaps two days."

"We'll get them all?"

"We'll get all or most of the missile launch sites," Porter corrected. "But we won't be able to take out all of the nuclear sites."

"Why not?"

"They've moved most of their development program underground. We know where most of them are located but I'm certain they have sites we don't know about. And even with the ordnance we have we won't be able to completely eliminate all of the underground sites that we hit."

"But they'll be damaged beyond immediate use?"

Porter nodded. "Yes, Mr. President. We can include the nuclear development sites in the targeting package but not on the first strike. They would work better as follow-up sites."

The furtive glances between Porter and Mattis had not gone unnoticed and Trump wanted to be certain the nuclear sites were included. "But you have a follow-up strike planned?" he asked to press the point.

"Yes, Mr. President."

"And you have targets already planned for the follow-up strikes?"

"To some degree. We know that we will hit these locations." Porter gestured to the map. "But we also will do bomb damage assessment to make sure we've disabled all of their known launch capability. That will require some additional strikes on these targets. When we do that, we can also hit the nuclear development sites, along with two chemical weapons sites and fourteen airfields, which are already on the list."

Haspel spoke up. "Mr. President, once we begin the attack we have to hit the most critical targets first. It is critical to Israel's safety that we prevent Iran from launching any missiles at all. It's the only way to ensure Israel's safety. To do that, we have to focus our attention on the missile launch sites."

"And while we're doing this, what would the Israelis do?" Trump asked. "Would they participate in this?"

"They would not participate in this strike," Admiral Porter explained. "In order to attack locations in Iran, they would have to use aircraft. It's a long way for them to fly and would require midair refueling along with permission to use neighboring air space. It's just too risky for them and for us. We need to hit Iran hard and quick with no advance warning."

"And the Israelis know this?"

"Yes, Mr. President," Porter replied. "We're coordinating with them to keep their focus on the Iranian ground forces approaching through Syria and Lebanon."

Haspel spoke up. "We've also detected some chatter about a threat from Gaza and the Sinai."

Trump frowned once more. "I thought the threat from Gaza had been dealt with."

"It was addressed earlier," Haspel explained. "This looks like a renewed effort."

"What is the threat from the Sinai?"

"ISIS," Mattis explained. "They have training camps there, and we're seeing some indication of increased activity."

"The Israelis know about that, too?" Trump asked.

"Yes, Mr. President," Porter replied. "We're in constant contact with them now."

"Ever since your earlier conversation with Prime Minister Netanyahu," Coats added. "The first call you made with him—in conjunction with Lieberman's visit to see Jim. We've been working together since then."

Trump nodded approvingly. "Good." He glanced down at a memo lying on the table at his place. *Operation Daniel*. He liked that name, remembering that Daniel was a figure from the Bible. He also liked the idea of striking Iran early, before they had a chance to attack Israel. After a moment for thought, Trump looked across the room to Porter. "Anything else, Admiral?"

"No, Mr. President. I think we've covered it."

"How long before you'll be ready to attack?"

"To put us in our best position, twenty-four hours. But we can be ready to go in twelve."

"Does that time frame still give us the ability to hit them before they can hit Israel?"

"Yes, Mr. President. Based on our estimates, they will be ready to launch in sixteen hours. We can be ready in twelve."

"Get everyone in position to execute the plan. And count on going in twelve hours. But don't go until I give the order."

"Yes, Mr. President."

✦ ✦ ✦

Not long after the Security Council meeting ended, Netanyahu phoned the White House. Trump took the call at his desk in the Oval Office.

"General Eizenkot has briefed me on our latest information," Netanyahu began. "He and our intelligence agencies agree with your assessment—that Iran is preparing a large-scale missile strike and that Israel is the target. Hezbollah is preparing to strike us as well."

"You've confirmed your intelligence from reliable sources?"

"We have drone images and reports from operatives on the ground."

"Any indication when they are likely to launch?" Trump asked.

"Based on what we know about their hardware," Netanyahu replied, "and the progress they've made so far in their preparations, our best guess is that they will be capable of launching an effective strike in about sixteen hours. Sources tell us that Iranian troops in Lebanon are preparing to speed up their move toward our border."

"That's what our people say, too," Trump concurred. "I have spoken with our National Security Council. Admiral Porter has a plan to launch a strike against Iran."

"How soon can you launch that strike?"

"We'll be ready to go in twelve hours. I understand our commanders are working together on this."

"Yes. They began to do that after our earlier conversation."

"Right. They also tell me that we will address the missile threat from sites within Iran while you address the threat from Syria and Lebanon."

"That is my understanding, too," Netanyahu replied.

"We're hearing chatter about increased activity in the Sinai, and in Gaza," Trump continued. "Have you heard anything about that?"

"No, but it would not surprise me. ISIS has camps in the Sinai, and Hamas is always ready to stir up the people of Gaza against us."

"You might want to ask our people about that. They can give you the details."

"I will pass that along."

"Okay, then," Trump replied. "We'll stay in touch."

✦ ✦ ✦

Later that same day, Admiral Porter appeared at the Oval office, where he met with President Trump, Jim Mattis, and John Kelly. "Mr. President, all of our assets are not yet in position to provide the optimal attack capability, but we've received intelligence that suggests the Iranians are preparing to begin launching missiles from their bases in Iran sometime in the next eighteen hours."

"You think we should go now?"

"Yes, Mr. President. I do."

Trump looked over at Mattis. "Jim, do you agree?"

"Yes, Mr. President, we need to begin Operation Daniel immediately."

"What about the Israelis? Have you coordinated this with them?"

"Yes. Lieberman insists we go now. He would have preferred we started earlier."

"I always thought of him as being reluctant for war."

"He is reluctant. We're all reluctant, Mr. President. He knows what's going to happen."

"What do you mean?"

"He knows that many of his people will die."

"I thought this was designed to prevent Israeli deaths."

"It is. But it can't prevent all of them. And that's the part that bothers all of us. He's doing his best. We're doing our best. They have as much support and help as they know they can get. And still, Lieberman knows some of his people will die."

"Then we should get on with it and make that number as few as possible."

"Yes, Mr. President."

Trump glanced in Kelly's direction. Kelly nodded his approval, then Trump looked back to Porter. "Okay, Admiral. You have the order. Begin Operation Daniel."

"May I use your phone?" Porter asked.

"Certainly."

Porter lifted the receiver on the Oval Office landline and placed a call. Moments later someone at the Pentagon answered and Porter said, "We have a go order on Operation Daniel. Start the clock."

When the meeting ended, President Trump once again telephoned Netanyahu and informed him about the operation.

"Yes," Netanyahu agreed. "We are very much aware of your pending operation and very much in favor of its execution at the earliest possible moment."

"Very well, we'll proceed and leave the operational details to our generals."

"As it should be."

✦ ✦ ✦

Shortly before midnight, US Air Force stealth bombers took off from a NATO base in Aviano, Italy. Four hours later, they slipped into Iranian air space and, before being detected, let loose a torrent of smart bombs on Iranian radar, communication, and command-and-control facilities. A second sortie followed close behind and cleaned up remaining sites, along with most of the fourteen airfields originally listed as secondary targets. Admiral Porter suggested the change in priority to limit the use of Iran's air force.

Not long after the second sortie completed its work, warships traveling with the USS *Forestall*—a ballistic-missile submarine, two guided-missile cruisers, and ten guided-missile destroyers of the Arleigh Burke class—by then entering the Gulf of Oman, launched a barrage of cruise missiles toward twenty of Iran's prime missile sites. The *Forestall* itself launched a dozen more cruise missiles as immediate follow-up.

While the cruise missiles streamed toward their targets, a fourth sortie of aircraft from the base at Aviano—this one including both stealth bombers, stealth fighters, and high-flying B-52s—dropped bunker-busting bombs on additional missile sites. As they were in the air, a fifth wave was being readied to attack airfields, chemical weapons facilities, and the most crucial sites in Iran's nuclear weapons development program.

✦ ✦ ✦

News of US missile strikes against Iran reached Prime Minister Netanyahu's office as soon as the planes left Aviano on the first bombing sortie. Bomb damage reports from that aerial attack were available shortly after the planes returned from the first run. Lieberman was with the prime minister when the results were delivered.

"Iran is powerless against the Americans," Netanyahu announced.

"This is only the beginning," Lieberman cautioned. "The first wave of cruise missiles and now the initial bombing attack. They still have far to go."

Netanyahu remained confident. "Whatever the Iranians do, it will come to nothing."

"Even so," Lieberman cautioned, "the threat remains from Hezbollah. And Iran has moved Zelzal missiles into the Beqaa Valley. They can reach any city in the country with those."

"What about Iranian troop movements?" Netanyahu asked.

"They're still advancing toward the border."

Netanyahu looked puzzled. "Without Iranian missiles to cover them?"

"They have thousands of missiles at their disposal from Hezbollah. In addition to the ones the Iranians have recently added to their own units."

"I am sure General Eizenkot is aware of this situation."

"Yes. IDF is planning preemptive strikes now, but I am not

certain we can make enough of a difference in time to avoid an attack on our cities."

"We knew that might happen."

"Yes."

"Anything else?" Netanyahu asked.

"We have reports of chatter about new action from Hamas and movement in the Sinai."

"The Sinai? I thought our neighbors were not showing any signs of aggression toward us."

"They aren't. This isn't Egypt. This is ISIS."

Netanyahu looked worried. "And no one anticipated they would be involved?"

"We saw no indication of activity from their camps."

"Is there a plan to do something about this?"

"We have contingency plans to reposition troops from Central Command to reinforce those in the south, should they be needed. General Eizenkot assures me they can be repositioned quickly. The stronger, more conventional threat is in the north."

"Keep me apprised."

An assistant appeared at the door. "The White House is on the line for you."

Netanyahu glanced at Lieberman. "I need to take this call."

"Very well," Lieberman replied as he turned toward the door. "Thank you, Mr. Prime Minister."

✦ ✦ ✦

Within hours of Lieberman's meeting with Netanyahu, Hezbollah launched a missile barrage from Lebanon, striking locations all across northern Israel. In Galilee, warning sirens wailed as Israelis took cover. The missiles hit Israeli troop positions near the border, but also struck northern Israeli cities. Damage was only moderate, but the disruption of daily life was complete.

In order to facilitate a heavy and sustained response, NSA provided the IDF with US satellite information and analysis from US battlefield management platforms that backtracked the missiles to specific locations. Using that information, IDF aircraft conducted multiple air strikes on Hezbollah positions from which the missiles had been launched. Precise information at that level allowed IDF to eliminate dozens of launchers and large stockpiles of weapons before they could be used.

Still, missiles continued to rain down on Haifa, Tiberias, Nazareth, and numerous communities in between—then the missiles began to fall on Tel Aviv. Rather than random explosions, like those experienced during the Gulf War when Iraq fired Scud missiles at Israel, these were precise attacks on specific targets—the HaKirya section of Tel Aviv, the Diamond Exchange District of the city, the defense ministry building—all of which sustained heavy damage.

General Eizenkot was in the command center, an underground bunker near IDF headquarters, when the attacks on Tel Aviv began. Built to withstand a direct hit from a nuclear bomb, it provided a safe and secure location from which to conduct a war while providing access to IDF regional command centers through video, telephone, and radio connections. Access to the world was facilitated through a secure Internet connection. Eizenkot had anticipated just such an attack and was prepared for it. Nevertheless, the need for constant bombing sorties strained IDF's capacity for quickly turning around aircraft. It also placed considerable stress on IDF pilots, many of whom never left the cockpit of their plane while undergoing refueling and reloading.

Unlike other officials, however, Netanyahu, had remained above ground at his office in Jerusalem. None of the missile attacks reached his location, or any other area of the city for that matter, and it was more convenient to work from his desk where he had access to information, notes, and files to which he was accustomed. No one seemed to be in immediate danger.

Still, the nature of the most recent round of missile attacks—their pinpoint accuracy and the strength of the weapons employed—left the prime minister's security detail in a quandary. Should they continue to man his regular office or move him to the bunker? Then, despite repeated attempts to shoot it down, a missile struck a joint IDF–NSA facility on Mount Scopus. Suddenly, the question of the prime minister's safety was no longer academic.

When news of the strike against Mount Scopus reached Shin Bet's security protection department—that aspect of the agency tasked with protecting the prime minister and other high-ranking officials—the prime minister's detail swung into action.

Miki Rozin, the agent in charge of Netanyahu's detail, gave the order. "Take him to the bunker."

Moments later, the door to the prime minister's office opened and six Shin Bet agents entered the room. Rozin was with them. "It's time to go, Mr. Prime Minister."

"I heard the explosion, but I don't want to leave just yet. I still have—"

Rozin nodded to the agents. Two of them stepped forward and took Netanyahu by either arm. "You're going," Rozin said grimly. "We can do it the easy way, or the hard way."

Netanyahu's assistant appeared. "You have no choice," she said. "You can direct the war from there."

"But everything I need is right here," Netanyahu protested.

Suddenly a missile struck a few blocks away. The building shook and windows rattled. The two agents standing with Netanyahu hustled him toward the door.

"What was that?" Netanyahu asked.

"Zelzals," Rozin replied. "Zelzal-3, to be specific, Mr. Prime Minister."

"Can't our defenses take them out?"

"They're doing their best. But the Patriot system isn't one hundred percent effective."

In the hall, Rozin led the way to a stairwell. "We'll go this way, in case the building takes a direct hit."

"They would never do such a thing," Netanyahu scoffed. "They value the city as much as we do."

"These are Iranian missiles," someone said. "They can hit us without hitting everything else."

Just then, another missile struck, this one even closer than the last. Rozin shouted, "Hurry! We've no time to waste."

✦ ✦ ✦

Meanwhile, aboard the USS *John F. Kennedy*, lying one hundred miles off the Israeli coast, Rear Admiral Bill Agee stood in the carrier's command center with his weapons assistant and studied the latest reports from the recent strikes in Iran. "These missiles are coming from sites inside Iran?"

"Yes, sir."

"Forward this information to the group and tell them to prepare cruise missiles for launch. Tell logistics to prepare targeting packages for each of these sites. When their sites go active for a launch, I want our missiles to take them out."

"Yes, sir. Do we need to coordinate with the *Forrestal*?"

"Yes," Agee replied. "Notify them that we intend to launch when ready and keep them in the loop going forward. This is an ongoing operation."

"Yes, sir. Do we need any other authorization?"

Agee frowned. "Authorization?"

"To engage the Iranians on this basis."

"Son, the rules of engagement say we are to 'engage and destroy,' and that's just what I intend to do."

"Aye, aye, Admiral."

In spite of wave after wave of counterstrikes from Admiral Agee's forces, Iranian missiles continued to strike Israeli targets. Even the Patriot and other anti-missile batteries couldn't keep all of them from reaching key Israeli locations.

"Nothing will stop this but a ground offensive," General Eizenkot fumed.

At his command, IDF troops, which already were amassed on the northern border, crossed into Lebanon and the Golan Heights to take up the fight on the ground. By the afternoon of the following day, major battles raged along a front that ran from Tyre on the Mediterranean coast to Mount Hermon near the Lebanese border with Syria. Pitched battles ensued along the eastern side of the Golan Heights where Iranian units had attacked from their strongholds in Syria.

Disruption brought about by advancing IDF troops, along with repeated waves of cruise-missile strikes from the *John F. Kennedy* carrier group, brought a lull in the long-range-missile strikes against central and southern Israel. As those missile attacks dwindled, US aircraft operating from the deck of the *John F. Kennedy* joined IDF aircraft flying from bases in southern Israel to execute coordinated air strikes against Hezbollah and Iranian troop positions in Syria and Lebanon. Those attacks slowed, but did not halt the advance of Iranian troops toward the front where fighting raged.

CHAPTER
28

WHILE FIGHTING continued near Israel's northern border, ISIS units rolled out of the Sinai, crossed the Israeli border near Ezuz, and swept northward, opening a southern front in the war. Advancing rapidly, they burned and pillaged their way through villages and communities that lay before them, commandeering trucks and other equipment along the way. Very quickly, they advanced beyond Sde Boker and bore down on Beersheba. Dimona, site of a key Israeli nuclear reactor crucial to its own nuclear development program, was suddenly in peril.

At the same time, to the west of that initial thrust, additional ISIS units crossed the border from Egypt near the Mediterranean coast and stormed the Kerem Shalom Crossing on the Gaza barrier. With little difficulty, they overwhelmed IDF units that manned the crossing and entered Gaza. Their arrival and success in overrunning the checkpoint incited Palestinians in southern Gaza to join them.

Eager to make amends for the collapse of the earlier border protest, which he felt was at least partially his fault, Mohammed Khalafi rallied his group of Hamas operatives at the house in Umm al-Kilab and urged them to join the ISIS effort.

Ibrahim Atweh was skeptical. "What can we do? We tried before, but failed."

"I agree," Hisham Shomali added. "ISIS is on its own."

"No," Jabra Shahid spoke up. "We can't let this opportunity pass us by."

"What opportunity?" Atweh asked.

"ISIS has the muscle we need," Shahid argued. "Did you not see what they did in Iraq?"

"That was Iraq," Shomali countered. "This is Gaza."

"How is it different here?" Shahid asked.

"In Iraq," Atweh explained, "the Americans spread weapons everywhere. All ISIS had to do was overrun a few Iraqi army units and they could have any weapon they wanted. Here we have no weapons to take."

"We have *some*," Khalafi argued. "We are not completely defenseless."

"I appreciate that," Atweh responded in a conciliatory tone. "But we have no one from whom to steal the weapons we need, as ISIS did in Iraq. They will fail here, just as we failed." He looked down at the floor and lowered his voice. "I do not want to die in a failing effort."

The group fell silent for a moment, then Samir Jubran spoke up, "I don't want to go on living in a failed country, either. And the only way we can change that is to die for our country. If we are willing to die for the freedom we say we cherish, then perhaps we can win that freedom."

"Dying to live?" Atweh chuckled.

"Yes," Jubran replied. "Exactly that." He had an intense look in his eyes and his voice was firm and forceful. "The ones who are willing to die for their cause, and keep dying no matter how many times it takes, are the ones who can win." He looked at each of them. "Shahid is right. We cannot allow this opportunity to pass without taking full advantage of it. But it is a moment that will require all that we have. Even our very lives."

No one responded at first, then Atweh asked sarcastically, "And just how do you propose that we die and keep on dying?"

Jubran ignored the tone of his voice and looked over at Khalafi. "You still have the pickup truck?"

Khalafi nodded slowly. "Of course."

Jubran continued. "If we ram the pickup truck into the fence at a vulnerable location—beside the gate, or somewhere other than at the crossing—we can rip open a space wide enough for some of us to get through."

Atweh shook his head. "And when the patrols see us coming and are waiting for us on the other side?"

"That is not a problem. All we need to do is overpower one soldier—just one—and get one of his weapons. Then we use that weapon to shoot two more. We get their weapons and then we shoot two more each. And we keep going until we have killed them all. That is how ISIS does it. That's how we can do it, too."

"And many of us will die," Shomali added in a dismissive voice.

"Yes," Jubran acknowledged. "The first through the opening will die. But the ones coming after them will reach the soldiers. And the ones after them will kill a few. And the ones after them will kill many more."

"But we will die doing it," Shomali argued.

"Yes," Jubran replied. "We will die. All of us will die. But some of the soldiers will die, too. Then the ones of us coming next will pick up those weapons and more soldiers will die. And we will keep coming and dying until all of them are dead, even if it means all of us die in the process."

Shomali seemed to consider the idea. "And freedom from this hellish life will live from that?"

Jubran smiled. "It is the only way *freedom* will live."

"I know where we can find some explosives," Khalafi intoned in a deadpan voice. "That would make it much easier to open a way through the fence." Those in the room turned to look at him, waiting for him to say more. "Al-Qassam has it in a storage building in Al Zahra. Near the university."

Atweh frowned. "How do you know this?"

Khalafi shrugged. "I just know."

"And where did this explosives cache come from?"

"They harvested it from unexploded Israeli bombs," Khalafi explained.

Atweh's mouth fell open in a look of realization. "Not all the bombs exploded."

Khalafi explained. "Not every bomb they drop on us explodes. Not every grenade. Not every missile. Cluster bombs spread hundreds of small explosive charges over a wide area. Not all of them detonate. Al-Qassam has a crew that collects them and another that dismantles them and removes the explosives."

"And you know where they keep it?" Jubran asked. "You know the location of this storage building?"

"Yes," Khalafi replied. "I know the location."

"But how would we use it?" Shomali asked.

Before anyone else could answer, Jubran answered, "We load it into the pickup truck. Drive it into the fence. Detonate it on impact."

"But how do we detonate it?" Atweh asked.

"With a grenade. As I said before, I still have a few left."

Jubran grinned. "This might work."

"Yeah," Shomali acknowledged. "It might work. But there's just one problem."

"What's that?" Atweh asked.

"We have to get the explosives out of the storage building."

Khalafi smiled. "I think we can take care of that."

✦ ✦ ✦

An hour after sundown, Khalafi took Shahid and Jubran with him in the pickup truck and drove north, toward Al Zahra, a municipality in the Gaza Strip located a few kilometers south of Gaza City. The trip was not as easy as it sounded. Already the region was in disarray from the arrival of ISIS, and a rivalry was in play between Hamas and ISIS for control of the minds and hearts of Gazans. A physical confrontation between ISIS and members of Al-Qassam Brigades was not yet out of the question. Because of that, Khalafi took care to follow a route that avoided neighborhoods he knew to be brimming with unrest. Doing that added time to the trip but several hours later they succeeded in reaching the storage building where the explosives were kept.

As the truck came to a stop near the building, Shahid asked, "How did you know about this place?"

"My friend Nabil Bahour worked with the recovery crew a short time. Until he lost a leg in an explosion." Khalafi glanced in Shahid's direction. "Do you know him?"

"No."

"Removing explosive charges from unexploded artillery shells is dangerous work," Jubran commented. "Your friend isn't the only one to lose a limb in the process."

No one picked up on Jubran's comment and they climbed from the truck in silence. The building was guarded by only a few strands of barbed wire and they made their way inside without difficulty.

Once inside, Khalafi pulled a flashlight from his pocket and flipped the switch to turn it on. A faint beam appeared and he shined it to where the light fell on three plastic buckets.

Shahid stepped closer for a better look and found the buckets contained a granular substance that was gray in color. "What is that?" he asked, pointing to the buckets.

Khalafi came to his side. "This is the explosive charge from the shells."

"It won't explode like that," Jubran noted.

"Why not?"

"It has to be confined to explode."

Khalafi pointed across the room. "We could always use that," he suggested. "I think it would explode under the right conditions." He shined the beam of the flashlight on a pile of artillery shells, mortar rounds, and RPGs that stood on the opposite side of the room, apparently awaiting disassembly.

"Why do they bother taking it apart?" Shahid asked. "Why not just shoot it back at the Jews like it is?"

"We have no way of firing most of it." Khalafi walked over to the pile. "But what if we loaded these in the truck." He pointed across the room. "With those plastic buckets in the middle. Then we drop a grenade in one of the buckets and detonate the whole load."

Shahid glanced over at Jubran. "Will they explode like that?"

"I don't know," Jubran replied. "They'll explode if we drop them on the end. Most of the artillery and mortar shells that don't detonate fail to do so because they didn't hit correctly. They have to hit at the right angle or the fuse on the end won't set off the primer."

"You seem to know a lot about this," Khalafi noted.

Jubran did not look in his direction. "My cousin worked in one of these places."

Khalafi raised an eyebrow. "One of?"

"They have several. The Israelis dropped a lot of shells on us. There's unexploded stuff everywhere."

"Did your cousin survive?"

"No," Jubran replied. "He died. All who work in these places eventually die. The ones like your friend who lose a leg or an arm are the blessed ones. They get the honor of the work, plus the honor of the injury."

Shahid stood up straight, as if at attention. "And the honor of others who see them and know what happened. As do we now."

"They are blessed three times over," Khalafi added in a reverent tone.

With great care, they succeeded in loading the unexploded ordnance into the back of the pickup truck, along with the three plastic buckets that contained raw explosive material. A canvas tarp lay on the ground near the pile of unspent shells and they used it to cover the load, then climbed in the cab for the return trip.

"Maybe you should drive slowly," Jubran cautioned. "We don't want to rattle those shells too much." The others laughed but Khalafi slowed the truck and did his best to avoid potholes, of which there were many in Gaza.

✦ ✦ ✦

The next day, Khalafi and the others who had been with him in the earlier border protest spent the morning rallying a crowd to storm the border fence. Not many were interested in a repeat of what had happened before, but when Khalafi began suggesting ISIS might join them, the residents of Umm al-Kilab grew curious. After several hours spent going from house to house, Khalafi and his men succeeded in badgering another hundred to participate. Not exactly the crowd Jubran had envisioned but it was better than nothing.

Khalafi and the others tried a little longer to convince more people to join them but finally there was no more time to wait. The crowd, such as it was, was getting nervous and Khalafi knew they had to go now or abandon the plan. He brought the pickup around to the front of the house and peeled away the tarp. "Okay," he shouted. "Who's driving?"

Everyone became quiet and still and stood with their eyes focused on the ground, then Jubran stepped up. "Give me the keys," he said. "This was my idea. I'll drive." He took the keys to the truck from Khalafi, then glanced around at the group expectantly. "Who wants to ride in back and detonate the grenade?"

As before, no one replied and once again stared at the ground, then Atweh stepped toward the rear bumper of the truck. "I'll do it." He swung a leg over the tailgate and climbed into the back of the truck. When he was in place, he leaned over the side and thrust his hand toward Khalafi. "Give me the grenade." Khalafi opened the driver's door of the cab, took a grenade from the front seat, and handed it to him. Atweh took a seat on the floor of the truck bed, an arm's length from the buckets. "Let's go. We have work to do."

Jubran took a seat behind the steering wheel, closed the driver's door of the truck, and started the engine. As it came to life, he glanced out the window toward Khalafi with a grin. "Tell my family I love them and make sure you get the crowd to follow."

"We will," Khalafi promised.

Jubran backed the truck to the street and steered it toward the road that led to the border fence. He drove slowly, giving the crowd time to follow, but as he made the turn onto the road he noticed they were not yet moving in his direction. He pressed the brake pedal and brought the truck to a stop, waiting to see what would happen next.

A moment passed. Then a moment more. "Let's go," Atweh called out. "We can't just sit here with a load like this."

Jubran gestured out the window. "I'm waiting for them."

Atweh turned to look behind them. "I think they're coming now."

Jubran glanced in the rearview mirror again and saw Khalafi leading the group from the house up the street toward where he'd stopped the truck. Assured they would follow, he lifted his foot from the brake pedal and once again the truck started forward.

Twenty minutes later, the group still was not halfway to the fence. In the distance, Jubran noticed activity on the Israeli side of the barrier and he became worried that he and the others had been spotted. "If they've seen us," he mumbled, "we'll be under fire soon."

Jubran was about to break off the effort and head in the opposite direction when two Humvees appeared in the rearview mirror. From the cloud of dust that rose behind them, he was certain the vehicles were traveling fast. Within moments, the Humvees overtook the crowd of people traveling on foot and closed in on the pickup truck. As they grew closer, he saw that the vehicles bore the insignia of the Egyptian Army. "Egyptians? They've never been in Gaza before. The Israelis won't allow it. At least, not any farther than the area at the checkpoint."

Instinctively, Jubran pressed the gas pedal and the pickup truck moved faster but it was no match for the Humvees and minutes later they came alongside the pickup. Jubran was unsure if they meant to stop him or shoot him, but then the window of the first Humvee lowered and a man leaned out the window. Through the open window Jubran could see the passenger held an ISIS flag. He gestured with it and then waved with his arm out the window for Jubran to join them, motioning for Jubran to take the lead. That's when Jubran realized the men in the Humvee were from ISIS. He acknowledged them with a smile and wave, then both

Humvees dropped in line behind him.

Soon, Jubran and Atweh were traveling at the truck's top speed and in the rearview mirror he saw there now were six Humvees behind him. At first he was excited to know that ISIS was joining them. "At last!" he shouted. "We have the chance to succeed." But in the next moment he thought of the great cloud of dust boiling up behind them now and fear struck at his heart. "This isn't good," he said to himself. "The Israelis will see us for sure and they will attack us at any moment."

Just then, a helicopter appeared before him. Traveling just above the ground, it popped up from behind the barrier and came straight down the road. Jubran held his position with the Humvees lined up behind him, but his eyes were wide with fear and his hands gripped the steering wheel tightly.

Suddenly, tufts of dust appeared on the road ahead of him and though he could not hear the sound he knew the pilot of the helicopter was shooting at him. Fifty-caliber bullets. Shells, actually. As big as his fist. Capable of plowing through the truck's engine. If one struck him, it would rip his body in half.

Jubran waited until the bullets were almost to him, then, at the last possible moment, he jerked the steering wheel to the right. The helicopter reacted as well but by the time it did, it was directly over the Humvees, and Jubran was almost to the barrier fence.

Behind him, Jubran heard the thump of the helicopter's rotor and the scream of its jet engine as it circled around for another shot at him and the Humvees that had followed him from the road and now were barreling toward the barrier fence. Any moment now, he would feel the jolt of the bullets as they struck the truck from behind. If they hit the cargo he was carrying, they all would be flying through the air in seconds. Jubran shook his head in an attempt to push those thoughts from his mind and concentrated on the fence that now was only a hundred meters away.

Around him, Jubran was surrounded by noise. The roar of the truck's engine. The thump of the helicopter. And now he heard the report of gunfire, some of it heavy, some of it light. "They're shooting at the helicopter!" he screamed. "That is why the helicopter hasn't taken me out yet." But he knew they would. They must. No matter how much the men in the Humvees did to protect him, the pilot of the helicopter had to stop them from reaching the fence and the only way to do that was to stop the truck.

Jubran clinched his teeth. "But maybe I can make it," he shoved his foot against the gas pedal with all his might. "Come on," he growled. "You can do it. Just a little more. Just a little more." The fence was now only fifty meters away. Then twenty-five. Then ten.

At the last moment, Jubran let go of the steering wheel and covered his face with his arms, shouting at the top of his voice, "Allah Akbar!" In the same moment, Atweh dropped the grenade in the bucket and the truck crashed into the fence.

The nose of the pickup truck plunged downward as the truck came to an arresting halt against the fence. Jubran's body, still traveling at top speed, shot forward, slamming his chest against the steering wheel so hard the steering column snapped in half. Blood splattered across the dash. Jubran's body continued forward and his head collided with the windshield, then crashed through it. Searing pain shot down his neck and into both legs.

Jubran sailed over the hood of the truck in silence and he wondered if the grenade had failed to work. Had it all been in vain? Had he sacrificed his life for nothing? Had they all been tricked by Khalafi? Were they really—then the seat from the truck flew past him and flames more intense than he'd ever known engulfed him. And then everything simply disappeared.

✦ ✦ ✦

Still three hundred meters away, Khalafi watched from the road as the pickup truck collided with the fence. He saw the rear wheels of the truck rise up from the ground, saw Atweh in the back as he dropped the grenade into one of the plastic buckets, then saw him as he sailed over the cab of the truck. Khalafi stopped and waited, but nothing happened and a sinking feeling came over him as he wondered if the plan had failed. Had his friends given their lives for nothing? Had they been duped by Al-Hadi? Had they been told lies by Hamas? Were they all going to die right there on the—

Suddenly, the truck erupted in a huge fireball. In the same instance, sheets of fencing and the posts that once held it in place flew out from the explosion in every direction. From overhead, the IDF helicopter took out three of the Humvees but the three that remained plowed headlong into the flames and smoke. By the time the sound of the explosion reached Khalafi's position, the Humvees were obscured by thick black smoke that billowed from the pickup.

"It worked!" Khalafi shouted. "It really worked!" And he found it impossible to suppress the triumphant grin that spread across his face.

After a moment, Khalafi turned to the crowd behind him. "Come on! Let's go!" He waved with his arm to encourage them forward. "All the way to Jerusalem!" The crowd responded and surged toward the fence.

As Jubran had predicted, Israeli soldiers on the other side of the fence fired at them but already a dozen lay dead from the attack by ISIS in the Humvees. Members of the crowd who moved through the gap in the fence paused to pick up the weapons the fallen soldiers left behind, then turned those weapons on the soldiers who'd dug in to defend the border.

Overhead, the helicopter circled back once more and opened fire on the crowd, but they ignored the gunfire from the helicopter's cannon and continued forward anyway. Khalafi, however, held back and made his way around to the driver's side of the pickup. He shielded his face from the heat with his hand and peered through the opening where the door had been. Through it he saw nothing but the twisted hulk of the truck's frame. Nothing remained of Jubran and Atweh except the overwhelming sensation that they were gone.

✦ ✦ ✦

As news of the barrier breach at Sufa spread, thousands of Gazans rallied to the cause and flooded through the opening created by Jubran and Atweh. Additional units from ISIS responded, too, and poured through the gap, bringing with them firearms, rockets, and mortars.

IDF units on the Israeli side defended the border with a fighting retreat—fight and fall back, fight and fall back—using it as a stalling tactic while calling for additional reinforcements. As a result, hundreds of civilians—most of them from Umm al-Kilab and surrounding communities—were killed in the process, as were almost a hundred IDF soldiers. And still people from Gaza kept coming.

Nor was fighting along the border confined to the area around Sufa. Intense fighting raged up and down the border fence as those who lived near the other crossing points adopted the same strategy as Khalafi, Jubran, and Atweh—ram the fence with a vehicle and sacrifice their bodies to the Palestinian cause, then charge across and scavenge weapons from IDF casualties. Other groups of Gazans did not have the advantage of explosives, but the group near the Erez Crossing had access to larger and heavier trucks, which they used with great success. Drivers crashed the trucks into the fence with enough force to tear a small opening, allowing thousands more to force their way through the fence. The tactic worked so well, ISIS had trouble keeping up.

When initial reports of the border attacks reached General Eizenkot at the underground IDF command center, neither he nor his staff was overly concerned. "We heard this might happen. Direct our regional commanders to respond as necessary," he ordered

Regional commanders in charge of the Central and Southern Commands did as ordered and directed additional units to the Gaza and Egyptian borders, respectively. But with thousands pushing through gaps in the border fence, and with organized, trained, and equipped ISIS units rolling up from the Sinai into southern Israel, conventional ground troops were pushed to the point of being overwhelmed.

After five days of pitched battles, General Matan Neubach of the Southern Command, called for air strikes. In response, F-15 Eagles from the base at Hatzerim responded with close air support, using bombs and missiles to destroy ISIS vehicles, then strafing the stranded ISIS fighters with their fifty-caliber cannon. The resulting human carnage was awful but unavoidable.

Along the Gaza border, General Assi Sagall of Central Command employed a similar tactic, deploying helicopter gunships to attack Gazans as they approached the barrier fence from the Gaza side. The attacks left hundreds dead but had the desired effect of stopping the surge toward the border. With the surge stymied from the Gaza side, armored IDF units operating on the Israeli side of the fence positioned tanks and other armored vehicles to block the gaps. Once the holes in the barrier were plugged, helicopter gunships turned on the ISIS and Palestinian fighters trapped on the Israeli side of the fence.

AWACS planes operated by the US Air Force, along with US battlefield management capabilities, proved useful in both efforts. Ten more days of fighting followed, but at last IDF units in central and southern Israel turned back the threat from Hamas in the west and ISIS in the south. Establishing order and control cost thousands of lives, mostly among Palestinians groups who attacked from Gaza and ISIS units that came up from the Sinai.

✦ ✦ ✦

Six weeks after the United States launched its offensive to eliminate Iran's offensive missile capability, IDF troops succeeded in routing Iranian ground forces from southern Lebanon and turning back the attacks from the Syrian side against the Golan Heights. Cut off from resupply and reinforcement by US interdiction, most of the Iranian units were depleted beyond fighting strength. Almost all of Hezbollah's rockets had been either launched or destroyed.

After order was restored, Trump and Netanyahu conducted a joint tele-press conference by satellite—Trump at the White House in Washington, Netanyahu at a communications center in the Israeli ministry of defense building in Tel Aviv.

"Today," Trump announced for the joint US network and Israeli cameras, "we have successfully concluded our joint US–Israeli mission to defend the sovereign integrity of the nation of

Israel and rid the Middle East of the threat posed by an armed and belligerent Iran. Our success came through the hard work and sacrifice of the men and women of the Israel Defense Forces and the United States military. We're both very proud of the discipline, courage, and bravery our fighting men and women showed."

Netanyahu responded, "On behalf of the Israeli people, I would like to thank our American ally for their willingness to step forward and defend the Israeli people against Iranian aggression. When our forebears declared Israel's independence, the United States stepped forward as our very first ally. They have remained our ally ever since and we are deeply grateful for their commitment to law, order, and the protection of sovereignty here and throughout the world. They are, indeed, the best hope among the nations.

"As they have in the past, the men and women of the Israel Defense Forces proved once again why they are known around the world as one of the best and bravest fighting forces history has ever produced. Through their diligence in the face of great adversity, our people have remained safe, secure, and free of tyranny."

The joint conference continued for almost an hour as reporters peppered both leaders with questions. To their credit, Netanyahu and Trump stayed on the satellite hookup until every question was answered. When the event finally concluded, both men were exhausted.

CHAPTER
29

WHEN THE US HAD BEGUN its attack on Iranian missiles sites, Yaakov Auerbach was at the Shin Bet office in Beersheba. He remained there throughout the conflict, living and working from the operations center alongside Elon Harel and most of the other staff and agents. When ISIS came up from the Sinai and crossed the border into Israel, Auerbach was concerned about his family's safety, but he monitored the situation and was never in doubt IDF would succeed in turning back the threat.

While keeping an eye on the situation with ISIS, Auerbach, Harel, and their fellow Shin Bet agents continued to work on uncovering the full extent of the plot behind the attack in Jerusalem. As a result, they succeeded in locating Masalha—the Arab teacher who organized the children for the Jerusalem attack—whom they found hiding in an apartment in Arad, near the border with Jordan. As fighting with Iran, Hamas, and ISIS came to an end, Masalha was in custody and held at a facility adjacent to Shin Bet's office in Beersheba.

At first Masalha refused to cooperate, but after lengthy interrogation and coaxed by the hint of an offer of punishment less than the death penalty, he began to talk. In bits and pieces, he divulged the details of the planning and organization for the attack, including information about Rajabian that confirmed he really was an Iranian operative and that he was the one responsible for coordinating the attack in Jerusalem with the earlier attempts to protest and attack at the border crossings. "He tried to make those occur at the same time, but I do not think he was successful."

"You don't think?"

"No. I don't think he was. We did our part, but after that, you guys showed up and I have not learned the details of what happened after that, but it is my understanding those events did not go off as planned. Rajabian was good with ideas. He was not so good with getting them done."

Auerbach and Harel participated in the interrogation sessions, but not all of them. Other agents helped, too, rotating the sessions between teams of two in a way that kept fresh agents in the room at all times. That meant the interrogations were long and tiring for Masalha, but not so long and not so tiring for the agents. In this way, they hoped to maintain an advantage that forced him to participate at his weakest and allowed Shin Bet to participate at its strongest.

When Auerbach was not in the room with Masalha, he often watched from an adjoining room through one-way glass that afforded a view of the interrogation while obscuring his presence. An intercom speaker on the wall provided an audio feed. As he stood in the room, watching the end of a session and in preparation for his next turn at Masalha, he thought of an exchange he'd had with Masud Darwaza, the Palestinian informant who had been one of the first to suggest that a new kind of Iranian operative was present in Gaza. Pressing Darwaza for detailed information about the matter had gotten him killed. Auerbach wondered if Masalha knew anything about that.

Just then, the door opened and he was joined by Harel. "You ready to take our turn?"

"Yeah," Auerbach replied. "But I want to ask him about something else." Auerbach reached for the door. "Wait for me. Don't go in there until I get back."

The earlier session ended and the interrogators left the room, expecting to find Auerbach and Harel waiting to take their place. They found only Harel. "You're by yourself?" one of them asked.

"He'll be along in a minute."

"Don't let him sit too long. The point of all this is to keep the pressure on."

"And it's worked," the other chimed in. "We got some good stuff this time." Harel nodded but did not respond.

A few minutes later, Auerbach returned carrying a manila envelope. "Okay. We can go in now." He opened the door to the interrogation room and led the way inside.

The room was sparsely furnished with nothing on the walls except a coat of gray paint. Light came from a single fixture suspended from the ceiling directly over a plain black table that stood in the center of the room. Masalha was seated on one side, his back to the wall opposite the door. Auerbach and Harel were seated across from him.

Auerbach opened the envelope and took out a photograph of Darwaza. It was an older image and Darwaza appeared much younger than when he'd died, but Auerbach was certain it would be sufficient to identify him. He placed the picture on the table in front of Masalha and pointed to it. "Do you recognize this man?"

Masalha glanced at the photo and shook his head. "No, I have never seen him before."

"Are you certain you don't know him?"

"As I said," Masalha repeated, "I have never see him before."

Auerbach reached inside the envelope once more and produced a second photograph, this one recovered from Shammas's apartment on Cyprus. The picture was of Shammas standing with Khalafi, a known Hamas operative but someone Shin Bet had not been able to locate. Auerbach pointed to Shammas. "What about this man? Do you recognize him?"

Masalha smiled. "If you have that picture, then you already know I am acquainted with Shammas."

"How do you know him?"

"We were friends in school." Masalha leaned forward for a closer look at the image. "How did you obtain this picture?"

Auerbach avoided the question and pointed again to the photograph. "What about this man?" He tapped the image of the man standing next to Shammas. "Who is he?"

Masalha shrugged. "A friend of Shammas, I suppose."

"You recognized the picture," Auerbach insisted. "It meant something to you. That's why you asked me about how I came to have it." He glared at Masalha. "You know Shammas. And you know the person standing next to him in this picture. Tell me who he is."

Masalha sighed. "Mr. Auerbach, you are asking me things you already know. You and all of your fellow agents. You come in here with your documents and photographs and questions as if you are on a quest for the truth. But the questions you ask me are questions to which you already know the answers."

"I know what I know," Auerbach responded. "Tell me what *you* know."

"Okay," Masalha snarled. "I know the man."

"And what is his name?"

"Khalafi." Masalha gave an exasperated sigh. "His name is Mohammed Khalafi."

"And how did you come to know him?"

"Through Shammas."

"And how did Shammas know him?"

"Shammas and Khalafi are cousins." Masalha leaned back in his chair. "You already know these things. Why do you ask me about them?"

"You know that Khalafi is a member of Al-Qassam."

"Of course. As you yourself already know. Khalafi is the one who introduced me to all of this."

"All of what?"

"The resistance. The Palestinian cause."

"How did you meet him?"

"We met on several occasions while Shammas and I were in school. He came to London to see Shammas. We went out to the clubs together. That sort of thing."

"So, Khalafi worked with you before Rajabian."

"Yes," Masalha admitted. "Long before."

"What was Khalafi's involvement with the protests in Gaza at the border crossings?"

Masalha had a questioning expression. "The most recent ones with the trucks ramming the fence and our people crossing to freedom?"

"Yes."

"I do not know."

"What about the earlier protests?"

Masalha smiled in an arrogant expression. "All of them?"

"You know what I mean." There was a hint of impatience in Auerbach's voice. "The one before the last one."

"There is no last one," Masalha snapped. "Only the most

recent one. And the one before that, I do not know of Khalafi's involvement. Though knowing him as I do, it is difficult to imagine that he was not involved."

"What was Khalafi's involvement with you and the attack in Jerusalem?"

Masalha shook his head. "Khalafi was not involved with me in that at all."

Harel spoke up. "You expect us to believe that?"

"You are, of course, free to believe whatever you wish. But I suspect you already know that Khalafi and I have had no contact since Rajabian arrived. After Rajabian contacted me, I dealt solely with him. He told me I should know as little as possible about the other operations. So I did not ask about anything or anyone else."

Harel pressed the point. "But you knew Khalafi and others in Gaza were attempting to organize protests at the border crossings."

"Of course."

"And how did you know that?"

"Because our event was to coincide with theirs. But that is all I knew. Only that they were to happen. Not anything about how they would come to pass."

Auerbach took up the questioning. "If you wanted to find Khalafi, where would you look first?"

"In Gaza."

"Where in Gaza?"

Masalha stared at him a moment. "Are you really going to

offer me something other than execution?" he asked finally.

Auerbach shook his head. "An offer is not up to me. But I can assure you of one thing."

"And what is that?"

"Unless you cooperate with us, you'll have no hope of living."

Masalha sat quietly. After what seemed like a long time, he shifted positions in his chair. "Khalafi has a place. One of those metal cargo containers. Where he keeps things that he does not want anyone to know about."

"How do you know about it?"

"His cousin—Shammas—told me about it."

"Where is it?"

"As I said, it is in Gaza."

"You've been to Gaza?"

Masalha replied. "No, but Shammas has been to it. He followed Khalafi there once."

"Can you tell me where it is?"

"Shammas said it is by the sea. Near Khan Yunis. You know the place?"

"Where in Khan Yunis?"

"By the sea," Masalha repeated. "That is all I know."

✦ ✦ ✦

A few weeks later, Ismail Yassin, a Shin Bet informant, walked into Café Jabalia, a coffee shop in Gaza City. Two men sat at a table in back. Yassin recognized them both immediately. The one on the left was Hossein Rajabian, wanted by Shin Bet for his part in the attempted Sarin gas attack in Jerusalem. Seated across from him was Abdullah Al-Hadi. Everyone in Gaza knew Al-Hadi by sight, though no one would admit he even existed.

Yassin took a seat near a window and faced the opposite side of the room. A few minutes later he was joined by a friend. While they sipped coffee and chatted, Yassin used his smartphone to capture images of Rajabian and Al-Hadi, doing his best to seem casual and nonchalant to avoid raising anyone's suspicions.

That evening in his one-room apartment, Yassin connected his phone to a laptop and, using a VoIP connection to mask his identity, sent the images to a contact at the Shin Bet office in Jerusalem.

The message was received by Yoram Imry, the Shin Bet agent who had worked on the Jerusalem investigation after the bomb maker's house exploded. He reviewed the photographs from Yassin, realized how important they were, and referred the matter to Noga Milgrom, Auerbach's supervisor who also managed the office at Beersheba. "I thought you'd want to see these," Imry related. "I think you still have the lead on the Masalha/Rajabian investigation."

After only a glance at the information, Milgrom contacted Nadav Argaman, Shin Bet's director. They met at Argaman's office and reviewed the matter.

"Normally, I would send this through channels," Milgrom began. "But time is of the essence."

"Yes," Argaman acknowledged. "If we're going to do anything, we need to do it quickly." He looked at the pictures once more, than turned to Milgrom. "So, what did you have in mind?"

"I realize that under normal conditions we would stay out of Gaza. But these aren't normal conditions."

"These are not."

"Rajabian participated in a plan to destroy our nation," Milgrom continued. "We know where he is. We can't allow him to slip away."

"You are thinking of a wet team." It was a statement, not a question.

Milgrom nodded. "Do you need a memo for it?"

Argaman shook his head. "The less paperwork on this, the better."

"I'll see to it." Milgrom stood and turned toward the door to leave.

Argaman called after him, "Do you think Auerbach would be suitable for this?"

"If he finds out about it, we'll have a difficult time holding him back."

"As I suspected." Argaman smiled. "Add Auerbach to the team."

"He's not been on one of these in a while."

"Send him anyway. He can help with the identification. Not much time to plan and practice. Might be helpful to have someone like him."

When Milgrom returned to Beersheba, he called Auerbach to his office. He was seated at his desk when Auerbach entered the room. "What's this about?" Auerbach asked as he closed the door.

Milgrom pointed to a chair on the opposite side of the desk and when Auerbach was seated explained, "We have a tip on Rajabian."

Auerbach's eyes opened wide. "Great." He scooted forward to the edge of the seat. "Where is he?"

"Gaza."

"That's a big place. Anything more particular than that?"

"Gaza City. Apparently, he's been meeting with Abdullah Al-Hadi." Milgrom showed him the photographs they'd received of the two men at the coffee shop.

"Any plans to get him?"

"We have a team preparing for it now," Milgrom answered.

"They're going to Gaza?"

Milgrom smiled. "Care to join them?"

Instinctively, Auerbach stood, as if ready to leave right then. "You know I would," he blurted. "When do we leave?"

"Sit down," Milgrom gestured to the chair again. "This could be a dangerous mission."

"I know." Auerbach took a seat once more. "But things are always dangerous for us. That's what we do."

"But things have changed for you," Milgrom noted. "It's not like it used to be."

Auerbach frowned. "What do you mean?"

"You have a wife and children now."

"I know. But they understand this is what I do." Auerbach leaned toward Milgrom and lowered his voice. "Look, I've worked a long time on this case. We found Masalha. We took care of his contacts on Cyprus. The only piece we're missing is Rajabian, the Iranian who masterminded the whole thing. I'm not giving up now. My wife wouldn't ask me to do that. *You* can't ask me, either."

Milgrom grinned. "That's what I told them."

"You told them I would want to go?"

"I told them they would have a difficult time stopping you."

Auerbach stood. "When do we leave?"

"Tomorrow."

Auerbach seemed surprised. "They don't want to prepare?"

"We've known this for a day or so. They've been flying UAVs over the area where he was seen. Collecting photos, that sort of thing. Analysts are reviewing them now and creating maps. But it's more important to act. We need to capture Rajabian and to do that we have to act before he has time to get away."

"Not much reason to wait," Auerbach acknowledged.

"Right." Milgrom stood. "The team is meeting in the conference room. You should join them."

CHAPTER
30

THE SHIN BET TEAM preparing for deployment to Gaza was comprised of six members: Hossam Wilchek, the team leader; Saul Feige, the team's primary long-range marksman; Reshef Talmi, Idan Tauber, and Tomer Spitzer, who were listed as operations specialists; and Auerbach. He was familiar with Wilchek. The others were brought in from a Shin Bet facility near Haifa. Auerbach had never worked with them.

For the remainder of the evening and most of the following day, Auerbach and the team reviewed video footage captured by drones hovering over Café Jabalia and the surrounding neighborhood in Gaza City. They pored over enlargements of still photographs taken from the video, detailed images taken from street level by Ismail Yassin and others operating in Gaza on Shin Bet's behalf, and maps prepared from drone and satellite imagery.

Finally, as the team's deployment approached, Wilchek turned the conversation to their assignments. "We'll begin at the coffee shop. Set up surveillance there for a few days. See if Rajabian comes around again."

Feige, who functioned as second-in-command, spoke up. "Remember, Rajabian is our primary target. But don't pass up a chance to take out Al-Hadi."

Auerbach asked, "Any thought to capturing them?"

"This is a wet team," Wilchek replied. "Not an arrest team."

"And this mission could get very wet," Feige added. "If you know what I mean."

Auerbach acknowledged, "I know precisely what you mean." *Wet team* was a euphemism for an assassination squad, usually on an assignment that was likely to be quite bloody. "However," he continued, "it would be helpful to talk to them."

"Too dangerous for us to do that," Wilchek said. "We'll have enough difficulty just getting ourselves in and out without getting killed, much less bringing someone else out with us."

"Especially if that someone else is Al-Hadi," Talmi noted.

"Or Rajabian," someone added quickly.

"And then we'll have international complications."

"Iran will never acknowledge he's one of theirs."

"They'll make up a story about how he is a diplomat or a student and paint us as the bad guys."

"Back to the task at hand," Wilchek broke in. "We'll have to do this the old way."

"No radios?"

"If they hear us talking," Feige explained, "they'll know who we are. So everything according to standard procedure and no radios."

"Which means?" Auerbach asked.

"Like I said," Wilchek answered, "we'll start with the coffee shop where they were seen. Talmi will take the sharpshooter's position." He pointed to Feige and Tauber. "You two take the front." He glanced around. "Spitzer and Auerbach will cover the rear."

"And if this doesn't work?"

"We'll regroup and find another way. Anybody gets a shot at either target, take it."

Auerbach spoke up again. "What's the plan for getting us out?"

"Make our way to the border checkpoint and call for a ride.".

"Think you can handle it?" Feige quipped.

"I've been on a few ops before."

"Then you'll know what to do," Wilchek replied in an authoritative tone. "Get your gear. We leave in an hour."

Late that afternoon, Auerbach and the Shin Bet team divided into pairs and climbed into the cabs of three transfer trucks making deliveries through the Erez border crossing. They crossed with only the usual difficulty and made their way down to a house near the Church of Saint Porphyrius, which they intended to use as a base of operations.

The following day the team walked down to the neighborhood near Café Jabalia and took up the positions Wilchek had assigned them. Auerbach and Spitzer were stationed behind the café. Talmi was situated in the third floor of a building across the street from the café entrance. Feige and Tauber were farther up the street in a building from which they had an unrestricted view of the front of the café and along one side.

Two days later, Al-Hadi appeared on the street where he was met by a man no one on the team recognized. They went inside the coffee shop, were there for ten minutes, then Al-Hadi came out alone. As he walked back in the direction he came, Talmi positioned himself for a shot but as he was about to take it, three women walked from a nearby building and blocked his line of sight. When they were out of the way, Al-Hadi was gone.

From their position up the street, Feige and Tauber spotted him also. Feige watched through binoculars. When the women appeared he looked over at Tauber. "I'm going after him."

"Talmi will get him," Tauber cautioned. "Stay here."

"No," Feige replied. "He won't get him. Those people are in the way."

Tauber seemed not to realize what was happening but knew better than to let Feige pursue Al-Hadi alone. He waited a moment while Feige took the lead, then crossed to the opposite side of the street and followed at a distance.

Two blocks up the street, Al-Hadi came to a corner grocery store where Rajabian was waiting for him. The two men talked for a moment, then Rajabian turned in Feige's direction and gestured for Al-Hadi to look. Feige realized he'd been made and opened fire right there on the street in broad daylight. Tauber backed him up. In the hail of gunfire that followed, Rajabian was struck three times in the chest and fell backward onto the sidewalk. Al-Hadi took cover in the doorway of the store, then slipped inside and disappeared from sight. Four men emerged from the store and began shooting in the direction of Feige and Tauber, momentarily pinning them in place. Tauber was certain they would die at any moment when the report of a fifty-caliber rifle shook the air and one of the shooters from the store sailed backward through a store window.

"Talmi," Tauber whispered.

Indeed, Talmi heard the gunfire and saw what was happening from his station. He made his way to the rooftop and found a position near the corner from which he had a clear view of the store. That's when he opened fire on the gunmen shooting at Feige and Tauber.

From his position with Spitzer in an alley behind the café, Auerbach had been unable to see Al-Hadi, but he heard the gunfire when Feige and Tauber began shooting.

"We gotta go," Auerbach urged.

"We're supposed to remain in our position. That's the procedure."

"Al-Hadi and Rajabian are down the street. Come on."

The alley where they'd been hiding ran the length of the block.

Auerbach and Spitzer followed it in the direction of the gunfire. When they were about halfway down the block, they heard the report from Talmi's rifle. The sound of it was unmistakable.

Just then, a door opened from the right and Al-Hadi appeared, dressed in a Bedouin's robe with a keffiyeh covering his head. He glanced in Auerbach's direction and his eyes opened wide in a look of realization. In the same instant, he turned away and ran. Rather than shooting him, Auerbach chased after him.

At the far end of the alley, Al-Hadi reached the street and turned left. Auerbach followed. In the next block, Al-Hadi crossed to the opposite side and called out in Arabic for help. A car was parked nearby and when he spoke, two men got out. They turned in Auerbach's direction, drew pistols from their waistbands, and began firing in his direction.

As bullets whizzed past, Auerbach ducked behind a truck that was parked at the curb. Spitzer, who had followed, took cover behind a car a short distance away. "What do we do now?" he called.

"Shoot back!" Auerbach leaned out from behind the truck and squeezed off three rounds in the direction of the men who'd been shooting at him.

One of the gunmen tumbled to the pavement, writhing in pain. The other fired until his pistol was empty, then ducked out of sight, reloaded, and continued firing. As he did, Al-Hadi ran toward the corner. Auerbach caught sight of him as he disappeared around the end of the building.

Auerbach reloaded as well, then shouted at Spitzer, "Cover me!" Spitzer raised up from hiding and opened fire while Auerbach came from behind the truck and ran after Al-Hadi.

By the time Auerbach reached the corner, Al-Hadi was halfway to the next street. Auerbach ran after him but as Al-Hadi came to the corner, a gray Mercedes screeched to a stop alongside him and the rear door flew open. Al-Hadi climbed inside, slammed the door closed, and the car moved away. Desperate to keep up, Auerbach commandeered a motorcycle that was parked at the curb and started after them.

Auerbach followed the gray Mercedes as it moved in and out of traffic, often moving into the oncoming lane as cars and trucks approached, then darting back in line at the last moment in an effort to lose him. Horns blared and once or twice vehicles crashed around them. Still, the Mercedes kept going, making its way toward the southern end of the Gaza Strip while edging closer and closer to the Mediterranean coast.

Forty-five minutes later, they reached Khan Yunis, the neighborhood near the southern end of the strip where Darwaza had lived—and where Masalha had said Khalafi kept a hideout. For a moment, Auerbach lost sight of the Mercedes, found it again, lost it again, and then caught a glimpse of it as it turned into an alley in the next block. Despite the threat to his own safety, Auerbach turned into the alley after them. As he did, however, the car was already to the far end and turned onto the cross street. Auerbach gunned the engine of the motorcycle and raced after them.

When he reached the cross street, Auerbach looked to his right and saw the Mercedes in the distance. He sped after it, weaving in and out of traffic, trying to catch up. In the distance, he noticed the blue water of the Mediterranean and realized they were closer to the coast than he thought. Soon the beach appeared and for an instant the smell of salt air overpowered the stench of crowded urban life, then the Mercedes came to a stop in front of a small café, and Auerbach pushed all other thoughts from his mind. Only one thing mattered—capturing or shooting Al-Hadi.

Just then, the driver's door of the Mercedes opened and the driver stepped out. Dressed in gray slacks and a linen shirt, he wore black loafers and dark sunglasses. He smiled in Auerbach's direction as he walked calmly around the front and went inside the café. Auerbach brought the motorcycle to a stop alongside the car and looked through the rear window to the back seat, only to find the car was empty. That's when he realized Al-Hadi was long gone.

"The alley," he said to himself angrily. "That's where he got out." He struck the handlebar of the motorcycle with his fist. "I should have known that."

For a moment, Auerbach thought of returning to the alley. Perhaps he could pick up the trail again there. Perhaps he would find Al-Hadi walking casually along the sidewalk, chatting with those whom he met as if nothing had happened. Then he thought of Masalha and his mention that Khalafi had a storage container near the coast that he used as a hideout.

"Somewhere in Khan Yunis," Masalha had said.

By then, Auerbach was long since separated from the Shin Bet team. Any hope of finding them was as remote as the possibility of finding Al-Hadi. But he was in Khan Yunis and he was near the coast. Perhaps he could find Khalafi's hideout. Maybe even locate Khalafi. And if he found Khalafi, maybe he could learn more about what happened to Darwaza.

All afternoon, Auerbach roamed the streets near the beach, searching for a shipping container, but all he found were bomb-damaged buildings, squalled residences, and vacant lots that were littered with trash and refuse. Late in the afternoon, he was near the southern edge of Gaza, not far from the Egyptian border. The border fence formed a thin gray line in the distance and locating Khalafi's hideout seemed even more futile than when he began searching for it earlier in the day.

Auerbach was about to give up the search and head for the border crossing, but as he turned the motorcycle to leave, he caught sight of yet one more storage container sitting a few meters from the beach. It had been obscured by the rubble of a bombed-out building, but as he turned the motorcycle his line of sight changed and he saw it. Rather than leave, he rode over to it, only to find the door was locked. That was encouraging—no one who hid the kinds of things Khalafi was reported to hide would do so without locking the door—so Auerbach decided to wait.

Up the beach a hundred meters was the burned-out remains of a delivery truck sitting near the edge of the road. Auerbach parked the motorcycle on the opposite side and sat down in the shade. A breeze wafted in from the ocean and felt cool as it tousled his hair. For the first time that day he realized how tired he was and he closed his eyes to rest.

Sometime later, Auerbach was awakened by the clank of metal on metal. His eyes opened wide at the sound of it and he turned to look through the remains of the truck to see a man standing at the door to the storage container. Auerbach recognized him at once from the pictures he'd seen in the apartment on Cyprus and from photographs in Shin Bet's system. The man was none other than Mohammed Khalafi.

Auerbach waited while Khalafi unlocked the container and went inside, then came from behind the burned-out truck and moved quickly toward the container. He approached carefully, making certain he created no sound, and drew his pistol from his waistband. Auerbach held it at the ready as he stepped inside.

Khalafi stood at the opposite end, sorting through a stack of boxes and was startled by Auerbach's sudden appearance. He wheeled around to face him, then saw the pistol in Auerbach's hand and froze. "You're not fooling anyone with that getup," he smirked. "You're a Jew and everyone knows it. They've been talking about you all over. You and your friends. What do you want with me?"

"I want to know about Masud Darwaza."

Khalafi's smirk turned to a grin. "The traitor got what was coming to him. Same as your kind does to your own traitors."

"You knew him?"

"Why are you concerned about him?" Before Auerbach could respond, Khalafi's eyes opened wider in a look of realization. "Ahh. Yes. You were his Israeli contact. You are the one who got him killed."

"Who killed him?" Auerbach asked.

"I do not know that. But I know it wasn't me."

"Darwaza was a good man."

"Darwaza was a weak man."

"Who killed him?"

"As I said before, it wasn't me. But if I knew, which I don't, do you really think I would tell you?"

Auerbach was tired. It was late in the day. And right then, seeing the look on Khalafi's face and hearing the tone in his voice, a sense of frustration swept over him. Darwaza was a decent guy. He had worked for several handlers, always without pay. Khalafi knew what happened to him. He *had* to know. They *all* knew and this one was going to pay. This one was going to suffer. This one was going to—Without warning, Auerbach pointed the pistol at Khalafi's leg and squeezed the trigger.

Confined by the metal storage container, the shot rang out with a deafening roar, and for a moment Auerbach did not notice Khalafi's screams. He only saw blood splatter the wall. Saw Khalafi grab for his leg and tumble to the floor. But as Auerbach's hearing returned he heard Khalafi shout, "You stupid Jewish pig! I will never tell you anything!"

At the sound of the first shot, Auerbach felt a sense of relief wash over him as the tension rushed from his body. Still in the glow of that release, he squeezed off a second shot, this one striking Khalafi's other leg. "Tell me who killed Darwaza!" he shouted.

Khalafi was scared now and bleeding profusely. He tried to scoot away but there was no room and he was pressed against a stack of boxes. "Okay. Okay," he shouted. "I'll tell you. I'll tell you what you want to know. Just stop the bleeding before I die."

Auerbach raised the pistol for yet another shot. "Who killed Darwaza?" he demanded.

Khalafi held up his hands in protest. "Wait. Wait. The person you are looking for is . . ."

Just then, a shadow fell over them both and Khalafi looked past Auerbach. He smiled and Auerbach turned to find Al-Hadi behind him. He stood at an odd angle, his body sideways to the length of the container, and his right hand was obscured by the folds of his robe.

"I knew you would be here," Al-Hadi spoke with a calm, even voice and seemed unfazed by Auerbach or his surroundings.

"How did you know that?" Auerbach asked.

"You are a Shin Bet agent. You were Darwaza's handler. I knew you would never let him go. Just as I knew you would not stop following me, even though the car was empty and I was long gone. But I am wondering one thing."

"What is that?"

"How you knew Khalafi might know about Darwaza."

"It's a long story," Auerbach replied.

Al-Hadi, who was blocking the doorway of the container, said, "I do not think you have anywhere to go just now. So tell me, how did you know to look for Khalafi?"

Auerbach was thinking about whom to shoot first—Khalafi or Al-Hadi—as he raised his pistol. At his first motion, Al-Hadi moved his right hand from beneath the folds of his robe. In it he held an automatic pistol, which he now pointed in Auerbach's direction. "I would not try anything just now." He grinned. "You will tell me what I want to know and then I will shoot you. But first . . ." Al-Hadi pointed the pistol in Khalafi's direction and fired, shooting Khalafi in the head, then he turned to Auerbach. "Now it is your turn." He smiled and held the pistol to fire it. "This is your last chance to tell me what I want to know."

Suddenly, Al-Hadi's head exploded. Blood splattered Auerbach's chest and covered the ceiling. A moment later, the report of a rifle reached him and he knew Talmi and the others had found their location.

CHAPTER
31

LATE THAT EVENING, Auerbach and the Shin Bet team returned to Beersheba. He dropped his gear in the office, then headed home to see his family. He arrived at the front door dirty, sweaty, and exhausted. His wife, Yarden, greeted him at the door and he collapsed into her arms. Their children gathered around them and they embraced in a family hug.

After a moment, their daughter spoke. "Papa?"

"Yes."

"I think you need a bath."

"I think you're right."

Auerbach freed himself from them and started down the hall toward the shower. Yarden followed and helped him undress.

"Are you all right?"

Auerbach turned to face her. "I was so afraid."

She gave him a look of concern. "You were worried the fighting would reach Beersheba?"

"No." Auerbach shook his head. "I wasn't afraid about that."

"Then about what?"

"Jerusalem," he whispered. She nodded for him to continue. He began to cry, "They were just kids. They could have all been killed."

Yarden wrapped her arms around him and pulled him close. "But you rescued them. You saved them. You kept them safe." Auerbach sobbed and she pulled him closer.

"When will it stop? When will they stop trying to kill us?"

"It will never stop," she replied softly.

He pulled away, a puzzled look on his face. "What do you mean?"

"They hate us for who we are. We can never change who we are. This is our life. A life of struggle. That is the way it always has been. As we are who we are, and they are who they are, things will always be this way." She kissed him gently and smiled. "That is why we have you." She kissed him again. "My brave, strong husband. The brave, strong father of our children."

BOOKS BY: MIKE EVANS

Israel: America's Key to Survival

Save Jerusalem

The Return

Jerusalem D.C.

Purity and Peace of Mind

Who Cries for the Hurting?

Living Fear Free

I Shall Not Want

Let My People Go

Jerusalem Betrayed

Seven Years of Shaking: A Vision

The Nuclear Bomb of Islam

Jerusalem Prophecies

Pray For Peace of Jerusalem

America's War:
  The Beginning of the End

The Jerusalem Scroll

The Prayer of David

The Unanswered Prayers of Jesus

God Wrestling

The American Prophecies

Beyond Iraq: The Next Move

The Final Move beyond Iraq

Showdown with Nuclear Iran

Jimmy Carter: The Liberal Left
  and World Chaos

Atomic Iran

Cursed

Betrayed

The Light

Corrie's Reflections & Meditations

The Revolution

The Final Generation

Seven Days

The Locket

Persia: The Final Jihad

GAMECHANGER SERIES:

  GameChanger

  Samson Option

  The Four Horsemen

THE PROTOCOLS SERIES:

  The Protocols

  The Candidate

Jerusalem

The History of Christian Zionism

Countdown

Ten Boom: Betsie, Promise of God

Commanded Blessing

BORN AGAIN SERIES:

  Born Again: 1948

  Born Again: 1967

TO PURCHASE, CONTACT: orders@TimeWorthyBooks.com
P. O. BOX 30000, PHOENIX, AZ 85046

MICHAEL DAVID EVANS, the #1 *New York Times* bestselling author, is an award-winning journalist/Middle East analyst. Dr. Evans has appeared on hundreds of network television and radio shows including *Good Morning America, Crossfire* and *Nightline,* and *The Rush Limbaugh Show,* and on Fox Network, *CNN World News,* NBC, ABC, and CBS. His articles have been published in the *Wall Street Journal, USA Today, Washington Times, Jerusalem Post* and newspapers worldwide. More than twenty-five million copies of his books are in print, and he is the award-winning producer of nine documentaries based on his books.

Dr. Evans is considered one of the world's leading experts on Israel and the Middle East, and is one of the most sought-after speakers on that subject. He is the chairman of the board of the ten Boom Holocaust Museum in Haarlem, Holland, and is the founder of Israel's first Christian museum located in the Friends of Zion Heritage Center in Jerusalem.

Dr. Evans has authored 93 books including: *History of Christian Zionism, Showdown with Nuclear Iran, Atomic Iran, The Next Move Beyond Iraq, The Final Move Beyond Iraq,* and *Countdown.* His body of work also includes the novels *Seven Days, GameChanger, The Samson Option, The Four Horsemen, The Locket, Born Again: 1967,* and *The Columbus Code.*

✦ ✦ ✦

Michael David Evans is available to speak or for interviews.
Contact: EVENTS@drmichaeldevans.com.